THE WHITE BOAR

Here is a dramatic historical novel that vividly re-creates the life and times of England's controversial King Richard III. Shakespeare portrayed him as evil incarnate, a hunchback who gained the throne by murdering his two nephews. Conversely, many historians argue that he was an innocent scapegoat and might have been one of history's great monarchs had his reign not been so tragically short. In this novel one issue concerning Richard's life is never in doubt—that he held the unfaltering devotion of two extra-ordinary men, Philip and Francis Lovell. And it is through their eyes that the reader sees the last Plantagenet—the man and the King.

The White Boar

Marian Palmer

CORONET BOOKS
Hodder Paperbacks Ltd., London

Printed in Great Britain for Coronet Books, Hodder
Paperbacks Ltd, St. Paul's House, Warwick Lane,
London, E.C.4, by Cox & Wyman Ltd., London, Reading
and Fakenham

ISBN 0 340 12808 9

To my father, Leonard Postill

THE WHITE BOAR

"Loyalty binds me"

DEVICE OF RICHARD OF GLOUCESTER

PART ONE

A Crimson Sky at Dawn

January 1465

CHAPTER ONE

THE women had left wax torches burning, and hung the chamber walls with tapestries of unicorns made tame, because the bride was a maid. Echoing up the twist of stair, the last voices drifted of the withdrawing guests; they had stayed to see the children bedded, and to make, broadly smiling, the olden jokes. Then they left boy and girl together, and went back laughing to the dancing and the feast. A few more years, they said comfortingly to the bride's father; then he could see it done again, and know in truth the lace was tied. Henry Fitz Hugh, lord of Ravensworth and anxious still about his prize, could only assent. There was no sense repining; the fact was that Anna was too young, and the boy too, though well enough grown for his years; but Fitz Hugh had been surprised as much as made grateful by the offer of Lord Lovell's heir of Tichmarsh for his girl, and he would not be happy until he knew that as surely as in church, they had been joined in bed.

In the tower room, the hissing of the torches sounded louder than trumpets. Stiffly lying under the sheets and blankets and embroidered coverlet, the boy watched the shadows move. Why he was there, he knew full well: a bribe to Fitz Hugh of Ravensworth to keep him faithful; Francis Lovell for a son-in-law, to make a good King's man of that uncertain Yorkshire lord. They had never, Francis told himself, persuaded Lord Lovell from his fealty with such a gift. But his father was dead, body and heart together broken by the defeat of Lancaster on Towton field, and his heir and lands had gone into the ward of other men for how they chose to use them until the boy was grown, and, it was to be hoped, by then a bred-up Yorkist too.

In the farther half of the bed the little girl was equally still. He could see her nose over the edge of the drawn-up covers, and the tips of her fingers where she clutched the sheet; what she was thinking, he was able neither to conceive nor care. His eyes stung; he turned on his side, curling his knees to his breast, and fell miserably asleep.

Next day there was more strangeness, more that was

unfamiliar and new. Having arrived at Ravensworth only the day before, Francis found he was to leave it again that morning; it was not under Fitz Hugh's roof that he was to be set to his training, but fifteen miles off, in the household of the Earl of Warwick at Middleham.

His escort for the journey was Warwick's captain, Sir John Blount, a genial veteran of the great Earl's wars, who looked him over with a friendly eye and told him, for encouragement, that they'd an interest in his bridals at Middleham, Mistress Anna being own niece to my lord of Warwick. Francis, unheartened by a fact which he already knew, confined himself to a murmured comment; but throughout the ride Sir John continued unabated discourse, pointing out landmarks, dropping scraps of information about Middleham, and remembering aloud his adventurous days when he had fought in the bitter struggle between Lancastrian King Henry and his Yorkist kinsmen, and Richard Neville, the young and valiant Earl of Warwick, shook out his banner and rode to battle beside his doomed uncle Richard of York, to right the wrongs of England. That time was long over; Richard of York was dead, his head struck from his shoulders and placed mockingly over the gates of his own city of York by Henry's savage queen; and Richard Neville in rage and grief had risen up and plucked the crown from weak Lancaster's greying head and set it triumphantly on the bright hair of his cousin Edward, dead York's eldest son.

Cheerfully reminiscing, the broad North Country voice ran on. Francis, who had been instructed in a quite different tradition, gazed at the bear and staff of Warwick on the pennon which preceded them, and played with his hackney's reins. The short winter light was beginning to fail; as they forded the river below Leyburn, Sir John raised his hand and pointed. "Look now, lad: we're nearly there. That's Middleham."

It lay on the heights of the village of its name, thick-walled and grim; girdled successively by outer and inner wards with rising above them the great stronghold of the keep. The north gatehouse had guarding figures of stone spaced about the battlements; as well as the outer ditch there was a moat around the inner walls, and the slitted windows had been made for archers to shoot from. Sir John, at home once more, swept the march of buildings with a satisfied glance; his companion regarded the massive fortifications and stark towers with apprehensive eyes, and, shivering, drew his cloak more tightly around him. Yorkshire was a wilder place, bleaker and more lonely, than any he had known; this mighty fortress could have sprung from its hill, a rock to watch over a country like to it: rough, forbidding, and bare.

The wardens of the gate were expecting them and passed them through, lifting hands in greeting. It was true, Francis found, that everyone had an interest in him. In the swarming outer courtyard he swung from his horse: a dark boy, some years still from the abrupt growth of adolescence, with a mouth at once sensitive and expressive, and fine-grained skin uncomfortably warming under the scrutiny of a few score pairs of eyes. As he stood in doubt, wondering what next he was to do, a youth in squire's dress ran down from the parapet wall and came over, saying with a smile, "Well, coz. Wishing yourself south of the Trent again? But you'll grow used to it, as I did, and soon think there no better place to live in England."

There was a likeness between them, less of colouring than of feature; Francis, both grateful and shy—he had not seen his cousin Philip for three years—smiled in return as they walked towards the inner gate. In Oxfordshire, when Sir Thomas Lovell, Philip's father, had followed the Earl of Warwick for York, there had been estrangement between their families; later, when Lord Lovell, crippled at Towton fight and slowly dying, had wanted Yorkist friends, he had been reconciled with his younger brother. For a while then Francis had seen a good deal of his cousin, until Philip turned fourteen and went away to the Earl of Warwick's household to learn to be a knight. Glancing secretly at him as they crossed the courtyard, Francis thought his kinsman altered, and yet much the same. The dying light fell slantwise across his profile, and the swing of hair against his cheek showed hardly browner than his tan. It would be a year or so yet before he finished growing, but the promise of the man was already visible in the lightly muscled bones, and when he looked down to meet his cousin's gaze, Francis saw it in his face too.

Sir John had gone in search of the steward, and the servants who had attended them had vanished also, Francis discovered, with his gear. With relief he understood that for the time he was in Philip's charge. He was beginning to be curious about what he saw, and lagged a minute to watch the blacksmith shoeing a warhorse at the forge. In the inner court a party of riders overtook them, plumes and pennons fluttering, to dismount at the keep stair; they had been hunting, and Francis noticed there were boys among them no older than himself. Philip started to tell him their names beginning with those nearest; one of them, a strapping, red-haired youth, turned as he heard and said grinning, "Cock's bones, it's the bridegroom, and not even the civility to wear my lord of Warwick's colours in his service. Have we a Lancastrian come among us, do you suppose?"

Some of his companions laughed. They were all in scarlet, the Neville livery, with the Earl of Warwick's badge on the sleeve; it came to Francis that by tomorrow, likely, he must put it on himself. He took a step forward, his hands doubling into fists, and gripping him hard by the shoulder Philip said under his breath, "Don't be foolish, you can't fight them all and they mean no harm besides. Let it pass, and by tomorrow they'll be your friends." Redhead was waiting at the top of the stairs, a mixture of mischief and malice in his eyes; he looked about to descend when behind him someone spoke.

"Have the Percys ever been such servants of York, Rob, that you are so forward an advocate? I thought your kins-man, the sometime Earl of Northumberland, still lay in Fleet Prison, heartily suing for pardon of King Edward for his late services to Lancaster." It was a young voice, low but carrying, with the unforced pitch of one who expects to be heard. The youth called Percy turned as if surprised; then, his colour heightening, he walked without replying into the keep.

In the gap made by his departure a boy was standing. He was older than Francis by a little, grey-eyed and slightly made, and closely inspected there seemed an awkwardness about his right arm and shoulder, as if the muscles had grown thicker there. He stood looking down at Francis, gently teasing with his fingers the sleek, settled feathers of the hawk on his fist; he appeared amused, but not un-friendlily so, and Francis instinctively smiled in response, warmed by an attraction as instantaneous as it was un-reasoning. For a moment it seemed as if the grey-eyed boy would address him; then, changing his mind, he made

14

a small sign of acknowledgment to Philip, and went inside.

The other lads, as if awaiting the example, had followed him. To his cousin, Francis said hesitating, "Who is he?" Philip answered, "King Edward's brother, the Duke of Gloucester. Didn't you know he was here?"

Astonished, Francis could only stare. It was true he had been told, and from Oxfordshire to the Trent endured unbroken reinforcement of reminder that he was to share Richard of Gloucester's tutelage at Middleham; he had imagined some flame-haired young giant, boisterously self-assured and splendid with consequence, a younger version of the usurper Edward, whom he had seen once from afar. Robert Percy, indeed, had been much in the fancied mould. He thought again of the boy just gone, and remembered the ungainly shoulder; and as if he had spoken aloud Philip said quietly, "You show what you're thinking. Take care you don't do it to his face: he knows about it, better than you."

It was getting on for supper; light from the great hall of the keep laid a streaming sword across the dusk, and there was a murmur of voices within. The boys, Francis learned, ate all together under the Master of Henchmen's eye; the Earl of Warwick being from home, his wife and daughters dined in the inner chamber, and the steward of the household kept his state on the dais. Afterwards, Philip took his cousin across the courtyard and showed him his bed in the dorter where the henchmen slept.

Richard of Gloucester came in with some other lads towards complin; his eye caught Philip's, and Francis saw from the way the rest made room for them that they were old companions, and given as much privacy together as their manner of living allowed. Many people, Francis reflected, would have counted on something from it, the favour of the King's brother; and Sir Thomas Lovell was a country gentleman who had improved his fortunes by marrying a wool merchant's daughter. Benevolently meditating, Francis regarded with approval his cousin's straight shoulders and slender waist, mentally dressing them in court velvet, slashed and puffed and pleated, with a collar of King Edward's new device of suns. A place at Westminster was the least that might be expected, and perhaps lands to add to the modest holdings Sir Thomas could bequeath his son; many gentlemen had bettered themselves so.

As if feeling the younger boy's gaze, Richard looked up

from where he sat talking with Philip, his thin, unevenly muscled body hunched forward against his knees. This evening he had a scrubbed appearance, and a new graze over one eyebrow from late practice in the tiltyard after supper was done; King Edward, Francis remembered, was a famous warrior, and had worn armour to fight beside his father at Saint Albans when he was only thirteen years old. Across the space of two empty beds, the grey eyes of Edward's brother met the contemplative brown ones, and Francis, made abruptly conscious of his calculations, went scarlet with a hot, inexplicable shame. He would have looked away like a coward, had he not feared the betrayal it would bring; but after an instant Richard said, "Francis, I heard tell your father died this winter past. I have heard his grace the King say of him he had rather Lord Lovell for his honest enemy until he could make him otherwise, than many a one about him now that came hurrying after Towton battle to be his friend. I am sorry your father did not live long enough for it to be so." His sudden smile had a singular directness and warmth; in that moment, Francis entered upon his life's service.

A fortnight after the marriage of Francis Lovell to Fitz Hugh his brother-in-law's daughter, the Earl of Warwick returned to Middleham. He had been long in the south, busy about his great affairs; for days the banners had been looked for, and rumour working outwards now from the south walls and square watch-tower gave it to be known that the Duke of Clarence was riding with him. The astonishment could hardly have been greater had it been King Edward himself. Although Edward had cheerfully left his brother Richard for months at a time to his undisturbed training under the Earl of Warwick's roof, it had long ago been noted that when it came to his other brother, George of Clarence, the King preferred to have him closer under his eyes; and there were those who doubted it was for affection's sake. The Duke of Clarence was King Edward's heir until the Queen should provide her husband with a better one; and for all that Edward's impulsive and clandestine marriage to Elizabeth Woodville—dowerless, unroyal, widow of the Lancastrian Lord Grey and twice the mother of his sons—had disgusted Edward's barons and provoked a quarrel with his mighty cousin of Warwick from which, it was said, the ashlars of Reading Abbey were still quaking, the commons of England

16

were ready to forgive both the new Queen and her seem-ingly endless accompaniment of ambitious brothers, sisters, and uncles a very great deal, if only she would give the King a son.

It seemed to the steward, bowing low to the master of Middleham and his guest, that his lord was looking both tired and more than a little grim. Lately it had often been so, particularly following the occasions of those hurried visits of the Earl to Westminster and his cousin's court. Speculation as to causes was no part of the duties of a loyal officer, and the seneschal made none: only casting an assessing eye side-ways at the taut, preoccupied profile as he matched the Earl's quick stride through courtyard and keep, and down the wooden gallery to the great chamber where his wife and daughters waited. They were pretty girls, Isabel, not yet thir-teen, and Anne, some years younger: the only children of the marriage and sole heiresses through their mother to the princely fortunes of Beauchamp and Despenser; and it was an unexplainable thing that Warwick had not yet arranged the betrothal of either. If the steward was visited by a new and surprising thought as his gaze rested on George of Cla-rence a restless stripling, long reputed to be importuning his brother the King for a rich wife—he kept the suspicion discreetly to himself, and murmured in the Earl's ear that, when he wished to give him audience, there was a courier with letters from the French King who, having missed my lord at York, had come straight north to Middleham after him and been waiting these two days past.

The dark eyes lifted turning from their lingering con-sideration of the light track on Isabel's flaxen hair. "I was at Sheriff Hutton: he might have found me for asking," the Earl said briefly; it was plain his mind was already wholly on the messenger and his packet. Letters to the Earl of War-wick from King Louis once more courtly adjuncts to French diplomacies with King Edward were becoming more and not less frequent with the progressive English drift towards Flanders and alliance with Louis' hostile vassal and rival Duke of Burgundy: an inclining against which it was widely known the Earl of Warwick had argued passionately and in vain. Although he had barely greeted his wife, he went out at once, despatching a yeoman to seek out the courier and send him to his privy chamber.

Through a page of the Countess of Warwick's closet, it

was gossiped by suppertime that the Duke of Clarence had to come to Middleham to take his brother Richard back to Westminster. The story was true: Warwick himself, the French business dealt with, had waited on his young cousin to tell him his northern years were done. How unwelcome an imparting it would be, the Earl knew well: the changes the Woodville Queen wrought at Edward's court, the King's brothers had been first to suffer from. It would have been greatly preferable to Richard of Gloucester, Warwick was aware, if he could have spent his life through out of sound or sight of the royal court, serving jointly his brother Edward and his cousin Warwick on the wild Welsh or Scots borders for the kingdom's weal. But he heard the Earl calmly, saying nothing because it was apparent there was nothing that could be said to change it; and Warwick, unwilling yet to probe deeper, let him go unhindered away.

On the day before their departure he gave a great feast to honour his royal cousins. The air was soft with a gentleness like spring, and neighbour-gentry from as far off as Richmond and Bolton came streaming over the rutted roads to Middleham, swelling the numbers of barons who had attended the Earl from Edward's court. The castle had put on gaiety like a grim beldame tricked with garlands; new tapestries flaunted glowing colours on the smoke-blackened walls; gold and silver and pewter shone above the salt; and musicians in the gallery competed for attention with dwarfs and dancers and acrobats, jongleurs and comb-capped fools, all thrumming and twirling and posturing and balancing between the tables for the pleasure of my lord of Warwick's guests.

To mark the end of his sojourn in his cousin's household, the Duke of Gloucester had been elevated from his usual place to the dais where Warwick and his wife sat with their more important visitors. Not wholly at ease among so many strangers, Richard would have gladly exchanged his dignity for a seat by one of the lesser northern lords he already knew, but Clarence beside him was holding sparkling court. The King's heir was quite as great a person as most Yorkshiremen expected to see north of the Trent that year, and there was a trace of amusement in Richard's eyes as he watched the manoeuvring to catch his brother's notice; but as the hours wore on the gleam faded. A sly innuendo barbed the conversation of the southern nobles, whispers and jokes he did not hear well enough to understand; but he could read the smothered laughter behind the carelessly concealing hands. He looked at Warwick, but the Earl seemed unaware of anything amiss at his table; during a lull Richard heard him enquiring of his sister, Lady Fitz Hugh, about the health of his nephews and nieces at Ravensworth. Brimming cups passed and repassed, and the Duke of Clarence's server was busier than any three others. A Kentish baron at his other hand was addressing him now in a confidential undertone, and Clarence, lightly swirling the wine in the gilt and jewelled goblet between his palms, listened in absorbed silence. The torchlight made a radiance around his golden hair; the two heads bent closer, then separated as Clarence flung back in his chair, uproariously laughing and slapping the Kentishman's knee.

There was a sugared subtlety before Richard, Saint George and the maiden, stickily crumbling where he had already picked at it. He stared steadily at the knight's sword, half-vanishing in an untidiness of flaking pastry, and became conscious that the stout, comfortable Lord Scrope of Bolton was speaking down the table to Clarence's neighbour, the Kentish lord. It was an innocent question, but of vital concern in a country long wracked by disputed succession: Was there any possibility that the Queen was with child? Several of the northern barons looked up, eager for the latest court news, and the object of the enquiry gave a bray of laughter.

"No, Scrope, the widow isn't breeding yet, praised be God, for I tell you"—he leaned over his place, his bleared eyes roving down the board—"I tell you, it has come to this: our salvation is in it that she be barren, and you should fall on your knees to pray for it. Do we not endure enough, without her spawning a line of princes? By God's soul, she rules both king and kingdom while our dread lord Edward snores in her sheets." His arm, widely gesturing, indicated Clarence lounging indifferent beside him; the broad palm descended to the table with a smack. "Sirs, we have too long suffered, while the remedy sits to our hand!"

Curling like smoke among the shocked or puzzled faces, some approving murmurs rose; far down the board a voice shouted, "Well said." Darkly flushed, Richard sprang to his feet, his fingers closing murderously around the heavy goblet before him. Clarence had sat as if oblivious throughout, his hand shading his brows, but something of the movement caught his glance. He bent swiftly forward and, snatching his brother's wrist, forced it ruthlessly to the table. The great cup went spinning with a clatter, its contents splashing yards away, and above their incarnadining river Clarence's blue eyes blazed into his brother's grey ones, while the quiet deepened and the wine dripped down, and shadows leaped and quivered on the walls. Then the room sighed with the releasing of a hundred breaths; violently contemptuous, Clarence threw the pinioned hand aside, and, quick to the steward's signal, the trumpeters sounded. Everyone rose; the minstrels struck up in the gallery, and in an aftermath of reconstructed calm Warwick was able to hurry his cousins from the hall. The door slammed, and across the privy chamber they faced each other.

In the background Warwick hovered watchfully, his eyes flicking from one to the other, a frown of annoyance creasing his brow. Clarence's colour was rising dangerously, and in a voice which was thick with rage he demanded, "How dare you make such a spectacle of me before those lords?"

Richard said slowly, "Let my brother pardon me. I thought it was the paladin beside you who did that." He was shaking and pale, but his eyes met the angry ones squarely.

"And now you chop terms with me, would you?" Clarence breathed. "I warn you, Dickon, don't try me too hard, or for all the love I bear you—"

"Do you bear it me? I will renounce it all, do you return so much to the King our brother, who made you a knight and to whom you have given your oath. It is in your honour to remember it to him, and nothing towards me that am his private subject, like yourself."

His brother's hand, slapping flat across the mouth, sent him sprawling to the rush-strewn floor. "God's death, do you lesson me, Gloucester?" Clarence panted. "Here's instruction for you, then—" He reached down, twisting a hand in the slighter boy's collar as he dragged him erect; his clenched fist went up, and Warwick exclaimed in warning: "Cousin!"

Momentarily Clarence paused; then abruptly he released his hold. Sharply turning he walked to the window and cast himself down in the seat, staring sullenly at the murky glass. "Plague take you, Dickon, have you no more sense than to heed what a man says in his cups?" he muttered resentfully.

Richard made no reply; a trickle of blood was running from his lip, and he searched vainly for a handkerchief before wiping it with his sleeve. Clarence looked round, and, beckoning him over, threw an arm around his shoulder. "Listen to me, Dickon: you and I must not fall out. There are quarrels enough for both of us, ready to hand." The silence was unresponsive; irritated, he snapped, "Are you still fretting for that drunken tosspot out there? I tell you, he was cup-shotten!"

Richard said unsteadily, "He was talking treason, and you allowed it."

"I was drunken too," Clarence replied ingenuously, and gave a little crow of laughter. "Better be glad I had wit enough to hold your hand: there would have been a grand to-do if you had pitched your cup at the gasbag's head. He would have sobered fast enough."

"It is truly so." Warwick came from the shadows, his voice conciliatory, his gaze on the boy. "Do you think I would permit treason at my table, cousin?"

Richard flushed hotly, and shook his head. Warwick considered him in a thoughtful way, then put out a hand to turn the averted face towards his own, his hard eyes compelling the reluctant grey ones. "You have been three years in my household, cousin, and I have been your good lord. You do yourself and me small honour by doubting my faith." He felt a sharp wincing at the reproach, and added more gently, "These are cruelly troubled times. Lackwit though he may be, that man but meant to say what the old blood of this kingdom have lamented these many months. About the Queen we can do little, but something may be accomplished that will prune her kindred, and the King must be persuaded to see it. There is no treason in this." He smiled. "Will you have my oath?"

Silence fell, while a shower of raindrops pelted down the chimney to hiss among the embers, and Clarence watched, brooding, from the window seat. He would have put in a word himself, had he not been warned by his cousin's eye. Balked, anxious, not a little angry still, as he stared at his brother's smudged profile and set, bruised mouth, another picture returned irresistibly to mind: a hushed chamber, bright with banners; throngs of nobles and the straining shadows of rose and turquoise and amber repeating the window traceries across the marble floor; and tall on the dais, the

statue-figure of Edward of York, to whom Richard Plantagenet, newly made Duke of Gloucester, was promising his
faith.

Impatient, Clarence bit at his thumb. Warwick had not
moved, nor had Richard stirred from his touch; but as the
pause lengthened a tiny frown appeared between the Earl's
brows. He had never doubted, and he did not doubt now, the
power of his enchantment over his cousin Richard, but for
one fractional instant he had known the disconcerted astonishment of a man whose hand, reaching for malleable clay,
has closed on flint.

In the quiet, the snap of a bursting coal sounded with abrupt distinctness. Nearly inaudibly, Richard spoke. "I ask
your pardon, my lord: I have no wish that you should swear
to me. You have given your word to the King; if you will
keep it, it is enough: if not, it would serve no purpose that
you should be foresworn a second time to me."

An almost imperceptible irony struggled at the corner of
Richard Neville's mouth. He answered lightly, "Then
cousin, we are friends again."

As if it had never been, the cloud passed. There was a
private door to the gallery which led to the west wall apartments; Richard moved towards it, and the Earl went with
him, an arm linked in his, saying briskly, "It grows late, and
you must make your start betimes tomorrow. I should seek
my bed, if I were you."

With no desire to return to the company in the hall, Richard made a motion of assent, but on the threshold Warwick
checked him. "A word more, kinsman," he said deliberately.
"You go now to court, and there will be much that is new to
you, and much, perhaps, that will be little to your taste. I
would have you remember, cousin of Gloucester, that in
Richard Neville you have ever a true and faithful friend."

Something flitted through the boy's eyes: an unreadable
expression which might have been fear, or revulsion, or the
pain of a crumbling illusion which bore neither examination
nor acknowledgment. Putting ceremony aside, Warwick
clasped him warmly by the shoulders; from the window Clarence, his good humour restored, signed a friendly leave.
Together they watched him go, and as the door closed they
looked at each other and smiled.

PART TWO

The Youngest Brother

June 1469—November 1471

CHAPTER TWO

VESPERS was sounding from the priory which neighboured the holding of Willowford as two riders pushed past the clump of hanging branches that gave the manor its name, and, splashing across the stream which bounded the outer fields, mounted the opposite bank. At the crest of the slope they turned into a path which ran through progressively clearing brush, but their horses went unsurely in the solidified mud of the late spring rains, and the foremost rider caught his lip in vexation as he checked his mount from a steep ditch, nearly hidden by drooping boughs.

"We can see to this road now, Gregory," he remarked. "What a country squire I have become, that the first benefit I see in prosperity is the chance to repair our roadways!" His hazel eyes rested on the fields now visible through the thinning trees; as if to himself he added, "Well, it's been a long struggle."

Gregory Traynor brought his horse up beside the younger man's as the track widened sufficiently to allow the passage of two horsemen abreast, and they rode sociably on, now and then raising hands in greeting to the tenant farmers gathering firewood among the trees. "A long fight," he agreed contentedly. "Four years and more, Master Philip, but you've done your part well. Your lady mother will be well pleased with that bit of parchment you've brought from London."

"Clear title at last." Philip said with a sigh. "On my soul, there were times when I thought we should never be done with lawyers and pleadings, and but for my mother's firmness, and Lord Audley's good neighbourship at the last, I would have despaired of it all."

"There's not a man of us on the land that doesn't know what you've been through, sir, since Sir Thomas passed," Traynor returned roughly. "Bitter hard it must have been, giving up all your fine friends and losing your chance at service with my lord of Gloucester, just to come home and worrit about lawsuits over the Mistress' dower. But you've Woodstock manor sure now, with your mother's kinsmen bound over to keep the King's word in it; so there's an end, and happy I am to see it."

There was silence for a time, broken only by the shrill of birds calling, and the wind stirring among the trees. Philip looked down, turning on his finger the only ring he wore. It had been his father's, and until his death had never left his hand. "There were threadbare times," he said after a while. He smiled ruefully. "I can't think why there should be such a shame in being poor: I saw Rob Percy that was with me at Middleham in London once, and dived into an alehouse as if the Chief Justice pursued me. Rob looked prosperous, I recognised Gloucester's livery. He'll be a knight now, I suppose."

"Yes, and you've a grey beard coming and three parts of your life sped," the groom scoffed. Philip gave an unwilling laugh of embarrassment, and Traynor leaned over to put a hand on his arm. "Now you attend to me, sir. You're one and twenty now and your own master at last: can you not go to London and set about the life you want? You'll excuse my speaking, Master Philip, but I've known you since first you squalled your way into the world, and full well do we both know this isn't the life your father meant for you." And then, in a coaxing way, "Think on it, now. There's my lord of Gloucester at Baynard's Castle in London: folks say he's often there visiting his mother these days, not caring much for Westminster manners, as the story goes. Don't you think he'd be glad to have word of you again, after all this time?"

Impatient, Philip shook his head. "Do you suppose me cutting a figure about London, Gregory? To beg a little place about the court, and ape the manners of the fine gentlemen at Westminster and Shene—I never wished for such a thing. As for the Duke of Gloucester, I stand to my ears in his debt already for what he did in the matter of my wardship, and my sister's too, when my father died: I know it came from his purse for my mother to have got them as she did. I would serve him for it with my life if he needed me, but I'll not go asking new favours now. Better far to stay here, where at least I can see to my people's needs."

"And glad they may be of it," Traynor muttered, for it was well known that in good times or ill, Dame Alice's hand lay heavy on the manor rolls. He saw from the tightening of Philip's mouth that the comment had displeased him, and blandly changed the subject, observing, "Well, my lord Audley will have been glad himself to see this day. He did well for you in London."

As if doubting its presence still, Philip slid a hand within his doublet to feel the parchment roll. Even to his inexperienced eye, London that week had presented a spectacle of more than the usual confusion; rumours of trouble in Yorkshire flew like sparks, and Edward, stung at last from unwary nonchalance in regard to his northern affairs, was bestirring himself to go and inspect them. In such a hurly of mustering and marching, Lord Audley's success in getting the King's signature to the precious sheet seemed to Philip no less than miraculous; but Audley had said with his courtier's smile that it was a matter of knowing the right doors to knock upon.

They were breasting the last slope to the house now, but the tiled roof and its little pigeon-house were some distance yet when Philip drew rein. "We are expected, Gregory," he said, and, squinting after the pointing finger, Traynor made out a small figure at the top of the hill. Philip lifted his hand; and with a shout the watcher descended from her post to rush towards them.

As she came panting up, the young man's eyebrows climbed. There was a smile of greeting on the upturned face, and the child who wore it seemed blithely unaware of the rents and stains in her gown, but after a horrified glance at the ruin, and a second apprehensive one in the direction of the house, Philip sprang from the saddle, "Name of God, Meg, what has happened to you?"

The dark eyes fell, assessing the havoc with a kind of conscious surprise. Postponing repetition of the enquiry, Philip hurried her back down the path until the branching undergrowth hid them from sight. Traynor followed, struggling with a grin. Halting at length, Philip made a comprehensive survey of the draggled figure before him, and observed, "If Audley could see you, Mistress Devereux, he would not think much of my hospitality and protection—nor my lord your father either. Praise Heaven, fasting, for every Flanders mile! Unfortunately there is still my mother to answer to. What have you been doing, to get yourself into such a state?"

There was a pause, while Lord Devereux's daughter pensively regarded the shreds of her garment. Guiltily she said, "Well you see, sir, it was the tree."

"Tree?" Philip looked about, puzzled; his eye fell on the stand of beeches which crowned the hill, and returned in disbelief to the penitent before him. As he appeared temporarily without speech, Margaret seized the opportunity to explain disarmingly, "I was watching for you, sir, and I could see farther from the height. But I slipped, coming down—" Her voice trailed into depressed silence. Philip began to laugh, caught the expression of huge amusement on Traynor's face, and dutifully repressed his own. It would be, he knew, no occasion for merriment when his mother learned of it, and with some idea of averting another such disaster in future he mustered what severity he could to say, "Do you tell me you were climbing there, Meg? Child, what possessed you to do such a thing! Maids do not climb trees in England, and I cannot think it so different in Burgundy either. What would my lord your father say if he heard of it, and you a big girl nearly eleven!" As a beginning, he knew, it had fallen somewhat short of Dame Alice's eloquence. But whatever else he had meant to add perished unspoken as he realised that—quietly, trying in vain to conceal it—she was weeping.

"Meg!—no, you must not—" She had turned her head aside, blindly pretending absorption in the first buds opening among the briars by the path. He thought of the long wait in the ill-omened lookout; he remembered too having noticed a quenched air for all the eagerness of her welcome, evidence enough of yet another scarring collision with Dame Alice. Mentally rating himself for an insensate brute, he thrust the gelding's reins at Traynor and, sheltering the quaking shoulders with his arm, drew her down to a fallen log beside him.

He had not thought once, when his neighbour Audley asked houseroom at Willowford for his exiled kinsman's daughter, that the request would lay much charge on him; it would be his mother's business to repair the fearful holes in ten years' haphazard rearing, and if Lord Audley, a rising man in King Edward's government, discreetly preferred that even so small a Lancastrian should find harbourage for the present outside his household, it seemed a slight return for his efforts in London on Philip Lovell's behalf. But they had reckoned without the fact of Margaret Devereux. While other girls her age were growing into womanhood, learning all the fashions and graces of behaviour, of feminine negotiation and reward, she had passed her life in the cramping confines of two poor rooms in Bruges, companioned only by her father and one rough-handed serving girl whom Lord Devereux—somewhat absent-mindedly—had remembered to take with him in his flight as his daughter's nurse; living hand to mouth on the beneficence of their more fortunate friends; and studying nothing but the exquisite manuscripts Lord Devereux had carried in a fishing boat all the way from Yorkshire, in preference to gear or gold. In such a state, eight years after Towton, had the conscientious Lord Audley found them; and nothing the child Margaret had learned from her father's books had prepared her for the cold-water shock of what, in Dame Alice Lovell's efficient, managing hands, she must now be moulded to. Philip had been no more able to stand aside than he could have watched one of the young lambs at Woodstock lie helpless on its back in the dimpled fields, until the shepherd or starvation came.

A breeze came freshening from the Chilterns, and the dipping sun made lances through the trees. He waited, smoothing the tumbled curls, while her tears were spent; when she was quieter he said compassionately, "Have you been in trouble again, Meg? Poor little maid, and what must I do but rail at you too. Tell me about it, then."

But she only shook her head, saying with a swallow, "It's nothing. I'm better now."

"Yes, I hope so. But you've not answered me: maybe I can help?"

Her eyes, like drenched pansies, were fixed stubbornly on the shirt cords at his neck. It was the first time she had shown reluctance to bring him her difficulties, and he reflected a moment before venturing a guess. "Was it the baths again, Meg?" He had found her once before, by the stream where he took his fishing line, scrubbing herself in the chilly water with her skirts kilted to the knees, in a vain effort to forestall the loathed ritual in the solar. She turned her head away without reply; judging it a fair surmise, Philip drew his brows together in perplexity. "Well, but Meg, people must bathe. There was a man fined in London last week for sending his prentices dirty to bed—Surely you had baths in Bruges?" He had never fathomed the reason for her intense hatred of the procedure, but suddenly it came, in a violent, rebellious cry.

"Not—not all in a tub!"

In that first blank moment of comprehension, Philip had to bite hard on his lip. She was child enough to him still so that ridiculous solution had not occurred to him; but then he looked again at the anguished colour that had flooded even to the nape of her neck, and he understood how it must be to her: the huge bath which he and his mother and sister shared with whatever relatives or guests might be visiting them; the throng of attendants with the hot towels and bowls of sweet herbs. In Bruges there had been only the sketchy comfort of a bedside pannikin, and fat Janet, who had cared for her from a baby.

"Meg." She had been trying to evade his gaze, but she lifted her head with a palpable effort when he spoke. "Meg, why ever didn't you let me—" Something made him pause. "—Let my mother know?" But she only shook her head again, and in mercy he let it go. "Well, never mind. We'll arrange—something."

A tremulous smile stirred the corners of her mouth as their eyes met. As if in apology, Margaret said presently, "I suppose you're thinking that— that we lived so poorly in Bruges, I can't get used to a proper household."

"Not quite," Philip returned lightly. "When my lord your father is restored to his due state, his daughter need expect to share neither her chamber nor her bath. Master Philip Lovell could count himself honoured then to be given a place very far down the table in Lord Devereux's hall."

"That's not true!" A fierce anger wiped the last unhappiness from her face. Smiling at the passion of the denial, Philip stooped to drag up a handful of wild strawberries, and gravely divided them. When she had sat nibbling for a while he said, "I had news of your father in London, Meg: Audley has been your good kinsman. The King has promised a pardon, and Audley believes my lord will be able to sail from Flanders next month."

Her eyes flew to his. "Next—next month?"

"Does it seem long to wait?"

A mixture of expressions strove in her face as she stared at her lap. The berries were soft between her fingers, and the juice ran in a bright stain across her skirt. "And he'll come here then—and we'll go to Yorkshire?"

Touched by the odd desolation in her voice, Philip said. "I know, you've been much uprooted in your life. But you were born there, Meg, and it's a fair country, the north."

"I can't remember. It was so long ago, you see—" Abruptly she put the last of the strawberries in her mouth, and made a business of enjoying them. "They're sweet."

"It was an early spring." He touched her chin. "I will be sorry when you go, little maid."

Studying her hands, Margaret said after a moment, "I was wondering if you—if you might care to visit us in Yorkshire one day, sir. My father would be right glad to welcome you in his hall."

"That's kind of you. If ever I am in the north, it may be we shall meet again."

She pulled nervously at her skirt, trying to straighten the rumpled folds. "You've been so good to me, sir, and it would be a joy to my lord to—to be able to repay it if he could." She looked up, resolute. "Don't be angry. But I heard my lady say there were new barns needed, and fresh roofs for the old ones—"

"And failing that, there's a tapestry of Arras I saw in London that would hang two of the four walls of my closet, and could be had, I daresay, for as little as five hundred pounds," Philip suggested. He was only half smiling. She opened her lips, but, thinking again, closed them in miserable silence; and he reached over to take her hands.

"Meg, I'm not angry. If there is one particle of yourself that has come to you from my lord your father, I know his gifts would be very gladly given. But you must understand how it is. Though my mother's dower is secure at last, and we shall want for neither necessities nor comforts now, not all the entries in my bailiffs' rolls, not all my rents and the spring clip from Woodstock could make up a tithe of your father's revenues. So you see—don't you?—why there can be no talk of presents between us. Now promise you will think no more of this. Do you promise?" She nodded, visibly unhappy still, and Philip leaned back with a barely controlled sigh of relief. The hotness of his body was like a flame; he was in a fury with himself for being unable to master it, and afraid too that the child would notice and be hurt. She was already in distress enough at the prospect of removal to yet another strange abode, for all that Lord Devereux, by Audley's account, was—in his absent scholar's fashion—a both sympathetic and indulgent parent. Audley had been very chatty about his relative and that gentleman's present activities in Flanders, but certain of his gossip Philip was keeping

31

for the moment to himself. Trying to divert her with a joke, he said at last, "You'll like it in Yorkshire, Meg. Lord Devereux has many friends there, and I should be surprised if a trackway three fingers deep isn't worn to his gates by Michaelmas, only with the train of Mistress Devereux's suitors."

As an attempt at humour, it enjoyed no marked success. Flushing to her hair, Margaret said, "I don't want them Must I be married, sir? You aren't, or Kate."

"But I ought to have been, at least ten years ago. Only my father put off seeing to it, being much occupied with other things, and afterwards our circumstances were changed. Law-beset heirs don't make the kind of marriage my mother wanted; nothing less than a baron's heiress would have suited her!" He did not add that he was devoutly thankful it had happened so. Margaret gave him a considering glance from beneath her lashes; not a conceited man, the trend of her reflections would have astonished Philip if he had been invited to share them, but some of Dame Alice's strenuous efforts at social training had told. Cheerfully unaware, he handed her to her feet, and they turned together towards the house, Traynor going before with the horses. At the courtyard gate Margaret slipped away, throwing a last bright look over her shoulder; tacit between them was the understanding that the postern would be a more prudent entryway for her, offering a line of unobtrusive retreat to the upper chamber, and the conspiratorial good offices of Dame Alice's tirewoman.

As they watched her from sight Traynor remarked, half in question, "You did not tell the little maid the rest."

"There may never be the need. It's not certain yet that Devereux means to marry; Audley only knew there was talk of it at the Duke of Burgundy's court. Devereux is very warmly received there now, being so near again to the King's favour. But he may well be thinking on it; his first wife died when Meg was born, and they say the Burgoner lady is fair, and well dowered."

"Likely my lord is wanting a son to follow him." Traynor hitched a slackened rein, and cast a speculative look at the abstracted profile. "You should be taking thought for it yourself, sir. It's in your own hands now, but my lady would like it well to see you married."

"So she has said, and named me off a string of likely maids

and widows. Don't you be starting too, Gregory. There are girls enough without those heelropes yet." The silence was disapproving, but Philip was staring over the fields to the distant hills. "There's deep trouble in the north. I hoped—I thought there might be commissions of array coming to the Midlands, but—" He shrugged, mocking himself. "The King will deal with his rebels very well, I daresay, without any help of me."

He pushed open the gate, which was unlatched in expectation of his coming. Crossing the yard to the house, he saw in the unshuttered window of the antechapel a bounce of movement, and his sister's lifted hand of welcome. She was fifteen, and still unbetrothed while her marriage portion remained in question; she would be anxious, he knew, to learn what had passed in London. He waved, and smiled an answer and went inside.

Early in July Lord Devereux set sail from Flanders, a newly married husband. His affairs had gone more speedily in the end than he had once dared to hope; Duke Charles of Burgundy, lately heir to his father's dignities, had shown himself all kindness, adding his voice to Lord Audley's at Westminster on the exile's behalf. A magnanimous prince, Edward had been disposed to listen; he had, besides, recently married his youngest sister to Charles of Burgundy, and was very willing to firm the alliance by pleasing his brother-in-law. Lord Devereux's enlistment of Charles' support had been itself not without price, but, still relishing the sweets of his new domesticity, he confided to his bride that for all the Duke's bargaining, they had gone quite well. A fresh wind carried them briskly towards England, and the tall cliffs shone like marble in the sunlight as they neared the coast, veering slightly from their course as an inconspicuous vessel slipped past them out of Sandwich, bound for Calais. The identity of its passengers might have surprised William Devereux, but, happily scanning the familiar shoreline, he barely noticed as the sails dipped from sight. Lord Audley was waiting at Dover; he had a warm greeting for his kinsman, and a hearty kiss for his lady.

It had been Devereux's intention to present himself gratefully at Westminster without delay, but Edward was in the north, wholly engaged in the suppression of a disturbance which had unexpectedly assumed the proportions of well organised rebellion. Edward's concern would have been the greater had he known that, in his absence, his wayward brother Clarence and the Earl of Warwick had fled together to Calais, where Isabel Neville and her mother were already waiting. A few days later the marriage which Edward had striven four years to prevent finally took place, and within the month Warwick and his new son-in-law were back in London, recruiting an army which, it was given out, was to help the King with his northern rebels. The banner of the rose and sun of York was hoisted, and, sped on by London's loyal cheers, the Earl of Warwick and the Duke of Clarence marched away.

Shortly before Lord Devereux began to consider embarking upon his leisurely journey from London to Oxfordshire, Philip was making a departure of his own from Willowford. He had had no further message from Audley, who in fact was too preoccupied with making smooth his returned relative's way in London to have had a thought of sending one; and it seemed probable to Philip that, with or without a wife, Margaret's father had not yet sailed for England. A complexity of affairs clamoured for attention at Woodstock, where the household intended to remove until harvest time, and there were visits as well that he should make to the intervening demesnes of Tuttenham and Little Barking, left too many months only to the supervision of the bailiffs. He would be a fortnight gone at very least, he told his family, and laughed at Margaret as she stood in the courtyard, wistfully watching the sumpters loaded. "Little maid, I cannot take you in my saddlebags to Woodstock! The place must be made fit to live in, and in twenty years I daresay my mother will trust the steward." He pinched her cheek, and swung his cloak over his arm. "Is hawk management new to you? You shall have your own merlin at Woodstock; we'll try what we can bring down together, once we're settled there."

He mounted and nodded to Traynor. A scant escort of servants was already horsed and waiting; with Traynor leading they followed him under the gatehouse, around the beeches at the head of the path, and out of sight.

The prophesied fortnight passed with no more incident than the appearance of a liveried rider at Willowford, enquiring for its master. He seemed pressed, but, directed to Woodstock, spurred away without explanation; and two weeks had stretched into three before the dusk of a summer evening brought the party from Woodstock once more clattering up the narrow path. The gate was locked, but a hammered summons brought the porter, and, his customary deliberate stride lengthened with urgency. Gregory Traynor pushed past him into the courtyard. Leaving a trio of companions to answer the gatekeeper's astonished questions—for it was long past the hour when the household might have expected them—Traynor made his way to the house at a near-run. Neither Dame Alice nor Kate was in the hall; an aproned serving girl confided with a giggle that they were entertaining a visitor in the great chamber abovestairs: Sir William Secott from Ipsden way, a rich knight six months a widower, and didn't Mistress Kate know well why he should be calling at Willowford now. Traynor's exasperated stare around the hall failed equally to discover the steward; he hesitated, and with a glance at the darkening windows muttered finally, "Well, too late this night anyway. I'll have a sup in the kitchen, wench; do you send word to my lady." He turned back to the narrow passage behind the screens, his mind dwelling pleasurably upon the prospect of a jack of ale; but in the half-lit gallery a pair of hands clutched at him. "Gregory Traynor!—is it you then, Gregory?"

"Nowt else," Traynor rejoined sourly, and with difficulty freed himself of the clinging grasp. He was tired, and would have been glad of the chance to rest his legs before Dame Alice sent for him; but a second look at the blotched, distraught countenance made him pause. "So you've heard? Give over, woman: it's none so bad as that! Blithe as a lad free of the schoolman, I left Master Philip, and if my lady and Mistress Kate can sit happy with that great lump Secott, there's no cause for you to be setting up a cry."

A smothered sob answered him. She was an untidy, full-breasted creature – who waited in Dame Alice's chamber, of large sympathy and easy tears; they were falling fast now. "Then he's *not* with you, the master? Oh, angels have mercy—Gregory, it's the little maid. She's gone."

"Gone?" Traynor repeated stupidly. "Gone where?"

"There's no knowing. I've been looking since supper—we thought her abovestairs, and paid no mind when she didn't come down to table—small reason she had to eat, poor little lamb, I wasn't going to worrit at her, and with Sir William here the mistress never noticed—But then I went after to fetch her up a bite, lark pasty it was, her favourite, and—and she was gone."

Holding hard on his patience, Traynor said, "Talk plain, for love of God. Why should she be gone anywhere?"

There were more tears, with the words coming indistinctly through the flow. "Well you may ask! Oh, it was wicked cruel—I'll say nothing of my lord Audley, it was none of his doing, but for the little maid's own father— A fine new wife he brought with him, spoke foreign she did, with never a word the mistress knew, but Mistress Meg understood her well enough. Gregory, they've promised her to one of the Burgoner Duke's barons. A great lord, with two wives already laid under the earth, and I had it from my lady Devereux's woman that he's a hard, proud-stomached man, and twenty years older than Mistress Meg's own father. She didn't believe it, asked her father to explain to her in English, for it must be she'd been too long from Burgundy to understand their French tongue clear any more. Then they told her: there's papers sealed, and she's to go this very month. It was the Duke of Burgundy's own wish—seems he said he'd had good service from my lord Brezy—that's his outlandish name—and it was as cheap a way of paying him as he knew, out of my lord Devereux's moneybags. Wants an heir too, my lord Brezy does, and neither of his wives before gave him one: the Duke said he might do better this time, the third time being lucky as the saying goes. Aye, they told her that too, making a joke of it, and her only standing there with her face like snow. My lord Devereux looked red before he was done, but he wasn't changing his mind for all that. She didn't ask him to—just cried out that if he'd wanted a husband for her he needn't have gone so far to find him, though dear knows what she meant by that—and then she ran from the room."

A pause followed, while Traynor chewed scowlingly at his lower lip. "And she's been gone since then? And you've told no one? Woman, you're a fool."

"I was afraid for the trouble she'd be in. They all went back to Stratton Audley after—the mistress said they'd do better to go and leave the little maid to her. She wasn't above half pleased, I could tell that though she wasn't saying so; she hadn't taken to my lord Devereux's wife at all— And then, while they were all leaving, Sir William came. I've been looking and looking, but I can't find her and it's coming on for night—"

But Traynor was already halfway along the passage to the door. Passing for the second time the hall entry, he glanced briefly at the stair to the upper chamber, but the point as to Dame Alice's wrath had been well taken. Mentally allowing himself a few minutes for a look-round first, he went out into the courtyard. It was empty now, and a slip of moon showed above the walls; beyond, the huge tops of the beeches floated in a darker mass against the sky. The mere thought of a girl roaming the countryside at such an hour made his scalp tingle; though Willowford lay some miles off the London-to-Oxford road, there was enough travel in the neighbourhood to draw the thieves' bands which no prudent wayfarer kept far from remembrance, or roving beggars who would kill for what the corpse yielded them. The groom's frowning eyes rested on the locked gate; it was a puzzle to him how she could have got out without the porter having seen her. Then he remembered the postern.

He made use of it himself, as little inclined as had been the fugitive before him for the gatekeeper's enquiries. Once outside, he made a grim survey of the slopes of meadow and ploughland, looked for an instant in the direction of the stream, hurrying and murmuring towards the mill, and, about to give it up, paused on a thought. Presently he pulled the gate to behind him, and, cautiously skirting the walls, made his way around to the front of the house. Moonlight threw a tracery of shadows along the path and brightened the dust to silver; not a breeze stirred, and the leaves hung like shapes of stone. In the deeper blot of the beeches he halted and stared up. Everything was still, but after a moment he put a foot in the gnarled crotch of the lowest one; it had been pollarded once, and the knotted boughs had grown into fantastic forms. Hoisting himself to the first level, Traynor stopped and peered again; and he heard the breathing stop above him.

"Mistress Meg," he said softly. "Little maid, you cannot stay here. Come down, now; here's my hand."

He held it out coaxingly. His eyes were adjusting to the darkness, and he could just make her out, perched like a squirrel on one of the thick branches. She leaned towards him, the tips of her fingers finding his, and the movement brought her face into the moonlight.

"I heard you come back, Gregory," she whispered. "I was sure you'd come today. Gregory—" Even in the dimness he could see the shy colour flooding to her brows. "—Gregory, will you fetch Master Philip for me? Tell him, it's—it's very important."

Traynor swallowed, awkward with pity before the hope in her eyes. After a long pause he said, "He's not with me, Mistress. He's not come back from Woodstock."

She neither moved nor spoke; desperately he hurried into explanation. "It was a message fom the Duke of Gloucester came to Woodstock, Mistress. The King's been taken prisoner by my lord of Warwick and the Duke of Clarence, and my lord of Gloucester's gone into the west to raise a strength to deliver him. He needs men cruel bad, little maid, and he's sent for Master Philip to help him—the steward will be taking all the men at Willowford that can bear bill or bow tomorrow, to join the master at Corfe. I was sent back to tell my lady, and bring master steward the word."

Margaret said slowly, "Then he—he's gone? He's not coming back?"

"He was friends with the Duke of Middleham," Traynor responded gently. "He'd never refuse him, in so great a need."

He was still gripping her hand; the fingers had grown cold in his with a chill that reached the bones. "You should not be out here, Mistress Meg, it's not safe. Think of my lord your father, and how he would be fair beside himself, if only he knew—" He felt her flinch, and went on resolutely. "Truly now, a father knows best for his little maid. Do you think he'd do aught but what was for your good? And it's a fine, great place he's fixed for you to have, you've no cause to complain of him for that."

He waited anxiously, trying to see her face, but she had turned it from the light. "Will you not come down? My lady knows nothing, I promise you—and you cannot stay here, little maid."

He heard her soft breath again in the leafy stillness above. Leaning her other hand on his shoulder, Margaret straightened painfully from her difficult position. "Yes," she said quietly. "Yes, I'll come down."

Still clutching his arm, she let him lift her after him to the ground.

CHAPTER THREE

WARWICK and Clarence had run their quarry to earth in Buckinghamshire. Days before, the Herbert brothers' loyal troops, hurrying from the west to Edward's relief, had collided bloodily with the northern rebels' well-equipped forces; Warwick and Clarence, coming up from the south, fell on the King's friends from behind to finish the rout. The captive Herberts, hated for the favour Edward had shown them, were taken to Coventry and put to death.

Ignorant of the disaster to his reinforcements, Edward was cautiously making his way south from Nottingham when news of the defeat reached him. A copy of the rebel proclamation was in his hands, and a glance was sufficient to identify its authorship. All Warwick's grievances were set out: the thrusting ambition of the Woodvilles, the increasing prominence of Edward's favourites which was ousting the ancient power of the King's own blood. It was Warwick and Clarence speaking with one voice, and, driven to the wall, Edward yielded. His small force was quickly disbanded, and the two Woodville brothers-in-law, with their father, Earl Rivers, were urged to flee for their lives. Incontinently they did so, and when Warwick's brother the Archbishop of York, suave in steel and plumes, came up with Edward at Olney, he found the King alone but for a handful of servants, his chamberlain the lord Hastings, and his brother Richard of Gloucester.

Courteously the Archbishop invited his cousin to ride with him to Coventry, and with an eye on the mailed escort at George Neville's back, Edward pleasantly agreed. The Neville troops surrounded him, falling in swiftly before and behind; Richard made an instinctive movement and halted, his hand falling from his sword. Leaning sideways from the saddle, Edward embraced him cheerfully, and bade the silent Hastings an unconcerned farewell. George Neville's instructions had included no reference to either; Warwick still had hopes of bringing Hastings, never a lover of the Woodvilles, to a new way of thinking, and the Duke of Gloucester, although having proven a less tractable subject for persuasion than Richard Neville had once supposed, was not yet seventeen and manifestly of no importance. They were carelessly bidden to take themselves where they would, and flushed with triumph, the Archbishop set off with his prize for Coventry.

As the sound of hoofs faded Richard and Hastings drew apart from their attendants to speak quietly together beneath the trees. Presently, their plans made, they separated on their different ways. Hastings to go into the north and the younger man riding hard for the western counties. Richard's messenger, charged with a number of errands in the area, was disappointed at Willowford and, turning north, met its owner on the road scant hours after he had embarked upon a leisurely return journey from Woodstock. Thinking from the Yorkist livery that there had been, perhaps, a further development in the recent suit, Philip took unsuspecting the letter he was offered, broke the seal without glancing at it, and spread the sheet. After a moment he turned it, frowning, and his eyes found the signature, black and emphatic beneath the secretary's regular hand. Suddenly pale, he flicked the paper over and began again.

A minute later he looked up. "This letter is from the Duke of Gloucester, Gregory. He commands me to join him in the west with all speed—there's no time to return to Willowford, so do you take word to my mother; tell her I don't know how long I shall be away, but I will send word soon. And see to it that as many men as are able come to me at Corfe; tell the steward I look to him to bring them without delay." His mind, blazing with excitement, was running on armour too; but his father's was no fit for him. He must make do with what he could find at Corfe, and have his own made when time allowed, now there was excuse for so great an expenditure. Questioned for details, the messenger explained and enlarged upon what his master had been too pressed to write, and Philip listened in silence, staring at Richard's letter with its heavy seal: a ship, for the Admiral of England, Ireland, and Aquitaine, with the leopards and lilies of Plantagenet on the sail. The device of three words was new since their Middleham days: *Loyaulté me lie.*

The party at length divided, Philip taking the southwest road to Dorset, and Traynor with the two remaining servants hurrying on to Willowford. Despite the chances that impended, the groom could not help a chuckle as he rode; for

Philip had been transparently delighted to be slipping his domestic hobbles, and Traynor, who had been some months apprehensively telling over in his mind all the temptations into which young men were commonly drawn through boredom or no fit occupation, breathed on the summer morning a sigh of satisfaction and relief.

Darkness was falling next day as Philip made the steep ascent to Richard's West Country hold. Groups of men were busy in the outer and middle baileys, working with pieces of harness and weapons of every description; my lord, they said, was on the walls, and a sweating smith's helper left his bellows by the forge to indicate the stair.

The walkway behind the parapet was narrow, and Philip had to pick his steps in the dying light. Near the bulge of the gatehouse tower a man stood alone, gazing down at the approaches to the bridge; he turned when the footfall sounded, saying half in question, "Philip?" and held out his hand.

He was taller by a little, and his hair had darkened from mahogany to brown; but even in the shadow Philip saw these were not the only changes. Whatever had been of youth in his face was gone; his eyes looked wary, as if he had learned more easily to doubt than trust, and he carried self-command like a weapon. They embraced, and stood back to regard each other, and Richard said with a gleam, "I knew who it must be when I saw you ride in. There is no other gentleman in England that would not think shame to show himself abroad with a train of two men at his back."

It was an old joke between them, but already there seemed no strangeness about his remembering it. Philip responded smiling, "There will be more to follow; your courier took me on the highway as I rode back from Woodstock," and Richard said carelessly, "Then you are satisfied in your business there? You were a great fool about that, Philip; name of God, I could be angry that you were four years in sending me word. You have had a weary wait in consequence for your just rights."

A little silence fell. "Woodstock?" Philip repeated. He had stiffened in spite of himself. "What do you know of that trouble, my lord?"

Richard said mildly, "Why, Audley came to me about it in London in the spring; he was concerned for the progress of your suit, and reasonably so, it appeared to me. Didn't you know?"

41

Philip bit his lip. "No—no, I did not. I am grateful beyond words for your grace's favour, but I already owe you too much—"

The depth of his reaction surprised him; he broke off, ashamed and struggling with himself, and Richard said coolly, "Something less of my gracious favour, by your leave; I pleased myself as much as anyone over that little affair. You've been fighting Woodvilles, Philip: Didn't you know? Your kinsman Jennings was wiser than you; he took the trouble to get Earl Rivers' good lordships before ever he turned to thinking about your mother's dower. It is a rich property: Lord Rivers would have been not ill-pleased with his share."

He leaned an elbow in the crenellation of the parapet, his chin on his fist, his eyes dwelling as if in irony on his companion's face. A spear of light springing from the guard tower gleamed on his hair, showing warm chestnut still. Philip was silent, but a deep colour burned on his cheekbones; presently looking away, Richard added in a different voice, "If you are supposing you have had justice measured out to you in proportion to my interest, get rid of the notion. The King was angry when he heard of Rivers' meddling, but he would not have stirred one finger if I had not been able to satisfy him of the justice of your claim. His grace does not tinker so with his courts, although others may do so in his name." His face darkened, and he was quiet for a time, tapping with his finger on the ledge. "You think you have been injured by the Woodvilles? You are not alone. They have made the court a very sink; they crawl like caterpillars through the chambers of the justices, and there is not a corner of all England they have not filthied with their slime. Rivers is only one, but he is the model for them all."

Philip knit his brows, remarking, "But if this is your mind, my lord, why should you be here? The rebels have never claimed they meant anything but to part the King from his wife's kindred."

Across his shoulder, Richard met his eyes. "Do you think me a fool? The rebels may have been persuaded they are taking up arms only against my brother's favourites, but the Earl of Warwick has quite another ambition. Believe me, I have known these three years past what my cousin of Warwick is about."

"His grace of Clarence," Philip observed carefully, "does not seem to share your opinion."

After a long pause, Richard said only, "No." Expressionless, he stared down through the gathering dusk at the long road winding away from the bridge. It had been a hot summer; the water in the ditch was low, and flies buzzed over the muddy banks. He slapped at one, and turned away.

"Philip, in a few days I expect to ride to join Hastings; he is raising a force in the north. Will you come with me?"

Philip smiled at him, flicking his boot with his riding whip. "Why else should I be here?"

"The times are uncertain; I can't swear you will make your fortune in my service."

"I wasn't seeking it, my lord."

They looked at each other, and suddenly the younger man was smiling too. "Oh, you have not changed a whit. I've been sick for Middleham sometimes, Philip—Rob Percy is below, did you see him? Come then, we'll share a cup in my chamber."

He went towards the stair. His cloak was lying where he had left it, flung over the parapet; as he turned to follow, Philip picked it up. The wool smelled of herbs from the chest, and warm sun. Years after, he was still able to recall the feel of it, swinging across his arm, as they went downstairs.

On the evening of the day that Philip Lovell arrived at Corfe, the Earl of Warwick and King Edward were confronting each other in Coventry. It was an encounter for which Warwick had unconsciously braced himself, but Edward greeted him amiably, signed unprotesting the bale of parchments—gifts of property to Neville supporters, rewards of office to Neville men—which had been prepared by Warwick's clerks, and endured without visible annoyance the replacement of his personal servants by the Earl's watchful retainers. His hope now lay in persuading his captors he could be as docile a puppet as the biddable Clarence, his waiting heir; and he knew what the price of failure would be. Compliance notwithstanding, the Earl soon had his cousin conveyed to the better safekeeping of Warwick Castle; two weeks later he decided that Middleham would be surer still, and by rapid marches himself conducted his prisoner north to Wensleydale. To any eye he held both king and kingdom in his hand; he had given himself the pleasure of sending Edward's father-in-law Rivers and one of his sons, captured at Chepstow, to execution outside the city walls; he enjoyed besides the discreet good wishes of King Louis, who had sheltered the exiled queen of Lancaster, Margaret of Anjou, and her son long enough in France to make clear his unfailing delight in Yorkist embarrassments; but reports of riot and rebellion were coming in from the southern counties, where men seemed unaware that the obedience they had once owed King Edward was now due his keeper, and the parliament Warwick had hoped to assemble to confirm him in his authority proved an illusory hope. September came, itching and uneasy, and an abrupt new peril exploded in the north: a rising of Lancastrians inspired, Warwick wrathfully learned, by one of his own kin. Viewing from afar his great relative's preoccupations, Humphrey Neville had seized his graceless chance; and when the call to arms went out to deal with him, Warwick discovered the summer's business had done its disastrous work. Increasingly suspicious of the Earl of Warwick's purpose, men said openly they fought no more for the house of Neville until they knew what it was about. They were King Edward's subjects, saving only the need, now past, of persuading him from the influence of certain evil advisers; when the King himself told them he had want of soldiers, they would come.

In the end, it was the Archbishop of York who went to Middleham to treat for terms. He found Edward in the presence chamber, unconcernedly playing at tables with a dark youth whom the Archbishop remembered as the Earl's ward, Francis Lovell; it was a cosy scene, the King's cup standing ready to the boy's hand for serving, and a fire on the hearth to take the chill, and it crossed George Neville's mind that it could be no part of his brother's design to have the members of his household on such friendly terms with their guest. Edward, however, was almost unbearably obliging; he said affably that he would be glad to support his cousin's writ in exchange for a more congenial place of residence, and mentioned Pontefract, his own castle near York, as a suitable choice. It was also much nearer the centre of his affairs, and considerably more accessible to those friends who might want to get in secret touch with him; but, wedged on the horns, the Archbishop had no alternative than helplessly to agree.

A few days later King Edward entered his city of York. Citizens and gentry from miles distant swarmed to offer homage, and, their King once more among them, the northerners turned out loyally for his service. Desperate as the situation had become, Warwick could have found comfort in discovering his second appeal to be as ineffective as the first; but with humiliating alacrity the recruits streamed in, and scant hours after Edward had gone in state to Pontefract his cousin was speeding north with a bright array of scarlet jackets and fluttering pennons, his lacerated temper only slightly helped by the prospect of bringing Humphrey Neville to understanding of the error of his ways. Retribution, swift and terrible, descended upon the insurgent Neville and his band as the Earl of Warwick whirled down on them, and pausing only long enough to fling away their arms, the Lancastrians took to their heels. Within days the last flicker of rebellion had been ruthlessly stamped out, and the captive leader brought in fetters to York to answer for his treason. Edward was pleased to ride over from Pontefract for the occasion, and with his cousin of Warwick beside him on the dais which overlooked the square watched with unmoved countenance as Humphrey Neville paid for his misjudgment with his life. The axe swung; the crowd whispered and was still; and a gasp, quickly suppressed, came from the youth who stood behind the King.

"For shame, Francis: fainting at a little traitor blood?" Edward remarked without turning his head, and there was a choke of denial from his attendant. "No, your grace. But, he's still moving—"

"A just end for a pestilent traitor," Edward said coldly. "He has led many poor folk to their deaths; I do not pity him."

Francis swallowed, and was silent. There was a warm clamminess about his midriff; he fixed his eyes on the platform boards, and by keeping an ear to the comment of the onlookers managed to judge when the executioners had finished their work. Trumpets blew; heralds proclaimed in old Norman; and with the blind eyes of Humphrey Neville staring after him from a pike's pole, the Earl of Warwick attended his cousin through cheering throngs to the gates of York. There, in an atmosphere redolent of the friendliest goodwill, Edward parted from his faithful kinsmen. He had solicited the Earl for the continued companionship of his ward, declaring him more lively company than Pontefract's solemn men-at-arms, and Warwick shrugged an assent. He was hardly thinking of Francis Lovell then, having just had from a servant the whispered tidings that a man in the Duke of Buckingham's livery was believed to have been seen in York, watching among the crowd below the executioner's platform in the square. As Warwick bade his cousin farewell, it was with abstracted eyes and a mind wholly bent on speculation as to what a servant of Harry Stafford should be doing hundreds of miles from his young master's West Country lands. Buckingham was a stripling, no older than Richard of Gloucester, but after the heirs of York and Lancaster he was the prince next in blood, and if the nobles of England—for the most part Lancastrian once, now weakened and embittered by defeat—were to rouse themselves to interfere in the struggle between York and York, the Stafford name was one they would follow. Intently brooding, Warwick remembered too the Duke of Clarence, sullenly awaiting him at Sheriff Hutton; the young man had expected to be offered his brother's crown, and was accepting with poor grace his diminished importance in the Earl of Warwick's schemes: his, too, was a name that people would heed. For the course of the ride back through York the Earl pondered with hardening eyes, and by mid-afternoon he was racing before a train of breathless followers for his castle of Sheriff Hutton. The Duke of Buckingham might or might not be himself in the north of England, for what purpose could only be guessed; but, Richard Neville grimly promised himself, whatever else befell, the Duke of Clarence was to be allowed no opportunity to slip from the peril of his present entanglements into the safe shelter of King Edward's bosom.

Hardly an hour after Edward had quitted York, an unobtrusive horseman passed through the Mickle Gate and started at full speed after the royal procession. Edward had set a leisurely pace, and the afternoon was barely spent when Francis overtook the cavalcade and brought his neat mare up behind the King's great charger. He was received with a round denunciation for neglect in failing to present himself when the party left York, and, the pricking ears of Warwick's soldiers thus satisfied, Edward consented to be appeased. Later there were more signs of a return to favour when he granted the truant the honour of his company as they drew slightly ahead of the rest of the party. The cheek-strap of his horse's bridle seemed to worry him; he bent as if to examine it, and with primmed-up mouth and dancing look Francis met the questioning eyes.

"All well, sir. I had word with the Duke of Buckingham as soon as you had gone, and he meets with Sir John Howard tonight. My lord of Essex arrived as I was leaving, and the Earl of Warwick and the Archbishop have gone off to Sheriff Hutton, at furious speed, I was told."

Edward considered a little. "They may have heard something," he conceded. "In which case, may God grant wings to our friends! You had better be very busy at your prayers tonight, Francis: I shall be heartily rehearsing my own." He gazed towards the hills, adding reflectively, "And you would do well to make sure the Earl of Warwick learns nothing of this day's work. I will protect you while I am able, but I can't take you from his keeping yet: your wardship has been worth a deal to his coffers since I told it to him, remember. I must gain my ground slowly, so it is never quite worth the risk for him to move against me: Do you understand?"

Francis made a light reply. To the members of his household, Richard Neville was a remote and awesome figure whose comings and goings were as little questioned as the courses of the stars; but his authority had always made itself felt through his officers, and it seemed unlikely that the Earl would descend from Olympus to concern himself with his ward. So voiced, it appeared a rashly optimistic point of view to Edward, whose experience with his cousin had long ago taught him there were few things the Earl of Warwick overlooked; and there was a trace of curiosity in his voice as he said, "I wonder why you took the risk? It's not a small one, and as I recall your father was a faithful servant to Lancaster. What do you care for your Yorkist troubles?"

Embarrassed, Francis avoided the speculative eyes. The chance to participate in the affairs of Richard of Gloucester, however distantly, was one he would not for half his inheritance have relinquished, but he had no intention of admitting it. Presently he grinned and said, "Why not? It's a pleasure to disoblige my wife's family."

Edward was amused. "You have done that, for a certainty. But the Fitz Hughs are no greater enemies to York than some of your own relatives, my dear Francis, and the family were good Lancastrians before ever your respected father-in-law made himself busy with Neville schemes. I daresay there are many feel it a very suitable match for you."

A warm colour had risen in the boy's cheeks. "It was no choice of mine, sir."

"No, it was mine in the beginning," Edward acknowledged cheerfully. "And the Earl of Warwick has made as fine a profit as I did from your bridals, for which I trust he thanks me. And yet—" His eyes narrowed. "Yes, he's been wonderfully friendly with old Lancastrians lately. How strange it would be if he took that way in the end! Really I can hardly think he would be so foolish: Margaret of Anjou is not the woman to forget my cousin was one of those that said her son had the Duke of Somerset for father."

The sun sank, westering; the shadows grew longer. From the corner of his eye Francis studied briefly the profile of the man beside him, half-hidden by the loosely curling auburn hair. Ruthless, intelligent, sensually self-indulgent, it told him as usual nothing its owner did not wish. The familiarity of a dozen weeks had brought a certain ease, but it would have taken a coarser grain of assurance than Francis Lovell owned to proceed from that to carelessness. In whatever state he kept, no stranger, seeking him, would have asked, "Which is the King?"

Pontefract lay ahead, its tiled roofs and Norman church tower clustered like toys around the fortress rock. In the last twilight they rode up the castle hill, and the gate dropped after them.

Less than a week later, the Earl of Warwick was storming up the same rocky slope. A scattered retinue streamed in his wake, and to the rear a reluctant Clarence rode knee to knee with the Archbishop of York, the younger man's near arm within easy reach of an instant archiepiscopal grasp. Ignoring the progressive delaying action behind him, Warwick swept into the courtyard and, brushing aside the greetings of his seneschal, demanded to be conducted to his cousin.

Edward was on the west curtain, leaning against the battlements as he looked towards the distant Pennine peaks. He turned, politely questioning, as the Earl exploded into his presence, and remarked, "Why cousin, I had not expected you. Your lordship is in a considerable haste: Do we have another rising?"

Warwick spoke curtly, ignoring the gibe. "I shall be glad if your grace will accompany me. We leave on the instant for Middleham."

Edward replied gently, "I think not, my lord," and Warwick came a step closer.

"I had not solicited your opinion, cousin," he said softly. There was murder in his face, but the blue eyes stared back, unmoved.

"I am aware. But have you spoken with the Earl of Essex? He is below, taking refreshment in the hall with Howard and Mountjoy. It may be they will be surprised to learn of your plans."

Warwick was silent for an instant, shocked into immobility, and the pause was interrupted by Francis Lovell, who came racing down the nearer tower stair and burst through the arched entry, exclaiming, "Sir, the Duke of Buckingham is coming, and my lord of Arundel is with him!"

"Thank you, Francis," Edward said calmly, and simultaneously Francis identified the looming height above him. Checking with a gasp, he muttered an excuse and was backing towards the stair when a chilly voice halted him.

"One moment, Francis," Warwick said evenly.

Francis stopped, apprehensively enquiring, and warily retraced his steps. "My lord?" His heart was thumping painfully, but it did not occur to him to look at Edward for help. An unresentful realist, he expected none.

As he came nearer Warwick reached out to grasp his shoulder, turning his face into the sunlight. "I have been thinking about you, Francis. I didn't see you with his grace when he left York a few days ago: will you be good enough to tell me what you were doing?"

Francis opened his mouth, hesitated, and retrieved his voice. "Wenching," he said defiantly. Desreputably inspired by other lawless occasions, it was the best his invention could do. Jerking him closer, Warwick said in a hard tone, "Don't play games with me, malapert. What were you up to in York?"

A sudden colour burned in Francis' cheeks. He was passionately inclined to inform the Earl of Warwick that it in no way became a jumped-up Yorkshireman, sprung from obscurity barely a generation before, to mishandle a descendant of the Lovell barons who had held their lands from Henry Fitz Empress' times. The particular impulse was, with difficulty, repressed; but his voice shook as he said, "I was at the Dove, in Bawd's Lane, for an hour after his grace left York. There's a trull called Greasy Doll that will remember: Why don't you ask her? Call her Dollie, she likes that!"

It was the echo of his own voice, lingering horribly through the shock of Edward's lashing "Francis!" which sobered him like icy water. He saw the swift movement of Warwick's hand, and tried instinctively to recoil from it, but the iron grip doubled back his arm and pinned him hurtfully to the ramparts. He stood trembling, his teeth in his lower lip and blinking to keep back the watering tears: it was in his mind he was about to be thrown from the walls. There was a pause, while he heard above him the sound of Warwick's unhurried breathing, and felt his eyes, like obsidian, opaque and unreadable in the mask of his face. Then abruptly the Earl unclosed his hand. "You have leave, Francis. I will send for you later: be ready."

Edward was still leaning against the parapet. He paid no attention to Francis' hasty reverence, having been for some minutes absorbed in turning the jewel on his thumb, but as the boy's footsteps died he remarked neutrally, "I quite agree, cousin. An unpardonable exhibition." He took a fleeting glance at Warwick's profile, and added in a disinterested way, "I haven't any notion what he was doing while he was in York. If he did go to that noisome hovel—the Dove, did he call it?—I must be sorry I did not oversee his conduct more closely while he was in my company. He might easily have ended being poisoned, or having his throat cut."

Warwick said steadily, "Cousin, do you take me for a fool?"

Breaking a bit of mortar from the ledge, Edward tossed it over the side and watched the tiny splash in the water below. "No, my lord, I do not. But you will look sorely like one if you make a tumult in the stews of York searching for a harlot called Greasy Doll." He saw the Earl's mouth tighten, and went on smoothly, "Consider your dignity, my lord. Think of the tale it would make in Lille, where the Duke of Burgundy is no friend of yours: that the Earl of Warwick let his cousin slip through his fingers, and thought his own ward to blame. Think of your enemies at Louis' court; they would be glad to tell the story in France, and as you know Louis has his own sense of humour. Think of the rhymes of the ballad-

50

mongers in London, embroidering the theme." His blue eyes, limpidly resting on the dark ones, took due note of the involuntary flicker of expression; he dropped a hand to the rigid arm. "My dear kinsman, you will have only yourself to blame if this story goes abroad to your enemies. I have no reason to publish a tale which, after all, both you and I know to be quite untrue."

There was a short silence. Fixedly considering the younger man, Warwick could discern nothing but a detached and sympathetic interest; and slowly the Earl turned away.

"I must concede your grace the advantage. I agree, not a tale that would add to my credit at any time."

"I am sure no one realises the need for discretion more than your ward," Edward said carelessly. "I have passed some pleasant hours in his company; I should not like to think he was punished too severely for the sin of having enjoyed my favour." He was gazing at his rings. His lip curling, Warwick said, "I don't make war on schoolboys, cousin."

Edward controlled a smile. "I had not supposed it, my lord. And don't lay on too hard for that unruly tongue; it's easier to govern spirit than to instil it. So, many a time, you used to say to my father: Do you remember?" He nodded over the wall. "Buckingham and Arundel seem to be upon us. Shall we send word for them to wait upon us here?"

Tense with anger, Warwick met the equable regard. "Do you really think to impress me with these gentlemen? I have men in the courtyard: I've not heard the noble lords troubled to bring many such with them."

"No, of course not," Edward agreed. "But here is something that may interest you, my lord." He moved aside and, turning, stretched an arm across the battlements. Warwick hesitated, then stepped to his side, following the pointing finger with swift anxiety. His eyes searched the skyline, and his breath caught. Along the edge of the hills a brilliance sparkled: a frieze of lances, pennon-decked, their thousand polished tips gilded by the sun to fiery gold. He leaned forward in disbelief, straining to make out the standards, and Edward said cheerfully, "They're a little far yet to recognise. One belongs to Hastings, you'll know that when you see it. The other, my lord, is Blancsanglier—the white boar of Gloucester. This time I mean to have an army I can trust." He swung round, his shoulders against the crenellated stone, his back to the nearing brightness threading like a ribbon the

Pennine folds. "I think, cousin, that it is time I returned to Westminster."

In the extending pause they measured each other, and it was the Earl of Warwick, that never in his life had been outfaced by man, who looked away. In a white flash of brutal clarity he saw himself: an ageing adventurer who had out-lived the opportunities of a finished time. The red-haired, merry-eyed youth with whom he had thrown back and crushed the ancient chivalry of England had better read the omen and its meaning: for Richard Neville, blazing meteor-like across the turmoil of collapsing feudalism, the arc of his passing was a printless light.

Even as the hammer strokes of recognition beat against his brain, he thrust the knowledge from him. He saw quite plainly the trouble in Edward's eyes, and in the same instant haughtily rejected it; they stood at pause, divided as by a wall of glass—mortared of bitterness, reared high by anger bred from their widely diverging ways—and through it neither touch nor tongue could reach: only the clear sight of strangers who have met and passed by the way, and grief, and remembrance of the fled years. The moment ended, and the balance beam which for a breath had tilted and trembled in doubt came down forever.

"My dear cousin, there is no need that we should quarrel," Warwick said graciously. "You are right of course; you have been too long among us in the north, and the Duke of Gloucester and Lord Hastings have very properly brought a fit escort for your return."

Serenely smiling, Edward inclined his head. "Then will you be so kind as to bear my greetings to the gentlemen? I shall be with you presently."

Warwick bowed, and took his leave. Within the tower he halted in his descent to stand for a while at the slit of window that faced the hills. Nearer Pontefract the ground levelled to make easy going, and the first horsemen were shortly in the town, narrowing their files to single column as they threaded the twisting streets. Without looking more he went on down to the courtyard.

Leaning his weight on his crossed arms, Edward gazed at the bright array beneath the castle walls. In the market square someone had set up a standard; the coloured leather of the horses' trappings swung and fluttered, and the soldiers moved like dolls, dark in their padded brigandines or flashing with plate and tabard. Far below, a herald rode forward to the thin crying of pursuivants; back of them, as he sat waiting for answer, Will Hastings' great girth made one statue with his destrier, and there was another, slighter figure beside him. As if feeling his brother's eyes, Richard raised his own; and they both smiled. The bridge was down, and the first riders clattered over it beyond the watcher's sight.

Edward was about to follow Warwick down when the Archbisop of York appeared, breathless, in the tower door. He had Clarence behind him, nervously lingering in the shadow of the stair. After a single glance Edward would have gone by in silence, but Clarence caught his sleeve, whispering. "A—a word with you, brother." He was trying clumsily to kneel, but there was no room for it.

Edward halted, standing so near that the younger man had to lean back his head to meet his eyes. "Not even so much, George. You have your life, for which thank the power of our cousin your father-in-law, and no love of mine. Let that content you until the day I can remember again the same belly carried us. At this moment"—he paused, his voice thickening—"by the very tears of Christ, you offend my sight."

He went on down the stair. Near the foot it angled sharply; as he reached the curve there were hurrying footsteps beyond, and his face lightened as he strode to meet them. "Dickon—" And then, lower, "No, then—so. Ah, God be thanked for having given me such a brother."

The well of the other tower carried the voice upward, although the speaker had passed from view. Clarence listened, resting his head against the stonework, while the footsteps faded. The Archbishop had gone too, with clutched-up robes hurrying anxiously after Edward down the stair; another time, Clarence thought, he would have laughed to see the sight. For a space he remained, wondering what he would do now, or where he could go. Dimly he remembered he had a wife somewhere, a girl he had been put to bed with so he could get the Earl of Warwick's daughter with child of a Plantagenet; he had believed once it would mean something, to be the son-in-law of the great Earl, but he had soon understood his function. There was no one, from the dirtiest kitchen scullion to the horseboys in the courtyard, slyly grinning at his stirrup, who did not understand it too.

A light footfall above made him start. He straightened,

flushing hotly and wiping his face, and slipped quickly through the turret door to the battlements. Francis, cautiously descending from his refuge in the upper tower, caught only a glimpse of his back as he disappeared.

Below there was no one in sight. The inner court, circumspectly attained, looked to Francis to have attracted every soul within the walls: lords and knights, pages and squires and grooms; men-at-arms in Neville scarlet, their expressions apprehensive or bewildered and trying, Francis thought smugly, to appear as if they knew what it was all about. He saw his kinsman Buckingham, deep in conversation with Sir John Howard, the Norfolk landowner whose service had been worth more to Edward than many barons'; nearby the Earl of Warwick was talking easily with Essex and Mountjoy, as genially welcoming as if their arrival in Pontefract had been his dearest wish, and on the steps before the keep Edward stood with Richard and Hastings, greeting each by name the men who pressed round him. There were some riders just inside the gate, waiting under the boar standard; one of them, in a metal-sewn leather coat astride a bay stallion, showed only half his face as he spoke to a companion, but Francis stared, took a doubtful step, and started across the yard at a run. A few paces from the gate arch he checked, and walked up to lay his hand on the bay's powerful shoulder, observing with a gleam, "You might have found a sprig of plumes for the nag, anyway. Do you make shift for the working day, cousin?"

Interrupted in mid-sentence, Philip regarded without recognition the youth at his stirrup, then said, "By the Cross, Francis," and leaned down while they laughed together to grip his arm. "Cousin," he said warmly. "I'm glad of this. How is it with you?"

"Come down a while and I'll tell you," Francis invited. Another of the waiting knights—a huge young man, copper-haired and freckled from brow to chin—turned as he spoke, and with a shout of surprise urged his destrier forward to join them.

"Francis?" Blue eyes inspected him, wicked with a familiar gleam. "Faith, what a gentleman grown is the babe! And to think I remember him at Middleham not three years past, bent over a chest for getting caught in the hayloft with the alewife's daughter."

"Did you like her too?" Francis said innocently. "You should have told me, Rob: she used to say you weren't ill looking, taken on a dark night with the candle behind you." He had an arm over the bay's withers, gently working his fingers down the shining hide, but the back of his neck was hotter than a three years' reminder warranted. Expertly evading a retaliatory buffet to the ear, he moved round to the stallion's other side, and one of the younger knights came up to say abruptly, "We're having a new arrival, Philip. Will you look there?"

He jerked his head towards the gate. A mounted party beyond was waiting for passage through; those who stood nearest, identifying badge and livery, hastily made way, and as the newcomers rode in there was a stir in the courtyard.

"Northumberland," Robert Percy murmured, his eyes on the Earl of Warwick's other brother. "Now I wonder who he has come to see?"

Ignoring the stares and whispers, John Neville drew unhurried rein in the middle of the yard, dismounted, and gave his charger to an attendant. For many there it had taken an effort of memory to know his face; since receiving the earldom of Northumberland from Edward for services given, he had been infrequently seen south of the Trent. In deepening quiet Warwick came to meet him; though the courtyard had seemed packed to its walls, yet as they embraced a little space opened, and across its breadth the brown eyes of the third Neville brother met the blue ones of his cousin, standing motionless on the steps before the keep.

Warwick was hardly conscious of the direction of his brother's gaze. For one flying instant he had looked past him, trying to estimate what meinie might have accompanied him; when he saw the Earl's escort of gentlemen, few and gaily dressed with no gleam of arms, it was a last, violent hope unalterably gone. To seem indifferent, he slid an arm through the younger man's, speaking a light greeting; Northumberland, hardly acknowledging it, had turned already towards the keep.

"Well, Dickon, a pretty brew you've concocted," he said heavily, and at the half forgotten diminutive from his childhood Warwick started slightly. Keeping pace with the long, soldier's stride, he answered low, "It might have been different had you stood with me. I sent you word, but you did not come."

Northumberland's expression was unchanged. "I serve King Edward. As he deals justly with me, so do I with him."

Warwick drew in his breath, and was silent. As they approached the keep he dropped his brother's arm to fall back a little, and Northumberland, kneeling, bent his lips to the offered hand of the King. "My liege and kinsman," he said deliberately, and smiling Edward drew him up. "My well-beloved cousin of Northumberland. I am very glad to see you."

Simultaneously the Duke of Buckingham advanced in a sweep of brilliant colour to exchange civilities with his Neville relative. Warwick gazed at him pensively; young Buckingham had been planted in Queen Elizabeth's household for the profitable period of his minority, and in course of time bound to the inevitable Woodville bride. The lad's resentment having been open, his arrival had shaken Warwick, for he had believed Harry Stafford to be less inclined than many to wish his kinsman Edward well. Yet here he was, all ingenuous delight as he held court among the lesser barons, flaunting his Plantagenet lineage in his heraldic colours, trading sallies with Hastings, and from time to time looking round to include Richard of Gloucester in his lively jokes.

"Is it true the Duchess of Clarence is breeding?" he was asking now of Northumberland, with bright unconcern for the near presence of the Earl of Warwick. "Mass, my cousin Clarence goes briskly to work: the marriage is not three months old."

"I have heard it is so," Northumberland rejoined, impassive, and with unimpaired calm Warwick joined them. "True indeed, kinsman. I had word from my wife this past week, and she says the child is expected at Easter next."

Buckingham chuckled and flicked a glance at Richard. "And where is the happy father today?" he drawled. "Is he not receiving felicitations from every side?"

Warwick's shrug disclaimed all knowledge of his son-in-law's whereabouts, and Edward said tranquilly, "I spoke with my brother a short time ago, cousin of Buckingham, so you will find him somewhere about." To the Earl he added cordially, "But he did not tell me of this excellent good news, my lord. My compliments to the Duchess of Clarence, and all good wishes for a fair conclusion to your hopes."

Warwick bowed, veiling a gleam of sardonic humour. Plainly Edward had no idea of provoking an open quarrel with his relatives, and several gentlemen who had been listening immediately came up to offer their congratulations. Bestowing a radiant smile upon the Earl of Warwick, Buckingham said behind his hand to Hastings, "I hear the Duke of Clarence bribed our papal agent in Rome to get dispensation for the marriage to his cousin's girl. We live in busy times, my lord."

His eyes invited the Duke of Gloucester to join with Hastings' snort of contemptuous laughter, but Richard was addressing a low-voiced question to his brother. Edward nodded briefly, his gaze still on the throng below, and a square with the boar badge of Gloucester on his sleeve detached himself at a word, crossing the courtyard to the horsemen by the gate. One of the captains went off to reform the ranks of the escort waiting beyond the walls, and a groom appeared, leading the King's white charger. Richard had left the crowd around the keep for a few words with Francis, shyly smiling at him across the yard; suddenly moving from the hand Will Hastings had laid affectionately on his shoulder, Edward said loudly, "My lord of Gloucester."

Clear and effortlessly carrying, his voice cut through the hum and chatter, and Richard turned, looking a question. Presently he began to walk slowly towards the keep. At the steps he halted, and Edward beckoned him up. "Beside me, Dickon." Over his shoulder he added, "If you would make room, Will?" Hastings had been standing at his elbow; he drew back without a word.

The sun had dropped beyond the towers; within the courtyard, only the height of the east wall still threw back the light. The first breeze of evening blew softly, and the swallow points of the knights' pennons stirred. Unsmiling, Edward waited while one by one the faces turned towards him; when the last sound had died, he spoke.

"My lords and sirs, you are aware of the death this summer past of the Lord Constable, Earl Rivers. By it, his titles devolve upon his eldest son, Anthony Woodville, the lord Scales, and under the terms of the letters patent whereby the office of Constable was conferred, this title also should pass to Lord Scales, now Earl Rivers." He paused, and a spark kindled in Warwick's eyes. He took an unconscious step forward, but Edward had seemingly abandoned interest in the absent Woodville brother-in-law. Raising his voice, he continued smoothly, "But we are ever mindful of the wishes of our barons, and in particular of my lord of Warwick, who has done so much to secure our throne"—he glanced at Warwick, who bowed gravely—"and after consideration it has been thought expedient that this condition of the grant be forfeit. It is therefore our pleasure that the office of Constable be settled upon our beloved brother Richard, Duke of Gloucester, of whose loyalty and devotion we have long been aware."

No one moved. Edward went on, his words falling like stones into a widening hush, "The Lord Constable, by ancient right, commands our armies, administers our Courts-Martial, and presides over the Court of Chivalry. Bearing in mind however the troubled state of this kingdom, it is our wish that in addition it shall fall to him to investigate all acts of treason, to punish offenders as he sees fit, and to be answerable for his judgments only to ourselves. And this office and these duties we do bestow upon our brother Gloucester for his life."

He turned slightly, and Richard, who had stood motionless throughout, went down two steps to kneel before him. Momentarily his hands rested within his brother's; then Edward, stooping, raised him.

Two gentlemen brought up the King's stallion, and lords and knights began looking for their own mounts. Hastings was still meditatively regarding the new Constable, but even as he moved to offer courteous good wishes the Earl of Warwick forestalled him.

"I must take some credit for this occasion," he said pleasantly. "My felicitations, cousin of Gloucester: you have not shamed your training."

Pausing, Richard met his eyes. "Despite your best endeavours, cousin," he said evenly. He did not take the Earl's hand. They had spoken low, but Edward heard, and he looked down with amusement from his sidling charger.

"Dickon, Dickon, gently I beg. My lord of Warwick and I are excellent good friends, are we not, my lord?" His heel pricked the stallion's flank; steadfastly smiling, Warwick swept cap to knee. They were both of them saying without speech: Another time.

The first horsemen were beginning to stream from the courtyard, and Edward turned his horse towards the gate.

The straggling files advanced; there was a final leave-taking of the Earl of Warwick and the Archbishop, a smile at Francis; and they were gone.

As the last riders galloped over the bridge, Francis ran up the tower stair to the wall which overlooked the south road. With his hands in the crenellation of the parapet, he stood watching as the long columns wound across the plain. The light was going; a scarlet stain spread through the opal and amethyst of the evening sky, and shadows deepened in the folds of the hills. The pennons dipped, and vanished. From a thicket of willows beyond the ditch a thrush addressed a last conclusive comment to an argumentative chorus of crickets; and the first star appeared.

It was growing late, and Francis shivered in the breeze. The rest of the household would be assembling for the late-day meal; he started irresolutely towards the stair, changed his mind, and lingered as the toothed blocks of the ramparts softened and merged into the uncertain grey of twilight. His imagination rested, only half believing yet, on the empty chamber below: the lazily tumbled day bed, still marked by the weight of the man who had lain there; a folio of Boccaccio's tales, forgotten in the window seat; and the chessboard swept of pieces between the hearthside chairs.

A little later a page came looking for him; my lord of Warwick had mislaid his riding-whip, and would be glad if his ward would find it for him and bring it to the solar after meat. Francis said wryly, "I suppose a birch rod wouldn't do?" but the child only gazed at him in mystification before he went away again.

Supper, Francis calculated, would be another hour at least. There seemed no advantage to be gained, and a great deal of dignity to be lost, by delaying past the appointed hour of assignation; when he heard the voices of the men-at-arms in the courtyard once more, he sighed and went downstairs.

CHAPTER FOUR

ON a wild spring day, so raw the labouring horses' breath blew white before them and all the Channel was a waste of foam, the Earl of Warwick fled from England. He took with him his wife and daughters, his son-in-law the Duke of Clarence, and as many loyal followers as he could find shiproom for at Exeter; some that for lack of space he had to leave behind were captured by Edward's pursuing deputy Worcester, and promptly beheaded, their quartered parts impaled on stakes for an example to those who still called the Earl of Warwick friend.

By that time Warwick's fleet was long away. It was bitter weather, with a knifing wind that carried the rain in sheets across the decks. English Calais answered his request for sanctuary with a cannon blast, and while he parleyed with the governor his daughter Isabel, attended only by her mother and sister, gave birth to a son. She had been nearly a month short of her time; the Easter child, so hopefully awaited, came dead from her body, and with neither priest nor prayer was buried in the sea. Hove-to all night beyond range of the guns, next day the ships stood away westward. From Calais the sails were visible for quite a while, shrinking squares against the grey of sea and sky, but at last they dropped from sight.

Philip had spent the winter in Wales, where Richard was dealing with certain chieftains for whom Edward's English distractions had offered temptation too great to resist. Some royal castles had been seized, from which through the early winter Richard laboured patiently at prying the insurgents; it was a generally dull business of siege trains and midnight negotiations through ill-lit posterns, but by Christmas the last defiant standard came down over Cardigan keep, and the sometime occupants went sheepishly home, grateful for the continued retention of their skins. The work that followed Philip found, on the whole, hardly less trying; the inside of Cardigan might afford more comfort than the mud and wattle village huts in which they had camped before it, but Welshmen had got unused to the idea of a law which took account of poor men's rights, and their scepticism assumed exasperating forms. A traditional compensation remained: if men were inclined to stand off yet, the girls, as Percy observed, were friendly enough for both.

It was in early spring that news came out of England of turmoil in Lincolnshire, and it proved a hornets' nest in which the Earl of Warwick had been meddling. The Lincoln rebels, crushed before Warwick could join them, were quick to demonstrate contrition by the betrayal of their confederates: it was no Lancastrian they had meant to crown, but the King's brother George of Clarence.

Long before then, Richard was hurrying to Edward's support. Marching from Wales, his troops stumbled unexpectedly upon followers of the West Country lord Stanley, just as Stanley, appealed to by his brother-in-law the Earl of Warwick, was cautiously mustering them. Richard was unaware of Warwick's entreaties to his sister's husband, but he knew Stanley's men had no business in arms, and methodically scattered them. Stanley, a prudent man, took the hint and stayed in Lancashire. For Warwick and Clarence, in headlong flight from Coventry, it was their last hope gone, and when Richard joined the royal forces at York there was nothing more to do but oversee the arraignment of the few remaining rebels yet unheard, and receive with his brother the news that the two mightiest ones had eluded Worcester after all.

Edward swore about that, but made only formal protest when he learned with what surpassing warmth King Louis had welcomed the lords of Warwick and Clarence into France. To his indignant council he recommended they wait for worse hearing, and that summer it came: at his palace of Angers, Louis had brought together in amity and love Richard Neville, the one-time sword of York, and the exiled Lancastrian queen.

Even at Louis' court there were unfriendly eyes to witness the scene, and a report of proceedings was shortly in English hands. Margaret of Anjou kept the Earl of Warwick fifteen minutes humbly on his knees, begging pardon for past errors; that granted, Louis, charming and persuasive, oversaw the forging of the pact by which the house of Neville undertook to restore the house of Lancaster to past dignities, and be joined with it by the marriage of the Earl of Warwick's

61

younger daughter to the Prince of Lancaster, Margaret's son. The joke of Europe was what the Duke of Clarence got from it, which after a year of pains was nothing: Lancaster had small use for him, needing none but its own prince to furnish its heirs, and King Edward and his wife, the French ambassadors had been told, expected within months the birth of their next child, whom both were confident this time must surely be a son.

Edward did not need the warnings of his spies to know he could look for a Lancastrian landing on his shores; the north was his weakness, and he passed a wary summer listening for echoes of new troubles which rarely failed to come. Riot upon riot exploded in Northumberland, whose people had never reconciled themselves to John Neville's supplanting of their ancient Percy earls; in the end Edward was forced to release the last Percy from Fleet Prison where he had lain since Towton, and send him back to claim his father's earldom. He made good the loss to Neville as best he could with the lands and title of a marquisate; but the name was the better part of it, and when Percy, hardly home again, sent word of insurrection among the Earl of Warwick's supporters that was beyond his power to suppress alone, the new-made Marquess of Montagu showed little disposition to help him. Richard, hurrying back from a return trip to Lincolnshire, heard rumours that disquieted him. At Westminster Edward showed him the Earl of Northumberland's last despatches, cursed the fellow for a wavering dullard, and said there was nothing for it but to go north himself to deal with the trouble. He wanted Richard to absent himself a further time from Wales to accompany him; Yorkshire was the heart of Warwick's power, and above all must be made secure. There was a map of yellowed parchment between them, and his spread fingers showed the danger: the naked coast from Scarborough to the Wash, any one of its numberless coves or beaches a gift for secret disembarking, the country beyond it boiling with disaffection. With his eyes on the sheet Edward said, "Do you think it's where he'll make for? It's his best hope, he has friends there to help him and he knows the land like his own courtyard. It's what I'd do, if I were in his shoes."

Richard stood looking at the map. In both their minds was a picture of the Channel coast, equally bare once the King had moved north, hardly better manned with friends to guard it from the invaders. "I think he'll choose the north," he said at last. "It's what I would do too."

He went off to his own apartments soon afterwards. Although it was only hours since his arrival from Lincoln, he shortly disappeared again, and Philip, rousing from a brief sleep in the congested dormitory where the bulk of the Duke's tired followers had been packed, learned in the supper hall that my lord of Gloucester was not expected back at Westminster until after complin. A graceful, much-jewelled young gentleman, overhearing, paused to contribute the information that the Duke of Gloucester had gone by barge to—so it was believed—Southwark. A laugh followed, indicative of profound enjoyment, and Philip, who never encountered Sir Thomas Grey without a reaction of acute antipathy, was annoyed at himself for flushing. The Queen's son watched him with a smile, tossing a pouncet box in his hand. "Southwark," he repeated pleasantly. "And what would you suppose my lord of Gloucester is doing there, Sir Philip?"

Holding fast on his temper, Philip replied coolly, "I imagine he has gone to see how his son fares, sir. He is an attentive father."

Grey laughed again, gave a last sniff at the scented box, and restored it meticulously to the pouch at his girdle. "Ah yes: Master John of Gloucester, so called. I had almost forgotten. And of course my lord will also be enjoying passage with the trull who bore the bastard. Now I would be the last to object to such pastimes, but if Gloucester means to own his little sideslips, it's a pity he couldn't have chosen his harlot with more discrimination." His eyes on Philip's rigid face, he rounded a shoulder, adding gently, "To be sure, it cannot be easy for one who is—shall we say, disadvantaged?—to get a lady's favour; I daresay my lord has done as well for himself as he could expect. Doubtless we shall soon see the Southwark bawd installed at court with a clutch of brats around her."

"Unlikely, sir," Philip said levelly. His hands had knotted uncontrollably, and he pressed them hard to his thighs. "My lord of Gloucester's good taste in that particular could serve as model for us all." It was a random shaft—he had been too angry for calculation—but none knew better than Thomas Grey by what ladder he and his brother were climbing to their golden fortunes, who, had their mother not been raised

63

from obscurity by Edward of York's wilful fancy, would have gone their lives unknown. The sudden sparkle in the round Woodville eyes provided Philip with a minor degree of satisfaction as, bowing curtly, he walked away.

It was past midnight when Richard came through the connecting outer rooms of his palace apartments, and, dismissing the single servant who had accompanied him, entered the bedchamber beyond. His page's pallet was in its customary position at the foot of the bed, but the usual occupant was not stretched upon it. Kicking the door shut behind him, Richard walked to the bedside, demanding with amusement. "Do you squire me tonight, Philip? Where the devil is my page?"

"I exchanged him my bed for his, and got the better bargain," Philip responded, as he rose yawning from the couch. "I think ill of your Westminster warrens, my lord."

Richard gave him a shrewd glance which Philip, kneeling to pull off the Duke's high leather boots, failed to notice. "Looking for sanctuary, Philip?" There was a twist to his mouth, and Philip, embarrassed, smiled an acknowledgment.

"As you say, my lord. It was different in Wales."

"Yes, I saw Tom Grey as I came by a moment ago; he told me he'd been talking with you."

The lifted brows implied a question which, by keeping his eyes lowered, Philip was able to ignore. He finished his ministrations in silence, and brought a taper to the thick night candle on the chest beside the bed. Making himself comfortable among the pillows, Richard said casually, "By the way, the King tells me he is having Francis brought from Middleham. He may come to court later, but until we've dealt with Warwick and his friends, Francis is to go and practise at marriage with his wife—who is, I understand, in Gloucestershire."

"With the Talbots: Lady Talbot is Anna's aunt. Talbot himself, of course, is kin to Shrewsbury. God, poor Francis," Philip said ruefully, and Richard grinned.

"Yes, I thought he wasn't too pleased with his domestic arrangements, last time I spoke with him. What seems to be the trouble? Is the girl so objectionable?"

"The single time they met, I doubt Francis paid her

enough notice to form an opinion. No, it's her family con-
nections he hates, being Neville and Lancastrian both. I saw
Anna once before I came away from Middleham; there's
nothing ill in her looks, but it would be all one to Francis if
she were the wild woman of the forest and warts from head
to heels."

Richard frowned, biting his thumb. "I'm sorry about that.
Unfortunately we can't risk offending Fitz Hugh or Talbot,
and if the King's approval of Anna's marriage will keep her
kinsmen home when Warwick lands, Francis must be the
sacrifice. The girl turned thirteen a year ago; since Warwick's flight the possibility of annulment must have been
giving Fitz Hugh some uneasy moments. Even so, I'm not
sure Master Francis' appearance at court would be much of
an alternative—not unless he's learned diplomacy since I
knew him." He smiled, remembering, and Philip chuckled as
he pinched the taper out.

"Not conspicuously, I believe. Good night, my lord."

Beyond the ring of the night candle darkness descended,
and the red coals of the fire paled to ash. Through the east
windows the shouts of boatmen plying their craft between
London and Westminster came faintly, and the river ran
softly on, past terraced gardens and battlemented castles of
the great, wide-windowed mansions and the maze of docks
and warehouses behind which, in a comfortable, crazy kilter
of plaster and timber dwellings, the London merchants lived,
traded, and prospered. King Edward lay at his place of Westminster, and the joined hands of Margaret of Anjou and
Richard Neville, called Dickon Make-A-King, cast only the
lightest of shadows on his peace.

The morning brought new messages from the harried
Earl of Northumberland. Edward consulted exasperatedly
with his captains, and, annoyed beyond measure at the Marquess of Montagu's continued sulky silence, made his plans
for the journey north with a small force to stiffen Percy's
resolution. Since it would be close on a fortnight before they
marched, Philip got leave to spend the interval in Oxfordshire, and a sunny afternoon several days later found
him with groom and squire making his way through the
wooded valley which struck north from the Thames towards
Willowford. Leaves lay deep along the path, muffling his
horses' hoofs; thickets of nut trees edged the way, and late-
blooming roses; and the air was heavy with thyme. As they

turned up the long hill beyond the ford, Philip looked involuntarily towards the crest. The spot was empty, as he had known it must be—his mother had written him long since that Margaret Devereux was gone from Willowford—but the blankness of the path reproached him that it was many months since he had spared a thought for the child. He wondered again about the man to whom she had been given: a rich marriage, his mother had said, but that was all.

As he rode into the courtyard there was an outcry and a bustle. A lad from the stables came running; in an open window above the yard the tonsured head of Dame Alice's clerk appeared, leaning out to see; and as Philip dismounted at the doorstep his mother came from the house. He knelt in greeting; remembering his unceremonious departure for Dorset the summer before, he was prepared for an excoriating rebuke, well salted from storing, but when she had looked at him a while she said only, "I should have thought it longer than a year."

In the days that followed, he found there were changes at Willowford too. His sister Kate was now a year married to the widower knight from Ipsden, and in the spring had much pleased Sir William by giving him twin sons. Philip rode over to offer good wishes; Kate, very satisfied with her new condition, welcomed him warmly, and a wet nurse, hugely smiling, brought the twins. William Secott himself appeared, expansively genial and quite ready to presume on an advantage of twenty years to advise his brother-in-law. He wanted all the London news, and, shaking his head, liked none of it: a chancy thing, meddling in the affairs of princes; many an honest gentleman had come to ruin by it. A wise man, Sir William said firmly, would stay at home until the Earl of Warwick and King Edward had settled their differences. Philip had to work at repressing a laugh; he was thinking that in William Secott, Dame Alice had got a son-in-law after her own heart.

For his mother continued unreconciled. She hated the world he had entered, as she had hated it in times past for her husband's sake; even the wonderful German armour, its last stage of travel completed only a month before by the London-to-Oxford carrier, had lain unexamined and ignored in its casings against the hour when her son must claim it. On the day of departure she watched, tight-lipped, while his squire brought down reverently from the upper chamber the awkward shapes in their soft leather wrappings; Philip, overseeing the bestowal of the packs, turned when the last of them had been secured and came to stand before her on the lower step.

"Give me your blessing, madam."

She replied bitterly, "It would be strange of me to give it for this journeying. Secott is in the right of it: there is no profit for you in these quarrels, only a great danger. What is one knight the less to the duke of Gloucester? But you are my son, however neglectful you have shown yourself in remembering it."

"Though I remember, it is not to the exclusion of other things. I have made promises you would not see me shamed for breaking." The reproach had cut, the more so for his wondering how far it might be true. She was silent, her jaw as rigid as his own, and Philip added more gently, "You wrong my lord of Gloucester, Madam. He has been a good friend to me."

"Oh, he has you fast now. And where does this end? Will you spend your life at his beck?"

He answered slowly, "When I rode out of London, there were no bands of soldiers in the streets, and the prentices were playing football in the fields beyond the gates." Yet it was not London his mind's eye was seeing now, but the scarred walls of Cardigan and Carmarthen, the goat-track Welsh mountain paths where no traveller went unarmed, the plundered Marches and the wildness of a country without law, before the Duke of Gloucester came. Her silence drew him back; the grief in her face troubled him, but there was no way more he could help it. He tried a joke instead, hoping to make her smile. "I must go. Forgive me that it's been only the butt-end of a visit; I promise the next time will not wait another year."

He stooped, kissing her fingers; she had barely time to touch his hair as he straightened. A moment later he was gone.

Philip came up with the King's detachments at Leicester, and not many days later they entered York. The disturbance which had so exercised the Earl of Northumberland had died, but it was Warwick's friends who had formented it, and, grimly appraising the ensuing uneasy calm, Edward established himself at York and took counsel with his brother.

There was tension in the air, and it was evident the Earl of Warwick's sullen adherents were waiting only for his return to take up arms again. Richard spent an energetic fortnight implementing measures to forestall the ambition, and Edward betook himself into Northumberland for a caustic interview with Henry Percy. That concluded, he descended upon the Marquess of Montagu, who received him with modified enthusiasm. Edward devoted some little effort to conciliating his ruffled kinsman before he rode back to York, where he told his brother that Jack was still sulky, but would come around.

Early in September the Earl of Warwick sailed for England. Galloping couriers brought the news to York that the Earl, ignoring after all his northern strength, had landed in Devon with the Duke of Clarence and was making for London. Despatching peremptory instructions to the Marquess of Montagu to follow him with all haste, Edward gathered his own contingents and started south.

Doncaster was the first halt, and, pitching camp on the outskirts of the town, the weary troops dropped into fitful sleep. In the King's tent lights burned late as with Richard, Hastings, and Rivers, Edward studied reports and made plans for the next day. Montagu was expected tomorrow, or at the latest by the day following, and with his strength joined to theirs it would be possible to make swift engagement with the invaders while Percy remained in Northumberland to hold the north. Midnight came; rising at last with a yawn, Edward declared himself satisfied, and said he was going to bed. His companions sleepily agreed, but as they took their leave there was a commotion outside the tent, and a white-faced sergeant pushed by the guard to drop on one knee before the King.

"Your grace, look to yourself. God knows where it's sprung from, but there's a force on our flank, and they're not our friends."

There was an instant's blank silence; the roughness of the intrusion, more than the announcement which accompanied it, had startled and annoyed the King's companions. Hastings started forward, exclaiming in anger; restraining him with a hand, Edward drawled, "Man, have you taken leave of your wits? The Earl of Warwick is several days' march from here, and hurrying from London; unless he's sprouted wings, I don't see how he can have landed in Yorkshire tonight."

Flushing, the officer rejoined stubbornly, "I know where the Earl of Warwick is, your grace. But my scouts fell into some fellows this side of Leeds—their main force is more than an hour away yet, but a band of them pushed on ahead and came on my men in the dark. We were sharp set for a while, but we got away in the end." Encouraged by the sudden intent look, he repeated earnestly, "I tell you, sir, they're no friends of ours. They swear they'll take you before ever you come up with the Earl of Warwick."

Hastings said doubtfully, "Stanley?" and Rivers remarked in his tranquil way, "Shrewsbury, more like. Stanley would never be so far from the west—not until he was sure of Warwick winning."

Edward had wheeled to his brother. "Dickon—" he snapped, but Richard was already lifting the flap of the tent.

"I'll look into it," he said briefly, and disappeared into the dark. Biting his lip, Edward frowningly contemplated the sergeant's worried face; the moments slipped by without a sound from the sleeping camp. Hastings began harshly, "If you've lied, fellow—"

"Leave it, Will," Edward interrupted. He stood motionlessly waiting, his big shoulders a block of shadow against the tent wall, the torches brightening his hair to flame. In a far-off house of brothers, someone was ringing the matins bell.

Richard came back a few minutes later. "It's true," he said, before anyone could speak. "More scouts have ridden in, and they've taken a prisoner. Ned, it's Montagu. He's told his men he stands with Warwick because you robbed him of Northumberland, and they've all thrown up their caps for Lancaster."

A shocked silence fell. Edward said slowly, "Jack Neville?" And then, whispering, "Oh, I have been a fool." He turned sharply, and, staring down at the table, mechanically straightened the litter of papers to symmetrical neatness; studied them, and with a flick of his fingers scattered the pile. Before them all hung their minds' picture of John Neville's decent, responsible face; so long he had toiled in his cousin's interests that even now it was a grotesqueness to imagine him their enemy, marching steadily towards them through the swiftly dissolving night. In the shadows Hastings and Rivers had started to argue urgent alternatives, and Edward swung round, his eyes fixing his brother's grey ones. "What is his power?"

"Greater than ours," Richard said quietly. "You knew that when you sent for him." He hesitated, and added in a restrained way, "There is not much time to make ready."

Edward gave a short, jangling laugh. "Oh aye, to fight a battle I am three parts sure of losing, with Warwick at my back to finish the business? I don't fancy my head on London Bridge." He glanced at the waiting sergeant. "Rouse the camp: tell the men to scatter as they will. As for us, sirs"—he considered them, and a hard smile crooked his mouth—"for the present it appears to be my cousin's turn. Collect what gentlemen you can: we are for Burgundy."

Less than a quarter of an hour later the little band of men was galloping from Doncaster. Behind them was chaos as the sleepy troops woke to the shouts of their officers and the clatter of departing hoofs; when, not long after, the vanguard of the Marquess of Montagu's forces came thundering down on Edward's camp, they found it all but deserted: gage carts overturned, empty tents flapping in the breeze, and plunderers already stealing in to loot the goods of the flying Yorkist host.

Wasting no time on the straggle of foot soldiers remaining, Montagu gave grim chase after his cousin. The hunt led through Lincolnshire to the shores of the Wash, but the fugitives outstripped their pursuers, and had set sail for Norfolk in what ever tiny craft were at hand when Montagu's hurrying men swept down to the bay. A squall was blowing up, and the floods of rain enveloped the flimsy boats as they laboured towards the Norfolk shore. Some fishing vessels at Bishop's Lynn rode peaceably at anchor, and were appropriated wholesale; two days later they were beating past Skegness point into the turbulent grey waters of the North Sea.

Out of the shelter of the coast the wind backed and stiffened, and a nauseous odour wafted from the hold. Sitting chest to knees against the taffrail, Philip said distastefully, "Ancient herring, presumably. A forecast of supper, do you suppose?" Robert Percy, for whom he had intended the comment, vouchsafed no reply; he was leaning saggingly over the rail, his attention passionately concentrated on the heaving deep. The ship lurched and wallowed; Philip took a good hold on his companion's legs to steady him, and averted his eyes from the scuppers, thankful only that for the moment

70

the gale was blowing a fury in the opposite direction.

Towards midnight the rain slackened, and dawn found them running before a brisk wind, with a watery sun breaking through the clouds and, to the south, the first suggestion of the flat Flemish shoreline appearing on the rim of the sea. Since daybreak Edward and Richard had been keeping watch for it, but even as they exchanged relieved glances, a seaman shouted there were ships off their port bow. Identification followed quickly; Warwick had lost no time spreading the news of Edward's flight, and the enterprising men of the Hanse towns knew the kind of reward there would be for those who apprehended him. The German carvels drew closer, and Edward's makeshift fleet raced south. Guns boomed behind them, and fountains of water rose, marking the balls; the shores of Holland spread and darkened, and as they ran in on the Alkmaar beaches the pursuers turned away in defeat.

CHAPTER FIVE

JUST below the pond's surface the shadow of a trout hung motionless, a dark shape in the clear brown waters below the busy falls. The one round eye which was visible stared steadily up at Francis, and, watching idly with his chin on his arms, he dropped a pebble. There was a silent flurry, and when the ripples cleared, the shadow had gone.

Francis remained a minute longer staring down into the stream, following with his eyes its bustling course through the overhanging brush, around a clump of beeches already touched with gold, and out of sight. The ground was like iron from the frost of the night before, despite the present thin warmth of the sun; it did not make a particularly comfortable resting place, and he was ferociously hungry besides. The ale and bread which were his prescribed rations for the rest of the day returned regretfully to mind: he had been, perhaps, a little hasty in rejecting them out of hand. Swearing under his breath, he picked up another stone to fling violently after the first, and put it down again as a step sounded above.

It was a steep path which led down the bank to the stream, and the girl descending it trod carefully to avoid her trailing skirts, having already both hands full. Francis turned over to watch her approach, and as she came near enough for him to see what she was carrying, the lingering stormy look vanished in a reluctant grin. He sat up, stretching out a hand, and after making sure of a safe place on the grass for the brimming horn cup, she sank down beside him.

"I've brought you some dinner." The food was wrapped in a napkin, which she proceeded seriously to unroll: good demain bread with beef soaking in sauce between the pieces, two sausages, part of a sugared confection, and a pear. She surveyed the collection anxiously before offering it, and he leaned over to kiss the tip of her nose.

"Anna, your aunt would whip you for this. I'm on short portions today: Didn't you know?"

"My cousin told me." She was looking distressed, and Francis' lips tightened. Not for the first time, he speculated longingly about the feel of Humphrey Talbot's throat; but three months of voyaging through the shoals of matrimony had brought caution. He addressed himself instead to the viands of his wife's providing, while Anna held the wine. Between mouthfuls he said presently, "So Humphrey's been busy already with the tale. Obliging of him! Did he think I wouldn't tell you myself, I wonder?"

Anna was nervously pleating the folds of her skirt. "He said—he said you spoke slander of the Prince of Wales, and insulted the Queen."

"Oh, did he consider it slander? I only said he needn't worry that Edward of Lancaster might take after Simple Harry, since it was good odds Somerset had had the fathering of him anyway. I should think he'd have been relieved. It's a pity I didn't know your uncle had come up behind us, though." Francis nursed his ear, which was vibrating still from the impact of the elder Talbot's palm. The memory of Humphrey's face went a long way to make up for it, but Anna's silence was disapproving, and after a sidelong glance he added, "I suppose I shouldn't have said that about Simple Harry. Old Lancaster's harmless enough, even if the Earl of Warwick has clapped a crown back on that addled head: I doubt he ever asked for it, poor fool." It was as much of an amend as he was prepared to offer, but Anna paid it no heed. Her face had gone prim.

"You are speaking of the King," she said coldly, and Francis raised an eyebrow at her as he lay down again, folding his arms beneath his head.

"Well, I said he was harmless, didn't I?" he objected reasonably, but there was a sparkle of anger in his eyes. After a short silence, Anna said carefully, "My uncle says the Earl of Warwick orders all as he desires while he awaits Prince Edward and the Queen from France, but there are some who believe he had best take care. He has many enemies, and lords like the Earl of Oxford and my uncle's kinsman Shrewsbury don't like to see a Yorkist lord take precedence before those who served Lancaster through all misfortune."

"And let's not forget my lord Stanley, who is now, it seems, a better Lancastrian than any of them," Francis jeered. "I hear he was in Warwick's train when his lordship entered London and rode to fetch Henry from the Tower—where he'd been since the Earl of Warwick put him there for King

Edward five years ago! A savoury mixture, by all the Saints!—Oxford and Stanley and Shrewsbury and Warwick—not to mention the Duke of Clarence, scurrying about on his father-in-law's errands. By God, I wonder what they find to talk about at table. There's scarcely a man of 'em hasn't been at the others' throats, any time these ten years past."

"And my uncle," Anna said icily. "You forgot to mention my uncle."

"And my lord Talbot too, then!" Francis snapped. They sat stiffly glaring; then abruptly he smiled and reached over to pull her down beside him. "Oh, devil take the lot of them. Don't sulk, sweetheart."

She hesitated, then, mollified by the contrition in his eyes, suppressed a giggle. Working unhandily with one arm around her waist, Francis cut the pear in fours with his knife; they finished the pieces together, and she settled herself against his shoulder. "That's better," he approved. "Now if we can just be rid of this—" He was tugging at her headdress, a heart-shape of stiff, dark stuff, with a trail of gauze veiling. When it was off her braids shone like beaten copper in the sun. He slid a hand under her chin; she wriggled uneasily, looking over his shoulder, and his fingers tightened. "Stop fidgeting: I want to kiss you."

A silence followed while that pleasant ambition was accomplished. After a time Francis remarked critically, "I don't think much of this gown, madam: it's plaguey discreet, you know. Still, making the best of all this drapery—"

Her skin was like new milk, flecked scantily on cheeks and throat with little spots of gold; they had been out so much together, all the bright autumn weeks, that the sun had laid a band of warm ivory to mark where her bodice ended. Her eyes, which were nearly green, looked blue now in the double shadow of her lashes and his bending head.

The rustle of a badger in the undergrowth startled the quiet as rudely as a human foot; hurriedly straightening, Anna adjusted the neck of her gown. Francis watched with amusement, but when she smiled shyly across at him he said nothing, only stretching out his hand to hers. While he stroked the blue vein inside her wrist, she said diffidently, "I—I wish you wouldn't quarrel all the time with Humphrey."

Francis considered that, his fingers still moving back and

forth over her palm. "Well, I don't," he said at last, adding with a gleam, "I couldn't; he's not here all the time."

"I suppose I should be glad only for that," she retorted, and he grinned guiltily.

"Even for you I can't endure your cousin, love. Better be glad he's mostly off in Oxford's household, nowadays; we should have broken each other's heads long ago, else." The smile vanished at her expression of reproach. Leaning on his elbow, Francis pulled restlessly at the faded grass, and the dry stems came away with a light tearing sound. "God. Well, I'll try, sweetheart. I suppose I owe so much an effort to your uncle anyway; he's done his best to be fair with me, and I know how I have tried him." Repossessing himself of her hand, he touched his lips to the fingers. "If you knew what was in my mind when first I came here! I was sure I was being used to keep your family still when Warwick landed, and I meant to make Lord Talbot sorry he had ever heard of Francis Lovell."

"I was frightened, a little." She was looking shy again. "It was so long since I'd seen you, I couldn't even imagine what you would be like, and Humphrey said—" She halted in confusion, and, hastily placating, added, "I've lived here so long, you see, and he's like my brother. Even when they sent for me to Ravensworth to be married, my father let me come back here again, after, when my uncle asked it."

Leaning her back in his arms, Francis stroked her hair. "Sweetheart, you've a wheen of brothers in Yorkshire and Humphrey Talbot's none of them. Do you think I've no wits? It wasn't just to learn stitching and serving that you came to your good aunt and uncle so far away from home; maybe Lord Talbot hasn't worried too much about it, but madam your aunt has expectations sure, until the Earl of Warwick whispered in your father's ear with another scheme. It's no wonder Cousin Humphrey would like to see me gutted on Tyburn heath." He was only partly smiling. Anna said fondly, "You're silly," and pulled his face down to hers.

Resting his cheek against her soft one, Francis recognised with astonishment and despair that she could not comprehend the thought. It would have comforted his jealousy a little, if he had not been aware that Humphrey Talbot comprehended it very well indeed. From the first hours under

Lord Talbot's roof, there had been no escaping his son; he was always there, serving before his father at table, welcoming guests, lounging in the great chamber above the hall: ever looking across to catch his little cousin's eye, to remember and reminisce with her over their childhood years, always pausing, just a moment too late, smoothly to excuse them both to the stranger, who could have no part in the joined memories. But that had been in their earlier, politer days, before the Earl of Warwick had driven his cousin Edward beyond the seas, and Lancaster was King again. The Talbots were no friends to Richard Neville, but Henry of Lancaster was their god and sun.

A silence very different from the other one had fallen between them. Anna could sense, without seeing it, the taut set of his mouth, the unhappy eyes in a face turned from her even while they embraced. Although she lay as close in his arms as any time he had held her in their bed, he had gone where she had no wish to follow, and a prick of resentment mingled with the desire to console as she slid a hand up his cheek, whispering, "Francis."

He looked down, his face changing as he met her eyes. "I love you, sweetheart. I suppose some day it will occur to my lord of Warwick to concern himself with me again, but—" She shivered, and he tightened his arms. "It may be I'll have to go away then," he said against her hair. "Having got my wardship back again, he may want me under his eye. But I'll come to see you often, even if I must beg him for it; I couldn't bear to be too long away from you. And in five years—less than five years—they'll have to give me back my lands, and I'll take you away to Minster Lovell." It did not strike him she might be less anxious for such a day then he; eagerly he ran on. "Do you know Oxfordshire, Anna? It's flatter than here, but there are hills around my part of it. There have been twelve Lovell barons before me on that piece of land; I'll be the thirteenth."

"That's unlucky," she said quickly, and he laughed, his fingers smoothing her brows. "You're my luck."

Turning on his back, he rested his head against her knees, his eyes on the slowly changing colours of the sky. "It's a fair holding, Minster Lovell. The house there now is quite a new one; my grandfather built it for his lady, the heiress of Rotherfield. There's a secret chamber within the walls, and when I was very young I used to imagine to myself who might have hidden once in such a place, or even died there perhaps. I'll show it you, one day. The castle at Rotherfield came to us with my grandam's dower—very big and old, with a vane like a fox. My mother liked it, and lived there as much as she could. But I was born at Minster Lovell, and though I have not set foot there since they brought my father home from Towton, I remember each stick and stone of it."

He broke off an overhanging branch of willow and was silent for a time, stripping the yellowed leaves from the bough. "My family has held the land since Norman times. A Lovell stood for Matilda when Stephen of Blois disputed her right; I was barely out of my cradle when my father, who did not come much into the nursery as a rule, told me about that, and explained what I was to understand from it. For more than three hundred years the men of my house have served the king—and now I sit fooling here, while the Earl of Warwick makes himself rich off my lands, and uses the gains to secure himself from his true prince." The twisted branch snapped abruptly. Throwing the broken pieces aside, Francis rolled over and put his face down against the turf.

Folding the discarded napkin in her lap, Anna looked sympathetically at the rigid shoulders. It occurred to her that the cuffing from her uncle might have been rougher than admitted; she would have liked to ask, but out of tact forbore. The alternative of a coaxing hand was curtly rebuffed; she sat a moment longer, debating, and then, picking up the empty cup, went quietly away.

So noiseless had been her departure that Francis did not realise she had gone, and the light footfall beside him stimulated no especial interest until a voice struck horrifyingly on his ear.

"Poor Francis. What an unfortunate thing is an ungoverned tongue, to be sure."

Studiously deliberate, Francis turned on his back and, shading his eyes from the light, stared up. The youth standing over him resembled Anna more than a little, sharing with her the same delicately pointed features and crisp, fiery curls, but the likeness woke no kinder emotions in Francis' breast, and, laughing to himself, Humphrey Talbot put a foot out, drawing it back and forth along the grass a few inches from the younger boy's head. "Well, Lovell, no stomach for correction? But rude manners call for lessoning, you know: surely you learned that much at Middleham."

Without moving, Francis said softly, "What a clamour the barnyard cock makes from his little dunghill."

The dallying foot checked. Thoughtfully surveying the recumbent figure, Humphrey was conscious again of that compulsive itch to violence which Francis Lovell never failed to rouse in him, and he wondered, as he had done countless bitter times before, what his sweet cousin could possibly have found to attract her in this objectionable stripling. His lips thinned, and Francis eyed him warily, an outflung arm tense with the expectation of contact. After an instant Humphrey said tightly. "By God, varlet, you're in need of schooling. I don't marvel my father's patience is at an end."

"Why, I thought he loved me as a son." Yawning, Francis closed his eyes. "You weary me, Humphrey. Go talk with the scullions, if there is no one else will bear your company."

"Ungrateful! Now, I had come to make you a present of some news; you deserve I should keep it to myself." Humphrey looked down at him, smiling and stirring the grass with his toe. "You're going to new keepers, Lovell; the Earl of Warwick's courier rode in an hour ago. And if you care to accept a word of advice, you'll mend your conduct while you're under their rule. They've a good understanding of how to deal with ignorant coxcombs in France."

If he wanted an effect, he got it in full measure. Francis' head jerked up, and for a minute he could only stare. Well pleased with the results of his gambit, Humphrey swung on his heel; there was a rustle behind, and a hand fastened on his shoulder.

"What's your meaning, Talbot? Christ, will you answer me or must I choke it from you!"

Stiff with fury, Humphrey wrestled free of the tight hold. "It's not my business to explain your future to you! But I'll tell you this much for your comfort, Lovell: it will be many a year before you come next or nigh my cousin again. She'll be well used to your absence, by the end of it."

"And marriages have been annulled, that were more surely made than this one. This is your doing, whoreson: Did you think I wouldn't know why? By God, you know how to

78

hold a hope, though priest, bishop, and king have said you the contrary."

Exaggeratedly astonished, Humphrey lifted his brows. "You're quite out. You've just yourself to thank, Lovell; my father has borne long with you, but his endurance has run out. You might explain it to my cousin, if you fancy she will cry for you beyond tomorrow week."

Something red seemed to float before Francis' eyes. His next clear awareness was the soul-rewarding feel of Humphrey Talbot's flesh beneath his hands, and Humphrey Talbot's body pinned neck to knee under his. No amateur, Humphrey reacted with promptness; they rolled together like dogs down the grassy bank, and a rapid step along the streamside path above ended in trenchant exclamation: "By God's soul!" A hand fell on the nearer of the combatants, which happened to be Francis; a boot thrust roughly between them. Panting, they rose, and in silence Lord Talbot's blue stare raked them.

"By God's precious soul," the baron repeated, after ominous pause. "Must I have the pair of you under lock for a little peace? Mother of God, was ever a man so beset!" He looked wrathfully from one to the other, adding sharply, "Humphrey, you've been instructed before: we'll have accounting for this. As for you, Francis, I have already lessoned you once today—" He broke off, patently revolving alternatives, and Francis interposed, "My lord, may I have speech with you?" The dead weight of an impossible fear hung above him; a curt nod granting leave, he said shakily, "Is it—is it true I am to go to France?"

Talbot's face altered. "So that's it," he observed. "I should be glad if you were less busy, Humphrey, in what does not concern you. However—" He hesitated. "Yes, it is true. The decision is not mine, Francis; the Earl of Warwick has sold your wardship to your uncle. Lord Beaumont," he added in explanation, for Francis was looking bewildered, but at the amendment his colour flamed.

"Beaumont! That—" Under the warning eye he choked the rest, but the scarlet sense of it hung in the silence, more expressive than a shout. Viscount Beaumont had spent the years of Yorkist power in exile at Margaret of Anjou's threadbare little court, but with the restoration of Lancaster the vigorous nobleman, brother of Francis' dead mother and closely related to the young Duke of Buckingham, had returned to England as one of the most important supporters of the uneasy new regime. Ringed with the resentments of old Lancastrians, Warwick was evidently trying to appease one of the most notable of them by relinquishing to him the immense Lovell holdings, but it was a confession of weakness which was unlikely to commend him to the recipient. There was emphatically no nonsense about the autocratic, high-tempered William Beaumont, and Lord Talbot, who knew and admired him, looked forward to delivering the Viscount his nephew with undisguised relief.

After a minute Francis said in a strained tone, "I see." Judiciously appraising his white face, Lord Talbot remarked, "I find the air of amazement somewhat surprising. Surely you knew when you came here that it was not your – your guardian's intention that the arrangement be a permanent one?" His voice changed on the last words; the guardian had been Edward of York.

Francis made an impatient gesture. "Yes, I knew it. But—" He stopped. "And what of my wife? Am I to be allowed to visit her?"

"So long as you are in England, there could be no conceivable objection," the baron said crisply. "It is your uncle's wish that you join him at Windsor for the present, and of course that is no impossible distance; while your wife abides under my roof, Francis"—his eyes rested grimly on his son, immobile beyond the younger boy—"you may be sure her husband will be welcome here. But Lord Beaumont has settled you are to spend the next few years in France, and the way would be over-long then for such a scheme, I am sure you will agree."

"The next few years?" Francis repeated slowly.

"Why yes: your uncle has naturally formed some close associations there, and he feels it would benefit you to see something of the world, and perhaps to spend some time in less controversial surroundings. In which I cannot entirely disagree with him," Lord Talbot admitted. In pity at the boy's horrified face, he added gently, "Come now, it is not sentence of execution, you know. Many young men would envy you."

That was unquestionably true, but Francis was not listening to him. Labouring to be clear, he said, "But you don't understand. She is—she believes she is with child."

In the absolute silence, he heard a sharp breath behind him. "Christ," Humphrey Talbot said softly. There was a sound of hurrying footsteps, and Francis knew he had gone.

An interval followed during which the shape and colour of each grass blade seemed graven on his eyes. Impassive, Anna's uncle spoke. "And why was I not told of this?"

Francis said jerkily, "No one was. We weren't quite sure—she's three weeks past her month time now, we've been afraid the women would notice—" He thought of the jokes and questions which from the first had been their unvarying portion: Anna's sharp-tongued aunt, herself nearly four months gone, prying, suggesting, criticising: the hints and whispers and surreptitious examination of the bed linen. With a kind of exhausted bitterness he said, "We wanted it to ourselves for a while."

"More fools you both!" the baron snapped. "Had I known of this—" He broke off, and stood staring with that mixture of impatience and honest perturbation which made it easy to understand how it was that, more than the father she hardly remembered, Anna so deeply loved him. At length he resumed, "Well, there's no helping it now. Lord Beaumont is determined you shall go to France, since the present climate of this country has such an undesirable effect upon you. I am sorry, Francis: I would have tried to help you if I had known."

Francis made no reply. His hands locked behind his back; as the silence grew he said, "When—when must I go?" and when the answer came—"This afternoon"—it was as if he had already known. Barely conscious of what he was doing, he turned and walked away.

In the courtyard there were strange horses waiting unsaddled as Lord Talbot's grooms shouted and hurried, and men in Neville livery stood round. The horse cloth and saddlebags of Warwick's emissary lay inside the porch; the man himself, being a knight, was taking wine in the solar with Lady Talbot while fresh animals were readied, and two servants carried down Francis' box from the upper room which, the household being small, had been his and Anna's alone. He looked for her there, but she was with her aunt in the solar, summoned because of the guest; like prisoners, they could speak only with their eyes.

In less than an hour it was time to go. The day was half

spent, and becoming colder; the sky was iron-coloured, and winter birds huddled in the hedgerows along the path. As they turned into the Gloucester road, the first snow began to fall.

CHAPTER SIX

IT was the evening before which had brought snow to Bruges, and a residue still lingered in the narrower streets where sunlight of a few hours since had only fleetingly reached it. Philip was crossing the Grand Place, deserted now with the fall of night, when he became aware of the footsteps behind him; he went on, not supposing himself concerned by it, until he began to understand the significance of the too-rapid overtaking, and the sliding scuff of boots on the cobbles trying to go softly. He had all the penniless alien's hard-learned mistrust of appeal to foreign law; where the Belfry tower cast a concealing shadow he halted, and instead of continuing across the square slipped quietly into an alley which stretched off the Place towards the black glitter of the canal. Their eyes, better adjusted than his to the darkness detected the manoeuvre; at the mouth of the passage they turned and came on after him, four figures spread from side to side of the gabled buildings, their shadows all grown into one by the flapping of their loosened cloaks.

At first he had supposed them some young townsmen who had heard him speak as he left the inn, and were out to give him a roughing; Edward's English were not popular now in Bruges, as foreigners are unlikely to be who cannot pay their bills. Then he saw the run of moonlight on their swords—each the broad, short blade exported through Europe by the Switzers of Basel: the unmistakable civilian equipment of the professional fighting man off the field. His hand closed with gratitude on the hilt of his battle sword, which since the first street brawl no man of Gloucester's that owned one went abroad without. Farther down the alley the shadows were thicker; he gave ground slowly, and too late realised his mistake; nearer the entrance there would have been better chance of interference or alarm by some passer-by. The flattened purse that had done the mischief swung at his belt, so nearly emptied he had not thought anyone could believe it worth the robbing: it was a joke for potboys, if he could live to tell it. His shoulders found a friendly angle in the row of houses at his back; he braced himself against it, and met with guarding blade the skidding, slipping, head-on rush of the opening assault.

A knight's battle sword has an advantage in length over the shorter baselard, but its weight makes it slow, and it was never meant for work against another man not equally encumbered. The first long sweep taught the thieves respect; they recoiled, separated, and elbowed forward again, each man trying to be second after his neighbour. All in a bunch, they engaged once more; a divergent rush, Philip knew, would have settled the fight in minutes, but no one wanted to be first in. The clanging and stamping seemed enough to waken half the town; his wrist was tiring fast, and his boots were having trouble keeping purchase on the icy cobbles.

Of a sudden the tail of his eye sensed a new movement; one of the aggressors with more imagination than his fellows had unslung his cloak. Parrying a stroke, Philip half-swung to protect his blade from envelopment in the swirling folds; his foot turned on a stone, and he fell headlong.

There was a moment when he thought he must surely wake. Moonlight winked on a lifted blade, and instinctively he flung up his arm; the next instant, the sword faltered and whisked away. The scuff of footsteps in the gloom was all at once immoderately loud; there were shouts, a quantity of curses, and the sound of running. Someone stooped, addressing a question in heavily provincial French. He made some sort of reply; a hand gripped his elbow, and he rose slowly to his feet.

Black and still, the alley stretched empty to the moon-washed brightness of the Place. Far away a diminishing din of pursuit drifted, but the newcomer—small, neat, and soberly dressed—was displaying no further interest in its results. While Philip leaned against the wall, catching his labouring breath, the little man bent and meticulously retrieved the fallen sword. Philip took it with a gasping word of thanks, and simultaneously discovered that they were not, as he had supposed, entirely alone. Half a dozen yards from the alley's entrance a solitary horseman waited; and the thick French of Philip's rescuer sounded again at his ear: "Monsieur?" He was offering his arm.

Out of the passage, the shadow of the Beffroi had only a little shifted in the moonlight. Standing at the rider's stirrup, Philip said as steadily as he was able, "My thanks, monsieur, for your assistance. I thought I was sped."

"There's a risk, sometimes, in going about the streets alone at night," the strange gentleman observed. Philip had an impression of a cool voice, an immensely authoritative manner, and the gleam of gold thread on a heavy velvet sleeve; but the face was in darkness, although his skin felt the prick of an inspecting stare. "Soldiers, I should judge, in between wars," he responded with a disjointed laugh. "And owning neither brains nor valour, from my experience of it. I should have had such fellows whipped from any company I have commanded, only for lacking the competence of their own profession."

"Well, they had the look of unemployment," the other agreed, smiling in return. "Yes, you were lucky: a cutpurse that knew his business would have settled the matter quickly enough with bowstring or poniard." He paused, and Philip was again aware of the searching glance. The moonlight was brighter now; with an unexpected shift to very fair English, the level voice added, "You are a long way from home, sir. I am afraid you and your friends have found but indifferent welcome in Flanders."

Disconcerted, Philip said guardedly, "The Seigneur de la Gruthuyse has been very kind, monsieur."

"Ah yes: I seem to remember being told he had offered his hospitality to the Prince of York and his brother." A slight lift of the heavy brows disposed of the Governor of Holland. "But I believe it is more for the sake of an old friendship, then as the Duke of Burgundy's deputy."

"If that is so, it is pleasant to find that friendship can still command so much," Philip said evenly. "Certainly the Duke of Burgundy has done his best to disclaim all interest in his wife's brothers, while he scrambles to come to terms with the Earl of Warwick's government."

"One remembers that this is, after all, a practical world." There was a faint amusement in the composed tones, but the smile which accompanied the words was a friendly one. "Well, sir, we must hope you and your countrymen will soon be in better case. Circumstances are variable, and I should not be surprised if I had the pleasure of very soon greeting you at Lille, all aglow in the sun of the Duke's favour."

Philip achieved a polite reply. There was an itch of warm blood crawling down his cheek; he wiped at it, annoyed to find his hand shaky still, and the older man said suddenly,

"But I am remiss: you are in no way to be lingering in the street. Are your lodgings near?"

"Quite near, I thank you," Philip replied mechanically.

"I will send one of my men with you, to ward off further adventures." Waving protest aside, he leaned forward, surprisingly extending a hand in farewell. Though he sat his horse like a young man, there were wings of grey in the dark hair at his temples, and a fine tracery of lines around the masterful mouth. "My name is Erard de Brezy: pray commend me to King Edward, and tell him I shall do myself the honour of waiting upon him soon. I regret I have not done so before, but I am newly back from Tours this day, and my affairs must take me north tomorrow for a time. No doubt we shall meet again, but meanwhile, my good whishes for the success of your undertakings." He touched a spur to his horse. His attendants had returned from their fruitless chase, and swung about to follow as he rode off down the street, the blue and gold trappings of his mount fluttering in the chilly breeze.

Rather thoughtfully, Philip walked back to the Count of Flanders, and under its rickety sign dismissed his escort with an expression of thanks which he felt shamed to be unable to complement with a coin, but appeared of itself more than the impassive servant had looked for. He was a Fleming, and spoke French very faultily; de Brezy, however, had addressed him, shortly, in that tongue.

The lower room of the hostelry, when Philip entered, was crowded, noisy, and thick with smoke. Glad to escape notice in the reeking murk, he went up the narrow stair against the wall to the loft chamber he shared uncomfortably with Percy and half a dozen others of the Duke of Gloucester's following. It was a small room, the eight of them sleeping head to heel with their squires wedged around the wainscot, and he was anticipating with distaste the commotion his dishevelment would bring; but when he pushed open the door he discovered only Percy within, sipping a cup of sour beer and gloomily contemplating the dying glow of a few coals at the bottom of the brazier. He glanced up as Philip came in, and his eyes widened. "Holy God—!"

"I do not die, Rob, for a cut cheek," Philip remarked irritably to the gape-mouthed stare and, unbuckling his belt, threw it still with its scabbarded sword into the window seat. Ignoring the objection, Percy dragged the room's single battered chest nearer the fire, and, stripping off his jerkin, flung it hurriedly over to improvise a settle. With a weary feeling that he was attracting considerable solicitude that evening, Philip dropped to its makeshift cushioning, accepted a tankard of beer, and drained it at a swallow while Percy, visibly eaten with curiosity, disposed himself on the joint stool opposite. He received the account of the scrimmage with relish, although inclining to be pointed about unaccompanied night walking in Bruges, but his brows climbed at Erard de Brezy's name.

"Monseigneur himself? You keep exalted company!"

"Do you know him?" Philip asked, surprised, and Percy spread his hands.

"Am I friends with the Duke of Burgundy? It's not far different. I saw him when he came to England with Antoine of Burgundy—as who did not! Great Bailiff of Hainault, Lord of Saint Aubin and Lenartsdijk, Knight of the Golden Fleece—He married an English heiress last year, having run through two wives' fortunes already: it takes money to play le grand prince after Monsieur de Brezy's style."

Percy sounded satiric, and Philip said defensively, "He was pleasant to me: I liked him."

"Oh, very pleasant," Percy agreed. "Quite typical that he should trouble himself with an obscure street brawl he's so much the grand seigneur in Hainault that it comes naturally to him to continue the role outside it. D'you remember the Earl of Warwick in the days of his glory? He had the same trick, but you'll not catch Monsieur de Brezy overshooting his mark in Warwick's fashion. A most excellent good friend, they say, and a bad enemy."

"He was at pains to send his good wishes to the King," Philip remarked, and Percy stared into the remains of his drink, tilting the cup towards the wavering firelight.

"I'm thinking that Erard de Brezy is reputed to be deeper in the Duke of Burgundy's confidence than any other man in the provinces," he said slowly. "And if the Duke can be said to listen to anyone it is to that same great lord. He was just back from Tours, you say? Now I wonder what he heard in France, that he should be so anxious to send loving wishes to the Seigneur de la Gruthuyse's guest."

"I haven't the slightest notion," Philip yawned. The aftermath of reaction was combining with the beer to make him drowsy, and Percy laughed at him as he divided the last between them.

"Sluggard. Even now our fates may hang in balance, while you sit snoring."

"I don't," Philip contradicted amiably, and to prove it sat up to direct a closer look at a heap of litter on one of the pallets. There was a slender-bladed misericord which he recognised as Percy's, with the curiass from his armour and a shirt. "What have you been doing while I was out?"

"Considering the question of tomorrow's meal," Percy responded, somewhat grimly. "Also, there's the landlord to remember again: he began to talk about his bill when I asked for the beer tonight. I was near stuffing his damned horsewater down his throat, cask and all."

"Why shouldn't he talk about his bill? It's not his business to house us free, though you'd suppose the honour to be all his sometimes, from the way he gets talked to under his own roof." Philip frowned at the pile. He knew why Percy was wearing his doublet fastened to the neck; the shirt on the pallet was the one he had been wearing when they fled from Doncaster, a little soiled, but otherwise in good condition still. "You mustn't sell any of those, Rob. If the Duke of Burgundy turns himself about again you could need your arms tomorrow, and it's too cold this weather to go without a shirt. Let's see what Ser Beppo will give for this." He pulled a ring from his hand and threw it on the pallet. Percy looked at it, and back to his friend. "Your father's? You can't part with that."

"Why not? He was a sensible man: he'd have been the last to expect us to be hungry while this would fetch something. Toss you for who deals with Beppo."

"Better let me, I'm bigger," Percy said humorously, but it was a half-hearted effort at best. Changing the subject, he said, "There was a courier came through near an hour ago, with news out of England. The King has a son."

"Well, it's about time," Philip remarked, thinking of the disappointing succession of girls that had been all the result of Elizabeth Woodville's past pregnancies. "And the Queen?"

"Safely delivered, and in sanctuary with the princesses still. The boy's to be named Edward." Percy's mind seemed elsewhere; he was playing with the laces of his doublet. "There was some other news too. Warwick has proclaimed that all who followed the King to Burgundy may return to England without fear for lives or lands. They need only swear fealty to Lancaster to keep all their property: he has promised it."

"Generous of him." Philip was examining his boot, still on the foot crooked over his knee. "Pest on it, here's another hole coming. There's a cobbler off the Place, I hear, that does a fair marvel patching leather; I'll walk over tomorrow and take your pair too, if you like." He fingered a lumped sole with disfavour. "When I am back in England, I'll never wear mended shoes again."

There was a short silence. Percy cleared his throat, rearranged his feet, and said at length, "I wondered—that is, I was thinking you might want to consider going back now and taking Warwick's offer."

"Yes, I could see you were," Philip told him unkindly. "And you'll be giving me your company on the same boat, I suppose?"

The big northerner flushed. "It's not the same. I must make my fortune somehow, and my father has an older son. What difference should Warwick's pardons make to me? But you have all your lands to lose, that you were four years working to secure." He added after a moment, "What about your mother? Do you know where she is now?"

"Gone to my sister at Ipsden: I've no need to worry about that," Philip returned absently. He half-lay with his hand propping his cheek, his eyes on the fire. The shadows hid his face, and Percy said roughly, "I'm a meddlesome fool then, and I know this is none of my affair. But then years from now, when you're wandering around Europe in the tail of any war that promises employment, I wonder if you won't regret what you're throwing away now? If Gloucester had one coin to spare for any of his men, we all know it would go first to you; but he's emptied his purse and exhausted his credit, and he depends himself on Gruthuyse's charity. He wouldn't blame you if you took the oath—not knowing how much you stand to lose."

"About the same as the rest of you, in fact," Philip said cheerfully, as he put the empty tankard on the floor beside him. "My given word."

"Very splendid!" Percy snapped. "You should try selling it to Beppo for something: I doubt you'll put on flesh out of the profits." Philip lifted an eyebrow as he pulled out the nearest pallet, and, the room being icy, made ready for bed by the simple process of stepping out of his boots. "I shall take to lifting purses, of course: Monsieur de Brezy tells me a bowstring is the very thing. Come to bed, thickhead: the fire's nearly out, and I don't suppose the landlord would thank us if we broke up his furniture to replenish it."

The single covering which each pallet owned was hardly more than a sheet, but the thin protection offered some comfort from the cold. Retrieving his shirt, Percy stretched himself on the neighbouring mattress, and by the time their friends came trooping up from the common room below, both were peacefully asleep.

The rapid beat of hoofs beyond the window more than an hour later failed to disturb any of the Count of Flanders' guests, and the courier went on by, urging his mount through the cobbled streets to the still-lighted house of the Governor of Holland. In his pouch he carried news for Edward that, notwithstanding all Charles of Burgundy's politic wooing, the Earl of Warwick had made cause with the King of France, and Louis' soldiers were already investing the Burgundian border fortress of Saint Quentin.

Christmas at the Duke of Burgundy's court, for all King Louis and his men, was kept with splendour, and the celebration was at its height when Edward and his train of followers rode to Lille. They were received with pomp by Charles and his Duchess, and if there were some smiles at the sudden warmth of the beleaguered Duke's welcome to his brother-in-law, no one, least of all Edward, was thoughtless enough to comment upon it. What emotions Edward cherished about Charles of Burgundy were an indulgence private to himself; and nothing could have bettered his manner—impeccably balanced between dignity and gratitude—towards the man who had at last chosen to help him regain a throne.

Richard had remained in Bruges, which was closer than Lille to the harbour of Flushing where the Yorkist ships lay, to oversee the ordering of supplies and deal with the wealthy merchants of Bruges who had decided that Yorkist credit was, after all, worth honouring; and it was February before he put in an appearance at Lille. Charles was receiving, and the hall was filled with bowing nobles. On the broad dais Edward sat with his sister the Duchess of Burgundy, while Charles himself—black-locked, swarthy, his dress a Roman simplicity among the extravagances of his courtiers—came halfway down the velvet-spread steps to greet his wife's youngest brother, and lead him back to join them. With a suggestion of a grimace Richard resigned himself to the requirements of diplomacy, and Philip took advantage of the ensuing polite confusion among the ranks of attendants to slip from the Duke's escort, and withdraw to the shelter of a massive column midway down the hall. From its discreet vantage he stood watching the ritual ebb and flow of gorgeous peacock figures which Richard's errands of the winter had made a familiar sight. Erard de Brezy, the bleached wings of his hair like snow under the torches, encountered the young man's distant eyes, and acknowledged his signed salute with a smile. The affairs of their respective masters had brought them together several times since that first meeting in the Grand' Place, and Philip had shortly been surprised to find himself on very friendly terms with Charles of Burgundy's most formidable courtier. He was aware of the distinction: he had long ago guessed the Lord of Saint Aubin to be unremarkable either for informality of manner, or readiness of affection.

The fresco of figures was altering again: some ladies of the court had been summoned to attend upon the Duchess of Burgundy and her brothers. Percy, who had preceded Richard's party to Lille by some days, came over to Philip, remarking with a smile at the scene, "The King is sparing no effort to assure himself of friends in Burgundy. De Brezy's wife is there: Did you know?"

"The English bride? He said something of her coming when I saw him in Bruges last week; she goes with him on to Lenaertsdijk tomorrow. Her first visit to court, I understand."

"And likely to be made memorable. Observe the attentions of the majesty of York." Percy's voice was dry. Philip said carelessly, "If the King thinks to get Monsieur de Brezy's good will by impressing his wife, he may be disappointed. I don't see Monseigneur being dandled into alliances by a woman."

"Not this woman, anyway," Percy responded, amused. "She must be all of twelve years old."

His brows rising, Philip turned to stare down the hall. He saw a slight child, stiffly gowned in damask, and swathed in the diaphanous folds of an enormous wimple.

The crowd shifted and swallowed her, and, shrugging, he looked away. "God above, talk of December and May. Rather an unlikely match for him to settle on, I should have thought."

"Two ugly heiresses, both buried," Percy countered good-humouredly. "And still no son for the Brezy name. She's a taking little piece, and will be pretty in a year or so: I daresay this time he wanted some pleasure to go with the dower."

The audience from the dais was concluding; Charles, his wife, her brothers, and the whole winding paraphernalia of attendants swept their stately course from the hall. The Duke and his guests dined that night in what went in Burgundy for privacy, and Philip saw neither de Brezy nor his wife again; partly rousing from sleep early next morning, he but hazily identified through the open transom the squeak of carts and clop of palfreys and sumpters, departing north to Lenaertsdijk.

Early in March a battered carrack slipped warily through the tumbling black waters off the Yorkshire coast, and dropped anchor above Ravenspur. A storm had scattered the Yorkist ships, and as Richard brought his tired men ashore there was no sign of the rest of Edward's fleet. Beyond the mouth of the Humber the wind was lifting the waves to impossible heights; it was raining hard, and darkness concealed alike the whereabouts of their companions and the Earl of Warwick's vigilant patrols. In the utmost discomfort they made camp, bolting their cold rations quickly before, not daring to kindle a fire, they rolled themselves in their dripping cloaks and fell into uneasy sleep.

During the night the wind dropped, and morning dawned mercifully fair. They struck south, alert for hostile scouts, but the skyline was bare of watchers, and at Ravenspur they found Edward's camp. They were, with Duke Charles' borrowed Flemings, some fifteen hundred strong.

Losing no time, Edward marched his forces towards York. After some anxious temporising the city admitted him, reassured only in part by the petitioner's suave protestations that he came as Edward, sometime Earl of March, claiming no more than his dead father's dukedom of York. It was a straw at which the mayor and council had, perforce, to grasp; the Earl of Warwick was far away, and his brother Montagu, who should have been standing between them and the invader, was still at Pontefract and showing no disposition to move.

Next morning Edward turned south, swinging wide of Pontefract to gain a lead on Montagu, who would surely be following soon with his power. But although galloping couriers were carrying word of their landing over every highway in England, of opposing forces they saw nothing, of pursuit no sign. No pennon showed, no flash of spearpoints behind them along the northern hills. Quiet locked their passage like a spell.

"Plague on the man, why does he not move and be done!" Hastings exploded, as Edward, establishing himself at Warwick, took counsel with his captains. They were in the great solar where less than two years before Edward had waited, a prisoner, upon his cousin of Warwick's pleasure; and he smiled now as he fingered a rolled despatch.

"Better be glad he hasn't, this direction; he could have finished us that first week any time he liked." He looked down at the roll again, biting his thumb. "Meanwhile, the Earl of Warwick has garrisoned himself within Coventry, and Margaret of Anjou lingers still at Calais, waiting and looking for him to accomplish what he has promised her. Something of a change for Henry's delightful queen; she used not to be so backward."

"They say she fears for the prince," Rivers remarked, and Edward's lip lifted.

"Well she may, but what a fool the woman is! Does she think to keep her whelp safe in Calais while Warwick conquers a kingdom for them, and then present the young gentlemen to the English people as their future king? Mass, Dickon was younger when he went to Wales, and I sent no nursemaid with him to make sure he kept his feet dry in the rain."

"You came near being well served for your callousness," Richard observed. "Good God, how green we were! I marvel you ever got your castles back."

"This is the seasoned warrior speaking now," Hastings suggested, with a wink at Rivers. Richard glanced at him, and said after a moment, "No, my lord." He was smiling too, but a current of dislike ran between them like summer lightning. As if by accident Edward leaned in front of his brother, flicking the paper in his hands to the centre of the table.

"I have here sure report that the Marquess of Montagu's purpose is to make rendezvous with the Earl of Warwick at Coventry. Together they have a considerable power, and Oxford and Beaumont are marching from Newark to swell the gathering. A mighty array, my lords, and one we are in no case to meet at our present strength, for all the growing numbers of our friends. But my cousin has become cautious. Even with his allies, he is waiting for more: he'll not budge until the Duke of Clarence arrives in Coventry with his following."

"Clarence?" Rivers' voice was sharp. "Have you word of him, Ned?"

"Most comprehensive word. My lord of Clarence reached Burford with the western levies two days ago; by now he is well on the way to Banbury, and the Earl of Warwick doubtless expects him in Coventry before the week is out." The ironic eyes shifted, considering again the crumpled despatch. "However, it has been given the Duke of Clarence, like Saint Paul, to see a great light. He joins himself with us here instead, three days hence."

"Bones of the saints," Hastings said softly. A pause followed in which the silent comments jostled; ending it, Rivers said slowly, "The Earl of Warwick has been singularly unfortunate with both his sons-in-law on this campaign."

"It would appear he has," Edward agreed, and laughed. "George of Clarence or the princeling of Lancaster: Which would you choose? By God, I could be sorry for him."

His accompanying careless nod signified the conclave's end. There was general movement towards the door; the ushers sprang to open, and Richard went through without a word. Rivers was about to follow when Edward, who had strolled to the window, turned from it to say curtly, "A word, Tony."

His eyes questioning, Rivers came back into the room. The table at which they had been sitting was near the window, out of the servants' ear; throwing his leg across a corner of it, Edward said casually, "Will you see to it, Tony, that word goes to the London magistrates without delay? I want Henry of Lancaster put under arrest and lodged in the Tower."

The fine brows lifted. "A large order, Ned. Warwick's council is still in London; the magistrates may not be ready to accept a Yorkist warrant."

"Dice you for it they do," Edward offered, and, chuckling, Rivers shook his head.

"Oh, I am poor to you already. I'll see to it," and then, his voice sinking, "What order for the Tower?"

Edward said gently, "Am I a fool? He has an heir in France."

His brother-in-law gone, he sat a while longer, idly turning the scattered papers on the table. He was whistling softly to himself, but his eyes were cold.

London received them with pealing bells and gates flung wide. Fugitive Yorkists came pouring from the sanctuaries, making room thereby for Lancastrian replacements, and all the city lined the way, ran at their stirrups, leaned from upper windows to touch hands and throw kisses and garlands. No one was sparing a thought for the Earl of Warwick and the mighty host advancing from Coventry; disentangling himself, not too hastily, from the arms of a citizen's daughter, Philip reflected with inward laughter that one might have supposed that fight already won. But it was a joyous havening, and balm to their tired, anxious spirits after the grudging exile of Bruges, the havering at York, the few friends coming to meet them on the ride south, half-looking over their shoulders even then, it had sometimes seemed.

Two days later—rested, provisioned, their numbers mushroomed to ten thousand men—they marched out by Moorgate, heading north on the Coventry road. Dusk was falling when the first troops entered Barnet; the place seemed deserted, and after a quick survey of the emptied town Richard sent a message back to the main body of the army. Shortly after Edward himself arrived for hurried consultation. Somewhere ahead of them the Earl of Warwick and his allies lay in the deepening dark; how near, the busy scouts soon brought word. The Earl's army was hardly a mile out of Barnet, swung across the path of Edward's forces and settling there for the night. After a moment's thought Edward told his brother to go on. He had no desire for Warwick to think better of closing with him and slip away instead, perhaps to join Margaret of Anjou and her Frenchmen, whose sailing from Calais, spies reported, now appeared imminent. The solution was to get so close to his cousin during the night that, next morning, the Earl would be compelled to fight, but it would be dangerous work in the total darkness which now surrounded them.

Cautiously, without lights, the Duke of Gloucester's men stumbled clumsily along the muddy track, keeping a tortoise pace to soften the thud of their chargers' hoofs. The minutes passed; all at once lights flickered before them through the misty dark, and scurriers returned with word that the Lancastrians lay hardly a bowshot ahead. Despatching a herald to the King, Richard turned from the road and began deploying the Yorkist right wing across the common immediately opposite the Earl of Warwick's left. Following close behind, Edward took up his position with Clarence in the centre, and Hastings' detachments fanned off on the other flank. Baggage carts creaked to a halt in the rear, horses were led behind the lines, and the difficult business of pitching camp without lights on unfamiliar ground was finally accomplished. The sudden explosion of cannonfire directly ahead was a startling interruption to the rustling quiet; Richard, about to enter his tent, checked to stare towards the sound, watching the flashes with narrowed eyes. "They're shooting over us for Barnet," he said presently. "I suppose they never thought we'd stir beyond it tonight. Let them waste their balls: my cousin is due for a surprise, come morning."

"They say he has three men for every two of ours, even yet," Philip rejoined wryly. "God send the surprises may be all his, my lord."

A pavilion had been raised near the Duke's tent where the knights of his household would sleep. Philip found a place, and settled himself for the remainder of what promised to be a noisy night.

A touch on the shoulder had the shock of insult. Rebelliously rousing, he rolled over and sat up; Percy, already armed, was standing at the pallet's foot. "Up with you, John-a-bed. Come look at the day, and wish yourself in Oxfordshire."

Though they could hear noises outside as the army wakened, within the pavilion there were flambeaux burning. Philip, following Percy's gaze, looked towards the lifted tent flap; the torches killed the dawn. When he went to the entrance, he understood why. Fog, thick and impenetrable, shrouded the camp; sight was impossible beyond a stone's cast, and the white boar standard above Richard's tent hung limp in the chilly, windless morning.

"Holy Saint Michael, fight on our side," someone muttered behind them, and Percy laughed in agreement.

"With a phalanx of angels too. Still, Oxford and Warwick will be treading no dance of joy either. God have mercy on poor sinners this day."

There was quickened movement in the pavilion as the Duke's knights armed by the smoky flares. The squire who attended Philip worked with a mixture of nervousness and excitement, his soft cheeks alternately flushed and pale; he was a good lad, eldest son of a smallholder near Willowford, who had endured the privations of Bruges with cheerful placidity, but Doncaster was the nearest he had come to pitched encounter, before today.

Outside, the thick grey was slowly lightening. The Duke's followers gathered beneath his standard: sergeants and officers, veteran captains and lords whose experience would be the makeweight for his own lack of it; squires, heralds, and the knights of his household. A messenger in the King's colours rode up, dismounted, and disappeared into the tent, and a minute later Richard came out. He spoke briefly with his captains, but the order of array had already been planned, and he did not worry the officers with last-minute changes. They were dismissed to their places, and the squires brought helmet and battle-axe. With a last glance around the shrouded field, he remarked non-committally, "Well, sirs, we must hope the cloud lies no lighter on the Earl of Warwick and his friends."

He flicked his visor shut as he spoke, and took his place before the household knights. Far to the left, thinned by distance and muffled by the mist, the trumpet sounded.

It was echoed almost immediately from the Duke of Gloucester's lines; a swarm of arrows soared into the air and vanished into the mist; and the roar of cannon shattered the stillness. Slowly, feeling their way over the rough ground, the knights and men-at-arms moved forward. The blank wall of fog which confronted them had a deceptive look of solidity, but somewhere within it the shadowy mass of the enemy left was advancing. Scouts, spying out positions the night before, had reported the lords of Oxford's and Exeter's Lancastrian troops formed the wings of the Earl of Warwick's array, with the Earl's own Neville followers under his brother Montagu's command between them. From far off the first noise of conflict drifted at Edward's centre crashed against his cousin's, and another flight of arrows whispered over their heads, but in the shifting, interminable greyness before the Yorkist right, nothing stirred.

Straining his eyes through the murk, Philip felt his foot slide on the coarse turf, and, recovering his balance, realised they were no longer on level ground. The land was tilting away from them; they were moving down a slope which angled more steeply with every passing moment. At first he was puzzled; then, sick with dismay, he worked it out. The broad common upon which Warwick and his captains had established themselves was protected on their left where the land fell away into a deep hollow; in the darkness of the night Richard's battle had stretched itself beyond his opponent's, and instead of facing the Lancastrians, they were swinging past them. The advantage was double edged; if the Duke of Exeter, no novice commander, discovered their position before they could climb the farther slope and regain the flat above, they would be trapped there with the Lancastrian left wing descending to butcher them at leisure.

Richard had already guessed what had happened; he quickened his step, lifting a gauntleted hand to hurry his men after him. They seemed to descend forever, but at last the perilous incline slackened and levelled, and minutes later they began to climb. In tense quiet the ascent was accomplished; the mist, so short a time before their unkindest enemy, now served them well. Panting and breathless, weighed down by their armour and trying desperately to keep firm footing on the muddy slopes, they reached the flat common above, and found themselves neatly astride Exeter's unsuspecting flank. Pausing only long enough to let the bulk of his men reach the crest of the rise, Richard signalled the line forward.

The surprise was absolute. Taken from behind, the Lancastrians gave ground, and for a moment the long, straggling wing protecting Montagu's centre position wavered and seemed near collapse. The last troops scrambled out of the bottom, pressing their fellows before them deeper into Exeter's cracking battle; companies of archers, drawn into hasty formation by their captains, loosed stinging volleys into the disordered enemy ranks, and cries of "York!" rang triumphantly along the lone. The next minute, the van of the reforming Lancastrian wing swept down on them.

Cursing and persuading by turns, Exeter had got his shaken men rallied. He knew the ground, having paced it over the afternoon before, as the attackers could not possibly know it; he understood very well his adversary's critical position on the lip of the precipice, and he was beginning to realise too that he had numbers on his side. For added surety a messenger went racing to the Earl of Warwick to demand support from the reserves; and Warwick, edgily conscious of the dislike and distrust of his Lancastrian allies, dared not refuse.

Like a ponderous arm, the long arc of mailed troops swung forward. The gunners had dragged their pieces round, and body-crippling stones began to thud among the rearward Yorkist ranks; their own guns lay useless on the other side of the bottom. Step by bitter step, the captains pulled their men back, hesitated, and withdrew again. A dozen yards from the edge of the plateau the bombards fell silent, their range lost, and then the arrows came, and a cruel, impossible tide of fresh men breaking like the endless, inexhaustible sea.

It was long past dawn now, but the mist hung low, and they could gauge the sun's progress only by the faint saffron glow in the eastern sky. Shortly after sunrise a herald from Edward struggled through the torn lines to the Duke of Gloucester's standard. He brought grim news: Lord Hastings' left, outflanked by the Earl of Oxford and with only a scattering of hedges for protection, had been driven back and broken against the Yorkist centre. The bulk of his men were fleeing back to Barnet, and only the greed of Oxford's soldiers, more eager to follow for plunder in the village than to stay and finish the work of destruction, had saved Hastings' wing from total rout.

Richard listened without interruption, his foot tracing a pattern in the sticky mud. He had come behind the battle only a few minutes before to speak with his captains; a squire held his left gauntlet, rusty with blood from a pikeman's thrust beneath the vambrace, and a surgeon was hastily stanching the wound while the herald talked. Lord Hastings, he said, was doing his best to drag the shattered remnant of his line back against the King's, but Oxford had gone to fetch his men from their sport in Barnet, and it would be only a matter of time before he brought them back to renew the assault. "The King believes the Earl of Warwick is sending his reserves against you, my lord—'a raw lad's folly,' says his grace, 'for the which my cousin himself had roundly schooled me, a dozen years ago. Let him break his teeth on my lord of Gloucester,' he says, 'my brother will hold him for the time I need to make the error plain'."

The bright voice ended, its owner's eyes slipping furtively from the unreadable steel cowls of the men clustered around to listen, to the mist-wrapped standard and the tossing confusion beyond the wall of household knights. The surgeon had finished his work, and Richard turned to the squire, holding out his hand for him to refit the gauntlet. While the straps were fixed, he said over his shoulder, "My greetings to his grace, herald. We do very well here: I pray you, tell him so."

"My lord—" It was Howard who spoke, a mailed hand on the younger man's, his red-rimmed eyes meeting the weary grey ones. "my lord, you cannot do it. In half an hour they will push us from the cliff: believe me, you must tell the King."

"Must I so? By Saint Paul, I know not what you can do, Sir John, but suffer me a little to understand myself!" There was a difficult pause, during which Howard, impassive, stared at the ground, and Richard took back his weapon from the waiting boy. "So I take no new men from him now, in half an hour his grace may have saved the day, and us too. You have leave, herald; I have told you, we do very well."

Philip had lost all idea of time. He thought they had been poised on the crest of the hill for many hours, but it was hardly brighter now than when they had climbed the slope. His arms rose and fell and stiffly rose again with the swing of the axe as if in sleep; the sickly half-light beyond the slitted helmet hurt his eyes, and he would have given all Willowford for one lungful of clean air. Having returned to the battle, Richard did not leave it again. His captains had no counsel left to offer; there was no purpose now but to cling as long as life endured to these few yards of violated earth, strewn with the wreckage of countless assaults, furrowed by the convulsions of the dying and soaked with their blood. Exhaustion lay in a dead weight upon them all; the ploughed mire seemed to clutch at their ankles with living hands, and when a foot turned on something that was moving still, no one looked to see.

The end, when it came, was so sudden it appeared the mocking illusion of a nightmare sleep. Tired to the point of fantasy, his padded doublet sodden with sweat beneath the suffocating weight of armour, Philip hardly noticed the first faltering in the attack. One moment it was gathering afresh; the next, the surging columns hesitated and began to separate. The wind lifted a curl of mist, and through the gap they could see the enemy centre buckling and falling away. Richard turned to signal; the trumpets blew advance banners. Suddenly a towering figure broke towards them through the rout, and Philip shouted in warning.

"My lord, guard yourself!" The tumult drowned his voice, but as if feeling the danger, Richard wheeled and threw himself sideways. The movement saved his life; the axe which should have cleft the mail at his throat fell glancing instead to his upper arm, and knocked him from his feet. Astride above him, the assailant was swinging up his blade when Philip reached them. It needed only one blow to bring the man down; he was a huge creature with arms that could have made him three men's work, but he had been too eager at what he was doing to look behind him.

One of Richard's squires hurried towards them, but Philip was already stooping to help him rise. Something dark flashed past his eyes, and a blow like a hammer caught his shoulder, spinning him back as if the load of armour were so much down. He felt an instant's wonder: then the shock of his face meeting the muddy ground, and an explosion of pain, licking viciously out and down through arm and midriff and thigh. With his last strength he tried to roll to his side; the clamour swirled and faded, and there was nothing more.

Consciousness returned slowly, coming and going in sluggish, indecisive waves with rifts of blankness between. Someone was fumbling with the straps and buckles of his cuirass; he knew a sharp terror, and gave a stifled cry of protest which came too late. A sudden wrench lifted him from inertia to an experience of agony more brutal than flame; the world turned blood-coloured, and then he was sliding weightless through a deepening twilight where voices flitted like bats in the crimson dark. A voice snapped, "Take care, fool!" and the clumsy tugging ceased abruptly. A slight bewilderment trickled through the clogging lassitude of Philip's brain; he knew that voice, and was convinced it did not belong here, but the effort to focus concentration on the problem offered only a fleeting check to his descent into oblivion.

Aeons later a hand touched his face, and he realised

dreamily that he was no longer burdened with his armour. There was a cushion beneath his head, and although an iron bar seemed to have been driven through his shoulder, the jagged teeth of pain had blunted to quite endurable discomfort: naggingly persistent, but no longer edged with fire. Thus far, good; with great care he essayed a movement, and was dimly surprised to find that his right arm, at least, still responded to command. In a little while, he told himself drowsily, he would try again. A delusive feeling of detachment floated down around him like a cloak, but even as he tried to draw it firmly about him, it wavered and dissolved. Fragments of voices pulled irritatingly at the fuzzy edges of his isolation, clarifying at length into a recognisable comment: "He's waking up." Percy, he thought vaguely; and then someone else spoke just above him. "Philip?" This time there was no mistaking it, and astonishment drove the last clouds away. He opened his eyes.

The glow of candles kindled against the misty obscurity which still lingered outside, broke harshly on his vision. By their light the face above him assembled slowly into perspective; Philip met the half-anxious, half-quizzical eyes, and tried to struggle to his elbow.

"Francis, what the devil—?" Reminder stabbed like a living thing; and, catching him behind the neck, Francis eased him to the pillows again.

"Keep still. There's the head of an arrow and three inches of shaft in your shoulder; you're to be quiet until the surgeon comes. Here's wine, drink it slowly."

He poured it from a flagon on the chest. Philip swallowed, and lay for a minute with his right arm across his eyes. "The shaft broke under me when I fell, didn't it?" he said presently. "It was a lucky shot for someone; I felt the gardbrace move, earlier, a strap gave somewhere and I wondered how much longer it would hold." He dropped his arm. Francis had resumed his interrupted occupation; he was stripping from his cousin's legs the lengths of padding which, worn beneath the greaves, served as protection from the chafing of the leg harness. With an obvious effort at distraction, he remarked irritably, "What in the world was your fool of a squire about to have these so tight? I wonder you've any feeling left."

"Enough for the moment, thank you. Where is he, by the way?"

"If you mean that milk-cheeked looby that was trying to

102

drag you from your harness, I've sent him to make himself useful with my young lad, outside with the horses. The blockhead was all for pulling the blanket from under you as well, disliking the sight of the blood on it, apparently. I've a poor opinion of your servants, cousin."

The deliberate lightness of Francis' voice was clearly meant to discourage enquiry, and Philip contemplated his profile in silence before observing mildly, "You had someone with you, then, on the road from Gloucestershire? I'm relieved: I'd supposed Lord Talbot saw you away with no more than his blessing to company you."

Bending to pick up the discarded swathes of padding, Francis said shortly, "I had no occasion to consult Lord Talbot. I've been in Lincolnshire since Martinmas, in Beaumont's household."

"Your uncle? Good God." Philip had heard of the Viscount. Francis smiled at his expression.

"Yes. Oh, he meant well by me, though his temper continues unimproved: I'm sorry for my aunt. But he was going to pack me off to France for schooling, once this little business was done"—he nodded jerkily towards the loosened tent flap—"so I took my leave three nights ago, with a pair of his geldings and a stable brat that caught me saddling up and raised a shout to go with me and see the world. Can you give him a place at Willowford, Philip? He's good with horses, and I've no notion what the King may intend for me now."

"A dozen stripes for horse-stealing to begin with, I should think." Philip shifted his weight painfully on the mattress. Incongruous among the litter of armour and padding cloths and torn-up wads of bandaging, the silver goblet he had drunk from gleamed beside him on the chest; he was suddenly aware he was lying in Richard's tent. From the doorway Percy drawled, "Not over Beaumont's beasts, Philip; my lord Viscount made himself too busy about King Lancaster's affairs for that. He was with Oxford; they'll be miles out of Barnet by now, and still running."

Through a jumbled chaos of pain and fatigue, recollection rushed in. Almost inaudibly, Philip said, "So we won."

Percy gave a shout of laughter. He had been standing at the entrance, peering into the thinning mist, but he turned then to come lounging over to the pallet. "Very notably we won. We'd luck with us; Oxford's men lost themselves in fog on the way back from Barnet, and let off their arrows into Montagu's flank instead of ours. Montagu's fellows, never having loved Oxford's from the first, promptly cried treachery, and both lots took to their heels. Our reserves finished the rout." He grinned unresentfully into his companion's drawn face. "A mighty day for York, Lovell, and I wish I stood in the shoes of the man that saved the Duke of Gloucester's life. He'll name his reward."

There was a stir at the door, and Richard's surgeon entered, cheerfully smiling and turning back the furred sleeves of his gown. A youth followed, bearing a collection of boxes and instruments, and two great-girthed servants who at a nod stooped to lift the pallet nearer the entrance. The morning's first pale sunlight glanced through to make an uncertain triangle on the blanket.

"But we'll have the candles too," the surgeon was saying genially as he laid back the covers, "for I'd as soon have fouled tools as not enough light to work by. Now then, sir—" Still pleasantly talking, he opened the blood-soaked arming doublet, and slit the shirt. One of the serving men squatted behind Philip's head, and the other knelt across his thighs. Francis began uneasily, "Rob, couldn't we—?" He was fingering the wine flagon. The surgeon, his examination concluded, looked round to say crisply, "There is little good in it, sir; he will do better to have it later," and Percy, who had been watching impassively with his hands on his hips, seemed to recollect himself.

'We'll be off, sawbones, since you're not needing us. Best come along, Francis, and find what his grace thinks of vagabonding wards—Philip, I'll not be far."

His large hand under the boy's elbow propelled him firmly from the tent. Francis went without argument; there was reassurance in that solid placidity, unadmitted though the desire for it might be.

Philip's chastened squire was outside, and the small Lincolnshire lad, on tiptoe from excitement and delight with a hundred questions pelting from his lips. The fog was lifting, and groups of men were combing the field, counting the dead, collecting prisoners, and bringing in the wounded. Gregory Traynor arrived, apprenhensively questioning, and a short time later the Duke of Gloucester appeared with the King. Richard gave Francis a quick smile in which surprise, pleasure, and amusement were equally mixed, before he walked over to the tent, lifted the flap, and vanished inside. Edward was conning a list of prisoners, not yet complete, and Percy's salute was only perfunctorily acknowledged, but he glanced up at Francis' shy bow, frowned, and smiled.

"By God's mercy, Francis Lovell, I had hardly known you. Have you been playing truant from authority? Surely this is something of which your keepers would not approve."

"I know they would not, if I had asked," Francis rejoined, kissing the outstretched hand. 'But Lord Talbot was at home in Gloucestershire, last I heard, and for Beaumont, do you suppose he will come looking for me now?"

"You've been learning court manners since we parted. So I am forgiven for delivering you to the yoke of matrimony? Poor Francis, you have suffered in my service! I remember my cousin of Warwick promising an hour with you at Pontefract, too."

Francis coloured violently, disconcerted by a demonstration of memory he would have preferred shorter by a length; but there were few things affecting his own advantage that Edward of York forgot. Behind the lazy eyes, the cool intelligence which never slept was busy now, tallying, weighing, appraising: Minster Lovell, Tichmarsh, Rotherfield Greys, Holgate Burnell, Acton Burnell, Deinscourt, Bainton—he knew them by rote, the roll of holdings whose revenues for six years had clinked a golden river into the coffers of other men; whose enormous power, not half a decade hence, must inexorably descend into this stripling's hands. He had taken trouble with the boy at Pontefract for that reason, and the attachment to Dickon was lucky too; but who knew?—who knew what time would make of him, Beaumont's nephew, the Duke of Buckingham's kin?

Richard had emerged from the tent. Edward turned to meet him, a question in his lifted brows; answering it, his brother said briefly, "In pain, and they're not done yet; he wanted me gone. I've had a word with Cannings, and he says Philip shouldn't be moved farther than Barnet for the next while, so I'm sending to arrange lodgings there. With your grace's leave, I should like Francis to stay with him for the time, and when Philip is well enough to travel again, Francis could come along too—by which time perhaps you will have settled on your intentions for him?" He was smiling as he finished, his eyes on Francis' anxious face. Edward considered, and laughed. "I'll give him into your keeping, Dickon. Let him finish his training in your household; he could learn his weapons in no better place, as I have had cause this day to know. "For the gentleman within"—he glanced towards the tent—"see to it he lacks nothing, and when he is healed that his name is called to my remembrance. I know how incalculably he has served me today."

A herald was running towards them through the mist, shouting and waving his arms. They turned together, and the man came racing up to drop on one knee. "God save your grace," he said breathlessly. "We have found the Earl of Warwick."

Suddenly tense, Edward leaned forward. "You have him fast?"

"Fast enough, your grace, he'll trouble you no more. We found him by their horsepark with his throat cut."

The words dropped like stones, heavy and unmeaning. Edward stood rigid; then he reached down to seize the silk-clad shoulders, saying in a low voice, "By the splendour of God, who has done this thing?" He was white with fury; getting no answer, he shifted his hold from shoulder to throat and dragged the herald to his feet. "Whoreson, I asked a question. Was it not published abroad that I would have no one do injury to my cousin of Warwick? Who has dared to violate my most express command?"

"Let your grace have pity"—the voice came thickly, rough as a crow's in the throttling grasp—"I do not know. Soldiers, it is thought, not knowing of the order, or—" He stopped, afraid to go on, and with a muffled obscenity Edward threw him aside.

"Or after his arms and jewels, the craven scavengers. By Christ, they had best sink their gains to the bottom of the Thames, for if I find who did this they'll pray for death—" Abruptly wheeling, he stood staring across the common. In the undergrowth some hedge sparrows cheeped softly. After a while the King spoke tonelessly: "And Montagu? Has he been found?" The reply was slow coming, and he glanced over his shoulder. "Dead too? I thought it. I saw him when we broke the line; there were only a few left around him." He paused again, then said, "Where are they?"

Hesitantly the herald pointed; to the north some green tree tops floated against the sky. Edward strode off with Richard, and after an undecided moment Francis and Percy followed. They kept a careful distance behind the King and his brother, but as they came nearer the Lancastrian horse-park they found it to have been a needless exercise in tact. The news had spread, and groups of people had gathered, peering and whispering. Edward brushed curtly past; they parted easily, their eyes on the centre of the clearing.

Warwick lay on his face, an arm still outflung towards the tethered horse for which he had been reaching when he fell. His armour was dented and muddied, and plunderers had stripped the gauntlets from his hands, seeking his rings.

Edward stood gazing before he knelt and turned the body over. Dirt clung to the face of the helmet, and the visor was twisted awry where it had been wrenched up for the daggers to thrust inside. Richard drew in his breath, and with a quick gesture his brother forced the visor shut.

Hastings pushed through the crowd, Clarence trailing behind him, as Edward rose to his feet. The burly Chamberlain regarded him in silence; then he said calmly, "Better this way, Ned. There wasn't room in England for the two of you: sooner or later you would have had it all to do again."

The wind blew softly against their faces; through the thinning fog sunlight fell warmly on their bodies in the heavy platings. Montagu had been brought to lie beside his brother; under the broken mail at his throat a piece of stained silk showed, the blue and mulberry colours of York, working from their long hiding place under the blazoned Neville quarterings. The three men looked at it without speaking; they were remembering how he had failed to pursue them on the march south from York, and how they had wondered why.

"Will—" Edward spoke after an interval, his eyes on the bare fingers of Montague's brother crooked like talons in the grass. "Will, how could this have happened? He was with the reserves, he at least should have been mounted—"

Hastings cleared his throat. "I've been making some enquiries about that myself. It seems there was a feeling among his own men, as well as Oxford's, that they wanted him afoot like the rest of them. They didn't trust him to stand with them if the fighting got too hard."

In the stillness Clarence's crow of laughter was like an indecency. Poking the body with his toe, he said lightly, "A long fall for the Earl of Warwick! He does not look so high now."

Edward turned on him, his eyes like blue flame. "He was a man, my little lord of Clarence. Run and play." They stared at each other; then Clarence swung on his heel without a word and walked away through the trees. The last flash of his armour vanished winking among the leaves, and Edward addressed the man beside him. "My lord of Gloucester."

"Your grace?"

"Have these bodies stripped, loaded into a cart, and taken to London. Let them be exposed two days in Saint Paul's before the people; after that the Countess of Warwick may claim them for burial." He went quickly from the horse-park.

Some soldiers lounged nearby, the white boar insignia on their sleeves; they came forward at a sign and started taking the armour from Warwick's body. Bored, the crowd drifted away. The sky was clearing to dazzling blue between puffs of cloud; the soldiers went methodically about their work; and Richard watched from beneath a stand of beeches, the shadows dappling his face. He had thrown a sleeveless tabard over his armour; the breeze caught it, and the golden leopards rippled in their scarlet field.

When the task was finished he walked over to the waiting men, reaching up to the jewelled clasps at his shoulders. The two lengths of silk parted and swung free. For a little space he was silent, looking at the bodies at his feet; suddenly he shivered, and gathering the pieces of silk in his hands he dropped them over the tumbled nakedness. Then he stepped back, saying shortly, "Take them."

Feeling sick, Francis turned from the sight. He heard Percy call after him, but only quickened his steps; the tent was not far, and in a few minutes he was standing at the entrance. He hesitated before lifting the flap, but inside all was still. The surgeon's boy was packing away the instruments, and Gregory Traynor looked round with a smile of welcome as Francis whispered, "Is he asleep?"

"Swooned," Traynor replied. "But he'll be all right now, don't you worry yourself." He was manipulating the blood-soaked shirt from Philip's other arm. Francis went to help; working carefully to avoid disturbing the stiffly bandaged shoulder, they got the rest of the stained clothing off, and a clean blanket wrapped round him. It was like handling one dead, but for the harsh, shallow breathing which never quieted. The piece of arrow lay on the chest, a stub of shaft, broken a little below the head.

Cannings was surveying his patient in a satisfied way, and sipping a cup of wine. "You'll be taking him to Barnet?" he remarked to Francis as he set it down. "My lord of Gloucester has told me to stay by him for a while, until we are sure of the healing. I'll call before supper; until then keep him warm, don't let him move about, and if he's thirsty when he wakes, mix water with the wine. Good day to you, sir."

Francis sat down by the pallet as Traynor moved to the door, saying, "I'll be seeing about a litter, sir."

Francis nodded, bestowed a contemptuous glance upon the pale-faced squire in the corner, and observed, "You might as well take him with you; he may be useful with the horses, but I'm not going to have him pulling my cousin about."

Alone, he settled back with his arms around his knees. He was tired; it had been a long ride from Lincolnshire, and he was aware of a lazy inclination for sleep. After a moment he pulled the chest nearer and propped himself against it, resting his chin on his arms.

A little later Philip stirred uneasily, tossed, and muttered. Francis, bending anxiously above him, thought his skin cold, and borrowed a cloak Richard had left lying by to spread over the pallet. After an instant's reflection he took off his jacket and added it to the pile, tucking the garment firmly, cocoon-fashion, around the blanket; he studied the effect doubtfully, but Philip turned over with a sigh; his swift breathing lengthened, and he grew still.

Outside there was a sound of wheels bumping and creaking over the meadow, and going to the door Francis looked out. The last of the mist had gone, and the sun shone brightly on a rough cart as it rolled from Barnet common, carrying the bodies of Richard Neville and his brother to London.

CHAPTER SEVEN

In the end, Philip was nearly three weeks at Barnet. Faithful
to his word, Cannings came again on the evening of the
move into the village, and found his patient restlessly installed in a chamber above the common room of the inn; it
was the best that could be offered, but Francis, sweeping the
premises with a distasted eye, had commanded new rushes to
the floor boards, and sent young Will, his cousin's squire, off
to London for linen sheets to replace the landlord's inad-
equate supply. Philip was unaware of the boy's going. The
day and the night following passed in a blurred fashion; he
felt, from a distance, the surgeon's hands. After a while he no
longer knew whether it was Francis or Traynor who spoke to
him; their faces merged and separated, and once he called
one of them Rob, demanding what he meant by leaving my
lord of Gloucester unattended. Somebody murmured
soothingly, and a cup, moist with cold, was held to his lips. He
drank avidly, and sleep like a well received him.

The evening of the second day came with a dying clatter
in the hall below, and the loft stairs' creaking signalled retirement of the last yawning guest. Traynor had gone to bed
in the antechamber, but in the sickroom a candle still
burned, and by its light Francis sat at the table, writing. The
work went slowly, with long considering pauses while he bit
at the quill; it was in the middle of one of them that the
bedclothes rustled, and he swung round to discover Philip
wide awake and regarding him with a smile from the pillows.
'Nobil ... Nobilis, mei miserere precor,' he remarked with
difficulty as Francis got up, thrusting the paper from him.
" 'Thy face is a sword, and behold I am slain.' If it's rhymes to
a lady's garter, coz, you're up late about it."

"Poetry? Not my gift, I'm afraid." Francis came to the
bedside, the candlestick in his hand. As he stooped to inspect
the bandages, Philip said, "Why aren't you asleep? You
needn't hang over me; send Will along, he can see to anything I need."

"As a matter of fact, I've sent him to London. I gave him a
note for Ipsden on your behalf; he should be back tomorrow,

but meantime you must make do with Gregory and me." Francis had been arranging the covers as he talked; offhand, he added, "I'd like to send him back again in a fortnight, with your permission. I've a letter the landlord's cart is taking to London tomorrow for the Gloucestershire carrier; there'll be time for a reply by next Monday week, and I'd be obliged if you can spare me Will's services to fetch it."

"By all means. Gloucestershire, did you say?" There was a glimmer of amusement in his cousin's eyes. Francis coloured, and said awkwardly, "It's for my wife, I'd not send him away otherwise. She is—there's to be a child, in about ten weeks as she believes. I've not seen her for some time; I'm a little anxious." He moved aimlessly to the window and played with the latch of the shutter. Philip said lightly, "Then you've become reconciled to matrimony?"

"You might put it that way." A new quiet followed. Philip lay without speaking, his eyes on the turned back; Francis had forgotten, nearly, the persuasiveness of those receptive silences. Without looking around he said, "It was in November that they sent me to Lincolnshire. I was allowed back once to see Anna—Beaumont had business in the west—but we had only a few days together, and—and it was not the same."

"Did you expect it would be? Even Eden was only once."

"Maybe, but I think I can put a name to the serpent in this garden," Francis retorted bitterly. He leaned his forehead against the casement, his fists knotting on the sill. "One day I'll kill him, Philip, I swear it, or he me. I can't breathe in the same room with him, and he's forever about Anna. Even in February—only three days I had there, and the better part of it and her was taken up with her cousin's knighthood feast. We even quarrelled over it, because I wanted to talk of something but the great place that had been promised Sir Humphrey Talbot in the Prince of Wales' household. It was my blame for plaguing her when she was feeling ill and miserable, and we made it up before I left, but—" He looked again at the unfinished letter on the table. Philip, following his gaze, wondered in just what fashion he had explained to Humphrey Talbot's kinswoman how he came to be in Barnet now.

"Why don't you go and see her yourself, Francis, when Will comes back? Take Gregory with you: young Will can see to me here. I'll make your peace with Gloucester."

"Don't be ridiculous!" Francis' voice, roughened with strain, eased on a laugh. "I fancy myself explaining it to the Duke of Gloucester: by God, I'd be wishing I was back with Beaumont. No, I'll wait and ask his leave when we join him." He saw his cousin's face was blanched with weariness, and interrupted himself to say remorsefully, "What a fool I am, keeping you awake with my talking. Are you in pain, Philip?"

"No, I promise you I'm feeling much better." Philip yawned, smiled, and rubbed his cheek. "Only I think it must be quite two days since I was shaved."

"All of that, I'd say," Francis conceded, after a brief survey. "I'll see to it for you tomorrow, if you like."

"I should be happier at the prospect if I thought you had handled a razor before," Philip observed ungratefully, and, ignoring a warm rejoinder, went almost instantly to sleep.

They were just finishing the shaving operation next afternoon when Gregory Traynor entered hurriedly to say that Will Parker had returned from London. Philip was lying with his eyes closed—he had been rather too optimistic about his improving condition—and, intercepting a significant glance from the groom, Francis made only a noncommittal reply. Gathering up the shaving cloths, he followed Traynor into the antechamber, and with the door shut securely behind them asked softly, "What is it?"

"Master Will's brought news from London: the French woman's landed. She put into Weymouth the day of Barnet field; my lord of Somerset has gone to meet her with a following, and she's brought the Prince."

Francis drew in his breath. "And the King?"

"At Windsor, they say, getting fresh men. She's going to fight, sir; Somerset's told her that Barnet finished the King's strength."

Francis reflected, chewing his lip. "We must keep this from my cousin," he said presently. "If he thought the Duke of Gloucester needed him, he'd fret himself to a fever at being kept here. Tell Will he's to guard his tongue when he comes up, and better he doesn't talk too much below either; there's no knowing what dolt might pass it to Sir Philip." He hesitated, and added casually, "Did he say—was it known what lords have gone with Somerset? Has Shrewsbury joined him, or—or any of the northern lords?"

'Not Shrewsbury, no, and Lord Fitz Hugh is still in York-shire, they say." Traynor gave him a straight look. "But you're right, sir; his brother-in-law Lord Talbot has gone, and Sir Humphrey too.'

Swearing quietly, Francis turned on his heel. He had not really supposed Anna's uncle would refuse Somerset his help; it was unreasonable to feel this lurching shock of dis-may. But how alone she would be now: heavy with child, in a misery of fear for her kinsmen, and with only that scolding shrew, her uncle's wife, for company. A mean-mouthed creature she was, with a nose like a pin; he had always dis-liked her and seen no reason for hiding it. He had felt the sting of her palm more than once, and heard her after, shrilly telling Anna that not all the holdings in the Midlands were worth such a shackling.

From the bedchamber he heard his cousin's voice. Auto-matically he moved towards it, trying to put from his mind the picture of the road west to Gloucestershire and the plod-ding carrier's cart. Five or six days, at most, and she would have his letter; another six, maybe seven, before he could receive her answer in his hand. He no longer wondered if she would be angry with him; he only longed for the days to pass until he could hear from her, to know she was well and as impatient as he for the time when he might come to comfort her.

It was a near fortnight before Will Parker set off for Lon-don again. Francis, fretting, would have sent him sooner if he could have borne to imagine an emptyhanded return; in the end he persuaded Philip to tell the lad to ask at the inn where the Gloucester carrier called, and if the man had not yet returned, to wait for him. The weather had become hot for April; the afternoon and the morning following dragged by. Francis told himself they could not possibly expect to see Parker again before another day; leaving Gregory in attend-ance in the stuffy upper chamber, he went out for an hour's restless wandering in the village, and the squire's sweating horse was standing in the courtyard when he returned. Will himself sat on the steps in the shadow of the innboard, cool-ing himself with a tankard of ale. He had with him more news of the Lancastrian advance through the western counties, a bulky parcel and letter from Dame Alice by the Oxford-to-London carrier, and from the Gloucester errand, no word at all. He had found the carrier at his inn, right enough, and the man even remembered having delivered the letter himself, Lord Talbot's house being on his way; but my lady had read what he brought her, he said, and told him there was no reply.

His cheeks flaming, Francis walked out of the courtyard. Not for all the world would he have faced Philip then with that blighting rebuff; it was bad enough to think of his hearing it from Will. A wave of wrath had swamped his earlier compassion, and as he kicked his way along the dusty street his palm itched to box his lady's ears. He understood very well the meaning behind that freezing little snub; as clearly as if she had said it, he knew what she expected he would do. Longing for him as equally as he for her, never doubting which in the end he would choose, she had taken this bitter, hurtful way to let him know he could not have her and his friends as well. No doubt it had seemed an admirable way to bring him to Gloucestershire; her dogs, he remembered furiously, had always been well trained too.

The smell of food met him, finally returning, at the door of the inn; in the common room the mid-day meal was already laid. Upstairs in the antechamber Gregory Traynor was doing something to a travelling chest, but neither the evidence of packing nor Traynor's grimly disapproving face conveyed any meaning to Francis until he walked into the bedroom, and discovered his cousin up and dressed, and flinging the last of his belongings into the small coffer which for the past fortnight had stood beside his bed. The bundle from Dame Alice—shirts and linen, one or two favourite books, and a purse of rose nobles—lay, only cursorily examined, at the bed's foot. Jerked from his preoccupation, Francis exclaimed, "Are you moon mad?" and Philip, having slammed down the lid of the coffer, sat on the bed and reached for his boots.

"Oh, there you are. Tell Gregory to come and cord that up, will you? And you might see if the landlord has his reckoning made, take something from that purse. It's lucky Will got back today; we should have had to go to the Lombards, else."

Crossing the room at a stride, Francis stood glaring at him. "Will you tell me what you're up to? Great God, I think you must be raving. Another fortnight abed at least—at very least—Cannings said before he went, and that was not seven days gone. Have your wits strayed?"

He stopped, for it was apparent Philip was not listening. He leaned back to pick up a letter, tossed down earlier on the coverlet; Francis instinctively looked at it, and recognised Richard's seal. Thrusting the paper into his doublet, Philip said coolly, "If you'd been here half an hour ago you could have spoken with the courier; he wouldn't wait past delivering this, being in haste to get on his way. I couldn't make out certain references until the man who brought it explained: I must have been the only person in a dozen shires round that didn't know the French landed on Barnet Sunday. Will you help me with these boots, Francis? They seem stiff."

"Only because you've not the strength to pull them on," Francis returned roughly. "To save you asking, it was I that told Gergory and Will to hold their tongues, and if you think I'll abet you now you're much mistaken. Are you trying to make me believe Gloucester sent for you, after what Cannings must have told him? Holy Mother, you'll have work to sit a horse!"

"You'll believe what you choose, of course. Cannings means well, but I know what I can do. Will you call my squire, since you're determined to be no help? And tell Gregory to send round for the horses." Philip had managed the first boot, and was reaching for the second. Francis saw in his cousin's fairer face a wilfulness of resolution which exactly matched his own, and made without hope a last attempt.

"But your armour isn't mended; it's still as we took it from you. There's no armourer in this miserable hole, it must go to London to be repaired. You can't possibly wear it, Philip."

"Will must do what he can, and we'll stop on the way to let an armourer have a look," Philip responded, unmoved. "And tell him to be quick about it; I want to leave in an hour."

He stood up, stamping his feet more firmly into the unaccustomed boots. With the explosive observation that it seemed to be some people's heads that had taken the worst hurt at Barnet, Francis strode violently from the room, hunted up Will Parker, and relayed Philip's orders to his groom.

In less than the stipulated hour they were on their way, a train of four horses, with the fifth – Francis' perquisite from Lord Beaumont's stables – acting sumpter under the weight of chest and coffer, Philip's armour, carefully polished and wrapped in goatskin, and the Lincolnshire stableboy. It was past noon, and the sun was beginning to stand down from its zenith, but London was behind them when Philip called a halt for the night. Francis surveyed his cousin's exhausted pallor in compressed silence before he went into a wayside hostelry to bespeak rooms for the night. The guesthouse of an Augustinian priory lay only a short way behind them, and would have provided far more comfortable lodging, but Philip had insisted upon going on until the last light failed, and Francis accepted the edict without verbal protest, having more sense, as he confided in an acid undertone to Gregory Traynor, than to argue with a lunatic.

They reached Windsor next day, and learned the King and his brothers had marched less than a week before in pursuit of the invaders, who were making for Bristol. Philip set a hard pace for Reading, which he hoped to reach before nightfall, but they were some miles from it still when Francis drew rein and announced defiantly that his horse had cast a shoe. This was perfectly true—he had loosened the cleats only an hour before—but Philip received the intelligence with lifted brows, and sceptically requested Traynor to examine the damage before admitting defeat. They were close by a house of Benedictines, a circumstance which Francis attributed to the greatest good fortune, and, feeling too tired to dispute the matter, Philip allowed him to lead the way to the abbey gates.

The porter came, a brisk, cheery-faced individual, and conducted them within. The Abbot, he said, was just now away, but his Prior would receive them; or perhaps—with a side glance at Philip—the gentleman would do better in his bed straight, and when they had eaten, if he desired it, the infirmarian would come. Philip shook his head impatiently to the last suggestion, but was wearily thankful when they were led directly to the guesthouse. He let his companions do justice to the excellent supper which arrived shortly after, and was lying on the bed, too aching-taut to do more than stare at the canopy and try hopelessly for sleep, when the outer door squeaked, and a minute later the Prior came in. He acknowledged Francis' reverence with a smile, almost in the same instant motioning to Philip, who had risen also, to lie down once more. He had not the intention, he said, of afflicting an overweary traveller with the burden of unsought company. Francis satirically volunteered that the overweary traveller was on his way to help King Edward fight the Frenchwoman, the inflection of his voice making his own opinion transparently plain. That drew an amused look, which vanished as Philip unwillingly explained; in a moment or two the visitor seated himself on the bed, and during the course of the ensuing conversation managed to suggest that he himself examine the healing shoulder. He had some knowledge of leechcraft, he said, and it would be a pity to rouse the infirmarian without cause.

The statement proved to have been a modesty; many a surgeon could have learned from that expert touch. Silently laughing at how easily it had been done—he was wondering if Dom Martin had left his unguents on the doorstep, or if he would have presently to send for them—Francis curled beside the hearth, too drowsy himself to marvel long at the sight of an abbey officer ministering to a guest of the house with his own hands. No less odd, after all, was it that he should know what he was doing in the bargain. It came of reading Aristotle, Francis heard him remarking to Philip's comment; one thing had led to another, and during the last season of the plague there had been a great need for help among the townsfolk.

Complin had long been sung; outside, the last green had dimmed and faded in the western sky, and the unwinding linen bandages made a tangle on the coverlet. Sighing, Philip rested his head against the pillow, his eyes on the monk's keen, absorbed face above the deftly working hands. It was impossible to guess his age, or from what condition he might have come; there were lines about his mouth, but the hair which ringed his tonsure was thick and untouched with grey. His fingers moved with light exactness, gentle and sure, as if guided by the very feel of pain. "An ugly wound," he said, as the last wrappings dropped away. "But it is mending; your surgeon understood his business. A spear thrust?"

"The clothyard shaft, or part of it, from one of Exeter's bowmen. It came from anywhere, I never saw the man. Our archers in the Welsh sieges used to shoot so; the figures on the walls were so high and far we could only send a cloud of arrows up, and count the empty places along the parapet, after."

A silence fell while the older man examined the hurt. The flesh had sealed, but the inner lips were full and raw-appearing still, the edges pulled and dry like crisp silk. Presently he rose, saying, "I shall not be long." The infirmary, a separate building, lay opposite the guesthouse; through the open doors they heard his steps fade, and grow clear again on the flagway. He came in with a covered jar which he opened, and sitting down, began smoothing on the salve.

"I see no unnatural humours here. This will help the outer part; for the rest, only your own good healh and good sense will serve. Don't lay too much on yourself too soon; also, for a few days more there would be no shame in a sling."

He was smiling as he finished. Philip said idly, "Can any man ask too much of himself?"

"How should he not? He is a body of earth, striving to see his God. In the days of the desert fathers, one of them being judged sinful was bidden gone from the church; and the holy Bessarion rose up and went with him, saying, I too am a sinful man."

The fire hissed and cracked; Will Parker, long bidden to bed, slept contentedly on his pallet, and at the room's farther end Francis sprawled before the hearth watching the flames. The voices came and went, threading his unregistering awareness like distant water, while he thought of Anna, and wondered how it was with her and how soon before the child would come, and when—for his temper had had time to cool—he could get Richard's leave to go and see her again. Still cloudily dreaming, he rested his head on his arms, and woke with a start to the impact of a pillow thrown by his cousin from the bed. There was a smell of wax from newly quenched candles; only the night light burned on its chest, and the Prior had gone.

Morning came, too soon for Francis' yawning taste, but the day promised to be fine, and Philip dealt ruthlessly with his protests. The sky was a sheet of coral, and as they struck westward their horses' hoofs left dark prints in the dew.

Wayside enquiry elicited the information that Edward was hardly a day's march ahead of them, grimly racing the Frenchwoman's weary troops to the Severn. Beyond lay Wales and the beckoning promise of Jasper Tudor's dissident Welshmen; but somewhere behind her, remorselessly thrusting its way through the narrow, crooked lanes of Gloucestershire, the Yorkist army was drawing nearer. When, two days later, Philip reached Bath, it was to hear that the Lancastrians had abandoned a temporary position in

Bristol and were in headlong retreat towards Gloucester and the passages over its bridge into Hereford. The gap between the two forces shrank to a few miles; the lanes were dusty, narrowing here and there to bare tracks through tangled woods, and there was no time to look for water. Gloucester closed its gates to the invaders; they dared not stop to rest. Tired. hungry, and tormented with thirst, the Lancastrians fled north for Tewkesbury.

Early on Saturday evening Philip arrived in Gloucester. Darkness was falling; by the time they had eaten it would be night. They found a hostelry just within the north gate from which, next day, they could be gone before sunrise, a prospect before which Francis groaned; but any hope he had cherished that his cousin would sleep late remained unfulfilled. Philip was awake at dawn; the landlord was obliging, and cheerfully consented to serve breakfast at once. They took it in the common hall, but the room was otherwise deserted, and the cousins were lingering over a last cup of ale while their horses were saddled and loaded when the outer door banged. A man appeared in the entrance, looking hesitantly around; dust clung to his boots and powdered his hair, and his face was corpse-pale beneath its dirt. Philip stood up, saying, "Francis, make room," but before either of them could move to help, the man stumbled draggingly to the table and sank to the bench before it.

Reaching for his cup, Philip refilled it from the flagon and set it by the stranger's hand. He took it with a mutter of thanks, drank, and put the tankard down again, rubbing his eyes. They saw then he was hardly more than a boy: some knight's squire perhaps, Philip thought, but the livery was unknown to him. He seemed dazed, and sat staring before him, unmoving, until Philip pulled a trencher across the table and silently put bread and meat in front of him. Rousing then, the boy looked up. "I'm sorry, sir. But I've been all night on the road without a horse—" His voice trailed off. Philip said gently, "From where?" He thought he already knew.

"From Tewkesbury." He picked up the bread, fingered it, and dropped it untasted. Pushing the food away, he leaned his head on his hand, murmuring tiredly, "But we lost." Half-hidden by his hair, they saw the swain of Anjou on his sleeve.

Across the tangle of fair curls, Francis met his cousin's gaze. The youth might have been asleep, so complete was his immobility, but for the trembling of his hands and mouth. Deliberately neutral, Philip said, "Then it was a rout?"

The boy turned slightly, regarding him with haunted eyes. "Yes, in the end. We were tired, you see—"

"It's a long march from Gloucester to Tewkesbury, and it was a hot day for it, as I remember. That would be Friday?"

"Yes. Five or six hours, I guess, it seemed longer. We were hurrying, you see; the next bridge over the river is at Tewkesbury. But when we got there, my lord Duke—that's Somerset, sir—told the Queen the men couldn't go any longer without rest, and by next morning they—they'd caught up with us."

"I see. Don't talk more now, unless you want to: Are you sure you won't have something to eat?"

It was coming faster now. "At first it seemed as if we might win. My lord of Somerset led an attack on their flank, where the Duke of Gloucester was commanding, and drove them back. Somerset thought he'd split their battle, but—but it was all deceit. They let him come, a little, and then loosed their arrows. The archers were hidden in the wood, and when our men broke they chased them across the common, cutting them down while they ran. When my lord of Somerset saw what had happened he rode to the centre, where the Prince was with my lord Wenlock—him that was the Earl of Warwick's friend—and shouted at Wenlock that he was a false traitor for not helping him, and had betrayed him just as the Earl of Warwick did my lord of Oxford at Barnet. And—and he struck him down with his axe. By then Gloucester was throwing his men against our centre, and the Prince was like to be trapped, so there was nothing for him—that is, for us—to do but—" He checked, shivering, and clasped his hands tightly before him on the wood. So he was with the Prince, Philip thought. His shoulder was aching again; he had been a fool to suppose he could manage without a sling. He pressed a fist mechanically against the throbbing while the shaken voice went on. "The Prince fled back towards Tewkesbury, but the Duke of Clarence was a little behind the battle, and followed with a troop of lances. When they caught up with us they dragged the Prince from his horse and broke open his armour, and killed him with their knives while—while he cried to my lord of Clarence for his life." He put his head down on the table, hiding his face in his arms.

Francis slid quietly along the bench, and, rising, went to the window. The wooden sign above the entrance porch swayed and squeaked in the breeze; the shutters were open, and the morning sounds of the street came clearly: bells for travellers' Mass, merchants and their servants, early abroad, a carter rattling by with his load, whistling and shouting to his team.

There were footsteps in the passage, and the landlord appeared. "I thought I heard a call, sir; was there something—" He broke off, his eyes sharpening. "What's this?"

Philip turned to look at him. "As you see, host: a boy, and greatly in need of food and rest."

"A boy, is it?" The landlord came nearer, peering at the slumped figure. "I heard no horse: What's his business?"

Annoyed, Philip replied curtly, "You heard no horse because there was none. He's been since last evening on the road from Tewkesbury, where"—his mouth twisted—"King Edward's enemies have been gloriously overthrown."

"Praise God." The response was instant; the hard eyes had not softened. "And I suppose this is a traitor trying to escape his deserts. Well, I've no room at the Rose for the like of him; he must take himself off at once." His plump hand fell on the motionless shoulder. Leaning swiftly forward, Philip caught the innkeeper's sleeve and twitched his arm aside. "By your leave, he will do no such thing! Can't you see he's spent?"

The rotund figure spun about; a spark of anger flared. "I'm a true subject of the King, Sir Philip; I'll harbour none of his enemies here." Their voices penetrated the boy's stupor; lifting his head, he stared from one to the other and tried to struggle to his feet. "I'll go now," he said shakily to Philip. "And thank you for—for the ale, sir."

Resting a hand on his shoulder, Philip pressed him back to his seat. "Wait a minute. Where are you making for?"

"Wiltshire," the boy replied faintly. "My family's there, it's not far. I'll be all right."

Philip studied him with a frown, ignoring the spate of protest at his shoulder. Presently turning to the landlord, he interrupted the commentary to ask brusquely: "have you a nag in your stables that you'll sell me? What's the price?" A silence followed, and a figure was named. "Pirate," Francis said conversationally from the window. Philip did a quick reckoning; it would leave them shorter than he liked, but there was no help for it. "Very well. I'll have my groom look it over first, though, and he can saddle up. When the lad's rested he'll go on his way and you can forget you ever saw him. Will that satisfy you?"

It appeared then there must be some further negotiation for the saddle, an article upon which the landlord placed considerable value, but the bargain was struck at last, and the innkeeper departed, stuffing coins into his purse. "Greedy bastard," Francis observed, as the door closed. Philip only shrugged, and stooped once more over the tired wayfarer. This time he had really fallen asleep, and all efforts to rouse him met with failure. In the end Francis and Will Parker carried him upstairs between them, and, easing the boy to the squire's bed, left him to his rest.

The day went by, for Francis, with maddening slowness. They were only a few miles from Tewkesbury and their triumphant friends, but Philip would not budge from Gloucester until their charge had been sent on his way. Though it was unlikely the King's officers would have any interest in so insignificant a Lancastrian, he placed no trust in the landlord's unconstrained good faith, and Francis spent the afternoon restlessly wandering the town, gleaning what further information he could from more orthodox messengers who had now arrived from Tewkesbury. The Lancastrian army was wholly scattered; the Duke of Somerset and his captains had fled into the sanctuary of Tewkesbury Abbey; and Margaret of Anjou and her son's frail widow, Anne Neville, had been run to earth in a convent across the Severn. Bells pealed; solemn thanks was offered in the churches; and still the boy slept. Shortly after supper, fuming with impatience, Francis followed their protegé's continued example, and went to bed.

They parted at sunrise next morning in the courtyard of the inn. Traynor had gone for the horses while Francis and Parker saw to the packs; sunlight was lambent on the house-fronts, warming the stone to honey, and the white rose of the innboard shone. Philip's eyes lingered on it with the boy's; beneath the crudely sketched Yorkist device, the original shape of the board was distinguishable still: a clumsily fashioned swan.

For a moment they stood looking; then Philip laughed and

turned his back on it, remarking as Traynor led up the land-lord's offering. "The horse at least can have no politics. Will you take some advice you never asked for? Once home again, stay quietly in Wiltshire for a while. If you are prudent, you've not ruined yourself forever; the King is not a venge-ful man, and memories are short."

"Mine's not," the youth returned curtly. He flushed then, and said awkwardly, "That was churlish: I beg your pardon. My name's Ferrers, Sir Philip. I'm in your debt; I hope one day I can repay your kindness."

"Don't trouble about it." Absently accepting his stallion's bridle from the groom, Philip regarded the drawn young face. "I'm sorry, but this is the end of Lancaster. You will be happier if you reconcile yourself to it."

Ferrers said lightly, "Have you forgotten Henry Tudor?" He had a toe in the nearer stirrup, ready to mount; and Philip smiled. "Oh, my dear boy! Bastard Plantagenet and bastard Tudor? Really, it would never do." He moved back as the lad swung himself up; the horse danced and sidled, and came round to a jerk of the reins. At the gate of the court-yard its rider looked back, raising a hand; they waved cheer-fully in answer, and he rode out of sight.

From Gloucester to Tewkesbury, Philip had calculated, would be a half day's easy journey, and the road being well travelled, they had no need to engage a guide. The day warmed rapidly, and about mid-morning they dismounted by the roadside to refresh themselves with bread, cheese, and ale from the packs. A shepherd passed, swinging his crook, behind a flock of black-stockinged sheep; he shouted a greet-ing before disappearing over the crest of the hill, and a little later a horseman in blue and mulberry swept past. Francis would have liked to stop him for news, but the courier went on by without looking up, his horse's hoofs spurning great clods of earth behind him.

It was not long past noon when they entered Tewkesbury. Beyond the town the army was still camped, and white chalk marks over the doors of several houses showed where the household officers were billeted. Archers and billmen lounged about the streets, mingling with throngs of curious citizens; towards the centre of the town the press increased, and the cousins finally relinquished their mounts to Traynor and continued on foot. A few minutes later they came into the market square.

It was from this place, they realised at once, that the crowd in the outer streets had been slowly filtering; even now a considerable portion of it remained, men and women, burgesses, alewives, and men-at-arms alike, all talking busily. In the middle of the square a rough scaffold stood, empty now but for a pair of executioner's assistants who were carrying the last body away. A farm cart drawn alongside was loaded with the trunks and heads of a dozen men, all piled everyway, the last head perched like a cabbage atop the rest. Philip gave the spectacle no more than a glance. He had never seen the Duke of Somerset, and if he had, would have derived no entertainment either from identifying his head, or, as a group of arguing prentices were trying to do, verbally matching it with the body. Francis, after one equally hurried look, seemed to share his incuriosity.

They had to pass quite near the cart to get across the square, and the mass of the crowd made progress slow. Ahead of them a butcher was telling his neighbour the tale: After the battle Somerset and his captains had fled into Tewkesbury Abbey, but the King, who had given ready pardon to the common soldiers sheltering there, had been pitiless to the Lancastrian chiefs. For ten years they had been the gathered head of rebellion which infected his peace, and some he had forgiven until he was weary: in God's name, he swore, let there be an end. It was the Duke of Gloucester who had tried them, with Norfolk, the Earl Marshal, beside him on the bench.

Philip was only half-listening to the butcher's story. He could see now what was holding the attention of the spectators: a covered carriage, just lumbering to a stop before a shuttered building opposite. A mounted guard of lances rode in attendance. They drew close as the carriage halted; the captain swung from his horse, and a cloaked figure appeared in the aperture of the open door. The captain's arm was only perfunctorily offered, and the woman hesitated, putting back her hood, before she stepped down into the street.

Years past, when Margaret of Anjou had come to England as a girl to be Henry of Lancaster's bride, the minstrels had made songs to her beauty. Philip wondered which of them, seeing her, would remember it now. For a moment she paused, her hollowed eyes moving across the rows of gaping faces, until they found in the distance the tower of the Abbey church shouldering against the sky. A fragment of the butcher's gossip returned to Philip: Edward, it was said, had given leave for the young Prince of Lancaster to be buried there. A kind of shivering ripple passed over her face; dragging the cloak around her, she hurried into the house.

Disappointed, the crowd began to disperse. Philip looked about, trying to decide where he would find Richard; he thought he glimpsed Robert Percy across the square, and was starting after him when Francis gripped his arm. Philip glanced over his shoulder, but his cousin was staring past him at the topmost object in the executioner's cart. Closer to, the thing no longer resembled a cabbage; they could see the blood dabbling the hair, and the fixed eyes turned sightless to the sun. "Oh God," Francis said softly. "It's my wife's uncle Talbot."

CHAPTER EIGHT

LATE in the afternoon of a spring day, two horsemen sat on the tree-capped hill above the Talbot manor, looking at the sprawl of fields and buildings which lay below. It was getting on for dusk; behind them the Cotswolds were slowly purpling, and some late birds gossiped as they made ready for sleep.

Francis gazed down silently, working his hand through the gelding's mane. To Philip, his profile spoke his doubt and reluctance as if he had said them aloud; all afternoon he had ridden with the single thought of reaching Anna before another messenger could bring her news of her uncle's death, but now, with Tewkesbury left far behind, he recoiled from his errand. He felt alien and intrusive, a reveller in a house of grief.

Philip wondered how much of this Richard had anticipated in Tewkesbury when he so readily gave them both his leave to go. It would be a while he had said, before he was in London again, and meantime Philip could serve him no better than in standing for him in arranging Francis' affairs. Philip had been grateful for Richard's consideration in the multitude of his other cares, but his thanks was brushed aside. There was nothing anyway that he was required for in London, and Francis would be the better for his company. It had been a hurried conversation; only hours later did Philip remember it again.

The wind blew gently against their faces, bringing the scent of clover. Francis touched a spur to his horse, and started down the slope.

The house was quiet as they approached it. A flock of ducks, unattended, gabbled softly in the grass beside the stream; the smithy was empty, the fire black out. Francis looked around the silent courtyard, and a ghost of memory stirred: his father's great house at Minster Lovell, its cheerful bustle stilled; anxious whispers and the sound of his mother's weeping; and himself, a boy of six, hearing of a place in Yorkshire where a battle had been lost. They had

carried John Lovell still living from Towton field, but it had
been the end of all he knew, for his son.

As they dismounted at the door a stable lad appeared,
coming forward to stare at them with big eyes. Francis
couldn't remember having seen him before; he seemed
young for the work, but likely there was no one else to do it,
with all the manor strength gone with its lord. The courtyard yawned before them, the larger for its desertion. Tossing the reins to the boy, Francis said curtly, "Where's your
mistress?" For however he disliked Lady Talbot, she had her
rights.

The lad's face changed and drew in, sullen with suspicion
and fear. "She's dead, of childing it was, and buried since last
Friday. There's no one but the young mistress, and—" But
Francis was already past him, and running for the house.

Within, there was not a servant about; it seemed impossible that a habited place could be so bare. In the great hall
Francis checked, debating. A flight of stairs against the wall
led to the upper apartments; his gaze hesitated between it
and the door left of the high table which opened on the parlour. He decided on the parlour first, and was making for it,
Philip a few paces behind, when somewhere a door closed,
and they heard the brush of skirts on the stair.

The flight angled towards its head, disappearing through a
tall arch into the rooms above, and she had halted at the
turn to regather her skirts, for she was heavy with pregnancy and the way was steep. The late sun patched the hall
with shadows; from the darkness of the stairs' foot Francis
said her name, and then took them at a run.

It was a while before either spoke. Her fingers groped to
his shoulders and clutched him close, and he felt her shake
with crying. For himself, he could have put off forever the
time when he must break in on this moment; it was another
life ago that he had wanted to be first with this, and add
another load to the burden of her griefs.

She became calmer after a time, and leaned her cheek on
his shoulder. "You know—you've heard my aunt died? It was
the burying day yesterday, hers and the little one's with her,
and then a man came with news from Tewkesbury—" Her
eyes lifted to his, ringed with hollows and the rawness of
tears. "Oh, what will they do to my uncle?"

He turned his face away, drawing her head down again so
he need not meet her eyes. "Sweetheart, it is already done.

Yesterday. Please, please don't think of it, there's nothing for you to be afraid of for him any more."

He thought that plain enough, to the edge of brutality, and was astonished when she seemed not to understand. "Yesterday? But the fight was before, was he hurt then and died of it, after—?"

He groped for words, and found none that were not like stones to strike her. Dumbly standing, his fingers smoothing her brow, he did not hear the little sound above them, the slither of a hand and clothing pushed for support against the wall as someone descended. Over their heads, a voice spoke like drops of cold water falling. "Anna, you're not kind to him. Don't you know still? He means he's dead, hanged and gelded and quartered like a sheep by the victors of Tewkesbury. Isn't that what you mean, Lovell?"

Francis jerked up his head. Humphrey Talbot leaned at the turning of the stair, deathly pale, his right wrist and arm bound in splints to the elbow and thrust into his doublet. He had a sword hanging next to useless, in his other hand.

Unmoving, Francis said after an instant, "That's not true, Talbot. Why would you hurt her by saying that lie?"

"Isn't it? Come then, what were you trying so mightily to tell? That they killed him kindly? Go on, let us hear the story. Who sentenced him? Who did the headsman's work at the block?—or don't you know all your friends yet to call them by name?"

Francis felt Anna tremble against him. He tightened his arms, and spoke across her hair. "The Constable of England sentenced your father, Talbot. It's his business, to deal with the King's enemies."

Humphrey bent forward. "And who is the Constable, Lovell? You like him well, as I remember. Have you told my cousin that?"

Like a sleeper waking, Anna moved against Francis' shoulder, trying to pull back from him to see into his face. He said steadily, "It was the Duke of Gloucester who tried him, Anna. The guilt was proven; the King demanded all their deaths. There was no choice for the Duke but to pass sentence. I spoke with him earlier today, and he asked me to say that if there is anything he can do, you have only to ask. He means it too; truly, he will be a friend to us both."

"You spoke to him?" she repeated. Her hands held him off

128

still; her swollen body pushed against him, resisting his effort to draw her near again. "You spoke to him today, and kissed his hand, and thanked him for his goodness—"

"What else would you have had me do? He has his duty to the King, as—as your uncle thought he had to Somerset. How should I blame him for that?" He was growing angry himself, because he thought he could see what she wanted, and was trying to persuade himself of its unreasonableness. But she neither wept nor pleaded; only her eyes searched his as if trying to comprehend him, and when she spoke the words were so low he had to strain to hear. "How should you blame him indeed?—when there is such profit for you in embracing him with both your arms?"

"Profit?" Shock made him stupid. Very carefully, he said, "What profit, Anna?"

"Why, your clear and simple gain of all my uncle's lands. That's why you've come, isn't it, to look at what you've been given? Your King will want a sure man here, you must have thought of that while you were hurrying to him in Tewkesbury, and who could be safer than you, having so well forgotten what your father fought to save? And so you take it all—my dower, that must always have seemed small to you, nothing like what you might have got if your King hadn't been making friends with my father by giving him a rich husband for me—and all this too, that should have been my cousin's inheritance. Did they offer it, or were you obliged to ask?"

He had, quite simply, nothing to say. In some yet unatrophied corner of his brain the passionate denial, already formed, clamoured for speech: more, if neither words nor witness would serve, time itself he knew must refute the lie; but his tongue refused command. All that mattered was that she had been willing to believe this of him. In a few short months, his image had been so scraped and scoured from her mind.

He felt her wince, and realised his fingers were making prints on her arms. Very gently, he put Anna aside and took a step past her. Behind her he heard Philip set foot on the bottom stair, and, from the courtyard, the clattering arrival of his cousin's servants, outstripped in the haste of the ride from Tewkesbury; the sounds reached him faintly, immeasurably far. He was staring at the man on the stairs above him.

'This is your work, Talbot. Did you suppose I wouldn't know?"

Philip spoke, in a low, urgent voice. "Francis, he's hurt."

"So much the worse for him." Francis did not turn. He was looking at the weakly dangling sword in Humphrey's hand, and feeling for the knife at his belt. He took another step upward, and heard his cousin's swift stride; someone dragged back his fist, trying to prise the dagger from his fingers, and without looking he beat the meddler aside. "Keep out of this, Philip!" His clenched knuckles, blindly striking, hit soft flesh. There was no sound, but something warned him what he had done. He wheeled, the weapon dropping forgotten from his grasp, and saw Anna crumple and fall down the long flight of stairs to the flagstones below. She lay motionless, her face half-hidden in her arm, only the mark of his fist showing like a smudge through her loosened hair.

Philip was already beside her when Francis reached them. Brushing past his cousin, he knelt to see, and Humphrey caught his shoulder "Take your hands from her, Lovell! Haven't you harmed her enough?"

Francis paid no attention. He was struggling with the laces of Anna's gown; the knots tangled, and he broke the ribbons with shaking fingers. "Get her women, Talbot. I'll take her upstairs."

Humphrey dropped to his knees, clasping Anna's hands. Her face was bloodless; after an instant he whispered, "If she dies I'll kill you, Lovell. I swear it."

Francis looked up. He said softly, "Get her women, fool. We'll settle our differences later, never fear for that."

As he spoke, Anna whimpered and stirred. She gazed up confusedly and pushed feebly at him, and Francis slid his arms underneath her, gripping her shoulders and knees. "Gently, sweetheart. I'm taking you up to bed."

She tried to thrust him away, then all at once cried out and clutched her waist. Humphrey covered her fingers with his, murmuring reassurances, and Francis snapped viciously, "God's Mother, Talbot, will you dawdle forever! Don't you see what is happening?"

He was trying to get to his feet, holding her in his arms. Straining her face away, Anna groped after her cousin's loosening clasp. "Humphrey," she said. "Humphrey, don't—" She stopped with a little catching breath; her hair was dark rust coloured where it stuck to her brows. Humphrey bent over her. "Yes, dear? Tell me what you want."

"Please," she said. "Please, don't let him touch me."

In the thick silence, a distant footfall sounded; Will Parker was approaching the hall. Moving with scrupulous exactness, Francis stooped, laid the girl on the spot from which he had raised her, and withdrew his arms. As he stood up, ignoring as if they had not been there both his cousin and Humphrey Talbot, his eyes had a curious blank look, something not quite of the apprehending of intelligence or pain; just such an expression had Philip seen once in a Welsh gunner, his arm sheared to the shoulder by the bursting of an overloaded cannon, in the first unbelieving moment before he could realise his loss. The door squeaked; across his shoulder Francis said sharply, "Parker."

Anna was twisting about on the floor, crying quietly. The squire hurried towards them, his cheerful face shocked, and Francis moved back to give him room. "There's been an accident. Be so good as to carry my wife to her chamber; this gentleman will show you the way." He walked to the long table below the dais and stood there, his back to the stairs, as the squire lifted her and, with Humphrey going before, hastened upstairs. A door slammed above; a few minutes later it opened again for Will to come out, and Humphrey's voice was heard, shouting for a servant. A frightened-looking maid rushed down and vanished beyond the screens, reappearing moments later with a cauldron of water. Francis was still standing at the table, resting his palms upon it; she gave him a hostile glance as she ran past. The door banged again. After that, there was silence.

It was late evening before the child was born. For hours the house had lain as if sealed from life; most of the servants had gone to bed, and the closed door to the upper apartments cut off all sound. Restlessly wandering about the parlour, Philip had been more than once on the point of going into the hall where he could see his cousin standing before one of the narrow, mullioned windows, gazing at the spring moon-light. His absorption was forbidding; each time, Philip turned away.

About ten o'clock Humphrey came out of Anna's room, and from the stairway spoke her husband's name. Francis turned, looking up; then he crossed the hall and went upstairs.

Philip continued his uneasy pacing. The parlour was a

pleasant room, one end of it almost completely taken up by a curtained bed. In a corner the dead Lady Talbot's loom stood; there were cupboards against the walls with plates and ewers and covered salts set upon them, and a table where the family took meals together when they had no guests, or wanted privacy from the hall. The remains of a light repast, largely untouched, were still spread out; Philip felt slight inclination for the refreshment a nervous menial had brought him, and Francis had disregarded it entirely. Sweating with weakness, intermittently nursing his bound shoulder and wondering with a kind of fury at his own helplessness how much longer it could possibly be before he was a whole man again, Philip was in the act of pouring wine he had no desire for into a goblet when he heard Francis enter behind him. He swung round, the question instinctive on his lips. "Is it—?"

"Yes, it's over." Francis came into the centre of the room, paused there, and went to the carved dresser opposite the table. The silver dishes on it shone in the candlelight. "Anna will be all right, they say. It was a girl."

"Francis—" Philip half-reached towards the rigid shoulder; when there was no answering movement he dropped his hand. "I wish there were something I could say."

"Don't trouble yourself: I've been listening to a good deal already." Francis picked up a basin, tracing the chased edge with his forefinger. Presently he put it down, and said coolly, "Well, there's nothing to keep us here. Can I tell Gregory we'll be away in the morning?" His face was like a mask. Philip appraised it carefully while he marshalled his tired wits; he knew what a wrong word now could do, and the silence seemed full of them.

"I'm afraid we must be here for a time yet. I have Gloucester's commission to act for him, and even if it had not been so, he would not expect us to be soon in London with the case as it is now."

"Possibly not. However, my wife has informed me my presence is intolerable to her, and that I will be doing her a charity by removing it. In the circumstances I can hardly do less than oblige her."

Philip spoke gently. "Francis: have a little pity. She's lost her aunt and uncle and the best home she knows; she's been hours in a pain neither you nor I would want to suffer, and the child is dead."

"For which I am to blame. That's been explained to me, you needn't remind me again." The spasmodic candlelight, leaning with the draught, showed a flickering change in the tight profile; when Francis spoke again, his voice shook. "Philip, it was an accident. I thought it was you behind me, you believe that, don't you?"

"There never was any question of it! Don't torment yourself with such absurdities: I know it, and so does Anna."

Hardly above his breath, Francis said, "Does she?" The hurt and shock in his face were so deep they looked printed to the bone. Philip gripped the slack arms, and said with slow emphasis, "Better than anyone, I assure you she knows. Don't you recognise her cousin's voice yet when you hear it?"

Francis made no reply. He had turned his head suddenly, listening; above the hall a door had closed. After a moment he walked to the threshold of the parlour and glanced towards the stair. "Talbot!" There was a pause, and they heard footsteps descending. Francis waited, then went back to the dresser and leaned against it, watching the door. A minute later Humphrey came in.

He stopped just within the room, looking from one to the other. He was even paler than when Philip had seen him earlier; the lines of eyes and mouth were drawn with pain, and he moved stiffly, his broken arm rigid in its heavy casings. There was blatant provocation, notwithstanding, in the cold challenge of his stare; with the spurting irritability of frayed nerves, Philip wished the fellow would assume a pose less suggestive of the last of the gladiators. Francis was looking at him in a considering way, running his fingers up and down the candlestick at his elbow; it was a relaxed, easy movement, but Philip saw his eyes. As if unthinking, he took a step nearer the table, dropping a hand to the stem of the goblet he had left there.

After a little silence Francis spoke. "Come in, Humphrey, you're hovering like a virgin with one foot into the marriage chamber. I promised you we'd have a talk; don't let's shout at each other across half the room."

Humphrey eyed him warily, and kept his position. He no longer carried the sword, but his left hand was sliding clumsily to the sheathed poniard at his thigh; the movement ceased abruptly as he encountered the derisive gaze. "I wouldn't, my chevalier. You've fallen into disadvantage, remember: one good hand to my two, and no lady to stand your defender."

"Keep your tongue from my cousin, Lovell," Humphrey said, very low. "She's no concern of yours, ever again."

"No?" Francis' eyes narrowed. "Well, that's as may be, but you're hardly in a way to be offering thanks for it. She'll be even less yours in a day or so, I shouldn't wonder."

"What the devil are you talking about?" It was more in confusion than anger; colourless under the bright coppery hair, Humphrey's face betrayed his weariness, and the laboured functioning of his mind. Smiling disagreeably, Francis remarked, "God, you're slow. Have you forgotten your late foray into arms at Tewkesbury? You've been taken in treason, fool: it's what men get attainted for, in case you didn't know."

Humphrey's lips parted, and shut again. Francis gave him a moment to assimilate the more distasteful aspects of his situation, and then asked carelessly, "Ever been in prison, Talbot?" Without waiting for a reply he went on, "Well, it doesn't matter, really. You might apply to Harry Percy for instruction, if he's available—which seems unlikely. Catch him stirring out of Northumberland! But he could tell you all about it; he spent nine years in Fleet Prison after Towton, and the only reason he got out then was because his northerners were being noisy about it. I doubt anyone would care so much for you, Talbot." He reflected on it, laughing to himself. "You know, it's very funny. When you think of the hundreds of pardons being granted, it does seem a pity you shouldn't share in the largesse. But you're a bit too rich, Humphrey, and your father was a bit too much a Lancastrian, so I'm afraid the King's mercy will stop short of a pardon for you."

He walked round the table, poured wine into a cup, and held it to his lips, looking at the other man across the brim. Another branch of candles was standing near; the flames made little points of light in his eyes. Philip said quietly, "Francis, enough. You've had your satisfaction; now let it be."

"In a moment, cousin: I'm not done yet. Besides, he's interested, can't you see?" Francis drank, and put the goblet down. Spacing his words with care, he said, "There is, of course, an alternative to the Tower. Have you considered that?"

The light brows drew together. "I don't understand."

"I'll explain it to you. It will be tomorrow or even the next day, maybe, before they come looking for you here. If you make a start tonight you could reach the coast by Thursday, and be on your way to France by the time they pick up your trail." Francis waited, studying the haggard face with malicious enjoyment. "So there's your choice, Humphrey. It's not much of a one, I'll admit. You've had a pretty soft life of it, you'll find it difficult, probably, to get used to begging your bread. Perhaps you'd even prefer the Tower; at least you wouldn't go hungry there, though I should imagine after a few years it would be a bit confining. Still, it's for you to decide. Rot in the Tower or starve in France, it's all one to me. I shall sleep very sweet, thinking of you."

Moistening his lips, Humphrey said tonelessly, "Yes, I fancy you will. However it falls, my father's lands are there for your claiming."

Francis regarded him steadily for an instant without moving; when he spoke his voice was compressed almost to inaudibility. "I wouldn't mention that again, if I were you."

Taut as a bow, his fingers sweating knots of impotence hurting the palms, Humphrey gave him back stare for stare. "Do you imagine I can't see what you're after? You want me cleared from your path: it's plain why. You'd be too glad to hand me over to your friends, if you were sure it was what they wanted. But you're not sure, so you're taking this way to be rid of me instead."

"Maybe I am," Francis conceded pleasantly. "But it will be pretty late to mend matters if you take a chance on it, and find I wasn't lying after all."

Falling cherry petals whispered ghostlike against the garden windows; a breeze rustled in the chimney, and the small fire leaped and crackled on the hearth. Humphrey stood with clenched hands, looking at the flames. Expedients, alternatives, fear and a quickening passion of grief, all raced picture-clear through his eyes, and Philip, repelled and angry, read them with a kind of shame at his own hardheld disassociation. Humphrey Talbot's pinched face belonged to a sick boy; he was plainly weak from injury, and the bandaging of the splinted arm showed all too obviously the roughness of an inexpert hand. Anna's, perhaps? Yes undoubtedly; and he would have ridden all the miles from

Tewkesbury with the thing untended, to end with this. Philip drew in his breath, and as if he had spoken Humphrey seemed to see him for the first time. He hesitated, and came slowly across the room.

"I don't know you, but I've heard of you, a little. You're Philip Lovell?" Hardly waiting for the acknowledgment, he continued, "He's got me, right enough. I can't risk staying here, and he knows it— Well, that's nothing to you. There were some Welshmen in Oxford's household when I was there, and they used to say of you that you kept your word. I wonder if you would keep it to me?"

Behind him Francis interjected, "Leave my cousin out of this, Talbot! This isn't his affair!" There was a note like metal in his voice, but Humphrey did not look round. "Would you?" he persisted.

Between pity and dislike, Philip said at length, "I can't imagine why you should want any kind of promise from me."

"You saw him today, and you don't know that." As pale as his shirt, the red-haired man's face spoke his meaning; and Philip said slowly, "Be careful, Talbot." He was watching Francis, a few paces beyond Humphrey's shoulder; unconsciously his fingers tightened on the massive goblet beneath his hand. Heedless of the warning, Humphrey reached across the table to grasp his arm.

"Promise me this," he said painfully. "Promise me you won't let—him"—his head jerked almost imperceptibly—"do my cousin harm. She's ill, you have seen the reason, and if he lays his hands on her again—" The words ended abruptly. Francis had gone for him without a sound; his fingers closed on the hurt man's throat, and a footstool went flying. Philip spoke once, his voice like a whiplash cutting Humphrey's choked cry; and then, rounding the table in a stride, he lifted the goblet and brought it savagely across his cousin's wrist. Half-fainting and gasping for breath, Humphrey heard Francis swear sharply; the strangling grip slackened, and, freed of it, he staggered to one side, groped for the cupboard, and leaned there, panting. White with rage, Francis flung round on his cousin. They measured each other, breathing hard; and it was the brown eyes that yielded. Flushing to his hair, Francis turned away.

"Get him out of here, Philip," he said huskily. He walked to the window, not looking towards the cupboard again.

Humphrey was still there, resting his weight on his one good hand, but he lifted his head when Philip addressed him.

"Sir Humphrey, you had better leave. You offend both my kinsman and me by what you have suggested: nor is it any business of yours to be concerned over the welfare of Anna Fitz Hugh. Should need arise, she has a father and brothers to stand for her; if it is a comfort for you to know it, they will have word from me."

Humphrey straightened, feeling his throat. Gathering himself together with a visible effort, he said, "I must see Anna; when I've told her good-bye I'll go. You—you will send to Ravensworth? My thanks, then, and good-bye." He moved haltingly to the door, opened it, and passed through into the hall. A minute later they heard him mounting the stairs.

Philip pushed the door shut, and turned to the window. Leaning against the casement, Francis met the expressionless gaze; he was keeping his wrist well out of sight, but Philip had seen him fingering it earlier. He walked over, saying briefly, "Let me have a look at that."

Francis resisted momentarily, and then, indifferent, submitted. Philip felt over the swelling, flexed the joint, and remarked, "Nothing broken, I should think, but you'll have it in mind for a day or so." He was brisk and undisturbed. Francis let him finish without speaking; when he had his hand to himself again he tucked it between his thigh and the wall. He was breathing as if he were concentrating on it; his eyes, a shade darker than usual, were on the leading of the casement panes.

Philip went back to the table and began cutting a slice from the demain loaf which had been left there. "I'm grateful for the extra men Gloucester sent with us," he observed while he worked. "I'll send one of them off with a letter for him tomorrow. There's a question also of how soon your wife can be moved and to what household. She can't stay here alone, and it's crown property now anyway, probably." He spread butter on the bread, added meat, and bit into it. "Fitz Hugh would have been the clear solution, once persuaded there was no intent to cast his daughter off by returning her to Ravensworth. Unfortunately, I don't see Humphrey Talbot's kinfolk receiving you as a guest in the next few years: not after tonight."

"Most unlikely," Francis agreed colourlessly. Philip sat on the corner of the table and slowly swung his foot. "Well, you're rid of Talbot, if you think it was worth the pains. Tell me, was it true what you told him, that there was a warrant for his arrest?"

Staring at the window, Francis said, "Why don't you ask the Duke of Gloucester?"

There was a pause. Sighing sharply, Philip said after a moment, "Touching the matter of your wife, I've a notion to write my sister. She's near Anna's age, and her stepsons aren't much younger. Secott's often away from Ipsden on his affairs; I think Kate would be glad of another girl's company." As Francis was silent, his head still turned away, he added gently, "It's not a lifetime, only four years more for your minority to run. You could visit her when you wished at Ipsden, and welcome, saving only Gloucester's leave and the convenience of travel. I don't know yet where he's planning to establish himself—it might be Wales, he has large holdings there—but wherever he chooses, it will be a long way from court. I'm glad of it; I had a life's dose of Westminster in two days, last summer."

"You'll continue in Gloucester's household, then?" Francis said idly.

"While he desires it, certainly. I expect I'll go back to Willowford long enough to get my mother settled again, since there seems nothing much he wants me for in London—" Philip's voice slowed. He was remembering again that conversation in Tewkesbury. Hasty it had definitely been, and it was natural that Richard should have appeared preoccupied; and yet— A vague suspicion, long buried, stirred and woke; a little coldness touched his heart. All at once, beyond any possibility of doubt or misunderstanding, he knew Richard had not wanted him in London.

The draught from the chimney freshened; one of the candles died with a hiss and a twist of smoke. Philip leaned over to trim the wick, and mentally called himself a fool. He was overdue for a holiday, that was sure; it would be night visions next, or meditations on the dance of death. Francis had noticed nothing; in a minute his cousin said cheerfully, "Well, I'll write to Kate in the morning; she'll come, I'm sure, and God knows I should be glad of a woman's hand. You'll want to travel back to Ipsden with Anna, of course?"

Crossing to the bed at the far end of the room, Francis

twitched aside the hangings and started to throw back the covers. "With your permission, no."

"Francis, you should. It's cruel to leave her this way."

"My wife has already indicated that she prefers solitude to any company of mine," Francis said shortly. "The case being such, I should be glad if you will excuse me." He walked round the bed and rummaged the second pillow from beneath the covers; it was Parker's business, but the squire had been dismissed to sleep in the hall. There were night candles on the cupboard; he brought one to the chest by the bed and kindled it with a twig from the hearth, shielding the light with elaborate care. Philip said levelly, "I can't compel you to charity, nor it seems even begin to make you realise what you've done tonight. For your wife's sake I'm sorry, and the day will come when you'll be sorry too."

Across the leaping flames their eyes met; then, his mouth setting, Francis looked away. "Your lad's abed, cousin: Will you have me to squire you?"

In silence Philip let him help him from his clothes. Francis undressed rapidly after him, snuffed the remaining lights, and slid into the far side of the bed. It could have held half a dozen, lying close, Philip thought. He lay motionless for time, aware Francis was too quiet to be asleep, but there was no movement from the other pillow. Gradually the small night noises of the house grew through the stillness; a shutter swung unlatched; somewhere a board creaked. From the garden a silver chorusing of crickets drifted, and the moon went behind a cloud.

About midnight Philip heard a door open above the hall. It closed again almost immediately; there were footsteps on the stair, and the grate of a withdrawing bolt. The minutes passed; then, far off, his ear distinguished the drum of hoofs. There was only one horse, from the sound of it; Humphrey Talbot had gone alone.

Wearied to his bones with the exertions of the day, Philip was on the edge of sleep when something brought him full awake again. He hesitated, and started to turn over, but despite his care he could not manage it quite noiselessly; the stifled sound did not come again. Half-raised on his elbow, he could see only a dark tumble of hair, and his cousin's head buried in his arm.

CHAPTER NINE

STANDING on the doorstep, Philip contemplated the day. It had been raining since dawn, and the courtyard cobbles rose like islands above the wash; he was already picturing, with depressing clarity, the state of the roads beyond the manor lands. Over his shoulder he remarked, "It's a foul morning, Kate. Are you sure you want to start today?"

His sister came down the step, pulling her hood more closely around her. "It may go on for weeks," she pointed out sensibly. "No, it's best we go. The sooner Anna leaves this place the better, it's as cheerless as a tomb for her now, and no wonder."

Philip looked down at her with a smile. She was hardly more than Francis' age, but already he could see Dame Alice coming. "I'm grateful to you, sister. How we would have fared without you these past days, I can't even think."

She coloured, smiling in return; and as if moved by common thought both pairs of eyes went to the centre of the courtyard, where Francis appeared absorbed in scrutinising his stallion's hoof. A stone had worked under the shoe a few days before; he was taking a long time examining the remains of the damage, and made a business of pulling some straw from the silky fetlock. Under her breath, Kate said, "I'd like to knock their heads together, the pair of them." The next moment the door opened, and Anna stood hesitating under the lintel.

There was a litter drawn up and waiting, but she paused, her lifted hands feigning some difficulty with the strings of her cloak, and Francis straightened and turned. They had neither of them had sight of the other since the night Humphrey Talbot had gone away. Across the courtyard they stared at each other, each with the identical mixture of curiosity and wistfulness and spite, to see how well or ill the other had done; and in each face was the same mute entreaty, the same stubborn waiting. Then Anna looked away, and Francis' sudden, fractional movement came too late. He stopped short and watched, unmoving, as she stepped into the litter. To Philip then, he said coolly, "Are you ready?"

and mounted without lingering for a reply. Philip helped his sister into the saddle of her palfrey; Gregory and Will took their positions behind, and the Duke of Gloucester's borrowed men followed with Kate's and Anna's servants and the sumpters. By the time Philip had led the company through the gate Francis was far ahead, cantering down the rough track towards the stream which divided the demesne lands from the hayfields and tenant farms beyond.

Past grazing common and outlying stands of timber, the main road ran due east towards Oxford and Ipsden, with a north fork to Coventry. There Philip halted and leaned towards his sister to make his farewells. Her eyes were on Francis, already kneeing his mount into the north road, and Philip shook his head. "Useless, Kate. I could drag him to Ipsden whether he would or no, but it would do no help now."

"He needs a sound birching, and for a groat I'd tell him so," Kate retorted. "Well, Godspeed, Philip. Come home often, won't you? Don't forget us with your grand friends: remember, we love you." He kissed her lightly, and spurred away.

By easy stages, it was a two days' ride to Coventry, where Richard had written the army was still camped. Given a choice, Francis would have made the journey in one, but Philip was not disposed to hurry, and Francis was compelled to adapt himself as he could to their leisurely progress through the dipping hills, easing his raw nerves by breakneck sorties down unexplored byways which he saw in a blurred fashion, and would never recognise again. Village after village slipped past, unnoticed; afternoon came and went, and they paused for the night at a priory; ate, slept, and rose again at daybreak to the continuing rain.

Towards noon the sun struggled through the clouds, and by mid-afternoon they had discarded their cloaks. They reached Coventry before nightfall, to learn the King and his brothers had departed for London a scant forty-eight hours before. It was too late to think of starting the long ride south that day; they found rooms in a house near the city gates, and the horses were led away. Francis shared a silent meal with his cousin, and at the end of it made his escape into the twilit streets of the town, pacing the cobbled alleys until the curfew and his own tiredness drove him back to the inn.

The landlord's courtyard, crowded a short time before with

the tumult of new arrivals, was deserted when he returned. Philip had gone up to the chamber provided for them, and the smoky common hall was emptied of the last reveller. A girl lingered, banking the fire; Francis remembered indifferently that she had waited upon them at supper. She had round arms, dimpled at wrist and elbow, and when she stooped over the coals the light made warm cups about her breasts. She brought him ale when he asked for it, smiling at him beneath her lashes, and seemed unsurprised when he slid an arm around her waist. Presently he put the tankard aside, feeling for the ribbons of her blouse. Acquiescent against his shoulder, she said softly, "They've all gone to bed," and moved her head slightly towards the darkened cavern of the kitchen. Francis reached for the cloak he had left earlier drying by the fire, and tossed it down before the hearth. "Put out the candle, sweetheart. There's light enough from the fire." She leaned from his arm, curving her palm to the flame. The light winked out.

The road from Coventry to London ran south and east through the Midlands, a three days' journey. They passed the last night of it in the guesthouse of the Abbey of Saint Albans, and late next morning entered London. The city was crowded, but Philip managed to engage rooms in a small place in Thames Street; he was unsure of Richard's plans, but had no mind to kick his heels at Westminster while awaiting the Duke's pleasure. The pole and bough of an alehouse looked inviting, and they made for it gratefully, Philip observing that after more than five days on horseback he for one would gladly accept the alternative of a barge to Westminster. Parker wondered aloud if my lord of Gloucester would keep them there so long it would be too late to return to London that night, and a sharp-featured urchin, clutching the skirts of an elderly man in a long merchant's gown, interrupted as they paused on the threshold of the tavern to state, in a piercing treble, that if they were in search of his grace of Gloucester, they would not be finding him at Westminster. He was at once cuffed and bidden to hold his tongue, but Philip looked back with a smile, and, encouraged, the boy dodged from his keeper's grasp and tendered his mite of information: the Duke had returned from Westminster late last evening, and gone to the Tower with a great company of gentlemen.

"And I saw him ride by, too," the boy went on, a little dashed by his listener's apparent lack of interest: Philip had not removed his hand from the doorpost, and was staring down at the neat brick step. "My lord Hastings was with him, and my lord Rivers, and I think Sir Thomas Grey—" He glanced at the older man for confirmation at this point, but received no assistance. His grandfather was, in fact, looking uncomfortable, and seemed not at all inclined to join in the recital. The boy hesitated, his eyes going from Philip to Francis and Will; then, finding a possible explanation for the young man's inattention, offered tentatively, "It was not so grand a show as when the King came by in the morning. He had the whole army with him; my lord of Gloucester rode at the head, and then the King and my lord Hastings, and my lord of Clarence. They had the Frenchwoman too, in a cart." He brightened at the recollection. "The King was very merry, but the Duke of Gloucester smiled hardly at all, and my lord of Clarence looked as sour as—as green apples. They say he has quarrelled with the Duke of Gloucester, because my lord of Gloucester would marry my lord of Warwick's daughter that was the Lancastrian prince's wife, and my lord of Clarence says he will not let her go, not for a kingdom."

"Clarence won't let her go?" Francis interjected, amazed. "What the devil has the Duke of Clarence to do with Anne Neville?"

The boy gave him a pitying look. "Why sir, he is married to her sister, and the Countess of Warwick is sent to a nunnery, leaving all her goods to her daughters. My lord of Clarence has his wife's share already, and claims the lady Anne's wardship now as well, so he may have the whole."

"Sounds like him," Francis remarked with distaste. "By God, Philip, I wonder how long the King will suffer him. A fine set-out it will be if he's no sooner dealt with Lancaster than he has his own brother to contend with."

Philip made no reply, for the excellent reason that from the moment he had learned of Richard's presence at the Tower with his unlikely assortment of companions, he had heard not one word more of the boy's gossiping. No human persuasion, he would once have said, could have lured Richard into such a company without the King. Only one link bound them: they were all members of Edward's inner council.

He turned to push blindly by Francis down the steps and

into the street. Traynor was coming from the inn after seeing to the bestowal of animals and gear; Philip heard his own voice saying that his horse must be saddled again, and was astonished at its tone of normalcy. There followed a time of waiting, colourless as the dusk of day; and when, the servant presently returning, he saw that Francis had ordered his own horse too, he made no protest.

Thames Street lay along the riverbank, lined with shops and warehouses, with here and there the tall gate and recessed courtyard of a wealthy citizen's house interrupting the frontage. At its farther end, ringed with battlements, the squat angles of its many bastions breaking the curtain, rose the steep walls and jutting turrets of the White Tower.

The warders at the Lion Gate opened to them at the Duke's name, and they crossed the outer bridge. Barrier after barrier admitted them: the Middle Tower, the Byward Tower, to their right Saint Thomas' Tower with the curved arch of the Water Gate and the river lapping coldly about its wharf; Wakefield Tower, the royal palace beyond; the Garden Tower: all with their gap-toothed ramparts and brisk garrisons. As they were passed from gate to gate, Francis heard the chink of coins. It was easy to get into the Tower, if you were known: the return journey was sometimes another matter. A few minutes later they were standing beneath the dazzling white walls of the inner keep.

Against the southern wall, a flight of stairs led upward. Philip made for it at a rapid stride; he was nearly at its foot when the door above opened, and Sir Thomas Grey came out. He was laughing and smelling a pomander stuck with cinnamon as he talked across his shoulder to his uncle Rivers, close behind. Checking abruptly, Philip swerved to a twist of stair just visible within the nearest turret. He went up as if pursued, Francis panting at his heels; paused, and continued up, emerging finally into a dim passage which ran from turret to turret through the thickness of the walls.

Here, for the first time he hesitated. His instinctive recoil from Grey and Rivers had taken him into a part of the White Tower that was new to him, and he was casting frowningly about, trying to get his bearings, when something brought him up short. Far off, they heard the sound of chanting.

Wheeling, Philip went on down the passage, his boots ringing on the stone. The voices were clearer now. The next minute they emerged into the long gallery which overhung the chapel of Saint John.

Standing between a pair of pillars, they looked down. Sunlight was fitful through the coloured windows, and golden pools of candlelight deepened the shadows, sparkled on the silver altar vessels, and turned the brown of the Saint's cloak to umber. Grouped around a bier, a handful of priests intoned from their books. An embroidered pall was spread over the body resting upon it, but the upturned face lay uncovered: marmoreally still, untidy greying hair straggling from the sunken cheeks and thin, pointed chin.

He had been crowned before he could speak, whose father's name had made France shake. All his father had won, he had let slip from his uncertain hands, and Warwick had ridden him through the streets of London for a public mock in the days before he took it in his head to make him a king again. The sad, puzzled eyes that had gazed so uncomprehendingly upon the world were closed now; it would be, Philip thought, the best sleep that Henry of Lancaster had ever known.

In the passage a step sounded. A man rounded the corner, glanced in their direction, and came to join them, saying brusquely, "So you're back, Philip? We hadn't expected you yet; you didn't stay long in Gloucestershire."

"Nor you in Coventry, as I found." Philip looked at him, disregarding the offered hand. "How was he killed, Rob?"

"Killed?" Percy put up his brows. "By what I hear, he died—from melancholy, it's said. Not surprising in the circumstances, is it?"

Philip said in a voice that startled them, "By the cross of Christ, do you take me for a fool! Three weeks ago his son was slain at Tewkesbury; no more than yesterday his wife made common show in King Edward's Roman triumph, and by now is doubtless somewhere within these walls—at which point King-no-more Henry of Lancaster dies, not omitting to apprise the Constable of the Tower of his intention in advance, so King Edward may send the chief men of his council to be at hand for the event. Great God, all London knows that Gloucester and Hastings and Rivers were here last night! Do you credit me with as few wits as poor Lancaster himself?"

"I know what I've been told," Percy rejoined woodenly. "And look you, Philip: it would be well if you rehearsed yourself in it too. You stand very high with the Duke of Gloucester now; there are those that envy you." He hesitated, trying to force down the other's gaze, and, failing, looked away. "Name of God, will you unmake the world? What other finish did you see? While his son was free in France to be his heir, so long he lived: the prince is dead, and this follows as night runs after day. Do you really tell me you didn't expect it?"

"Expect it!" Philip repeated passionately. "If I expected anything it was that Gloucester would have had no part in it."

"I doubt if you believed that, Philip," Percy said shrewdly. His shoulders moved. "How should he not be concerned? Yesterday at Westminster the King held a council at which the Duke of Gloucester was present. Whatever was decided then, it was Gloucester's business to carry the King's word to the Constable of the Tower: had he refused, another would have done as well. And so, farewell Lancaster." His voice changed. "Ah, Philip, let be. Will you break your heart for Gloucester's conscience? It's not in your keeping—"

But Philip had gone. They listened to his footsteps die along the passage; Francis made an irresolute movement to follow, and Percy caught him back. "Not yet. Let it alone a while; there's no use talking to him now." He considered the younger boy, chewing on his lower lip. "Well, young Francis? You're looking thoughtful: Are you out of charity with the house of York too?"

Francis said coolly, "No, why? It's not my affair: Who am I to tell the King his business?"

"Very sensible," Percy agreed tonelessly. His eyes swept the gallery. "I must go. They're looking for Gloucester below, there's a courier from Westminster waiting. One of Hastings' fellows thought he saw him come up here: the fool was drunk or dreaming, I suppose. Are you coming?"

With a last glance downward, Francis accompanied him from the gallery. In the chapel below there was a subdued stir; the door opened, and some soldiers appeared at the entrance. Their captain went to whisper to one of the priests, and the men came forward to form an escort around the bier. Four of them lifted it; the priests followed as it was borne from the chapel.

As the singing faded, in the thick shadows at the head of the gallery something glittered and flashed out. Half-hidden

by the archway, Richard leaned against a column, his arms
folded on his chest, the straying sunlight making sport
among the jewels on his hands and breast. Deep in thought,
he had been only distantly aware of the other voices drifting
through the chanting of the priests, and hardly noticed when
they came no more. Wholly absorbed, he continued to stare
down into the chapel. The tiled mosaics of the floor glowed
in the candlelight, hardly dimmer than the many-coloured
tapestries which hung the walls. Nothing had altered in the
years since he had come here to keep vigil before his knight-
ing. There still was the gilded throne-pew where the sovereign worshipped; there the vivid, stained windows with the
bright pictures which had irresistibly drawn his gaze as he
knelt, solemn-eyed, through the long night watches, gravely
rehearsing to himself the chivalrous responsibilities of his
order. "You shall honour God above all things; you shall be
steadfast in the faith of Christ; you shall love the King your
Sovereign Lord. . ." It was full half his life away. Edward had
been but a few months crowned; the name of Warwick was
famed through Europe as the sword and shield of York; and
Henry of Lancaster wandered a fugitive somewhere in the
north, harmless symbol of a dead cause, a spent moon lingering, forgotten, on the radiant periphery of the blazing Yorkist sun.

The room emptied, the chanting died away. The green fire
of an emerald burned angrily on the Lord Constable's hand.
By what dark pathways, what tangled thickets of doubt and
equivocation, had he come this way?

"My lord—" A squire, his approach unheard, waited uncertainly behind.

"Yes, what is it?"

"A messenger from Westminster has ridden in, with something of great urgency, he says."

"I'm coming."

The flaring candlelight touched his shoulder as he turned,
glancing along the crimson velvet sleeve and the motto
worked in gold upon it, *Loyaulté me lie*. He went hurriedly
from the gallery.

Late that evening, the body of Henry of Lancaster was
carried by torchlight through London to Saint Paul's. It was
laid there in state, with candles set around the bier, and the
citizens thronged the church to see. They came, and stared,
and went away again, whispering.

King Edward revelled late at Westminster, but his brother had gone from London. The Lancastrian captain Fauconberg, balked in an attempt to bombard the city, had withdrawn to his fleet at Sandwich, and by nightfall the Duke of Gloucester had gathered a troop of lances, and was racing in pursuit.

CHAPTER TEN

THE room was heavy with the silence of frustration: the deadlocked quiet that follows wordless rejection of an unspoken demand. Through the unshuttered window, sky and river offered each as to a mirror one shade of burning blue, and the younger man stood looking out, a foot in the recessed seat, his profile to the lounging figure at the table behind him. Watching the rigid mouth, Edward sighed and said, "Then you've done all you can with him?"

Richard replied briefly, "Yes, everything. But you know George. He doesn't let go easily, and the Countess of Warwick was a rich woman. He won't give up Anne Neville until he's made to." Again, the demand was implicit; again it dropped into a void.

"What about the girl? Have you seen her?"

"Nan? Yes, twice. Even that was something of an achievement! George has her surrounded with his creatures at le Herber; it was impossible to be private. But I know he's not using her kindly."

"I can believe he isn't," Edward said shortly. "Apart from which, he's probably anxious to get his prize from London, out of range of your inconvenient interest. It must have been a shock for him that you were back from Sandwich so soon; I daresay Fauconberg had all my lord of Clarence's good wishes on that expedition." His warm smile came. "For what help they were! You did good work there, Dickon."

Richard lifted his shoulders. "He was ready to give up before I arrived. Let's hope the Scots will be as obliging."

"Oh, there's no harm in Jamie Stewart," Edward said lazily. "It's all his plaguey borderers; once you've chased them back over the Tweed, young James will be only too pleased to guarantee they'll stay home in future." He frowned as he added, "Are you really going to take Fauconberg with you."

"He's a good captain," Richard returned lightly. "And very eager to show appreciation for being spared his head at Sandwich. I'll keep an eye on him." He was staring out the window again, watching the distant rush and boil of the river as it foamed around the arches of London Bridge. Beyond it, the chiselled turrets of the White Tower rose against the sky. "By the way, I shall take Francis Lovell too, with your permission. I'll make sure he restricts himself to the customary duties of a squire." He ended smiling slightly, and Edward looked amused.

"I admire your optimism. Take him of course, if you wish; I don't mean to meddle with your guardianship. You're not wanting for Lovells around you: Do you have an affinity for the breed?"

He was cracking a nut in his fingers; the crisp snap of the shell was the only sound in a sudden stillness. After an instant Richard strolled to the table, and, reaching for a cup, filled it from the flagon of malmsey beside it.

"Philip Lovell, do you mean? He won't be with me. He was badly hurt at Barnet, and I don't think he's in any way to put on harness yet. He's at home in Oxfordshire at present, I believe." He tasted the wine and put it from him, grimacing. "I don't know how you can drink this stuff: I'd as soon swill honey. Ned—" Pushing the cup aside, he looked directly at his brother. "Before I start for Scotland, I mean to speak with George again. Have I your leave to tell him you have promised Anne to me?" Edward did not reply at once; he was scowling annoyedly at his fingertips, and Richard said again, "Have I your leave?" Then, with a kind of suppressed violence, "Have I asked you for anything in my life before?"

"I wish you would ask for something else now," Edward muttered irritably. "Body of Christ, Dickon, is there no other woman in England—in Europe? In God's name, why must it be Anne Neville?"

"Why shouldn't it be?"

Goaded, Edward retorted harshly, "Because you and George will end at each other's throats over this, and I can't afford it. He's a nuisance and a troublemaker, but while I can keep him quiet, I will. If he wants Anne Neville's inheritance as well as her sister's, let him have it. You needn't be the loser."

"The devil fly away with her inheritance! I want Nan."

Checking on an exclamation of disgust, Edward searchingly regarded him. Presently he said in a milder voice, "Oh, so that's the way of it, is it?" He was silent then, swiftly reflecting and biting his lip. "Heaven preserve us, could you find no better time to fall green-sick with love! Well, I'll speak to him, Dickon. Maybe we can arrange something—" He grinned suddenly. "But I'm not going to tell him you'll take less of the girl's portion than your due. He'd pluck you bare."

A gleam of laughter shot through his brother's eyes, like sunlight flashing on a sheet of silver water. "It might get him talking, anyhow. I'll leave you be judge, but it's Nan I'm after; if necessary, only find out how much he wants to let her go. You've been generous with me, Ned."

"I don't know where you get your contempt for money, but I wish George shared it. Are you away already?" Richard was bending over his hand.

"With your leave. I shan't go back to Westminster with you tonight, there's a deal to do before we march, and London is more convenient. I'm thinking of taking a house here when I get back from Scotland; there's a place in Bishopsgate I like, if the builder is ever done with it."

"Very domestic of you, Dickon. Is it too soon to ask what Anne Neville thinks of all this?"

"Yes," Richard rejoined tersely, and departed on his brother's chuckle.

He set off for Scotland in June, reaching York by mid-month and the border soon after, to discover the Scots still happily occupied among the burning farmsteads of the northern marches. The Earl of Northumberland, whose business it should have been to pack the marauders home again, had expended his energies in vituperative promises of retribution to come; scolding apart, he appeared to have done little. Richard heard the tale out, and sent a message for my lord of Northumberland to wait upon him. It was a short interview, from which the Earl emerged rather flushed of countenance. Henry Percy went sulkily home to Alnwick, nursing the recollection of his first encounter with Richard Plantagenet in silence, and alone. To already bitter resentment was shortly added the realisation that the lords who had once come flocking for his advice and leadership no longer thronged his hall; they were pouring south to Middleham, where the leopards and lilies of Plantagenet had been run up over the great stone keep.

King Edward passed an agreeable summer, dividing his time pleasantly betweeen his palaces at Greenwich and Shene. He had a new, charming mistress; his wife was believed to be pregnant again; his handsome daughters and baby son throve. The Duke of Clarence, summoned once to Greenwich, went back to London in conspicuous ill humour. In August a long letter came from the King of Scots, offering apologies for his subjects, and suggesting discussion of those differences which had led to violation of the truce; James Stewart sounded harried, and Edward laughed as he read, reflecting that his brother had wasted no time. A little later he had a brief letter from Richard himself, confirming that the Scots had gone home, and were displaying no visible ambition to return. There was a postscript: Fauconberg, his gratitude for the Duke's clemency at Sandwich proving short-lived, had been apprehended trying to transfer his services to the Scots, and summarily executed.

Richard returned from Scotland in September, and, his business with Edward hurried through, the next morning found him on his way back to London. His arrival at le Herber was no surprise to the Duke of Clarence, who had had some weeks both to anticipate and to prepare for it. Lounging at his ease in the great hall of the Earl of Warwick's sometime London house, Clarence explained blandly that he had been told already he enjoyed no right of custody over Madam his sister-in-law, for all her young years and recent bereavements. He had sorrowed to hear it, but the King had spoken. This being so, Madam had long departed from his household and protection, and where she might be now, he did not know.

Richard looked down at him in silence, and as he met the lazily mocking eyes his fingers twitched. His grim-faced attendants, reading the thought, closed up behind; and over his shoulder Richard said tightly, "Sirs: we have men without. Fetch them, and search this house." Clarence, his amusement vanishing, started to spring to his feet in furious protest, and was flung back in his seat with a violence that sounded down the hall. For an instant they stared at each other like enemies, the younger man's unslackened grip pinning his brother like some new grotesque heraldry to the pompous blazonings of the chairback. Breathing fast, Clarence whispered, "Gloucester, you forget yourself, by our father's head," and in a low, still voice Richard answered, "Under favour, George: be glad I have remembered."

There were le Herber servants in plenty about the hall, but for some reason their master made no recourse to them.

Impotently raging, he sat wordless while the Duke of Gloucester's men went methodically through the house, startling the scullions in the kitchen and thrusting into the very garderobes of the women's chambers, before they returned to the hall in defeat. Wherever else Anne Neville might be, she was no longer at le Herber.

Only then did Richard remove the hand which throughout he had kept on the canopied chair. Gathering up his cloak, he said passionlessly, "We must try in other places, then." His eyes swung back to Clarence's smouldering blue ones, and a muscle moved in his cheek. "Be warned, George. If you have done her hurt—"

"I have not, I know not where she is," Clarence said huskily. "Look for her where you like, it's no trouble to me if you must go seeking your mistress in privies and cook-houses—"

But Richard had turned on his heel. The peering attendants of the hall scrambled to make way; his men shouldered unopposed after him as he left the house.

The mid-afternoon office bell was sounding through the monks' cloisters as a half-dozen parties of armed horsemen clattered from Westminster on their several ways to the Duke of Clarence's West Country holds. They were gone, some of them, more than a fortnight: time enough, it would have seemed, to unearth a score of girls; and my lord of Clarence's seneschals showed no disposition to challenge the Lord Constable's messengers. Bridges squeaked down to admit them; gates opened at their command; but one by one the little bands of men came emptyhanded back to London. At Westminster Richard sought out Edward in plain demand, and received a flat negative which allowed neither persuasion or plea.

"No, Dickon, I will not order him. I cannot, without I am ready to go to war to enforce it. You understand George as well as I: he would fight us both now rather than give in, and what is there to accuse him of that he has not already denied? Leave it a little. He's only hoping you will grow tired and look elsewhere for a wife, and you've a better patience than ever he had. Truly, he cannot keep her hidden forever."

"No, and when he comes to realise it, what then? You have said yourself he is—irresponsible."

"For the which very reason, if I force him now you might

cause what you fear. Whereas if he is left to come to sense alone—" Pitying in despite of himself, Edward looked from the haggard face. "On my honour, I do not think he would go so far. Only a little longer, Dickon."

Autumn winds blew colder along the Thames, and the trees turned rusty gold. Unobtrusive figures drifted through the hall at le Herber, loitered a while, and went away as inconspicuously as they had come; there were guarded enquiries in the houses of the Duke of Clarence's friends. All Hallows' passed; there was feasting for Saint Martin's at Westminster, and across the laden tables Richard encountered Clarence's ironic eyes. Shortly after, he removed his household to his mother's home in London; she was herself at Berkhamstead, living much retired, but she had written her youngest son, offering him Baynard's Castle for as long as he might care to use it.

November was half gone when Robert Percy, who had lingered in Yorkshire after the close of the border campaign, finally returned to London. He walked into the Duke's antechamber, caked with mud from heels to thighs, as the last supper tables were being carried away; and having exchanged greetings with several friends, sat down beside Francis, remarking, "Faith, it's a pleasure to find a seat that doesn't move; I've been on horseback since morning. Is Gloucester abed?"

He nodded at the shut door of the bedchamber as Francis moved along the chest to make room for him, laying the lute with which he had been desultorily amusing himself among the stalks of rush and lavender on the floor. "No, I don't think he is. He's often in there alone now, evenings."

Percy accepted that without surprise. "I've heard tales. Fiend have his whoreson grace of Clarence: a sweet brother he's proving himself." His restless gaze wandered the room. "Seems strange without Philip here; for two years he was never far from Gloucester's elbow. I don't suppose you've had any word from him?"

"No, nothing. I've not seen him since he left us that day in the Tower; I think he wrote the Duke, but he didn't leave a message for me."

"Didn't he?" Percy hesitated, his eyes on the downcast face. "Well, never heed it, Francis. He's serving us all the same, plague take him for the mule he is."

He strolled off shortly after, spoke briefly with one or two

154

others, and vanished, reappearing at length with the announcement that he was going out. He had changed his travel-soiled garments and washed his hands and legs, and a bright pin sparkled in his cap. Francis regarded him wistfully, repressing an impulse to offer his company; and Percy, grinning, shook his head. "No, I'm not taking you with me, young Francis. The Duke would not approve. Get you to your virtuous couch, infant, and pray for us sinners." Engrossed in assembling and delivering a suitable retort at the retreating back, Francis failed to notice that the usually gregarious Percy had managed to avoid other tenders of companionship as well, and departed alone.

It was ten minutes' leisurely walk to his destination, through streets of shops and warehouses, taverns, churches, and open markets, all crowded and noisy beyond belief. Hawkers and beggars shouted from their pitches and thieves lurked in the narrow alleys, but Percy went carelessly on foot, enjoying the city brawl and bustle after the silent northern moors. Beyond Saint Paul's he came presently to a dingy tavern off Newgate Street, mounted the steps, and halted on the threshold, scanning the busy common room. There was a man in a dark jerkin standing by the alcove of the rear wall; across the heads of the landlord's patrons their eyes met in greeting, and Percy pushed through to join him.

"So you're here," he said with satisfaction. "I wasn't sure you would be, but I left Francis at Baynard's Castle just in case. Since you've not written to him, I presumed you had your reasons for not wanting to see him."

"One very good reason, wouldn't you think?" Removing his foot from the window seat, Philip dropped to the settle and waved towards the place opposite. "He's Gloucester's squire; it would be highly embarrassing for him to be obliged to defend my comings and goings."

"You don't flatter him. However, I guess you know your own business." Percy was silent for a moment, looking down at him. "You're back, then, Philip?"

"Yes. It was good of you to write, Rob, I was glad to hear from you. But I was coming anyway. I suppose the truth is, I couldn't help but come."

Percy said simply, "Well, I'm glad." He sat down, crooking a leg over his knee, accepted a slopping tankard from a hurrying maid, and contemplated his companion across the brim. "You look something improved for your wanderings in

155

the wilderness, if you'll excuse the term: the shoulder's mended, I take it. What have you been doing with yourself?'

Philip smiled, and took a swallow of ale. "Shouldn't I be asking you that? You've had a busy summer, by what I understand."

"Now and again: Francis enjoyed himself. There's this business of Clarence now, of course, to help pass the time away. Another fortnight and it may pass him straight to hell, from what I'm hearing of Gloucester's mind."

"No loss," Philip commented shortly. The remark was almost drowned in a crash of platters; the hard-pressed maid, rushing to attend an impatient customer, had tripped with her arms loaded and gone sprawling. The onlookers cried out; the patron, drenched in hot sauce, swore and cuffed the girl; and in the kitchen an infuriated bawling from the cook ended distractedly in a command for someone to fetch up that idle slut belowstairs, for all the help she might be, before they had the place pulled about their ears. Philip turned his head to observe the melee, and Percy watched his profile, wondering why, with the summer's clear tan overlaying the tired pallor of six months past, he should look older by as many years. The maid was trying to brush lumps of meat and gravy from her victim's person; she flushed, then smiled, as she encountered their eyes, and Philip, amused by the look of recognition, said to Percy, "Is this another of your haunts? I'm sure I was never here with you before."

"I've taken a cup here once or twice. There was a captain of archers had his throat slit fighting to be first with that drab Bessie, last time I was here—more fool him. She'd have had time for him too if he'd waited." A fresh uproar had arisen in the kitchen, and Percy leaned from his seat to catch the girl Bessie around the waist as she ran by. "You're in a fair pother tonight, sweetheart. What's the matter?—all the servants gone off and left you to take care of us alone?"

The curfew had just sounded, and the room was emptying. As the chatter and noise of departure diminished they could hear the cook passionately calling upon God, and the thwack of blows. Giggling, Bessie disposed herself pleasurably on Percy's knee. "It's the wench from belowstairs, mad as Bedlam," she explained. "She's dropped a kettle of soup, taking it from the fire, and Master Cook, he's in such a way—"

"Careless of her," Percy said absently, busy exploring a gartered leg. "Well, she'll know better next time." There was a nearing disturbance in the passage, and a ragged child burst into the common room. An arm's length before her pursuer she tripped and fell, and the panting cook, employing the huge wooden spoon of his office, continued discipline. Intent upon renewing acquaintance with Bessie, Percy paid no attention, but Philip looked round and after an instant got up to walk across the room, saying, "For God's love, have done. Will you kill her for a pot of soup?"

Annoyed by the interruption, the man wheeled round to stare. "Oh aye, well for you to say so! Will that feed my master's guests? A full cauldron gone to waste, and all the fault of this witless stray that's been housed here from the kindness of my master's heart, God curse the day. And all she can do is stand crying for her hurt! Clean out of her wits, pestilence on her that came to trouble an honest man's kitchen."

"If she's simple, the greater cause to pity her," Philip interposed sharply. "Now put that instrument by, you've done enough. More than enough," he added with another glance at the crumpled figure at his feet. Between wrath and astonishment, the cook hesitated, and then, shrugging in contempt, he turned and stumped off down the passage.

Rather uncertainly, Philip looked down at the girl. She might have been unconscious, but behind the upflung arms, still shielding her face, he saw bright eyes warily regarding him. Beneath the ragged hem of her skirt her feet were puffed and scarlet and grotesquely blistered; he could not think how she had run upon them at all. She was older than he had first supposed, fifteen or so perhaps, and when she stiffened and shrank as he bent over her, he knew what she feared. Speaking very quietly, he said, "I won't hurt you. I wanted to see your feet, they're badly burned." In his mind he was rapidly revolving alternatives; a leech would be hard to find in this neighbourhood, so late at night. Then he remembered the nunnery he had passed coming from his lodgings at the George. The sisters would know what treatment she needed, and maybe let her have a place in their kitchens after, too, for the price of an offering.

Lowering her arm, she peered at him from the shadows. She looked like a trapped creature of the woods, wild with pain and ready to fly at the nearest hand; the desperate, half-fearful question in her eyes, patently belying the opinion of Bessie and the cook, told its own story. Straightening, Philip turned to the nearer cupboard; there was no wine upon it, but he had seen the maid reach inside, earlier. Breaking the lock with a kick, he took out a flagon, splashed its thin, sour contents into an emptied cup, and stooped once more. "Drink this. Might there be something in the kitchen for your hurts? Honey is good, or oil and yolk of eggs."

Her face contorted. Ignoring the offered drink, she leaned towards him. "For God's sake," she whispered. "For God's sake, please help me." The words died on a breath. Her lips had gone grey; all at once she sank back, knocking the cup aside with her head, and lay unmoving in the spill of torch-light, the wine still trickling down her cheek and into the tangle of her matted hair.

Philip crouched emotionless, staring at the pinched features. Her voice had startled him; it was not the speech of an illiterate kitchen drudge, although he reminded himself mechanically that she could have picked it up in some great household. Presently he bent nearer, lifting a strand of hair from the wasted temple.

His attention drawn by the quiet, Percy looked up from his entertainment in the window seat to say ribaldly, "Have a care what you're about, Philip! I believe I should come play propriety."

Philip disregarded the witticism. Kneeling by the girl, he said in a strained voice, "Rob, will you come here? I want you."

"I can't think why," Percy observed. He heard Philip swear softly, and got reluctantly to his feet. "Saints, if you must be forever setting the world to rights—" Grumbling, he detached himself from Bessie's hopeful clasp, bestowing a last slap on her backside as she flounced offendedly by. The door slammed; grinning, Percy joined his friend. "Well?" he said at length. "You've saved her a hiding, which seven days from now she'll never miss among the rest. What do you mean to do with her now?"

"Rob—" Philip turned, staring up at him. "You were at Middleham after me, it's seven years since I saw her. But if I'm not dreaming, it's Anne Neville."

There was an instant's silence, during which Percy's eyes flicked instinctively to the girl, and away again. Ending it, he said flatly, "You're raving."

"Am I?" Philip moved out of the light, letting it shine down full. "Look again. She's the Earl of Warwick's very picture, don't you remember it was always so?"

Compelled by the insistence in his voice, Percy shifted his gaze once more, impatiently running an eye over the thin, aquiline features and dark hair. His face changed. Philip said intently, "Now do you see?"

"She was sometimes at Westminster while I was in Gloucester's household there," Percy began doubtfully. "That was two or three years ago of course, but—" And then, more slowly, "Warwick's daughter! In this sty? God on the Cross, Gloucester will cut someone's heart out for this."

Philip was lifting the attenuated body in his arms. "Make a place on the seat, Rob, I'm going to lay her there. Use your coat for a cover; mine will do for her head."

"But it makes no sense!" Percy protested, hastily spreading the improvised blanket. "Every scullion in London knows Gloucester's been looking for her: Why didn't she speak?"

"She may have tried to, but don't forget she was brought here long before anyone supposed Anne Neville to be anywhere but at le Herber. The landlord was bound to be in it, but for the rest—you heard what Bessie said. They just thought she was mad. The wonder is it's not true, after their handling of her." Rolling up his jerkin, Philip slid it under the heavily lying head, and used Percy's to wrap her in; the room was chilling with the fire nearly gone, and it was evident that the ragged smock was all her clothes. Even insensible, she seemed to flinch from his touch. Sombrely watching, Percy said, "Has she been forced, do you suppose?"

"God knows." Across his shoulder, Philip met his eyes. "That's Gloucester's business. Leave it, Rob."

In the rear of the building, almost silent now with the onset of night, a door banged. Involuntarily they both turned; an authoritative voice could be heard in the kitchen. Philip went to the passage, listened, and came back again. "The landlord himself, I think," he murmured. "Rob, go and fetch Gloucester. It's not far to Baynard's Castle—and tell them to bring a litter, she's in no state to ride. Go on now! I'll stay and deal with things here."

In the kitchen voices were scaling upwards as the cook laboured to assuage his employer's wrath. Pushed to the threshold, Percy halted there long enough to say, "You'd best have this," and, unbelting the scabbarded sword at his hip, threw it to his companion. Philip caught it with a short laugh of thanks, and waved him on his way. The street was empty now, and white with moonlight; he watched the big figure traverse its length at a run, and, rounding the corner, disappear from sight.

Laying the sword on the table, Philip went back to the girl. Her colour, gradually returning, was deepening to fire on her cheekbones; he thought he saw her lashes stir, and was holding wine to her lips when the innkeeper's strident accents, overriding the excuses of the cook, came with excoriating clarity: "Bones of God, did I not say she was never to be taken from that room! Was ever a man so beset with fools! Could she not do work enough for you under lock, but you had to fetch her up here—aye, and even that was not enough—" In the pause while he gathered breath the cook broke in again. He appeared to have somewhat allayed the landlord's anger, for when the response came it was on a lower note, and Philip could not make out the words. The agitated voices died away, rising again more distantly in imperative summons; a door crashed. Outside the window which fronted on the stableyard, there were running footsteps.

Recalled to awareness of the cup still in his hand, Philip looked back at Anne. Wide-opened eyes, set deep beneath softly curving brows, calmly returned his gaze. As if continuing a conversation begun long before, she said quietly, "He has sent for help."

"I'm sure he has," Philip agreed. "But Baynard's Castle is closer than le Herber; I shouldn't like to lay odds on the Duke of Clarence outstripping my lord of Gloucester tonight." He glanced again at the cup. "Will you drink, madam? It's poor stuff, but you may feel better for it."

He knelt, offering it as to a great lady. She looked from the wine to him, then slowly put out her roughened hands to accept it. When she had drunk she let him take the cup away, and lay back with an arm across her face. From behind its concealment she said at length, "You know, then?"

He answered gently, "Yes. Rest a while; I promise you, it's over."

She made no reply. After a little while Philip went to the ash-strewn hearth, kicking at the smouldering logs. He stood for a time, watching the flames curl and grow, until he heard her move again; turning then with a smile, he found her regarding him. "I do not believe I know you, sir. Did you say—are you in the service of his grace of Gloucester?"

"You might describe it so," Philip admitted. The past months considered, it was an awkward question. "My name's Lovell."

She paused, alert, and then returned his smile. "Philip Lovell? I've heard of you. They call you the Duke of Gloucester's good spirit."

It was lightly spoken, but of a sudden her face grew warm. As flushed as she, Philip replied steadily, "You've been misinformed, madam. There are few things of which the Duke of Gloucester stands less in need."

The fire had broken into blazing at last; he threw on another log, and pushed it down among the embers with his heel. Leaning on her elbow, she pulled slowly at the ravelled hem of her skirt. "What part of London is this?"

"Aldersgate, about, back of Saint Paul's. East is Cheapside, where the fine houses begin."

"I knew it must be near Saint Paul's, I could hear the bells, but it was hard to be sure of them, quite." Her eyes travelled around the muss of overturned stools and benches, filthy rushes layering over stale food droppings, and mugs lying with their sour dregs spilling along the boards. "I never saw this room until tonight. There's a place below where I woke when they brought me from le Herber—the night wine was drugged, I don't know how long after it was. There was a man waiting when I woke. He said I was the tavernkeeper's niece, that my name was Mald, and when I learned to answer to it I should eat. He gave me this to put on—" Her low voice halted for a space. The minutes wore by; then Philip said, "Did you know him?"

"No. He went away after. I never saw him again, but he used to come at night to see the host; I could hear him through the door. Once I heard him say they need not be soft in their dealing— The tavernkeeper called him my lord. He—he spoke like a gentleman."

Through his teeth, Philip said, "Did he so." He had gone to the table, and was jerking the sword in and out of its scabbard; the hilt wealed a red pattern in his palm. He let it go abruptly, and turned away.

A deep stillness had settled over the house. Moving to the

window, Philip glanced into the street. He did not think it would be much longer before Richard arrived; Percy must be nearly to Baynard's Castle by now, and the Duke's men had learned speed as a natural condition of their employment. Leaning against the casement, he followed with his eyes the shadow of the innboard as it swung in the wind. Anne was so quiet he thought her asleep; he was startled when she said meditatively, "I have brought you to mind, Sir Philip. You were a squire in my father's household, weren't you? But you went away, rather suddenly, I remember."

"When I was seventeen. It was not my wish, but my father was dead and I was needed at home."

"You and Dickon were always together; I used to go down to the tiltyard after supper, and watched you practising there." They both smiled, sharing the recollection of that other time, and it seemed as if the cloud of a special trouble, a reservation partly of doubt, and half-withdrawn from her eyes. Divining its cause, Philip said, "He has been scouring England to find you, madam. This night will give him his first quiet sleep in two months gone."

Having returned from the window, he was reaching for the wine again, but his hand checked in mid-gesture. At the back of the building, a door had creaked.

Motioning for silence, Philip went noiselessly to the passageway. The kitchen door was shut, but beyond it there was a rumble of men talking. Presently he came back to the table, and, picking up the scabbard, slid the blade from its sheath. "I was wrong," he said, to her wordless question. "I thought he had sent to le Herber."

Even as he spoke footsteps sounded in the passage, and the landlord's voice, breathless and anxious: "In here, my lord, he's in here, and the wench too. They'll be robbing the place by now, I don't doubt. Jack Cook, get you back, there's no call for you here—" Still talking, trying at once to push the curious cook back into the kitchen and usher on the man walking before him, the landlord appeared in the entry way. Philip hardly spared him a glance; he was looking with narrowed eyes at his companion: a tall man, rangy but powerfully made, in a gentleman's fine woollen jacket and hose. He had a drawn sword in his right hand, and, Philip mentally calculated, a two inches' advantage of reach to go with it; and even in the uncertain torchlight it was possible to see the cruel, sensualist's mouth. Just inside the room he halted, his gaze moving warily from the one occupant to the other, and Philip said in a hard voice, "Come in, my lord, the host has invited you. Lovell is my name; I don't know yours, but I think—my lord—I have been this quarter hour very heartily wishing to meet you."

The tall man said harshly, "I don't know what you mean. I was dining nearby, and I know the landlord here; when he sent me word he had a madman loose in the place, I thought I could oblige him by throwing the fellow out." He paused, appraising. "Lovell, you said? Gloucester's spaniel, as I remember! Well, I don't know what your interest may be in this little drab, but you'll be pleased to explain to me what you're about, raising a tumult in an honest house. Do you suppose the slut virtuous? Why, God save us, she's—"

"Be careful!" Philip interrupted. Suddenly he was shaking. "Be very careful, before you use words of the Earl of Warwick's daughter." The silence stretched like a thong; mastering himself, he added softly, "Shall we reserve the explanation for the Duke of Gloucester—my lord? He will not be long."

For a heartbeat they measured each other. Then, to the landlord's putty face at his shoulder the older man said tightly, "You fool. You told me he was alone."

"But he was—he cannot have sent—God have pity!" With an inarticulate sob of terror the innkeeper spun round and plunged from the room. As the clatter of retreat died Philip said tauntingly, "Sensible man. Are you thinking to ape him, my noble lord? By God's eyes, you were brave enough when it was a woman. Stay a while, you're armed to fight—did you not mean to without the host? He's gone, my lord, and you've only a little, little while to do it all alone."

He had just time to kick aside the joint stool at his foot as the man closed with him. The clang of their engaging blades was the dearest joy Philip could have named himself; he had never in his life before fought a man for the express delight of encompassing his death. It was a short, bitter scrimmage, remembered after only in the ring of metal scraping and grating, the scuff of feet among the rushes, and his enemy's hoarsely labouring breath. Being desperate, he soon became careless; he was, besides, a good fifteen years older, and it told in his wind. Far down the street a sound of hoofs was growing louder; he lunged, missed, and went down, his hands still fluttering and plucking around the blade buried in his throat.

Panting, Philip leaned against the table. The huge gushes of blood were slowly lessening; his sword stood up in the cabining flesh like a staff. He dragged it out, a heel in the dead man's chest, looked at the running blade, and flung it rattling down. The noise expired in a silence through which he could hear Anne's short breathing; then boots were pounding up the outer steps, the door burst open, and the Duke's men swarmed into the room. Richard walked in among the first of them.

His eyes encountered Philip's and slid past, unregarding. If the stink and squalor of the place shocked him for all Percy's story, he made no sign; his gaze had gone already to the girl huddled in the window seat. She had pulled the men's clothes around her breast and ankles, but the tattered smock still showed. Darkly flushed, she tried to draw the coverings closer, and Richard went towards her. "Nan, I—" He checked, unsure. The summer wooing had been interrupted at its most delicate point; when she did not move he let his hands fall. "I've sent word to Saint Martin's, Nan. You're to go there for sanctuary; you'll have their best tending, and no one can touch you there, or force you from that house."

She answered, hardly whispering, "I thank you, cousin."

Richard said slowly, "I am not your cousin." Her eyes lifted, as if to judge his meaning; when he saw she understood him he dropped his hand to hers, still gripped around the cloth at her throat.

Percy came up the outer steps and stood beside Philip, dispassionately considering the sprawled object on the threshold. "Unconventional," he remarked, noting the angle of the thrust. "You were lucky he didn't open your guts." He glanced towards the window seat, adding, "What will you have done with this, my lord?"

Richard seemed not to hear. He was lifting the wrapping from Anne's swollen ankles; she stretched out her arms to prevent him, but was too late. There was an interval while neither moved nor spoke; then, gently drawing the cover up again, he kissed her cheek, and rose, and went to the street-side window to look through, but the litter had not yet come. He stood stiffly there, his hands open and helpless, staring like a blind man around the room until his eyes halted on

Philip. As if only then remembering, he went over to the dead man. Scarlet froth bubbled from the gaping mouth; the pupils glistened between frozen lids. Motionless, Richard said, "You've robbed me, Philip." He was silent then for a time; when he spoke again his voice was colourless. "Where is the keeper of this hovel?"

"A long way hence by now, I should think," Philip replied. The inflection of the enquiry made him thankful for it; he was feeling sick, and very weary, and longed only to be gone from the place. "Let it be, my lord. He was only a tool." Like this one, he nearly added, but forebore. It might be possible to prove the Duke of Clarence had delivered Anne Neville to her captivity, but that he had devised the details of it, only the abductor could have said. Philip wondered if, in his inmost heart, Richard really wanted to know.

Beyond the open door the clop of hoofs echoed. The Duke's men were waiting in a cluster outside; one of them entered to say that the litter was here. Himself raising Anne in his arms, Richard carried her towards the door. A page had laid a cloth over the body, so that my lady might not have to see; pausing beside it, Richard said, so low Philip could hardly hear, "Take that carrion and throw it on the doorstep at le Herber. Look to it, Sir Robert."

Grimly smiling, Percy jerked a thumb at a couple of servants in livery, and walked back into the tavern. Philip wanted only to slip inconspicuously away, but as he came from the house Richard glanced round from where he was standing by the litter to say curtly, "Philip, I want a word with you. Wait inside."

Sighing faintly—he had hoped to postpone the audience until morning—Philip retraced his steps. Percy had worked swiftly; rid of the abomination on its threshold the common-room seemed oddly bare, despite the tossed-about disorder of the furniture. Philip righted a stool and went to hold his hands over the fire. Someone had opened a window, and the air was sweeter for it, but very cold. The abnormal quiet of the house struck on his ear; the landlord's guests upstairs could not possibly have slept through the din, but he decided that, being veterans of the place, they had probably made off at the first outcry, and the servants too; it was a thieves' haunt if ever he had seen one. He was still reflecting on it when he heard Richard's step outside.

He came in briskly, nodding at a yeoman to stay beyond

the door, kicked it shut, and walked to the other side of the circular hearth. "Well, Philip." There was no reading his face. Philip said equably, "Well, my lord?"

An impatient thrust of Richard's boot scattered the shell of a log deep in the fire; a bright tongue of flame licked from the embers. "For what you have done tonight, Philip, you may claim what you will of me. You know that: let it pass. That's not what I wanted you for now." The grey eyes shifted, travelling upward from the playing firelight to rest on the other man's face. "I expected you in London some months ago; your letter was neither explicit nor overmuch a craving of my leave. I might, I suppose, have presumed you still unwell."

"Did you presume it, my lord?" Philip rejoined levelly. He looked down, moving his heel against the gritty ashes of the hearth. "I went back to Oxfordshire to think."

There was a dangerous silence. Expressionless, Richard said at last, "An agreeable luxury." Philip answered, "So in the end I also came to believe."

The fire snapped and smouldered; the torches were dull red eyes against the wall. Sitting on the corner of the table, Richard circled a knee with his arms.

"Philip, the King has given me Middleham. I am to hold England for him north of the Trent as Warwick did, and keep the border, with lordship over the Earl of Northumberland. I've given the Welsh lands to Pembroke's boy; that work's done."

As indifferent as if it had been a tourney prize of ribbons, he sat gazing at the emberglow. The light of a single candle alone now dispelled the shadows, informing the intent, purposive profile: the mouth at once circumscribed and emphatic, at once amplified by and belying the intelligent, observing eyes. Philip said slowly, "And you've not had one hour to enjoy what you wrought."

Shrugging, Richard responded, "I must be busy, and God He knows there's labour enough for six king's lieutenants in England, could his grace but muster them. It will be a task to go on with for a time; the Earl of Warwick is still remembered in the north. His people will see me as the heel of York, and Northumberland too is no well-wisher: he'll cast trouble in the way if he can." He turned a ring on his thumb. It had a red stone set in massy gold: a gift of the King on his nineteenth birthday, a month ago. "Taking thought for the which, it is in my mind that my household needs a steward. A minute ago I spoke of reward for you, Philip, but be sure this would be none: only bondman's toil with a face of honour until the north is won. Also, you hold this side the Trent and have no cause to serve me, unless it be for that reason it pleases me to believe, that you love me. Of your own wish then, Philip: Will you be my officer?"

He smiled, and in a moment, being answered, held out his hand. Philip took it, saying, "With all my heart."

PART THREE

Fair Stood the Wind for France

Summer 1475

CHAPTER ELEVEN

In the garden at Ipsden Anna Fitz Hugh sat alone, her head bent over the embroidery in her lap. Her solitude was a rarity in that busy household, but today the twins had been despatched on an excursion with the fowler, and Kate, who usually spent the afternoon with Anna, had discovered an urgent domestic task to keep her indoors, despite the clamour of the birds, and the warm beckoning of the May sun. Anna knew the reason for her privacy: pink-cheeked, she went steadily on with her sewing.

It was growing late; they would be laying the supper tables soon. The reluctant, fluttering expectation with which she had wakened that morning was being replaced by faint pique; it was, she reflected, all of a piece that her husband, who had kept her waiting so many years, should keep her waiting still. She had left his letter in her chamber, stubbornly refusing the impulse to keep it by her, but she knew the contents well enough without the hurried, uneven handwriting to prompt her: it was, anyway, rather short. It had been her first direct word from him since they had parted in Gloucestershire, although from time to time there had been correct, formal messages from Middleham in letters to Kate. The considerable care which had gone into their phrasing was unapparent to Anna, who after the first while began to find their stiffness trying. Her cousin Humphrey, she had lately heard, was now safely established under the protection of the Duke of Brittany, one of a group of English exiles in attendance upon the Duke's guest, young Henry Tudor; and although even the French King seemed to have lost interest in promoting the ambitions of the last Lancastrian claimant to the English crown, it was a reasonably comfortable situation for Humphrey. With the lessening of the original cause for bitterness, Anna began to think more kindly of her husband: even, as time went by, to wish for him again. His letter when it arrived was more welcome than she cared to admit, but with the passing hours her first tentative anticipation gave way to doubt. It crossed her mind that four years was a long time. He had written he would come, and had sent a messenger only days before to confirm the hour of his arrival, but such laggardness hardly suggested uncontrollable impatience to greet her again.

The gate squeaked. Anna had heard no step; the sudden sound made her start, and a bright spot of blood appeared on the embroidery. Furious at her rising colour, she put the work aside, lifting her eyes; then sat back again with a little sigh as Gilbert Secott came down the path. He was a mouse-haired youth, the eldest of Sir William's sons, who in recent months had shown himself assiduous with attentions to his father's pretty guest. Anna would have better relished the compliment to herself if she had not found him unlikeable; he spoke slightingly of his father to anyone who would listen, calling him pinchpenny and countrified and jaw-run-on; and once wondered idly to Anna if his stepmother received any of the squires at night behind her bedcurtains, on the occasions when Sir William was from home. He seemed at a loss when she grew angry, and not for the first time she was left speculating if he was in fact thick of wit, or simply impervious.

He sat down beside her on the grass, twirling a nosegay of primroses, while he remarked that the whole household had worn holiday dress long enough for a gentleman who appeared not all anxious to become their guest; he had left his father saying Lord Lovell must have travelled on first to Westminster, to make his duty to the King and be granted possession of his inheritance. Then he asked, with a side glance, if she would be sorry if my lord did not, after all, come today. She replied indifferently, a corner of her mind marvelling what kind of answer he could possibly expect to such a question, while the greater part of it was trying to imagine a man called Francis Lovell who was her husband. His very name was a strangeness; Lovell of Tichmarsh, Baron Grey of Rotherfield, Baron Holland, Baron Deinscourt—fine sounding titles, she thought tartly, for a gentleman who could not even come timely to greet his wife. Then she remembered how unknown to her now the man himself must be; she thought of her wide chamber above the hall, empty and waiting, the cool new linen and sweet herbs strewn among the rushes; and her heart tightened. It was four long years; and memory showed her only the boy she had known in her uncle's house in Gloucestershire.

Gilbert was talking desultorily on. It might be, he said,

that my lord would not even be here tomorrow. If it be so that the King had already left London, it might have been necessary to follow him all the way to Canterbury, where the army was mustering for embarkation to Calais. Drawn back from her private meditations, Anna conceded it might have been so. Edward's decision to resume the long-suspended war with France was a popular one, and caressing cajolery had wrung from her richer subjects—still half-surprised by their own bounty—a war chest to rival that which had launched Monmouth Harry on his march to the glory of Agincourt sixty years ago. Anna knew Francis was going with the Duke of Gloucester's huge contingents, and had even reconciled herself to it: a young man, after all, could hardly stay at home. Less easy to forgive had been the enrolment of his Midland followers under the Duke's northern banner, an omen for the future she could clearly read and already disliked; his knighthood too, she knew from Kate, had been left to Gloucester for bestowing when he should see fit. Lord Lovell's heir might have claimed it at Westminster when he chose, but, Kate said, he had told Philip he wanted to have deserved it, before he put Sir to his name.

On the other side of the ivied wall a clatter of hoofs sounded; through the quickening of her heart Anna was aware of voices speaking in welcome, and a crisp one answering. Her hands trembling a little, she picked up her sewing again, and discovered that Gilbert, unconscious of impending interruption, had selected this moment to try to lay the garland of primroses he had made around her neck. Footsteps approached the garden door; all at once reaching up to help him, Anna said softly, "Shall you be sorry when I go, Gilbert?" and leaned back her head to smile at him. He had turned eighteen last Lady Day, but she did not think he had had as much experience as he pretended. She tilted her chin helpfully, and it was that arresting spectacle which offered itself to Francis Lovell's amazed and wrathful gaze as he walked into the garden.

For an instant he could only gape. Then, his eyes sparkling, he strode forward, fastened a hand in Gilbert's collar, and jerked him rudely from his knees. "Master Gilbert Secott? Yes, I see. Be so good as to explain to me, then, just what the devil you mean"—this while propelling his victim rapidly towards the gate—"by trying to make love to my wife?"

He had shifted his grip to an armlock with which there was no arguing. Anna stood up, exclaiming in outrage, and Gilbert stammered, "Sir—my lord—you asperse my honour. I hold my lady in the deepest possible respect—"

"You had better," was the unsympathetic rejoinder. "And do it from a distance too. Out!" The gate slammed. From the wrong side of the wicket Gilbert looked upon defeat; and behind the fire of young rage and embarrassment a man's eye promised remembrance. Francis, dismissing him, swung on his heel. "And as for you, madam—" He was trying not to laugh; he had taken Gilbert's measure, and had a fair notion of the reason for his lady's wayward behaviour, but the circumstance was not evident to Anna. She took a hasty step backward, encountered the low kerb of the fountain against her ankles, and went over with a splash into the brimming basin.

"Blessed Mother—!" Reaching her at a bound, Francis grasped after a wet hand and lifted her up. "Of all the nonsensical— Are you very wet, sweetheart? Kind Heaven, you're dripping like a water spaniel; here, let me—" He stooped, wringing the water from her laden skirts while she leaned on his shoulder to kick off her shoes. After a minute he straightened. They were so close they could see each other's breathing; of a sudden his flush died, and with it every word he had so carefully devised to say. "Anna—" He searched her face, and her eyes looked back, all the colour of the sky reflecting up to deepen the blue. She had grown tall, he found; when he tipped up her chin he needed only by a little to bend his head. There was a slope of grass, warm yet from the day; she sank down, her arms around his neck drawing him after her, and his hands pinned her shoulders as he stooped, seeking her mouth.

Sunlight spilled molten over the garden wall; the shadows crept on the lawn. Against her cheek, Francis said huskily, "Sweetheart, where's your chamber?"

She turned in his arms, twisting nearer with a little languorous movement of sensual content. Involuntarily they looked as one towards the garden door; but it had no latch. He kissed her eyelids, and asked again. Smoothing a lock of his hair, she said uncertainly, "There's supper soon: shouldn't we be there?"

"Why, are you hungry?" She coloured vividly at the glinting expression then smiled in return, moving her head from side to side in denial on the daisied grass. Under his breath Francis said, "Witch. Do you mean to keep me waiting until Scott's bedtime?"

They shook with laughter to think of it and then lay still, unwilling to stir, until the gate squeaked. Francis glanced over his shoulder, and, unruffled, rose to his feet. "Give you good day, Kate. I must beg pardon for not presenting myself: I was renewing acquaintance with my wife."

"There's evidence," his cousin observed, her eyes on Anna's gown, and Anna said quickly, "I slipped. It's no matter, Kate, I'll find another dress." She had scrambled up, blushing and shaking the wet folds from her hips. As she turned towards the gate Francis suggested impishly, "Shall I come too and be your tirewoman, sweet?" but he had reckoned without Sir William. They met him in the hall, and at the point Sir William was quite unable to deny himself the pleasure of hospitality. He was full of questions too, wanting to know about the progress of the mustering at Canterbury, and, comfortably settling in his carven chair, sent off a servant for strawberries and wine. Conscious of his obligations, Francis allowed himself to be offered hippocras in the best cup, only whispering to Anna to go on upstairs, and he would join her soon. The open-mouthed stare of a serving maid who had paused, goose-wing duster in hand, to fix bemused eyes upon Anna's stockinged feet, Francis found less trying than Sir William's cheerful readiness to enjoy a chat; but, Kate in a few minutes reappearing, he made a thankful escape, and ran up the stairs to his wife's bed-room.

It was pleasant apartment with windows facing east and south, half-shadowed now with the going light. The fresh herbs smelled very clean and sweet; the walls were hung with bunches of lavender and rosemary, like a bridal chamber, and there were more sprigs among the rushes on the floor. Anna saw him smile, and said colouring, "It was the women did it, and Kate." He came to put an arm around her waist, saying, "And kindly thought of; I must thank them too, in the morning. Sweetheart, you're cold with this wet." He undid the fastenings of her gown, making so little of it that her breathing slowed; presently slipping the stuff over her hips, he helped her to step free. Her shift was white lawn, embroidered around the neck with bright silks, above, the curve of her breasts glowed like pearl. She had lost a little of her young slightness, although her waist was as narrow and supple as ever, but he was inclined to approve of the change and said so, laughing at her confusion. He would have drawn her down to the coverlet with him then, but she had had time to become self-conscious again; silently cursing William Secott, he turned her hand up and lightly kissed the inner wrist, and let her go.

There was bread for all-night on a chest, and meat and wine; he went to fill the cups and felt her relief. Throwing off his jerkin, Francis stretched himself on the bed, remarking teasingly, "Faith, I don't blame young Gilbert the attempt, anyway. You're an enchanting sight, sweetheart."

She gave him a look across her shoulder which nearly demolished his good intentions. "Poor Gilbert, you used him shockingly."

"Did I? I thought he got off very well; he might have ended in the fountain instead of you, my love." Watching her unclasp the necklace from her throat, he sat up and reached for his purse. "Which reminds me: I've brought you a present. There was an Italian merchant came to York, and he travelled on to Sheriff Hutton when he learned the Duke was there. It's a guaranteed charm for good luck and good health, and an infallible guardian of chastity besides"—he grinned mischievously sideways, inviting her with his eyes—"but I said I would have it anyway. See if you like it." He held it out: a collar of beaten gold links, with a blue stone in a square openwork setting depending from it. Undoing the catch, he said ruefully, "It was the Duke's money, I'm afraid. The King's kept me on no more than what was due me these years, but Gloucester knew I wanted to bring you something, and I was sure there'd be nothing like it in London— What's wrong, sweeting?"

He had put the necklace in her hands as she sat beside him; the slackened links ran through her fingers. Catching her breath sharply, she turned her face away. "I don't want it." The stillness grew and deepened like a palpable cold. She could feel him, motionless, behind her; the silence drove her on. "Don't you see? How can I hang his jewels around my neck? It was a different gift he made my uncle at Tewkesbury."

Quietly reasoning, his voice answered her, "Your father forgave it before he died. Your brother comes often enough to the Duke of Gloucester's court to make plain he has no quarrel there." She could not speak; her jaw clenched, trying to steady itself against the shake of tears. Now at last he was the stranger to her she had feared; unfamiliar at her shoulder she felt the newness of his physical man's presence, and where once would have been anger to match her own, a debating judgment. Presently he went on, "You have not spoken of your cousin. He is with Tudor in Brittany, I hear, and you have cause to blame me greatly for it. Since he and your uncle were more to you than any kinsmen in Yorkshire, it is understandable you should find it hard to forgive those persons who divided you from them."

She bent her head, groping to hide her face and the flooding tears. "I did not remind you of that. I have not reproached you, nor even wished to."

A long pause followed, while she wept on hopelessly against her knees, and Francis sat gazing at the jewel on its glittering chain. At last dropping it to the chest beside him, he slipped the bands of her garment from her shoulders and pulled her down with him across the bed. "Never mind. It doesn't matter, sweetheart; I never meant to make you cry."

Some while between dusk and dark, lying in his arms as the shadows gathered in the canopy above them, she turned her head to whisper, "Are you happy?" He replied as she wished, his mouth against her hair. It was not yet night, and around them the house still stirred with life: voices rising as they separated to their different rooms, the noise of locks and shutters being made fast. Soon Anna's maid scratched at the door; Francis got up to untie the hangings of the bed, letting the tapestries fall around them before he called her to come in. Through a chink in the curtains they saw the light spring up, and heard her steps, faint and muffled by the hangings, as she went about the room, opening chests and coffers to lay in trinkets and jewels and clothes. At length there was silence, and they knew her asleep. Too moved themselves to rest, they lay talking softly for a time; and reaching stealthily through the curtains took bread and meat from the chest to make a little feast, having remembered at last, as Francis said, to be hungry for supper. The night candle burned on its pricket, showing her body like marble gleaming through her unbound hair. Presently he put back what remained of the food, and drew the curtains shut.

They left Ipsden three days later, for Francis was expected at Canterbury within the month. He had written his steward at Minster Lovell, commanding him to summon the tenants of the manor to join him in celebrating the Feast of the Ascension in William Lovell's church. They made a leisurely journey, a string of sumpters plodding behind the stallion Francis rode beside Anna's white palfrey, all trapped in his colours, scarlet and gold. When they crossed the bridge over the Windrush to Lovell land it lacked a day yet to the appointed Thursday, but the parish priest was standing in the church porch, and waiting with him were all the manor officers.

They dismounted and went inside to make an offering. Sunlight blazed like fire through the stained windows, dappling the walls with colour and splashing amber and turquoise and vermilion across the alabaster figure on William Lovell's tomb. Francis lingered beside it, his hand on the carved feet. "This is where my grandfather is buried, Anna. He built this church, and the house too is his work. He ever loved his lands; when he was dying it was his joy to know he would lie here."

Outside the welcomers pressed round; there were more yet, they said, at the house. Presently Anna mounted again, and Francis walked before her holding the palfrey's bridle. Tall beeches joined above their heads; through the gaps they saw low hills, and yellow buttercups blooming over the fallow fields. Beyond a skirting of buildings and grey stone wall, they came to the east gate.

The manor house of Minster Lovell lay facing the river, its walls misted green with lichen, the huge arms of east and west wings flung out as if to embrace the court. On the slated roof a gilded weathercock flashed and wheeled, and the traceried windows were golden in the light. Francis was silent, drinking it with his eyes. "It is just the same," he said at last. "Sometimes I was afraid— But it is just as I remembered, the very same."

"Dear heart," Anna said humorously, and he turned, half-embarrassed, to face her. "And would they have tentings for a bath?"

He gave a strained laugh, and held out his arms to lift her down.

CHAPTER TWELVE

THE English army sailed in June, but it was the beginning of July before the King himself with the Dukes of Clarence and Gloucester embarked for France. They were expecting to be met in Calais by their ally and brother-in-law, Charles of Burgundy; but although the town was packed with English soldiers, of the Duke and his promised support there was no sign. His wife arrived instead, bearing gifts for her brothers, and the news that Charles, who for some months had been laying siege to the inoffensive German town of Neuss, had finally abandoned the project in disgust, and was salving disappointment by looting and pillaging in the territories of his indignant neighbour, the Duke of Lorraine.

In addition to her train of ladies, Margaret of Burgundy was attended by many of her husband's nobles, and before them Edward maintained a hard-held calm; but in the privacy of the council chamber the storm raged. "God, for a seat under the table," Francis Lovell murmured, an eye on the closed door, and Percy grinned in agreement. Decorous and unrevealing, the impassive panels kept their secret well; but the soft-footed ushers who came and went at summons from the inner room trod as if on glass.

It was nearly suppertime, and in the great hall many English were already gathered, waiting for the Duchess of Burgundy and her ladies to descend from the apartments prepared for them. A few of the Burgoner lords were present, although only one of them, a grey-haired man in blue and gold talking easily with Philip Lovell, appeared in the least comfortable about the occasion. Francis looked curious, and Percy said laconically, "Erard de Brezy. An old friend of your kinsman from our less prosperous days in Burgundy: we heard he was here. I fancy he has a thought or two about his Duke too."

But whatever the lord of Saint Aubin's reflections about his prince, he was keeping them to himself. There had been unfeigned pleasure in his greeting, but it struck Philip that he looked careworn and very much older, though it was less than five years since their last meeting. A kind of answer offered when a dark-browed young man wearing a sapphire velvet tunic stitched with yellow came at a sign to be presented, without elaboration, as Messire Auguste of Saint Aubin. He had an attractive smile and an easy, athlete's grace of movement, and Philip thought compassionately there could have been no greater evidence of Erard de Brezy's vain craving for a lawful heir of his body than the long delay in acknowledging openly this bastard son.

"No, he wasn't being shown about much last time we were in Burgundy," Percy commented, as they stood in an alcove after supper, watching a group of dancers moving through the figures of a galliard. They could see de Brezy at the other end of the hall, with Auguste, diligent and devoted, at his elbow. "I hear his wife miscarried of a boy last spring; I suppose that was the end of his hopes, and a sour finish it must have been. He's not young any more."

"But Madame de Brezy, I am told is very young and more than somewhat fair." A stout gentleman, gay in mulberry velvet with a collar of Yorkist suns around his shoulders, had come up in time to hear, and paused beside them with a suggestion of malicious laughter. "The Duke of Orleans got a son when he was past seventy, or so his Duchess told him. Monsieur de Brezy may yet be provided with an heir."

Philip contemplated the rubicund face with eyes from which all warmth had abruptly vanished. "That's not a speculation to be free with, Paston. Put a guard on your tongue, if you can't wag it to better purpose."

The plump body stiffened. "You are offensive, Lovell."

"It was my intention," Philip returned levelly. "Monsieur de Brezy has honoured me with his friendship."

Paston stared at him, weighing a retort, and Francis, who had been paying little apparent heed to the exchange, all at once looked round to ask innocently, "How's your brother-in-law, Paston?" He meant Sir John's bailiff, whom Margery Paston had run away to marry; years after the scandal her brother was still trying to pretend it had never happened. His small eyes, narrow with anger, jerked to the younger man's, hesitated, and fell. Without answering he turned and walked away.

"Will he send you a challenge, do you suppose?" Percy speculated to Philip, and Francis said lazily, "I've seen his style at Eltham: sits his horse like a sack of oats and handles

180

a lance like a quarter staff. I promise you, coz, you're in danger." Laughing, he strolled off.

The dance was ending. His attention caught by a blonde beauty, Percy departed to find, he said, if he might scrape acquaintance, and, restless, Philip turned back into the embrasure. Once he would have derived mild enjoyment from precisely the entertainment which was claiming Percy: he wondered at his bored disinterest now. Before God, I grow as staid as Secott, he thought irritably. The annoyance of the wrangle with Paston lingered in bitter aftertaste: his depression deepened. And what right had I to bite off the fool's nose, he reflected. Women don't love their husbands, usually; she may have betrayed him with half the duchy for all I know. Oh, a plague on the little emptyhead, and her dower too; he'll pay in trouble, probably, for every coin of it.

The archway curtain stirred. Someone said, "You keep private from our revels, messire."

Philip turned, mustering the expected smile. She was, so far as the shadows let him judge, a pretty woman: small and slenderly made, her face framed in trails of muslin; and for an instant, seeing her colour rise, he thought she had mistaken him for someone else. But she waited, considering him with bright, unwavering eyes; and responding politely, "I must beg pardon, madame; my mind was elsewhere," he moved to twitch back the curtain she had let fall behind her.

Laughter sprang into her face as she watched. "Oh messire, you are craven. Is this the gallantry of England? But I came only to ask if you would dance, Sir Philip."

Arrested in his adjustment of the hanging, Philip found himself regarding her again. The light was dim, but he had a sense of being minutely inspected in turn; discomfited, he said at length, "You have the advantage, madame. Did we meet at Lille five years ago, perhaps?" She shook her head; amused, he tried again. "Bruges, then?"

Her smile deepened. "Oh, it is as I have heard: the English have no skill at dalliance. Now a Frenchman, messire, would never have owned to such a fault of memory."

Philip contended unsuccessfully with a laugh. He could appreciate finesse where he discovered it, and was feeling progressively less inclined to worry about the curtain. A scent like flowers, sweet and disturbing, rose from the dark wings of her hair, half-concealed by the hennin and its misty veils; coming nearer, he slid an arm around her waist. "I must atone for my countrymen. Since we have met before"—he took her chin in his hand, lifting her face to his—"in England we renew acquaintance—thus, belle." Close to, she looked younger than he had thought, and a little less composed; he could see the pulse beating at her temple. Light shafting through the partly drawn curtain laid a narrow blade against her cheek, and his careless fingers froze. "God in Heaven—" he said softly. "Meg."

She stood motionless, all the mischief dying from her eyes as he stared down, then while he was gazing yet slipped from his arm. "Dear sir, there is no need that you should tell me. It was a great shamelessness, and Madam your mother had well schooled me for such a thing in Oxfordshire." Her English was good still, and only a little unready from its long disuse; the swift, familiar colour staining to her brows had brought back yesterday. Philip caught her hands, holding them warmly in his. "Is it possibly so long ago? But indeed to look at you I must think it twice my life away. Meg," he leaned down gently, "I must greet you indeed."

At the last minute she moved her head aside; the kiss fell on her cheek. "I—I have become too good a Frenchwoman for your English customs, sir." Her hands lay in his, as if belonging where he had taken them. He answered lightly, "But I claim the special privilege of friendship," and behind them a pleasant voice demanded, "My dear Lovell, do I find you already on terms with my wife? I have been wishing to present you this hour past, quite unnecessarily as I see."

Philip turned slowly. De Brezy stood genial in the aperture of the curtain, the boy Auguste like a sentinel at his shoulder, watching with suspicion and unconcealed mistrust the smile gone like a lamp blown out from the Englishman's eyes.

Somehow he forced a recover. "Your—your wife, monseigneur? But I did not—I had no idea—" He knew he was stammering and sounded a fool or worse. Margaret said quietly, "Sir Philip and I were old friends in England, monseigneur. He was a gracious host to me in Oxfordshire while my father was awaiting his pardon."

"Is it so indeed?" de Brezy rejoined casually. "Why then, this is a happy meeting." But a constraint had fallen, of which only he seemed unaware. The musicians having struck up again, one of the Burgoner knights appeared to solicit Madame de Brezy's hand; she looked at her husband first for permission, and with a last smile at Philip left them. Barely regarding her departure, de Brezy talked cheerfully on.

"I have been having a few words with the King: our Duke has sent him word he arrives within the week, and then, Lovell, we may expect to move! However, it is His Majesty's suggestion that my lord of Gloucester accompany his sister back to Saint Omer tomorrow, with certain of his captains. I remain in Calais to confer with His Majesty while he takes matters in hand here." The bland voice betrayed nothing, but Philip could not help a ghost of laughter. Edward was taking no chance of another shift in his brother-in-law's enthusiasms; the presence of the Duke of Gloucester in Saint Omer would be a powerful reminder of what England expected of the Duke of Burgundy. Thoughtfully sweeping the room with his gaze, de Brezy added presently, "Between ourselves, it is understood that Monsieur de Saint Pol has agreed to yield Saint Quentin without argument: a most excellent beginning. What useful beings traitors are, to be sure; God send King Louis a few more such and we can throw away our swords to go a-Maying in his fields."

No sharer in his father's optimism, Auguste remarked discontentedly, "I had rather fight the Frenchmen than buy their castles from them."

"Patience, my eater of fire, in good time you will blood that maiden sword. You are a Frenchman yourself, remember, and one day when the wind of Valois blows less strongly on Burgundy, we may all of us know it again. Do you not agree, Lovell?"

"Perfectly," Philip said ruefully. "And so pack us English home again. I can't think why you haven't finished the process long since."

"Little by little. What need of haste, when time is on our side? One day, look you, even this"—he waved a hand around the castle hall—"even this proud stronghold will go. Does it trouble you, Englishman?"

"Not a whit. Leave me my English fields—Frenchman—and I'll not pick a quarrel with you for your vineyards."

His back demonstrating his opinion, Auguste walked abruptly away, and de Brezy's shoulders shook. "*Beau fils*, I see your head on London Bridge. But I entreat you, have a care for my standing with Auguste: you have long been held his model for an Englishman, and he used to credit my judgment."

A summons from the King's dais took him away shortly after, and Philip, who had been watching without approval a young gallant's attempts to lure Margaret to walk in the passage beyond the hall, was pleased to intervene. "Walk, forsooth," he observed, as he handed her into an alcove seat and settled himself opposite. "I misdoubt the invitation, madame. The gentleman too much resembles my cousin Francis, who never took a lady to walk in his life." He had not thought until then she might find him officious; suddenly recalling, he added with a smile, "If I intrude, Meg, don't hesitate to inform me. I am reminded it is no longer my business to scold you for falling out of apple trees."

"It was not an apple tree,' she retorted. "And sir, I did not fall." Resting her head against the cushioned seatback, she met his eyes with unguarded pleasure. "How glad I am to talk with you again. Do you know, I tried from suppertime to make up my mind to it, before I came across the hall to speak? I was afraid—that too much time had passed, perhaps. You made me very happy in England."

"No more so than you us; the gatehouse hill looked bare with no one waiting, next time I came home. But that was a year after, and my lord your father had long taken you away."

She looked down, examining the embroidery of her skirt. "Yes. And you, sir? Have you a lady and babes now at Willowford?"

"I'm afraid not. Now, what have I said?" Her head had come round; she flushed at the amusement in his eyes.

"I only wondered. All gentlemen marry; it seems strange that you have not."

"I'm fortunate, having neither need for a dower nor the wish to populate a nursery," Philip said with a smile, and realised too late how he had blundered. Sick with contrition, he touched her hand. "Meg, forgive me. I had forgotten—I heard about the babe."

She let her fingers lie under his for a moment, then gently withdrew them. "Don't think of it. Even I do not, not often. How should I have grieved as I ought? From the beginning it was not my child: only Monseigneur's son to be given into his hands when the small trouble of my bearing him was done. It happened—it is finished—for my husband's sake I wish I could think there would be another time."

Philip watched the light come and go across her face, and his heart constricted. "Meg, truly he cannot be so hard—"

She looked round, regarding him with grave, shadowed eyes. "Hard? He waited years for that babe—he never even considered it might be a girl—but he has not reproached me. He is generous, and"—she faltered painfully—"not demanding. I'm grateful to him." But to Philip, remembering the eager affection of her child's hand reaching up to his, that was worst of all.

The Duchess of Burgundy returned next day to Saint Omer, escorted by her brothers the Dukes of Gloucester and Clarence; and there followed days of entertainment on a scale to open English eyes. Of the wandering Duke of Burgundy there remained no sign, but Earl Rivers came soon from Calais to increase the party, and his arrival was occasion for a tournament during which the talented Woodville exhibited his customary prowess—as if, Francis said acidly, King Louis were a thousand leagues away. Philip only shrugged and laughed. It was high summer, and warm as love; Richard told him smiling to take a holiday, and the days were not long enough to contain their succeeding pleasures. There were pageants, and feastings, and hunters' horns winding in the silver dawn: on other days more private rides through the dappled woods with Will Parker and Margaret's maid loitering behind, and perhaps a page with cushions for when they sat to eat. It was not her first visit to court, she said, but he had guessed that from what he had already seen; Madame de Brezy was a favourite with the Duchess of Burgundy, who liked to have her by her as much as the affairs of their husbands would allow. Sometimes in their excursions they met a woodcutter, or a farm girl leading a goat; they were Flemings and despised by their French masters, but Margaret knew their speech and always used it. She mentioned diffidently that Monseigneur would not care for such a thing if he knew, and Philip took the hint, being well able to believe her. After that he even tried to follow a word or two, but the attempts went slowly; complaining at length that it was a barbarous tongue, he was informed he lacked application, and apologised meekly, promising reform. That made her giggle, and the lesson came to an end.

They had eaten picnic fashion in a beech-ringed glade, and he stretched himself on the grass, his chin on his arms. The brown and green of trampled stalks and the grey of little pebbles were all mixed, Margaret thought, in his eyes; it was only in the shadows they went dark. Catching her glance, he said smiling, "You put me in mind of the Duchess of Gloucester: she also laughs with her eyes. I used to wonder at Middleham where I'd seen it before."

"I accept the compliment," she returned demurely. "They say you are her chevalier."

"They should try saying it to the Duke of Gloucester: we don't specialise in courts of love in Yorkshire. I carry her colours sometimes in the jousting—Gloucester doesn't waste his time on such matters."

Sunlight sifting through the trees checkered a pattern across his face, and he turned his profile against the brightness. One hand lay unmoving among the green blades, slender and muscular, with the wide, disproportionate grip between thumb and forefinger which had had generations of Lovells sending its model in glove or wax across Europe to the armourers of Augsburg or Milan, only for a gauntlet that would match the pattern. His cousin Francis', she had noticed, were the same. With her gaze on the slackened fingers, she said suddenly, "Is it true you refused a barony when the Duke of Gloucester offered it?"

Philip said briefly, "Gloucester doesn't offer baronies."

"Well, the King does. It only needed a word from the Duke."

"I daresay." Half-annoyed, he moved his head to look at her. "Where in the world did you hear that?"

"The Duke tells the story himself; he seemed amused, your cousin said." Margaret leaned her cheek on her wrist, pulling slowly at the strong, tough stems. "Why did you refuse?"

"Vanity, most like," he answered humorously. "It pleases me to think I need take no gifts from him. A towering conceit, which fortunately I live inexpensively enough to be able to afford."

A companionable silence fell, broken only by the whispered coursing of the stream which traversed the glade, running with hardly a ripple between banks of drenched reed and overhanging willow boughs. The maid Marthe dozed beside the emptied wallets, and some way off young Will lay patiently above the catkins, brow creased with concentration under his fringe of dust-fair hair, a hook and line produced from his jerkin dangling in the water. It would be evening in an hour, Philip realised, but the sun was like a tender hand between his shoulders, holding him where he was until the last of it should be gone.

Something white moved on the stream beyond the willows, and through a screen of boughs they saw jewel-bright eyes fixed upon them. They signed to each other and waited, but in a little the stirring branches hung motionless again. With his cheek on his arms, Philip said smiling, "Do you remember the ducks at Willowford? You thought them swans, never having known either before, and looked to see them turned back to princesses by moonlight, until the dairy girl explained why you should cease watching for the miracle. I was angry for her not telling you more kindly, but I daresay it was just she had never thought." He reached down to trail his fingers in the water. "A great time ago, it seems now."

His arm lay across her skirt, the linen shirt sleeve pushed carelessly from the wrist as he leaned down the bank. Margaret watched the foaming eddies spread and sink away, and drew her skirt free. "It does seem so. We must go; it will be dark soon."

Far off in Saint Omer, the abbey church of Saint Bertin was sounding the day's end with complin. He rose reluctantly, and calling to Parker went to fetch the horses. Marthe had shaken the wallets on the grass; as they mounted and took the path which led from the clearing, the swans issued cautiously from their sanctuary among the willows and lumbered up the bank, looking for crumbs.

It was next evening that the Duke of Burgundy arrived in Saint Omer. He was accompanied by only a handful of knights, having left his army to its own enjoyable devices in Lorraine, but the circumstance had not embarrassed him. The English army, he pronounced coolly, was more than enough to meet and destroy King Louis' Frenchmen, and, that accomplished, it would be easy to drive across Louis' wasted dominions and make contact with Burgundian forces in Lorraine. That it was Louis who had already done the wasting—his campaign of the winter before had so razed the countryside that the English would find little to sustain them as they passed—seemed to have no part in the Duke's calculations; and Richard found him evading even the question of which of his towns he would permit his allies to enter on their march south, pleading for excuse the dislike of the citizens for foreign troops. Alternately exasperated and unbelieving, and plagued by a tertian fever which had come upon him in Saint Omer and grown steadily more troublesome with recurrence, Richard lost no time in hurrying the Duke to Calais for counsel with Edward. There Charles explained once more his design for victory; and behind his back the brothers exchanged glances. The matter of the Count of Saint Pol's mooted treachery was touched upon, and in the face of such willingness to surrender Louis' fortress of Saint Quentin, Edward allowed that the first step should be for him to march through Artois to occupy that important stronghold: following which there must be further deliberations. Since the affair at Saint Quentin was to be no more than a transfer of French authority to English, he added, with a glance at his brother's flushed cheekbones, that he would leave my lord of Gloucester with some few gentlemen in Saint Omer, to represent English interest in the Duke of Burgundy's councils. Charles accepted the provision with grace, and bore his brothers-in-law from Calais to consolidate the alliance with a last flourish of hospitality.

Having delegated to his brother Richard the role of watchdog over the Duke of Burgundy's good intentions, Edward permitted himself to be entertained in Saint Omer. They dined into the evening, magnificently and at length, with the King of England and his brothers enthroned by Charles and his Duchess, and dancers and tumblers caracolling between the boards. Burgundy, indeed, was showing itself anxious to placate; to Edward, Richard remarked under his breath that he would have foregone with pleasure the battalion of physicians and leeches with which Charles was promising to surround him, in exchange for roofs over his soldiers' heads in the autumn rains.

Next day they hunted, rising at daybreak to start the hare from the corn and follow with crossbows, French fashion, the harriers yelling before. Francis, going early from the room he shared with Philip to ask how the Duke of Gloucester did that morning, discovered him yet abed and refusing to participate in the sport: a disinclination Philip announced himself as sharing, when his cousin returned to find him still among the pillows. He had promised to take Meg hawking, he said, and the others might go chasing the hare without him. Francis regarded the truant without expression for an instant before he said briefly, "Just as you please, of course," and made his departure.

It was a not wholly successful excursion from which in due course Philip and Margaret returned, having been marred at the outset by a small unpleasantness which, it seemed to Philip, spread like a sourness forward through all the day. He entered her apartments while the morning was yet early, to find her not emerged from dressing. The bedroom door was open a crack; waiting by the window while the servants of the privy chamber came and went around him, he heard de Brezy's voice: "But it is your business to attend the Duchess; it is expected, and you should not fail in your duty. Had I known she rode with her brother this day, I should have charged you—" There was an interval while Margaret said something too low to hear, and her husband spoke again: "I am sure she gave leave, and as for the lad, the case is different; his work is yet to come, and from what I hear he has earned his leisure. But it is otherwise with you, no matter how easy Madame may be. Next time, remember."

Philip was staring fixedly out the window when the door swung wide, and de Brezy came out. He was in hose and doublet with the sleeves flung back, his shirt half-showing at the neck, and the strong light made furrows of the lines about his mouth. "So then, you go abroad for quarry of your own this morning, Lovell? The day promises fair too." The chill correction of the inner room might never have been. Philip hesitated, uncertain; and over de Brezy's shoulder he caught Margaret's glance. Smiling, he replied, "I am told prodigies of your French game, monseigneur, and must be proved every claim. Come with us, and see scepticism confounded."

De Brezy laughed, and jerked a thumb towards the bedroom. "I have the morning already spent. Good fortune, *fils*." There was a table with lists and maps, and a guttered candle standing among the litter, evidence of the previous night's labour. The bed was in a tumble still, his jerkin lying where he had discarded it at the foot. He had come from Calais with Edward the day before, and worked privately at Charles' plans until evening; Philip had forgotten he must be back in Saint Omer.

It was striking nine as they rode out of the city gates, Will Parker and the falconer, the maid, pages, and dogs, all trooping behind. Margaret was very gay, making no reference to what had passed, and Philip silently accepted the restriction; he knew she was ashamed he had heard, and there was nothing he could say that would not be fatuous, or disloyal, or a lie. They had good, if unspectacular sport, loosing their birds at small game along the riverbank, during which time he set himself to making her merry in truth, and as the hours passed it appeared to him that he had succeeded. Falconer and children went home, laden with spoil, but clear of the woods there was light enough still for a racing canter across the flats which an hour later the deep cuts of streams and ditches would make treacherous going. They took them easily, Parker and the maid falling gradually behind, until the sun sank behind the round polls of the trees, and, pulling up before a claybanked rivulet from which Margaret's mare was doubtfully sidling, Philip leaned over to catch her hands on the reins, saying half joking, "No." The place was too wide for jumping; yet he was only partly sure she had not meant to try. She sat motionless, breathing a little fast and gazing down at his hand lightly closed on hers; suddenly her mouth worked and she looked away, saying in a tight voice, "Sir, be so good as to release my hands."

Disconcerted, he let her go. He thought he might have hurt her; then, hotly embarrassed, he remembered the hard instruction of the morning. "Meg, I didn't mean—" But she wheeled the mare so quickly the clay flew in clods under the scrabbling hoofs, and, beckoning her woman to follow, spurred for the distant city walls. Will Parker came up to join them with Marthe, putting privacy at an end; in the courtyard as they dismounted Philip tried once more, but, resisting the coaxing pressure of his fingers, Margaret pulled her hand free and with her face turned from him went quickly inside.

Dinner had begun hours before, but there was to be dancing after; it was the last evening Edward would spend in Saint Omer. Erard de Brezy having returned before him to Calais, he had left word for his wife that he wished her to be present, and there would be those, Margaret knew, that would make sure he learned she had not been in the hall to dine. The greater portion of her mind could not even be brought to care. Bathed and freshly gowned, her face new-painted and gillyflower water touched to her wrists and breasts, as she descended the stair she was thinking only of Philip, whom she had grieved for no deed of his, and wondering if he would be there for her to speak to, or if he would come later, or if, being required by the Duke of Gloucester, he might not come at all.

The tables had been taken away when she entered the hall, and some couples were dancing a torch dance. Beyond the circling figures and their burning staffs she saw Philip, cheerful as a day in spring, with his cousin and one of the Duchess of Burgundy's ladies, the three appearing wholly engrossed in conversation. It was, in point of fact, the first time since his arrival in the hall that Philip had removed his eyes from its entrance, but the instant sufficed. When, a minute later, he took another surreptitious look around the room, he was permitted an excellent view of Madame de Brezy's enchanting profile as she yielded her hand to Lord Rivers to kiss. The studied deliberation in the tilt of her chin stung as the afternoon's wretched business had never done; after an instant Philip turned away. The next time Margaret stole a glance in his direction he was laughing with Robert Percy over some absurdity, and clearly undisposed towards any change of society. Her throat tightened; the polished compliments of the Queen of England's brother sounded no more than a jangle of inanities, and the dancers' bright flambeaux smelt revoltingly of pitch.

They were quenched at length; the players in the gallery tuned for the next turn; and everywhere gentlemen who had been watching were looking for ladies to invite out upon the floor. From the tail of her eye Margaret glimpsed Philip's profile, immovable against a tapestry of Jason in Colchis, and in bitterness of disappointment set herself to teaching the recreant a lesson in good earnest. Lord Hastings strolled over to dispute, he said, Tony Rivers' right of continued place—he was near neighbour to Lord Devereux in Lancashire, he told her cheerfully, and deserved better of his daughter than such slighting—and the pleasure of filling to overflow the noxious cup of punishment came when Edward of York leaned sideways to an attendant to request, in an undertone, the presence of Madame de Brezy by his chair. On bended knees before the velvet-spread dais, Margaret let her gaze go fleetingly beyond it, and had the satisfaction of observing that she had claimed Philip Lovell's undivided attention at last.

Turning a defiant back, she settled herself in the seat which Edward graciously indicated at his right. The musicians were playing a basse-dance; in a little while he led her out, modifying his very long steps to her short ones, and smiling appreciatively at her flushed preoccupation with, presumably, the correctness of the occasion. The hall was warm, and there were doors open wide to the summer night; suddenly turning aside, Edward drew her after him to the moonlit terrace beyond. A short way removed from the lightstreams of the windows, a stone bench carved with crouching beasts was discreetly set; and it was there, sitting in the shadows with Edward lounging beside her, his arm stretched along the high back of the seat, that Margaret awoke from her trance.

Unaffected by his companion's abrupt silence, Edward thoughtfully surveyed her. He knew quite well that Erard de Brezy lay that night in Calais: a convenient circumstance, if his bewitching little wife fulfilled expectation. The moonlight showed the young firmness of cheek and mouth, and her fingers gripping the couchant leopards of the bench's arm; following the gesture with his lazy eyes, Edward said softly, "Madame, you have England under your hand."

The hand removed itself quickly to join the other in her lap. "Your majesty is kind."

"Kind? Why no, belle: it is for you to be kind." He bent nearer, taking her averted face between his palms. "You are the fairest thing I have seen since I came to France."

She had not thought there could be so much difference in the touch of a man's finger. Her skin tingled as if with cold, then grew hot again with the direction of his gaze; trying to draw the veil of her headdress across her breasts, she lost the stuff in the gusting breeze, and as she snatched for it Edward calmly lifted the chased links of the necklace around her throat. Closely examining the work, he remarked at length, "A handsome bauble," and restored it carefully to its earlier position. She sat rigid, searching for words, and when he dropped his arm to her shoulders tried to pull back. "Please, you mistake, I did not mean—"

He laughed and slipped a hand to her breast. "Belle, I have

not known a lady, scarcely, that in the beginning did not—quite—mean. Courteously now, faintheart: that mouth was meant for kissing—" She fought the embrace, desperately afraid; his practised grip compelled her face upward, then all at once slackened and was gone. Behind them a step had sounded.

Hardly crediting the reprieve, Margaret shrank back. Edward waited an instant, looking beyond her, before he said deliberately, "You are inopportune, Sir Philip."

His expression a mixture of astonishment and embarrassed, if belated, deference, Philip halted a few paces off, and then came forward to drop on his knee. "Your grace, a thousand pardons, I was seeking the cruellest lady in Burgundy; I had no thought I should find her in your highness' company."

Relaxed, Edward considered him with faint amusement. "Well sir, you have done so. Madame, like David of old, numbers her slain in ten thousands."

"Manifestly, dread lord."

There was a pause. A knowledgeable courtier would have taken himself off without delay, but the intruder seemed tiresomely unfamiliar with the canon. Once more turning to the woman beside him, Edward said curtly, "I wish you all good fortune, Sir Philip, another time. For the present I fear the gods do not smile."

The dismissal was absolute; incredibly, the younger man did not move. "Your grace"—an outstretched hand entreated the impatient attention—"your grace, I beg for judgment. See in what case I find myself! Not an hour since, Madame charged me upon pain of her eternal displeasure to present myself to her for the galliard, and even now the musicians are striking up. I have pledged her my word I am her slave: am I to be foresworn?"

Edward swung round, his eyes hardening in slow, unbelieving wrath, but the disarming smile did not waver. "Sire, you are the very fount of chivalry. I pray you, be my judge."

In the deadly quiet Margaret leaned before him, her arms flung out in protection and appeal. "Of your pity, sire, do not heed him! He is mad, or drunk—"

Her voice broke in weeping. Ignoring her, Edward said slowly, "By Saint Anne, Lovell, you're a bold man." His glance shifted almost imperceptibly to the girl, white with despair, and back again, dissecting and appraising the compact, hard-muscled grace of body, the steady insistence behind the open, ingenuous gaze; and like some foreign burden he felt his own thickened girth. The time had been when his gay cloaked farings through London had persuaded half the city wives, all unsuspecting, from their virtue; but his body had betrayed him, and he got his pleasures unknown no more.

He looked back at Margaret, mutely imploring him, and his mouth twisted. He had always liked to be thought gallant with a woman. She was, moreover, Erard de Brezy's wife, and he was beginning to understand her to be unwilling in very truth. Putting a finger beneath her chin, he said lightly, "Belle, you have made a promise. In honour I must concede the prior claim."

Philip straightened, expressionless, and extended his hand. "Madame?" Her touch was icy; she rose wordlessly, gathering her skirts around her. Impassively watching, Edward remarked, "There was an occasion at Barnet when you did my lord of Gloucester service, Sir Philip. I waited long for you to claim reward of me, but it was my brother's opinion that you lack ambition."

"It must be so, your grace."

The heavy lip curled. "It is as well. I pay my just debts, sir: but only once." Their eyes met; then with a flicked gesture Edward glanced away. "You have leave, Sir Philip."

Her gown whispered on the grass as they crossed the terrace, rounded a corner, and so passed from his sight. The hall door lay a distance off yet, and the jouncing beat of pipes and tabors came fitfully with the night breeze, now clear, now thin and far, half-lost in the sea sound of the trees. In the deep shade of a copse of them Philip paused, and without turning said in a strained voice, "Wait here a little. We will have to go in soon, and you must smile. Is your dress—is it torn?"

Shuddering, Margaret said, "No." There was a ledge, formed where the tree's trunk gnarled and divided; he led her to it, and stood waiting while she sat. She looked up, trying to read his face, but the darkness was complete, and he had withdrawn his hand. After an instant she said, "You've ruined yourself. If there were one thing I could say—but it was all my doing, my folly."

"You must not think that. On my soul, there is nothing in

194

his gift that I have ever desired; and for the rest, how could you deal with such a circumstance? You should not have been left unguarded to the risk—but it may be Monseigneur trusted me to watch over you. Yes, undoubtedly that was it." A long silence followed, while she saw only the outline of his shoulders as he stared across the terrace. The sense of an inward turmoil, sudden and shocking, came strongly to her; but she could not feel its substance. After a little he turned and walked back to her, saying with great gentleness, "Are you quite well now? We should not stay here longer." She realised he was offering his arm for her to rise, and drew back, shaking. "I don't want to go in there—not yet—"

"Meg, you must. Already it is too long since you were seen leaving in his company; a little more and nothing will keep it from Monseigneur. You must show yourself, and quickly."

Blindly groping, their hands met. Her heart lurched; but he only guided her fingers lightly back to lie on his wrist. "Come, now."

She had no choice but to follow. He had spoken plain truth of her danger, and very soon she came to know it; the tentative, amused curiosity in the faces of the women, the speculative looks of the Westminster courtiers, were brutal reminder of what observation attended Edward's favour. Alternately cold and fever-warm, Margaret let herself be drawn across the threshold, where Philip lingered to exchange commonplaces with some French acquaintances before strolling on into the hall. Francis encountered his eye, and made his way over to join him; the silent message which passed between them was unnecessary, for he had been unobtrusively watching the terrace door ever since his cousin's departure through it a few minutes before. He was in high spirits, having just come from an audience with the Duchess of Burgundy, and was inclined to make parade of the distinction—"Faith, coz, there's a general for you; pity her husband can't stay at home and let her lead his armies for him. Is it true the Bishop of Cambrai is her lover?" Philip said blandly, "I've no notion: Surely your magnificence knows her well enough to ask?" Percy arrived in time to add his mite to the chastening, and several English who had paused to listen smiled as they turned away.

Margaret hardly heard the bantering voices. Dimly she understood that something was changing around her—even the women no longer whispered and stared—but for all she knew from what Philip was saving her, she did not care. She was conscious only of his arm beneath her hand, and his talk, light and continual, that was like a wall springing higher by the moment between them; and she thought her husband might punish her and welcome, if only Philip would look down at her, and be silent, and become himself again. It was in her mind that he must be angry despite all disclaimer, and was only troubling himself on her behalf because he had once had a naughty child in his charge, and felt responsible for her still. The blazing circles of the chandeliers hurt her eyes; she was sick and trembling with shame and hurt and grief, and wanted only a place to be quiet in where she could weep.

Endlessly later the high dais stood vacant at last; Charles and his wife and guests had withdrawn to sleep. Philip, unnoticing, was engaged with some friends; through the confusion of jests and laughter Margaret whispered, "Please, I can't any more—" They were standing near the entrance to the hall; it seemed impossible he would not understand and follow. A short way down the corridor she paused, leaning against a painted column while she waited for his step. But there was no sound except her catching breath, and when she looked back, the doorway was empty.

Early next morning Edward departed for Calais. Richard, who had arisen more briskly than in days, rode with him part of the way, and the afternoon was advancing before he returned to Saint Omer. Philip had not been among the few who attended him, and it was with faint surprise that the Duke found him waiting when he entered his apartments. He was leaning by the open window which overlooked the bustling courtyard and green prospect of fields beyond the walls; Richard came to stand beside him, remarking, "Pleasant, isn't it? We'll have to grow used to our ease, I fancy. Better send into England for your dogs and hawks, Philip: there'll be leisure to employ them."

Still gazing down, Philip said restrainedly, "I was wondering about that very thing. Are we to be fast here so long, my lord?"

"Several weeks anyway. It will be a time before the King establishes himself at Saint Quentin, and he wants us here until then." Richard went to help himself from the flagon of wine on the dresser. After a short silence Philip said, "In the circumstances, then, can you spare me from your service for that time? I had it in mind to go back to Calais: I could be with you again within the month."

Lowering the cup, Richard stared at him. "To Calais? Name of God, for what reason? The place will be emptied once the King has marched."

"I have interests in the Staple; my steward is discontented with the merchant who deals for us since the last clip went over, and I promised to look into it if there should be time. I can't see much to keep me here."

Deeply frowning, Richard came back to the window. "There's a better reason than my maladies for our presence here, Philip. Burgundy has mishandled his affairs so there's no knowing when he may decide to cry quits with Louis and try for his own terms with him. By remaining here, we prevent any such experimenting on his part, and discourage him from suspecting us of the same intention. We cannot trust him, and we cannot allow him to begin to mistrust us."

After a moment Philip said, "I see." It was a cold, sunless day; in the merciless grey light the tired lines added years to his face. "I don't see how my absence should arouse his suspicions. Could he really care if I choose to spend the next fortnight looking at a woolman's accounts in Calais?"

"I believe if I were the Duke, I should very much doubt that was what you were doing," Richard observed reflectively. "It wouldn't be the first time you'd attended to some private business for me, and if you suppose my brother-in-law doesn't know it, you're in error." He glanced sideways at the set profile, a mixture of amusement and affection in his eyes. "Are you chafing, Philip? If it's a change you want, you could always ask Erard de Brezy if you might go with him when he leaves on Thursday; he got back from Calais today. The Duke is sending him to drag some order into that foolery in Lorraine; I daresay he'd be glad of your company, though I shouldn't have thought freebooting in the south would be your idea of a summer's recreation."

Philip moved abruptly, picking up Richard's discarded goblet from the window ledge to turn and replace it on the ornately decorated chest. "No, it's not." He was silent for a minute, slowly revolving the cup between his palms. The carved goblin faces watched him mockingly from the polished wood. "It's Thursday he goes, then? I hadn't realized it would be so soon."

The door opened to admit a page, bearing sheets, sponges, and steaming basins of herbs, and followed by a small procession of servants carrying vessels of hot water. They went on to the bedchamber beyond, where a covered bath had been already drawn up before the fire, and, yawning, Richard came away from the window. A squire emerged from the inner room and knelt to assist in the removal of the Duke's dusty boots. With a quizzical look at Philip, unmoving beside the chest, Richard remarked, "It might do for Middleham, Philip, but if you propose to sit down to dine here in that attire, I cannot answer for the consequences. If you won't consider my brother-in-law's feelings, only reflect upon mine. Will you shame us all without one jewel?"

Glancing down at his plain doublet and hose, Philip seemed to rouse from a dream. "With your permission, my lord, I'll excuse myself from the hall today. I've an errand—that is—Will can find me something later." He went out blindly, letting the ushers close after him.

There were many ways in which a gentleman of means might occupy himself in Saint Omer, and during the ensuing weary days it seemed to Philip that he had tried them all. It was years since he had enjoyed such leisure; in England he had been busy with the Duke of Gloucester's affairs, and it was an irony that now, with days on end in which to pursue his own fancy, he had never so longed for the distraction of employment. Even to keep to his own chamber was impossible; from rise to set of sun the pastimes commanded him, pageants and farings-forth strewing the hours like burrs: varied, ubiquitous, and inescapable. Some of the women amused themselves with a court of love, arguing exactly and at length such heavy matters as whether a gentleman, cast off by his mistress, should be free to love another, and the precise duration of service requisite before granting of the naked embrace. Francis went to watch and listen, and came away saying he had as lief lie with the Chief Justice himself, and the earnest pleader identified as Sweet Speech could only have been Rob.

It was next day, while the decisions of the ladies' court were still under debate, that a diversion offered in the request of two burghers for the judgment of battle in an affair of honour. The complaint of the one and the defence of the other was of no concern to the Burgundian nobles, who nevertheless gathered to witness with fascination the spectacle of two Flemish tradesmen settling their quarrel by armed combat. As a display it could not compare with the judicial duel whereby the French patricians regularly adjusted their differences, but to Philip, an unwilling observer in the stands, there seemed just as much blood. In the skill and quickness of the formal joust he had a certain professional interest, but the only attraction in the present affray was the repulsive novelty of seeing two men trying to pound each other to death. By the time one of them appeared near succeeding, and the loser, his cudgel flung away, had been dragged with jeers and catcalls from the lists, Philip was already slipping off. Percy shouted to him to stay for the cockfight which a few of them had arranged as conclusion to the afternoon's pleasure; Philip, shaking his head, turned to pass between the tiers of benches and saw Margaret, two rows above, sitting behind a silk-hung barrier with the Duchess of Burgundy's ladies.

They had not been so near since the evening before Edward went back to Calais. For a space of years, across the frieze of heads their eyes clung; and then the constable's heralds came to the centre of the field, proclaiming the victor's name and the justice of his cause; everyone stood to applaud, and the Duchess' gallery was blocked from sight.

Philip went on down to the horsepark. To Will his squire, he said in a voice that seemed not quite his own that he would require him no more that day, and, mounting, rode off alone towards Saint Omer.

His absence from supper that night passed unnoticed by his friends, of whom he saw no more until Percy and some others returned with Francis after dining to the chamber which the younger man shared with his cousin. An argument had flourished at intervals since the cockfight, when Percy had unwisely laid his money on a bird who had displayed his whitefeathers after less than five minutes' fight, and the discussion was warming. Francis, who had reaped a handsome profit from Percy's mistake, left it to his companions to garnish the wound, coming instead to the settle by the chimney. Philip was standing with one foot on the raised hearth, his eyes on the empty grate, and after a glance in his direction Francis picked up a dice box, leaned back in his seat, and threw a main.

"Never put your money on a grey gamecock, Rob," one of Percy's tormentors was advising provocatively. "Pigeon livered, every one of 'em. Now, if it had been the dun—"

In the flurry of demur that followed, Percy took grateful second place to a number of affronted partisans. Heedless of the din, Philip went to the dresser to fill a cup of wine, and Francis threw the dice again. Detaching himself at last from the disputants, Percy said with a yawn, "Well, I'll come to you for advice next time, Ratcliffe. You're bound to have it: you always do." He walked over to Philip, remarked briskly, "Greedy guts," and helped himself unasked to the flagon. Half-smiling, Philip pushed him a cup. Percy drank, wiped his mouth, and turned away, saying with a touch of sour humour, "I've had my fill of the Burgoners' hospitality this day. There's a tavern near Saint Sepulchre with as good nut brown as any I've tasted since England— What's the hour?"

"Struck nine, past," Francis murmured.

Percy hesitated, debating. Philip emptied his goblet, started to refill it, and, changing his mind, went to the window. It was a thick, sultry evening without a breeze to stir the heavy air, and on the edge of the sky lightning flickered. To Percy, he said suddenly, "If you're going, Rob, I'll bear you company."

Percy nodded amiably and turned to the door. "I'll tell my lad to take himself to bed. So soon as I'm back, then?'

He went out. Stretching, Richard Ratcliffe commented, "Plague if I don't think it a good notion. By God, if we're to dangle our heels here another month, I'll be wishing myself with de Brezy."

"The last of his company went today: why don't you ask the Duke's leave to follow them?" It was Assheton speaking, a lank, shrewd-eyed northerner, long in the Duke of Gloucester's service. Ratcliffe shrugged, and laughed. "I should think the Duke has his own plans." He ruminated, scratching his head. "Today, you said, Ralph? I thought he was gone since Thursday last."

Assheton chuckled and made a gesture. "Gone, but not hotfoot to Lorraine just at first, from what I've heard. He had the bastard with him; there was a visit to Bruges, I'll warrant." He saw the others were looking puzzled, and grinned again. "Didn't you know? He has his leman there—or so she was once—the bastard's mother. Very splendidly he keeps her too, they say."

"Domestic little arrangement," Ratcliffe said lazily.

"Very. He's had her more than twenty years, doubtless at one time for more than Messire Auguste's sake. Mahaut of the swan neck, she was called: Haven't you heard the story? She was Sluter's daughter, the wool merchant, a rich man of standing. It was in the old Duke's time; one of his favourites noticed the girl and carried her off. There being no help to be expected from the Duke, Sluter went to de Brezy, who'd a better name for his dealings with the Flemings, and very quickly the favourite yielded his trove. Unfortunately for Sluter though, de Brezy also found the maiden exceeding fair. He'd just buried his first wife, so I daresay he was ready for a diversion; he was even faithful to her for a while, it's said."

"Well, he's provided well for her son, anyway," Ratcliffe commented. From the settle Francis said abruptly, "Come and throw with me, Ralph." He could see his cousin immobile at the window, his white shirt a pale, luminous blur against the darkening sky.

Amused, Assheton returned, "Why shouldn't he be generous?—it's all the issue he's like to have now. God knows where the lands will go in the end; he must gnash his teeth over that. Still, he's done royally for the bastard and hardly less for Mahaut—and Madame keeps lonely in her chamber. Faith, I'd go sit with her."

He cracked a nut. The door opened as Percy came back, and Philip swung round to pick up his jerkin. Ratcliffe said carelessly, "Philip, I'll make one of your party, if Rob will contract not to lesson me on the choosing of a cock."

Struggling into the jacket, Philip did not look up. He said curtly, "I've changed my mind. Dick will go with you in my place, Rob—Francis, I'll not be long."

His chin on his knees, Francis responded, "I am not your warder, cousin," but Philip had gone.

The garden was empty, although light still shafted across it from the mullioned windows. He went through and mounted the outer stair, walking far from the inner wall to avoid the patches of brightness lying in oblongs across the gallery. At its farther end a double set of panes was pushed wide. He stood watching from the shadow, then sat on the low sill, saying, "Will you have company for an hour, Meg?"

The maid was with her, doing something to her hair; she started at his voice and then gaped, open-mouthed to shriek. Margaret touched her wrist and replied smiling, "Very willingly. Bring wine, Marthe." She had not risen, but her hand went out to him; it was as if the week just gone had never been. The servant stared again, her eyes round with surprise, and of a sudden twinkled with delight. Hurrying fruit and drink from the cupboard, she caught up a half-sewn gown and, dropping many curtsies, backed swiftly from the room.

A shade uneasy, Philip said, "Will she—?" Margaret shook her head. "Not a syllable, I promise you." But they had both coloured faintly. They were in the innermost chamber of her apartments where he had not come before; it was a large room with woollen rugs on a floor of unpolished marble, and one great tapestry of a knight on horseback before a stag, with small forest creatures and bright flowers all thick between the charger's arrested hoofs. Philip nodded towards it, observing lightly, "You keep solemn company. I thought ladies' bowers were always hung with tales of Lancelot and Guinevere, or maybe a garden with maidens harping."

"I had rather this, it came with me from Saint Aubin. I always liked Saint Hubert since that picture; the violets are like your English woods." She picked up a book lying beside her and held it out. "Do you remember this? You brought it for me from London, the year I stayed with you at Willowford. It was the first gift anyone had given me in my life; we were too poor for such things in Bruges, even if it had come into my father's head to think of it."

Philip took it slowly. "I remember. You wept, and I could not imagine why. Poor little maid, they were hard times for you. And did you never see the north, that should have made it up to you?"

"No. My father has three sons now: the eldest is named for him. The Duchess of Burgundy heard of it and told me, last time she had letters out of England."

He could find nothing to say. He looked from the folio in his hand, a little crumpled now for all the plain care with which it had been guarded, and back again to the bright tapestry, like a wood in spring blooming for joy of itself in the shadowed room; and he was thinking there are people that are born to love, and will do it though their hearts have had no more to spend themselves upon than a pet dog, or a bird.

Her eyes still on the book, Margaret said, "I had never seen a bestiary before. I loved most the fabulous monsters, the cockatrice and the griffin and the manticore, that has the body of a lion and the face of a man with fiery eyes. I used to see you a knight going forth with a sword to slay them in my honour at a stroke."

He could feel her smile. Keeping his gaze on the gaily coloured pages, Philip said after a moment, "It was only copyist's work, I'm afraid; in those days my purse didn't run to what the brothers do. I was in some hesitation about it because your father had so much better."

A silence fell. The candles flickered in the draft and grew still; the wide bed with its heavy curtains stood half-lost in darkness at the other end of the room, the servant's little pallet pulled out ready at the foot. She must return to sleep in a very little; the other women would wonder if she stayed much longer with them in the outer chamber. Putting the folio aside, Philip went over to the reading desk. A massive volume lay open; amused, he said, "The Confessions? A heavy choice for a woman, surely."

She answered with an impish expression, "My father did not consider my understanding to be, of that reason, an imperfect one. I came to Augustine quite early. I remember you saying once that although it was not always possible to agree with him, there were few things of the human mind beyond his comprehending, and it was better to argue with him than to find comfortable accord with a whole library of others."

Sitting on the chest, she leaned back on her wrists to look up at him. The maid had laid her headdress by, and through the jewelled net which confined it her hair gleamed like night water under torchlight. Her eyes rested on his, undissembling, withholding nothing; and it came to him that this was easier in truth for her, having already consented with her soul to all he had striven in his to deny. Her clear gaze saw his mind as transparently as if he had spoken; indeed, she had understood it before himself.

For a heartbeat he was motionless, staring down at the book on the desk. The passionate, inflexible prose ran on, its delicate black script broken by the blaze of fantastically garlanded capitals: "But in these things is no place of repose; they abide not, they flee, and who can follow them with the senses of the flesh? For the sense of the flesh is slow ... It sufficeth for that it was made for; but it sufficeth not to stay things running their course from their appointed starting place to the end appointed."

The vellum leaves rustled as he turned them, the only sound in the charged stillness of a moment towards which he had moved, half knowing, all the hours of the day. He shut the book and knelt beside her on the chest, stooping his face to her mouth.

Her lips parted under his kiss. For long they clung together, contented only with the touch of hands and mouths, the warmth of their bodies shaping each to the other through the stuff of clothes. At last without speaking he lifted her and carried her to the bed. The curtains were looped back; he put her down among the pillows, and drew the hangings close after them, and lay down beside her in the dark.

CHAPTER THIRTEEN

" 'Lord Lovell stands at the stable door,
Combing his milk-white steed—' "

FRANCIS leaned sideways, balancing the lute on his knees, and, intercepting the garland being proffered across his legs, turned to bestow it blandly upon the intended recipient. Entertained, the lady directed a perfunctory smile of consolation at the original donor, still kneeling in discomfited admiration, and said, "Monsieur Francis, you are a villain to rob another gentleman of his tribute. Are they all pirates in England, then?"

"No, madame, it comes over us only in Burgundy," Francis retorted promptly, and disposed himself at her feet. They were in the garden, the women bent over needlework or playing at cards, the few Englishmen attentive around them. From the trumpet vines along the wall came a drone of bees, bumping among the flowers; for weeks there had been hardly a drop of rain, and the air was like honey, thick and golden, heavy with warmth and the long dream of summer. Like the country of lotus eaters in the old tale, Francis reflected sardonically. The lute strings twanged sharply as he laid the instrument down, and across the circle Margaret said, "You have not finished your song, monsieur. Was he an ancestor of yours, this Lord Lovell?"

"Very probably, madame: he was a great rogue and a very neglectful lover. The lady had cause to complain of him." Indolently stretching, Francis contemplated her with a smile. "Though it's not an invariable family failing."

She neither blushed nor simpered, regarding him with candid, unwavering eyes; and in a minute it was he who looked away. Her forthrightness disconcerted him, suggesting as it did a thing out of his knowledge or experience: if they had named her from the market cross, he thought, she would not care. Restlessly working his fingers through the matted turf, Francis wondered how soon it must be before others noticed what, to him, had long been so plain. She was like a flower that has opened to the sun; as for his cousin, coming and going like a shadow in the hours before the dawn, he might have been some wanderer from Merlin's isle, so remote from earth, so wrapped in enchantment he seemed. At least one person that Francis knew of had already guessed; once, rousing in the unshared bed as the first birds woke outside the window, he had risen anxiously on one elbow to hear if Philip might be coming, and saw between the parted curtains Will Parker, wide awake on his pallet and watching like himself the growing light. Their eyes met; but neither spoke.

There were footsteps beyond the garden wall. The gate swung in, and Francis said lightly, "Give you greeting, cousin. So you're back again? How goes it at Saint Quentin?"

"Badly: Saint Pol has changed his mind again. The King wanted discussion with his captains." Philip came down the path to the little group under the laburnums. Amused in spite of himself, Francis noticed he managed to find a place not too far from Margaret, sinking to the grass with his arms around his knees.

"Gloucester's wasted no time on the road, you've hardly been gone a week," Assheton remarked. "So Saint Pol wouldn't yield the town after all? Pest on the traitor: he's as fickle as a woman." A teasing look upward pacified the ruffling beauty beside him. "So what's toward now? There'll be warm work at Saint Quentin, the next while."

"Oh, they only meant to have it if it was going free. For the while they're in camp outside Péronne." Philip turned as Margaret leaned down, snatching after the heap of silk which was cascading from her lap. "If you will permit me, madame?" He helped her retrieve the pile; swiftly, furtively, beneath the stuff their fingers touched. Merciful God, Francis thought inadequately, and sat up with a jerk. Picking up the lute again, he applied himself to tightening a string, and one of the women said brightly, "You'll be glad to have returned today, Messire Philip: there's to be a fête tonight, and the Master of Revels has promised to show us Hercules conquering the dragon with live birds coming from his mouth."

Relaxed on the grass, Philip said, "Belle, the night is too long away." He smiled at her beneath his lashes; the tail of the glance slid away to Margaret. She had already risen and was moving towards the garden door; very soon, they both understood, he would make his excuses too, and follow. Her skirts brushed his hand as she passed; at the gate she looked back briefly, and he answered with a little secret sign, his cheek on his knees.

The gate snapped shut. Francis had resumed his interrupted ballad, singing to the sweet, halting chords:

> " 'Lord Lovell is buried in Mary's kirk,
>   Fair Nanciebel in the choir—
> And out of her breast there sprang a rose
> And out of the knight's a briar.' "

A murmur of greeting drifted beyond the wicket, Margaret's voice and a man's lightly answering. A moment later Richard Ratcliffe entered the garden and strode grinning towards them across the lawn. "By God, Philip, you were too quick out of the hall; you should have stayed to hear what Gloucester brought back from Péronne. The Duke of Burgundy's just ridden in; Gloucester's with him now, and one of the pages heard Gloucester say King Edward will make peace with Louis and go home to England. Our host of Burgundy is calling down thunder on English heads."

The lute slipped to the ground with a clangour of strings, and Assheton broke off a whispered aside to one of the women, turning an astonished face. His habitually grave face alight with laughter, Ratcliffe stood enjoying the stupefaction. "I swear it's true; we're away from Saint Omer tomorrow cockcrow. Best watch your tongues at supper tonight; there'll be few friends to Englishmen in Burgundy from this day."

Assheton whistled and scrambled to his feet, making for the gate without a word. Francis, his expression thoughtful, stood up with the lute under his arm; he refrained discreetly from looking behind him, but when at last he risked a glance across his shoulder he discovered he need not have troubled: Philip had disappeared.

The other Englishmen were hurrying after Assheton, eager for more news. Francis' curiosity being second to a worse worry, he was disinclined to accompany them, and lingered a while on the terrace before wandering down to the maze which bounded the garden's foot. It was a green, still place, hedged with box higher than a man's head; depressed and anxious, Francis followed the path unthinking until a flash of colour caught his eye, and his footsteps slowed. It was a woman's skirt he had glimpsed through a thinning in the boxwood walls, the bright silk tumbled unheeding around her on the grass. She was not alone, but sat blindly gazing, her arms cradling like a child the man lying with his arms about her waist. Francis could not see his cousin's face; it was hidden against her breast.

Heartsick, Francis drew back. The indecency of intrusion appalled him; concerned only with retracing his steps unheard, he did not see the little movement beyond the next turning of the maze, nor hear the whisper of a watcher's breath. On the other side of the hedge something blue and yellow moved, lingered again, and presently vanished as noiselessly as it had come.

Supper in the Duke of Burgundy's hall was late that day. Returning unexpectedly to Saint Omer after an absence of some days, Charles had arrived on the heels of the Duke of Gloucester, back from Péronne with his embarrassing burden of knowledge as to revised English plans. Charles, drawn hotfoot by terrifying rumour from a meeting of the Estates in Hainault, had descended upon the camp at Péronne as Richard was quitting it, to meet with like disclosure. The King of France had shown desperate readiness to buy off the invaders; in the light of Saint Pol's double treachery, the uncertainties of campaigning in a ravaged countryside, and—unmentioned, but perfectly apparent beneath the Englishman's impassive politeness—the proven unreliability of his ally, Edward saw no reason why Louis should not have his wish. French coin would make good the expenses he had already incurred, and secure his dynasty for years to come; once Louis had got his enemy off his shores, he would go on paying to keep him away. Edward knew his countrymen. They had been taxed to groaning for Monmouth Harry's glories; a second Agincourt would have warmed their hearts, until they saw the bill.

Richard discerned no profit in rehearsing the argument once more to Charles, who in any case invited no exposition. It was plain to the Grand Duke of the West that Edward Plantagenet had sold his greatness for gold, and his contempt was ocean-deep. Crécy, Poitiers, and, inevitably, Agincourt, were produced, shaken out, and flourished like banners before being laid away again with a withering valedictory on the decline of English enterprise. Richard patiently heard him out. He had doubts himself of the wisdom of his brother's course; of all Edward's captains, only the Duke of Gloucester had spoken for battle first and treating after, when even better terms might have been struck. As soon as the flood of rhetoric allowed him speech, he said merely that he would impose no longer upon the Duke of Burgundy's hospitality, it being his purpose to depart from Saint Omer with his followers as soon as possible; and, bowing, took his leave. In the antechamber he found a host of attendants, mouths stretched wide—the door had been not quite closed—and, the dust of the road still white on his boots, Erard de Brezy. He had arrived from Lorraine only minutes before and was awaiting audience with his lord; he exchanged enigmatic glances with Richard as he strolled past him into the Duke's cabinet. The roar of wrath which greeted him rolled like thunder to the fascinated listeners, half-drowning the sympathetic murmur of response. Leaving de Brezy to pour what oil he could, Richard strode from the room.

An hour later the English were assembling their goods, and the tale was in every mouth. Francis, having awaited his cousin in the Duke of Gloucester's chamber uneasily and in vain, finally gave up and went down to the supper hall, but although it was growing late the trestles had been barely dragged out for the tables, and urgent messages were reaching the steward from the kitchens. Charles had gone gloomily to his wife's apartments, there to inform her precisely what manner of sons her father had gotten, and the household—whispering, speculating, exclaiming—waited upon his offended pleasure. Of Erard de Brezy there was no sign, although a number of his men were about the hall; Francis nodded in constrained fashion, and was unsurprised at the stiffness of the response. The air sparked with anger; across the breadth of the room Englishmen and Burgoners eyed each other like dogs on the leash that a word would set snarling.

In a small room beyond the hall Percy and a few companions were casting dice. Philip was there too, studying a roll of last-minute dispositions for the removal of the Duke of Gloucester's household, and after a single narrow glance in his direction Francis joined the players, squatting at Percy's elbow to watch the fall of the counters. The box rattled; Ratcliffe leaned to see, laughed, and tossed down a coin. "Yours, Ralph. You've the devil's luck tonight, on my honour." Assheton picked up the money; there was movement behind them around the door, people separating to make way for someone to enter through the crowd, and in the pause while the dice were collected Francis heard his cousin's voice, very clear and steady, addressing the yeoman who waited beside him: "Fruges, then, for the first night's halt, and Frévent the second. This schedule to his grace of Gloucester, with my duty." The game resumed; Ratcliffe, half-attending, was making a joke with Assheton when from the doorway a man spoke.

"The honour of an Englishman? *Déa*, Messire, you must find another oath. The pity of the Turk, for example"—the soft French knifed through the quiet like the slip of a razor honing—"the incomparable sweetness of dung." Cold with foreknowledge, even before he saw his cousin's eyes as he lifted them, Francis understood. Philip stood like an image; and, moving very deliberately, de Brezy came into the room and halted, staring into his white face. "Well, messire? Instruct me, I beg, for I have wondered about it this hour past: Wherein shall be found the honour of an Englishman?"

"Splendour of God!" It was Assheton who broke the frozen silence, starting impetuously to his feet. Percy snatched his arm to drag him back, and hardly above his breath Philip said, "By your leave, Ralph." A searing colour burned of a sudden on his cheekbones; but, submerging by its weight of terror all the rest, there was a stark question in his eyes which, falling as if by accident on the man behind de Brezy, found there its answer. Close by his father, Auguste was standing. Over one arm he had the baron's cloak; in his free hand, its glossy leaves dark against his tunic of vivid blue, he carried a sprig of boxwood. There was only one place in the Duke of Burgundy's gardens where it grew.

After a long pause de Brezy spoke again. "Well, *mon fils?*" The calculated spacing of the words was a bitter parody. "You did not used to suffer from unfluency of speech: I am waiting. Will you tell me, for example, that I am misinformed? Even, perhaps, misled?" It was rage, not prudence, that kept his voice down; once he put a hand to his throat as if the shirt band choked him. Philip said, too low for the others to hear, "Monseigneur, there is a person you do no credit by accusing me of what you do. For the thing today that occasioned this report I am alone to blame, and you are right to be angry with me. On my given word, you have not right nor any reason to be angry with anyone else."

"Rest you, my dear Lovell!" de Brezy jeered. "I know the value of your word. I have been this afternoon proving it through the full witness of a harlot servant who has paid with stripes for what bribes she may have had of you. For you must understand, *beau fils*"—he leaned forward a little—"until that moment, I did not myself believe."

What followed was too quick for anyone to prevent it. Auguste brushed by his father, dropping the cloak; Philip saw what he had been concealing beneath it, and too late flinched back. The impact of the blow sent him staggering: that, and the blinding, threefold shock of a triple-thonged whip laid flat across the face from temple to mouth. There was a warm wetness stinging his cheek, and then Francis was beside him, an outflung arm around his shoulders breaking his fall.

"Bones of God," he whispered, "so you're after a quarrel, bastard! Have you ever seen my cousin use a lance? By the Cross, you had better have your Masses ordered!"

"Auguste—!" It was de Brezy's voice, cracking with fear; and with a violent effort Philip freed himself of his kinsman's hold. "Francis. this is not your affair." Instinctively he had lifted a hand to his face; when he dropped it, the blood poured down. Three livid weals, thick and disfiguring, flamed like a brand across his cheek; above, the metal tips of the lash had cut to the bone. Francis drew back without a word; already he had interfered more than he ought in another person's quarrel, but it was like watching one drugged trying to rouse from sleep.

Several people around the door were attempting to peer past the obstruction of Percy's big shoulders, and more were pressing up behind. An older man pushed through and came over to Philip, saying smoothly, "May I be of assistance, messire?" Philip knew him only to see; he was not a friend of de Brezy. Dragging a handkerchief from his sleeve, he wadded it tightly against his bleeding cheek. "I thank you, sir," he said huskily, "But I have no difference with Messire Auguste."

Someone sucked in a breath. Francis began harshly, "Philip, for the love of God—!" but the words pinched off. De Brezy had turned to shoulder his way from the room; pale with dread, Philip was trying to follow him when an ungentle grip locked his arm. "Oh no," said Francis grimly. Percy closed up swiftly on the other side, and Assheton, reading his look, moved to fling shut the heavy doors. From the dispersing crowd a single comment rose: "But of course, it was the Duke of Gloucester's steward. Why should they not quarrel? Like master, *mon ami*—" Fading to a murmur, the voices drifted away.

PART FOUR

The Golden Sorrow

June 1476—January 1486

CHAPTER FOURTEEN

ON a morning in late spring, a tall galley flying the scarlet
pilgrim's cross put out from Venice for Palestine. She carried
an assortment of passengers drawn from most of the corners
of Europe, and, the voyage being long and tedious, it was not
a great while before most had made shift in French or Latin
to brush acquaintance, piecing the deficiencies of language
with signs and smiles as became wayfarers launched upon
the half-sacred, half-secular adventure to the holy places. An
exception to the sociability was a knight wrapped in a cloak,
accompanied only by a squire, but his detachment having no
edge of hauteur, it was accepted with tolerance. They
thought him English, by what rare exchanges with his solitary attendant could be overheard; it was remarkable that a
man could find so much to engross him in the empty seas. At
Jaffa they disembarked, and, discharged from the examination of Moslem officials at the dockside, began the
journey overland to Jerusalem.

It was to be more than a year before Philip returned to
England. From Jerusalem he travelled across the desert to
Sinai, a difficult journey which only the hardier pilgrims
cared to undertake. They slept cold to the bone without fires,
out of fear of renegade Arab bands that harassed the way,
and each man, gentle and low, learned to gather hastily his
own handful of wood for the brief evening meal before darkness fell; thirst was a normal condition of their days, allevi-
ated only at widely regulated intervals by the small supply of
water which came salt from the waterskins, or gummy with
sediment. Once there was a short pitched battle with bandits
who experimented with more than the usual night visit for
surreptitious thievery, and a fat merchant from Padua fell
sick of privations he had never dreamed to know, and had to
be carried in a litter, steadfastly refusing the extra mouthfuls of water that Philip offered from his own dwindling
store. Soon after they reached the Monastery of Saint Catherine, a bare huddle of buildings in the shadow of the
Mount, where they rested a few days, attended service in the
church, and made the twin ascents to Sinai and Saint

Catherine peaks. Then—for the German friars were already talking of winter in the Alpine passes—they turned towards home.

In Cairo Philip separated from his companions, taking ship to Rhodes, for he carried greetings from the Duke of Gloucester to the new Grand Master of the Knights of Saint John. There was a hint of curiosity in Pierre d'Aubusson's eyes; the Hospitalers' order stretched through Europe, and the Knights were great travellers, but the Grand Master was inclined to think young Thierry had been overcredulous in a story he had brought back from Paris, despite the three odd little scars on his visitor's cheek.

All Hallows' passed; the smiling seas were roughening beyond the harbour mole, and the mountains of Rhodes sank away. Venice showed a slattern autumn face, rich and grim, and along the Rialto the courtesans leaned naked from their windows, shouting for trade. In Urbino Will Parker fell into a languishing for one of Battista Sforza's ladies, and wrought involuntary cure when the contents of the bowl in which she had laved her hands at supper, filched for worshipful private consumption, proved too rich for the most love-sick digestion. Philip looked mercifully beyond the green after-dawn countenance, and shortly after suggested that the Marches were too northerly for prolonged winter visiting. Spring found them journeying up the valley of the Loire, which rang yet with tales of the death of Charles of Burgundy, who had gone once too often to Lorraine and paid for it at last in the blowing snow before Nancy. More folk than his own still refused to believe the great duke could be dead; in his own time, they said, he would show himself again. At Bordeaux a Bristol master loading with Gascony wines agreed to take passengers; two weeks later they were standing in to the broad Severn mouth, and on Corpus Christi morning the anchor plunged down under the harbour wall.

England looked pale after the blaze and hurry of the renascent Italian cities. At Willowford little appeared changed; the lands were green, the steward placid with content, and Dame Alice governed both with the remembered hand. The addition of some outbuildings and the enlargement of the great hall had gone forward as Philip commanded before leaving, and a year had grown the number of lads who swarmed the courtyard: sons of neighbouring families, doing their service beneath his roof. At Ipsden his twin nephews scrambled around him, entreating an account of his travels in Paynimrie, and staring to see him so darkened by the sun. Hugh after supper begged permission to serve his uncle's bath; his eyes spoke his longing, and when Philip was leaving he offered to take the boy with him as his page to Middleham. Pleased and flattered, Sir William was happy to agree. It was a long while since he had shaken his head over his brother-in-law's politics; since Heaven had decided to prosper the house of York, William Secott was of no inclination to question the judgment.

Some time after that Philip rode over to Minster Lovell, but Francis was not there. He had not been home for several months, Anna said; of late the north had claimed all his attention. Philip would have accepted that readily if it had not been for the set of her mouth; as it was, he hesitated, weighing a comment, before discarding it in preference for an enquiry as to the health of his godson. Young William had been still in his cradle when Philip saw him last; he was beginning to walk now, a big, level-eyed child with his father's dark colouring and decisive features, but without, it appeared, Francis' receptiveness to strangers. Philip did not stay beyond the following day; the boy was still hovering behind his mother's skirts as he made his farewells.

Travelling north to Yorkshire, he reflected that if Secott's complaisance had not been demonstration enough, there was evidence on every side of the settledness of Edward's government. The cattle stood sleek in their pastures; a distant troop of horsemen was likelier the escort of some rich merchant than a body of lances; even the signboards of the inns had blossomed contentedly with Yorkist roses. Not many weeks before there had been a brief disturbance in the eastern counties, where the Duke of Clarence, newly a widower and enraged by Edward's refusal to promote his suit with the heiress Mary of Burgundy, had tried to stir trouble; but there being no dissatisfaction for the spark to feed on, it had quickly died.

About the end of June Philip arrived at Middleham. During the months before his departure for Venice, he had tried many times to persuade Richard to receive back his steward's staff, citing a dozen half-reasons, and one, as near frankness as he could bring himself to come, that the Duke no longer needed him, a stranger from south of the Trent to help him hold the north: that he should choose from closer his court some man of standing to be his officer. Richard had replied pleasantly that he had one already and was not minded to change; but although Percy had shouldered uncomplaining the burden of his duties throughout his absence, there were not a few who might have been glad to supplant Philip Lovell in the Duke's private favour, and he was surprised and touched to find it had not happened so. His presence at Richard's side was accepted as it had been in the past; no one had even a comment on the suddenness with which he had set out on his travels, although some remarked they found him less altered by them than those who had stayed at home. Ratcliffe, strolling next day into the hall as the steward's court of complaints was ending, said with a smile that he might never have left the seat.

Early in the summer Richard made a short journey into Northumberland, for one of those periodic exchanges of opinion with Henry Percy whereby the Earl's pride in his northern right of place was regularly soothed. He took his steward and a substantial riding household with him; and when they returned to Middleham there was a messenger from Westminster waiting. He carried letters from the King, in which Edward told his brother that the Duke of Clarence, having failed to explain to satisfaction his part in the late unrest in Cambridgeshire, had been placed under arrest and lodged in the Tower.

The wonder was that it had not happened long ago. Even from a distance of many miles tales of Clarence's doings had drifted. There was the barbarous business of one of his dead wife's woman servants, whom Clarence had arrested, questioned, and hanged on the grounds that she had poisoned her mistress. He had begun to cast mysterious doubts upon the lawfulness of the King's marriage with Elizabeth Woodville, and hence, by inevitable processes, on the legitimacy of her sons; it was said he had practised against the King's life with sorcerers, and—more dangerous—had raked from the midden of the past the assertion that Edward was himself a bastard, got of an illicit liaison of the Duchess of York with one of her husband's archers, while the Duke was beyond the seas.

Better than anyone, all this Richard knew; and yet Philip believed he was astounded as was no other member of his household. The reply he sent his brother, no secretary ever saw; but soon it became known that the Duke of Gloucester intended to go to Westminster in the autumn, for how long he did not say. Preparations for the journey went forward, and on a clear day in early September a train of knights, squires, and servants of every degree gathered in the courtyard for the departure. Anne came from the keep for a last word with her husband, and four-year-old Edward of Gloucester stayed by his father's side to the last moment, regarding him with wistful eyes. He had never been to Westminster, and heartily envied Sir Philip Lovell's page the treat. Reading the thought, Richard smiled down with a hand on the silky hair. "Perhaps another time, Ned."

As they mounted and kneed their horses towards the outer gate, Francis glanced at his cousin and could not forbear a lifted brow. The boy Hugh, face bright with expectation, rode pillion with Gregory Traynor, but of other personal attendants there was no sign. Will Parker had got his knight's spurs when he came back to England, accoutred for his new life with a handsomeness in unexplained disproportion to his father's modest estate, and since then, although there were youths from Willowford whose services were at his command, Philip had usually preferred to do without them. His liking for privacy in the past had often led him to dispense with what Francis considered the barest decency of retinue; lately the tendency was becoming more marked. It would have been more to the point, Francis reflected irritably, if he had left that chattering little daw Hugh to the schooling at Middleham for which he displayed so continuing a need, and taken instead even one of the half-grown lads who formed his nominal entourage. Two years ago Francis would have spoken his mind unhesitatingly about the omission, which he felt detrimental to his cousin's dignity, but for a long while now he had kept himself from even so insignificant a criticism. It was an instinctive restraint for which he gave himself no reason; but when he saw Philip turn with a smile at some ingenuous remark from Hugh, Francis found himself thinking the brat might have his uses after all.

It was a good time for travelling, early enough in the autumn for the weather to be fair, but without the throngs of pilgrims who clogged the roads during the last weeks of summer. A wandering mountebank with an ancient performing bear attached himself briefly to the cavalcade, much to the delight of its younger members, and was collectively mourned by them when he went his way again at

York. They spent a day at Pontefract, where Richard's bastard son, John of Gloucester, was receiving his tutelage; he was nearly ten now, a slight, erect boy with clear grey eyes and a gravely poised manner. His sister Katherine, born shortly before Barnet, had been similarly placed for rearing, and it was understood there would be a generous dower when the time came for her marriage.

Beyond Pontefract the road ran due south to Grantham, branched, and continued on to London. It was a slow progress, made cumbersome by the carts of domestic furnishings which accompanied the movements of nearly two hundred persons; three weeks from the day they had left Middleham, the travellers drew up before the gates of Richard's town house in Bishopsgate.

It was in London that he chose to establish himself, although there were days at a time when his household there never saw him. Crosby Place was his refuge from the court: his silent, contemptuous answer to the pervasive arrogance of the Queen's intolerable kindred. At Westminster, at Greenwich and Windsor and Shene, Woodvilles swarmed about the King. Earl Rivers had been given governorship of the little Prince of Wales and was presently at Ludlow with his charge, but all the rest were there: chattering, intriguing, constantly at the King's elbow. Even Hastings, long resentful of Woodville pretensions, had trimmed to the prevailing wind and married his stepdaughter to the Queen's eldest son, Sir Thomas Grey. Grey had a new style now: he was called my lord Marquess Dorset.

Parliament was sitting, and there were long, frequent councils which demanded both Edward's presence and his brother's beyond the council chamber, an endless series of distractions claimed the King's attention as preparations continued for the Christmas marriage of Anne Mowbray, daughter and heiress of the Duke of Norfolk, to Edward's younger son, the four-year-old Richard of York. With each passing day his avoidance of private converse with his brother, and the hourly less overt triumph in the faces of the Queen and her relatives, gave confirmation of what even at Middleham Richard had already guessed: Clarence's incarceration in the Tower was the first step only towards the goal of his death. The London citizens, well aware of what was happening, muttered among themselves, and recalled the fate of Desmond, the deputy lieutenant of Ireland, another who had raised his voice against the Queen. The Earl had probably believed himself safe in Dublin, until he was dragged before a tribunal, tried, and condemned before a new Lord Lieutenant who was anxious to do Elizabeth Woodville a service. He knew better before the axe clove his neck; the subsequent murder of his two infant sons completed the object lesson for the rest of the world. And if she required such vengeance on a man who had said only the King might have made a better marriage, said the citizens, what would she not demand of the man who had impugned the marriage itself? Francis, distastefully picking his way across New Palace Yard with a spiced pomander ball at his nose to ward off the stench of refuse piled about the gates, thought the answer plain. Ahead of him he could see the Marquess of Dorset with his brother, Richard Grey; the Tower clock was striking, and as the chimes died Francis heard the younger Grey's voice, echoing back on a trill of laughter: "Remember me, my brother, when you sit in Warwick Castle." It was Clarence's stronghold, ceded to him in his wife's right; Francis had heard of the Marquess' ambitions before, although he had wondered how much they were based on optimistic faith in his mother's persuasive powers. Surely Edward, even loving his peace as he did, would never set that scented worldling in Warwick's place. Scowling to himself, the young man stood thoughtful, and roused to a dulcet voice.

"Indeed, my kinsman, we have fallen upon evil times."

Gently persuading, a light grasp enclosed his arm. Francis turned unwillingly; he cherished no particular regard for his grace of Buckingham, although by marriage they were distant kin, and just now, irked by a snatch of conversation he was sure he had been meant to overhear, he was less than ever inclined to relish the condescension. Buckingham, unnoticing, tucked a friendly hand beneath his elbow, waving away the horde of retainers that trailed at his heels. Fixing a significant eye on the retreating brothers Grey, he sighed and said again, "Very evil times. Had anyone told me, a twelvemonth past, that my cousin Clarence would be in such a case today, I should have laughed, Francis. I should have laughed."

Unreasonably irritated, Francis remarked dryly, "But I am told you will act as High Steward for his grace's sentencing, my lord—should he stand condemned of that he is charged with."

A glance reproached him. "Ever at the King's command, my kinsman. Would you prefer the Duke of Gloucester should have my place?" Francis was silent; the brilliant smile flashed. "But I have not asked how you are enjoying your stay among us. Sometimes a visit at court is as good as a play: there is so much to amuse. Have you spoken with Mistress Shore? An enchanting piece: they say Dorset has an eye to her now, although she used to favour Hastings before the King—observed her. See what a question arises, Francis! Hastings is now Dorset's father-in-law; if Shore breeds, is Hastings made father or grandfather thereby? It would need a conclave of bishops to decide. I put it to my cousin Gloucester, but he seemed to consider himself unqualified to judge."

Amused in spite of himself, Francis murmured, "Not his kind of joke, I'm afraid," and Buckingham chuckled. "*Au contraire*, he seemed entertained enough. Ah, my dear cousin"—Francis allowed himself an ironic gleam at the promotion, feeling no special gratitude—"there is a prince! With poor Clarence come on such woeful days, it gives one to think, by the Cross it does. When one reflects that but for those two brats Dame Elizabeth induced our sovereign lord to father on her—"

Desperate to check him—the courtyard was alive with palace retainers—Francis stemmed the flow. "For God's love, my lord, have a care! Would you see the Duke of Gloucester where Clarence is?"

The limpid eyes regarded him. "Exactly so. I knew you would not mistake me, cousin: I but meant to say that—had Heaven so decreed it—my lord of Gloucester is a prince to whom we might all have given our hearts."

It was in Francis' mind that the Duke of Buckingham let out his heart only at good interest, but he kept the opinion to himself. His aversion for his noble relative continued undiminished; when Philip mocked him at supper for the high company he had been keeping, his cousin said shortly, "Codshead: I can't understand why Gloucester likes the fellow. Puts me in mind of Clarence, the first time I saw him at Middleham."

Philip said meditatively, "Yes, I was thinking the same thing."

It was later that evening, when the King was retiring for the night, that the Duke of Gloucester walked through the privy chamber into the crowded bedroom, saying briskly, "Can your grace allow me some minutes?"

The breach of ritual would have been tolerated in no one else, but Richard seemed unconscious of the innovation. Already in his shirt sleeves, Edward paused, then nodded to his attendants. While they withdrew Richard waited, peeling an orange. The bed was made up, its curtains loosened, the thick ermine coverlet folded neatly in place. On a cushion by the bed the crown glittered and gleamed; the custom of its nightly placing by the King's head continued still at Westminster, although long abandoned at Greenwich and Shene.

The door closed. Edward said tersely, "Well?"

Tossing the fruit aside, Richard said, "I'm sorry to break in on you like this, Ned, but it appears the only way I'm to have a private word. It's about George." Edward studied his fingers, making no comment. The door to the adjacent dressing room was ajar; Richard went to it, kicked it shut, and stood with his back to the panelled wood. "What's the charge to be, Ned?"

Unmoving, Edward returned coolly, "High treason."

There was a short silence. Breaking it, Richard said carefully, "It is not, I believe, good law to hold that a sum of smaller offences can be greater than their separate parts."

"Smaller offences? You're tolerant, Dickon! Ankarette Twynyho was done to death on as palpably absurd grounds as could be imagined; Isabel Neville died of lungrot, as every soul who saw her could have testified. But because George must have it that someone—nicely unspecified!—will stop at nothing to injure him, he claims his wife was poisoned and hales her servant to the gallows as if he were King himself—"

"I never condoned that: he deserved judgment for that."

"—As if he were King himself!" Edward repeated. "Do you think me blind? He sees himself one step from a crown, and if I sat still for him he'd take it joyfully."

"You can't prove that."

"I can come close enough. Why do you suppose he wanted the Burgundian marriage? Only as a vaulting board to higher things, Dickon: I've Louis' kind assurance of that—if I needed it."

"It's not treason to feel yourself wronged. You refused

George, and offered Mary of Burgundy your brother-in-law Rivers instead."

Edward grinned involuntarily. "I knew she wouldn't have him. Bess wanted the match for her brother, of course."

Richard said bitingly, "What a disappointment. Are you consoling her with a promise of our brother's goods for her spawn? Dorset, as I hear tell, already counts himself Lord of Warwick."

Hard-faced, Edward met the smouldering grey eyes. "I have made no such promise, nor do I mean to. As an attainted traitor George forfeits his holdings to the crown: Warwick will be kept for his son."

"Name of God, will you coffin him before even he is heard!" Momentarily they stared at each other like fighters, each considering and groping towards the other's guard; then Richard began again. "George has been as he is these many years: Why have you borne with him so long, to do this now? A nuisance he may be: What possible danger can you see in his drunken dreams?"

A curious silence had fallen. Beyond the candles which burned between them, Richard saw thrown large the outline of his brother's head: a dark, immobile shadow against the tapestry which hung the wall. After an instant Edward said tonelessly, "Drunken indeed: the merchant that sells him his wines much be rich. I've not seen him these two years gone that he didn't stink of it." He was quiet for a time, examining his rings. "I have borne with him, as you say: you know how long. I can no more." And then, with a trace of anger, "Why do you plead for him? How many grants have you let go because George made a clamour about it? How many offices relinquished? He's no friend to you; you found that when you gave up the greater part of your wife's dower to him, only to get peace and the girl of your own choosing."

"I suppose I remember him as you never knew him, when we were lads at Fotheringhay while you were with our father. I used to run after his balls, and carry the arrows back for him when he was in practice at the butts, and believed myself in Heaven for his suffering me." The quick, rare smile came and went again. Presently Richard said in an altered voice, "When can I see him, Ned?"

Picking up a little knife from the table, Edward began to pare his nails. "I see no necessity for your doing so."

"Necessity? I was hardly thinking of necessity!" Edward did not reply; making two strides of the distance between them, Richard stood confronting him. "Where have you housed him, Ned?"

Increasingly annoyed, Edward rejoined acidly, "Curb your suspicions, Dickon, they do me no credit. George is comfortable enough in the Bowyer Tower—cupshotten three days out of four, I'm told. If you think your presence would be a solace to him, you're wrong: he doesn't like you."

"I want to see him. Are you telling me I cannot?"

"I am telling you I would rather you did not, which should be sufficient. For the present he has no visitors, nor to my knowledge has he asked for them." The heavy lip lifted. "After his trial he may feel more disposed for company."

Richard said slowly, "By God's Mother, have you so penned him! This is never your doing, Ned: Do you suppose I don't know the hand? They waited a long time, these leeches and lechers you've chosen to surround you, but this is their revenge for Chepstow, when Warwick rid you of two of the breed, and George stood with him in it. Did you so truly mourn your father-in-law and his son that day? You shed few tears that I ever saw, and before God I'd think shame to myself to be so woman-tired now that I could be fondled and driven against my father's blood—"

"Have a care!" Edward interrupted softly.

"Have a care! I have had a care these many years, and not a few like me! Are we to bear this forever, and no end?"

"Guard your tongue, I say!" Edward straightened suddenly, the thick veins cording in his temples, and threw out an arm to point to the shining circlet beside the bed. "You may be uncrowned king north of the Trent, Dickon, but know this: I made you what you are, and I can unmake you too. I have long been urged to the reminder."

He stopped, breathing fast. His brother had gone rigid; of a sudden bending in obeisance, he backed to the door and wrenched it open with a shaking hand. "I am very sure you have been urged. My compliments to her grace, my sweet sister-in-law, but I am not the Earl of Desmond, nor is my name George of Clarence. With your majesty's permission—?"

His colour high still, Edward made a short gesture, and turning to pass into the crowded antechamber Richard almost stumbled against the petrified figure of the gentle-man usher outside. The man sprang away, stammering apology; close behind him, a mixture of curiosity and delight in their faces as they craned to hear, were the Marquess of Dorset and his brother, Richard Grey.

In arctic quiet the usher fumbled the door shut. Motionless before it, Richard said, "Master Marquess, you bar my way." His voice was low, but Francis, unobtrusively waiting in the shadows, felt his scalp prick. For a minute Dorset hesitated; then, his eyes narrowing, the Queen's son stepped back. Scarlet-cheeked, his brother imitated him. Richard delayed an instant longer, his gaze travelling slowly from one to the other, and swung on his heel. The quick, hard footsteps died away.

Christmas came and went, to a boisterous accompaniment of mumming and revel. In January the little Duke of York and his bride of six were played in triumph from nuptial Mass to the day-long merrymaking of their marriage feast. The following morning, the Duke of Clarence was arraigned for trial before his peers.

It was a short, violent proceeding. Across the hushed chamber brother confronted brother, tearing the silence with shouts of accusation and denial. Clarence could read his fate, and fought like a wounded beast to escape the nets he saw preparing for him; when at the bitter last he cried wildly the King should prove his justice by his own hand, body to body in mortal combat, no one even smiled. Not long after, the deliberating lords adjudged him guilty of the offences with which he had been charged, and the Duke of Buckingham passed upon him sentence of death.

There followed days of waiting. The warrant of execution lay, unsigned, before the King; Richard of Gloucester moved like a shadow about the court; alone in her austere retirement at Berkhamstead, Cecily of York prayed on her arthritic knees and wept for her son. Late one night, a messenger slipped into the princes' palace at Westminster with a scribbled, anonymous note for my lord of Gloucester which concerned the business of certain high persons with some unnamed members of the Commons. He left even more inconspicuously than he had come, rewarded with a douceur which had no corresponding entry in the Duke's household accounts. Next evening, Richard's barge put out quietly from Westminster, and was poled swiftly downriver to London.

The Constable of the Tower received his guest with unconcealed astonishment. He had had no notice, he said, of my lord of Gloucester's coming, although as Lord Constable no doors, of course, were locked to him. There was a quality of uneasiness in the hurrying protestations; the anxious expression deepened as Lord Dudley learned what errand had brought the Duke to the Tower. Briefly, the unhappy officer considered temporising, but as he met the cold eyes of the man facing him, the impulse died. With an inward shrug of resignation Dudley escorted his visitor from the Constable's lodgings.

The Duke of Clarence's quarters were on an upper floor of the Bowyer Tower. Guards lounged below, dicing and drinking ale; night had fallen beyond the slitted windows, and torches smoked against the walls. A warder unlocked for them. Dudley said, "I'll await you, my lord," and stood back.

It was a bare room occupied at mid-length by a table and bench, with a window beyond, and the gaping hole of a privy let into the thickness of the outer wall. Richard paused in the doorway, accustoming his eyes to the murk; in an iron bracket, a single light burned. After a moment he walked across to the table and halted, looking down.

Clarence was slumped across it, his head on his arm, an outstretched hand not quite finishing its gesture towards the half-empty flagon beside him. Richard had last seen him something less than a fortnight before; he had received his sentence calmly, but now, with the passion of the last months ravelling out in despair, he lay inert, filthy and uncaring among the squalid accoutrements of his defeat. Stale wine fumes mingled intolerably with the reek of the privy, and the rushes which strewed the floor were caked with refuse. Richard withdrew his gaze long enough from the slouched figure to kick aside an unidentifiable litter at his feet, and when he looked up again Clarence had raised his head. He stared, squinting bleary, reddened eyes against the light; then groped clumsily for the overturned cup at his elbow, filled it, and downed the contents at a swallow. "My little brother Gloucester," he said thickly. Something flickered across his face, an unreadable expression which might have been anger, or suspicion, or a half-formed, uncertain fear. He started to get shamblingly to his feet, bracing his hands on the table. "What the devil"—his voice blurred, and focused again—"what the devil do you think you're doing here?"

Richard said levelly, "I came to tell you what I presumed you'd rather hear from me than Dudley. When the Commons meet tomorrow, they'll present a petition that the Lords' verdict be acted upon. Some of them are the richer already for the intention."

Unblinking, Clarence met his eyes. Presently he said slowly, "Are they so." His wrists shook under the weight of him; he sat down, whispering, "Then he'll dare?—he'll dare?" Suddenly he leaned sideways, vomiting weakly into the straw.

After an interval during which Richard waited silently, Clarence sat up, wiping his mouth with his sleeve. His hands trembled uncontrollably; clasping them tightly together, he said at length, "A rare pleasure for you, Gloucester, to be first to inform me."

Going to the window, Richard stood looking out. It had begun to snow again; a flake drifted to the sill, settled, and thinned to transparent crystal against the stone. "Do you think so?"

A small hiccough of laughter, jagged with hysteria, sounded behind him. "Why not? I'd see you in my place with a good heart." Richard made no reply; the unthreading fingers jerked at a soiled cuff. "My upright brother. You sicken me, Gloucester: D'you know that?"

The snow was falling more quickly now, its thick, pale feathers furring the ledge. Richard watched it, his lips tight-set, and said after a while, "There's the matter of your children. The girl will have an honourable place and a fit marriage when she's of age for it. As for the boy—" He hesitated. "He will be Earl of Warwick: Ned's word on it. For the present he's to remain in the country with his govern-ors—"

Hunching an indifferent shoulder, Clarence fumbled with his cup. "Warwick or Clarence, what do I care? The brat's simple, I've known it these many months. So much for the heir I got from Isabel Neville." He was trying to pour more wine from the flagon, but his quivering hand refused him. Flinging the cup away, he dropped his head to his arms. "They named me successor to young Lancaster, parliament

did, after Warwick brought Henry from the Tower. I was to
be king after the prince, if he got no sons. And he had none,
but I rot here that should sit in Ned's place, until he sends
his headsman for me—" The ungoverned twitching of his
hands grew; he shuddered and twisted round to stare at the
younger man. Richard made an indecisive movement; mis-
reading it, Clarence snatched desperately at his arm. "Don't
leave me. For Christ's sake don't leave me alone—eight
months I've sat here, waiting—" He pulled his brother closer,
breathing in harsh, noisy sobs. "D'you dream, Dickon? Do
you never think of them—Henry, and Somerset and his
friends that you sentenced after Tewkesbury, and Fauconberg?—they put his head on London Bridge, I remember,
looking east to his Kentishmen, I used to see it grinning
there with the crows picking at it—Do you never remember?
I do—oh, I've been well companied, these months. The old
man and his son at Chepstow—we showed them, Warwick
and I—but there were others we couldn't catch, and I see
them now, nights, they all come round. Dorset, and my high
lord Bishop of Salisbury, and Rivers, they come and watch
and smile, and sometimes they reach out for me—" Lurching
erect, he plunged to the narrow window and hung there,
thrusting his arms wildly through the aperture into the
cool, moist air. Part pulling, part lifting, Richard got him to
the bed. Clarence was whimpering and pawing at him, at
once resisting and clutching at the steady hands; pushing
him to the pillows, Richard gripped him by the hair and
forced the convulsed face round to his. "Splendour of God,
remember who you are!"

It was the whiplash authority, absolute as a handslap
across the mouth, that got through. The frenzied struggles
ceased; sobbing, Clarence turned his cheek to the pillow.
With his fingers prisoned in the damp clasp, Richard looked
down at him. He was rank with sweat and vomit and the
shameful assertion of his body's fear, but the gloom was kind
to the flushed, wet face, shading the bloat from its coarsened
features to a dim reminder of other years.

After what seemed a great while, Clarence stirred. The
hot, sticky palm fell to the coverlet; in a thin, uncertain
voice he whispered, "What's the date?"

Richard answered quietly, "The seventeenth of February."

Clarence repeated it, plucking nervously at the sheet.

"Then it will be the eighteenth tomorrow. February the eighteenth—they'll meet in the morning, and send the speaker with their petition—Dudley should have the warrant before suppertime. That's what Ned was waiting for. I wondered about that, but he's waited long enough, years and years—he could wait a few more days for the Commons to make it right."

He was looking towards the table; Richard hesitated imperceptibly, then went to it, filled the cup, and brought it back to him. "He stood a long time between you and your own folly. You made your own pit; in the end even he couldn't save you from it."

Clarence laughed brokenly. "Is that what you think? He's marked me down this many a day, since I learned what I did of him and the harlot he calls his wife—and now you're with them in it too." He drank, his teeth chattering on the rim of the cup, and put it from him. "Do you like your new friends, Dickon? Do you enjoy louting and scraping to them? You never used to care for it—you were a sickly, long-faced brat, but you held to your own once—"

He stopped, for Richard had turned sharply away. His lips parted; but after an instant he said only, "I stand with Ned."

"God, what a fool you are! It's your rightful place you'll be helping his bastard to, once they're rid of me, that's the thanks you'll have of him. They must laugh together in bed of a night, thinking of it." He giggled, a shrill, unpleasant sound, and maliciously regarded the unmoving profile. Sighing, Richard asked, "Have you done?"

Clarence laced his fingers under his chin, peering derisively through the shadows. "Ask Stillington, Dickon. He could tell you: you should talk to him—except he may be hard to find. He was clapped up here too, last I heard, with only the mitre on it to save his head for what he knows. Ned would give half England only to stop his mouth as he's stopping mine." He leaned forward, his eyes glistening with mockery, trying to see his brother's face. "Dickon," he said softly, "did you have leave from Ned to come and see me tonight?"

A stillness spread through the room, eddying in little, unquiet ripples to its farthest corners. After a moment Richard said, "Stillington? That prim little mouse of a bishop?" His manner had that deliberate, defensive concentration which imposes itself over an unwelcome thought. "You're moon-mad, George; Ned never trusted a secret of his to that meek little shaveling." In an unconscious repetition of his brother's earlier movement, he went to the window, turning from the room's fetid closeness to the stark night air. Even outside the stench persisted, rising from the piled filth beneath the Tower walls: the noisome, unbearable refuse odour which was the consequence of too many people, too closely packed. From London to Westminster, one was never free of it.

He heard his brother's clumsy step behind him, the muffled curse as he discovered the emptiness of the flagon on the table, the lumbering progress to the wine cask beside the buttress. He wondered if he had been wrong to come, if it would have been kinder to have let him drink out his last hours, unsuspecting, in the sodden stupor that was his preferred state. But it had seemed impossible that any man could wish to be so patronised and denied the final dignity, the final acknowledgment of his human condition.

Clarence had managed to replenish the flagon. Carrying it back to the table, he filled the goblet and snapped roughly, "You've discharged your errand, Gloucester. You can leave when you want: I've not asked your company."

Richard said briefly, "Just as you please." He moved to the door and paused, looking back. "If there is anything I can do—"

"Still easing your conscience, little brother?" Clarence snarled. "Or is it Ned's you're concerned for? Don't trouble yourself, in another twenty-four hours Dudley and his fellows will have seen to it all for you—" His voice cracked. The sullen truculence ebbed, carried on a wave of terror; he swallowed, and put a hand to his neck. "It's the axe—they hack at you so, I've heard tales of it. They say you don't feel it after the first stroke, but how would anyone know?" He laughed hysterically, gulped from the cup, and lowered it. "Dickon—" He came nearer his brother, gripping his shoulder. "Dickon, stop a moment. Will you speak to Ned? Will you ask him one thing for me? Ask him—ask him if I might choose the way of it. I'd not mind it so, if it could be another way—"

Richard guided him to the bed, helped him lie down, and used a handkerchief to mop the tear-stained face. "I'll ask him, George. It will be all right, I promise you. Nothing else?"

Clarence shook his head listlessly. He was still clutching the empty goblet; before he left the room Richard took the stoup of wine from the table and set it quietly beside the bed. The last sound he heard was the thick gurgle of the liquor as it was slopped into the friendly cup.

Dudley was waiting outside, his expression divided between impatience and involuntary curiosity. Richard said curtly, "This kennel's not been swept for days: Was it your order that his grace be kept in such a sty?"

The Constable hastily disclaimed. The condition of his grace's lodging—and, he might silently have added, his grace's person—was no doing of his. My lord naturally had his own people to minister to his wants, but he had sent them away some days since, saying he wanted none of their mammering about him. The explanation had an authentic ring; Richard considered him grimly, and decided to accept it. "Leave him by himself, then, while he wishes it. Later, if he should change his mind, see to it he is attended on the instant."

A little resentful of the hard, instructing tone, Dudley murmured a stiff assent. Richard was tracing a pattern with his boot among the rushes; lightly stirring the straw, he said, "Lord Dudley, have you had a prisoner here of late called Stillington?"

The Constable's face changed. "Stillington, did you say? No, my lord."

Richard looked up. From his seventeenth year he had commanded men, and he had learned very early how to know a lie. There might have been any number of reasons for it; but in the moment before they evaded his, he had seen the fear in Dudley's eyes.

The next day, the Duke of Gloucester removed himself and his followers from Westminster; less than a week later he was on his way back to Middleham. About the same time a covered cart rumbled from London, draped in sable and escorted by a small body of horsemen. They formed all the company which had been decreed for the burial in Tewkesbury Abbey of George Plantagenet—drowned, as the wry account already ran, in a hogshead of Malmsey wine.

CHAPTER FIFTEEN

As Edward of York grew older his rule harshened. There was violence over the seas, where King Louis was remorselessly tearing the heart from Mary of Burgundy's inheritance; there was murmuring at home, where the tribute annually extracted from Louis as the price of English indifference, no longer sufficient to meet the expenses of government, was being supplemented by unpopular taxes; and on the northern border, urged on by their perpetual ally France, the Scots were gathering.

James Stewart had a treaty of friendship with his English neighbour, having promised his son in marriage to Edward's daughter, and a portion of the princess' dower was already in James' hands. Suddenly the Scottish King sent a herald to Westminster to say that if Edward did not forego his aid to Burgundy, James must come at once to the succour of his friend, the King of France. In a rage at the sophism, Edward retorted in kind, and a bitter war flared. Tired and beset with troubles, after months of difficulty he was obliged to consign its prosecution into Richard of Gloucester's hands; in hurried consultation at Fotheringhay he gave his brother what men he could supply, and watched them march away.

Richard had already got matters in train with the siege of Berwick, and when he returned with the King's southern contingents the city fell. He was impatient now to push on to meet the army James was bringing against him, and, a core of defenders having retreated into the castle keep, its reduction was left to a detachment under Lord Stanley's command. The appointment, advisable though Stanley's power in the west made it, was not one Richard had been eager to bestow; it was twelve years since a young Duke of Gloucester, hastening from Wales to help the King, had fallen upon the troops Stanley was mustering for Warwick's support and incontinently scattered them, but Richard had not forgotten, and although Stanley, narrow-lipped, uncommunicative man with little conversation and less humour, had long made his peace with Edward, it seemed likely he remembered too. In the end Richard left Philip

Lovell to second Stanley's command, of which honour Francis, his mouth expressive, wished his cousin the utmost joy.

The English army pressed north, and the quarrelling of James and his nobles made of Edinburgh a bloodless conquest. Sardonically appraising King James' domestic upheavals, Richard accepted with equanimity the offer of the town burgesses to repay from their own coffers his niece's dower, and took submission of the Scottish lords, from whom a sally out of Edinburgh had drawn suit for peace and suggestions of a new marriage treaty. The last proposal Richard rejected, seeing nothing to be gained from it, but before he relinquished Edinburgh he wrung from James' nobles an inglorious guarantee of no interference in the unfinished work at Berwick, which he wanted very much indeed. Then he turned south once more.

The garrison at Berwick was still resisting gallantly, but with the collapse of the northern army their last hope was gone. Stanley had been vigorously pressing the siege, and the mined and battered walls bore witness to the efficiency of his work; there was justification for his report that even the rats must be ready to abandon the place.

Less than a fortnight later the citadel surrendered. The arrival of Richard's courier in London was the signal for bonfires, processions, and a cannon salute from the guns of Calais; by Christmas, his army disbanded and Berwick secure, he was himself at Westminster. Although almost everything he had to discuss with his brother was bad, Edward was not neglectful about showing his appreciation to the Duke of Gloucester's captains, and Philip, hurrying back from a visit to his Oxfordshire estates, returned on a day of investitures. He was too late for the ceremony—the winter roads, always doubtful, had surpassed his worst expectation—but the chatter of the palace confirmed what had been half-conveyed before in a diffident note from Francis. When he had washed and got himself into dry clothes, Philip climbed the stairs to his cousin's rooms, accompanied by his nephew Hugh. The bedchamber was empty, but a wild disorder of garments proclaimed the haste with which the owner had earlier quitted it; smiling to himself, Philip accepted refreshment from one of his cousin's pages and, leaning against the window, watched the slow course of the raindrops running down the mullioned panes. Hugh, uncharacteristically silent, curled by the hearth and looked at the fire.

It was full dusk when Francis returned. The little page had reappeared with a branch of candles; on the heels of his departure there was a bustle in the outer room and Francis came in, his squire behind him. He was robed in scarlet furred with miniver, the hood dropped back, and a collar of Yorkist suns glittered around his shoulders. He stopped when he saw Philip, his face lighting, and, sweeping the blaze of velvet with a glance, Philip said smiling, "My felicitations, cousin."

Embarrassed, Francis looked down at the trailing robes. "Thank you. I wasn't sure you would be here today: the roads must be very bad now."

"Yes, a slough this side Oxford. That's why we're late, and I'n more sorry than I can say. Still, tardy though it is—" He made a flourishing reverence and straightened, holding out his hands. "My gracious lord, Viscount Lovell. You'll have many good wishes this day, Francis: Will you pardon your slothful kinsmen and accept theirs too?"

He glanced behind him as he spoke, but Hugh was gazing stubbornly at the glowing hearth. Disburdened by his attendant of the heavy mantle, Francis stretched in relief and turned to help himself from a dish of sweetmeats. The squire was folding the velvet to lay within the chest, handling it in awe like a relic; and Philip said, very quietly, "Hugh."

The youth started and crimsoned under the warning eye. Scrambling to his feet, he muttered, "I b-beg your pardon, my kins—that is, my lord. My uncle has spoken for both of us: I am sorry if I did not seem attending."

Francis contemplated him in a thoughtful way, and of a sudden his lips twitched. "Hugh, you take me back. Yes, never mind, run along now." He flicked a gesture at the other lad, and waited while he followed the younger one out. The amusement had vanished from his eyes; he said abruptly, "The boy's right, you know. There's no justice in it, Philip."

"If you mean what I believe you do, you're talking great nonsense," Philip returned equably. "The King has owed you this a dozen times over since Gloucester knighted you three years ago. Hugh is only suffering from a misapplied prejudice of affection—not unlike yourself, if I may say so."

235

"My arse," Francis said crudely. "Whatever service I was to Gloucester in Scotland, you did ten times more at Berwick."

"And was amply thanked for it," Philip interrupted. There was a note in his voice which was at once a termination and a warning. Seated on the chest, he slowly swung his foot. "Well, coz? Are you content?—or is it a step on the way, with the stair still climbing?"

"A gilded step. Give me another ten years and we'll both have forgotten this ever seemed important—" Shrugging, Francis played with the shining chain. "Well, that's another day. For the moment the gilding's well enough. I can make the Stanleys give place to me now, and I could not begin to describe to you, Philip, how that pleases me."

Philip was silent, clasping his knees. It had almost passed from his memory that, for a short year before she grieved her way after John Lovell to her death, Francis' mother had been given to Lord Stanley's brother for wife. It was possible only to guess how astonishingly Francis had hated and resented William Stanley for that: stranger still was the lingering preoccupation in a man grown, married and with a son of his own. But Philip had long given over speculating what peculiar disappointments in his marriage had gone into the shaping of his cousin's manhood. How he was living now, he took no trouble to hide, and in the variety of his mistresses he was neither discreet nor discriminating. What Anna felt about it, no one knew. If she was angry at her husband's less and less frequent appearances at Minster Lovell, she made no sign; all her life turned now on the dark, reticent child to whom his father was a remote figure, busying himself in some disapproved-of way far from Oxfordshire.

Shortly afterwards Philip went back to his own quarters, which Francis would share with him no more. He experienced a prick of nostalgia at the reflection, and then laughed at himself for it: his own situation had altered too. He was made sharply conscious of it in the enormous supper hall that night, when Sir Ralph Hastings was at pains to seek him out and invite his company over a cup of wine in his brother the Chamberlain's apartment after meat. Although William Hastings was a man as expansively genial as he was hospitable, not even his great chamber was open court for every gentleman in from the shires; and Philip began slowly to understand that the favour of the Duke of Gloucester counted for as much at Westminster now as King Edward's peerages.

It was a stark reminder of how Edward's fortunes had declined. Mary of Burgundy's Hapsburg husband, his valiant resistance at an end, had been forced to terms with France, and Louis, his triumph complete, had repudiated the treaty with Edward, cancelled the tribute money, and terminated the betrothal of his son to Edward's daughter. How much the last circumstance should be regretted by the Princess Elizabeth was debatable—the Dauphin Charles, even by the most charitable, was regarded as a repellently backward youth—but there was no mistaking the insult to her father. That Louis had dared offer it brought the English to bitter understanding of how dear those seven years of tribute had cost them. In that gloomy winter the Duke of Gloucester's Scottish successes provided the only brightness; ashamed and raging, the country seized on them as the one palliative to the national disgrace.

Richard wanted his brother to press the Scottish war. He had left James with enough on his hands to prevent more interference in English affairs for a while at least, but the best answer to the mounting threat of France was to reduce Louis' ally to a condition of permanent neutrality: in time it might be possible to break the traditional association of Scotland and France, and draw the Scots into alliance with their southern neighbour. With craft and patience the thing was not out of reason; there was even precedent for it, in bygone days.

"While Louis' privateers raid up and down the Channel at will," Edward remarked savagely. "Oh, you're in the right of it, Dickon: there's no other way now."

"None that I see," Richard said calmly. They were in the green-walled dressing-room which adjoined the great bed-chambers, the door closed against intrusion. A small table stood heaped with papers, with a couch beside it, and Edward lowerered himself to the cushions with a sigh. "Well, by summer then: it's no weather now for campaigning. The devil's in it that I can spare you so little."

Smiling slightly, Richard said, "It will be enough." He knew of old his brother's fanatic preoccupation with his treasury; his enemies called him gibingly the Merchant King, and for all his delight in the Scottish victories, he had groaned aloud when he learned the cost.

Studying the younger man from beneath his lids, Edward reflected with a tinge of irony on the inscrutable ways of Providence. It was not many years, as time seemed to him now, since his brother had been a shy, self-effacing figure on the fringes of the Woodville court: less than twelve, since Edward had given him the north and sent him beyond the Trent to govern it for the crown. The taut wariness of his uncomfortable adolescence had long settled into aloofness which could, at choice, become formidable, and few traces remained of the awkward youth who had provided Elizabeth Woodville and her sons with such unwearied entertainment. The imbalance of his shoulders was hardly noticeable now, although a vestigial consciousness lingered: even his intimates seldom surprised the Duke of Gloucester in his shirt-sleeves.

Richard was flicking through the litter of despatches; sighing, Edward turned his eyes away. The bare sight of that compressed, restless energy was dispiriting reminder of his own failing resources. He was not old, he told himself—God's eyes, was a man old at forty?—but he had lived hard, and his body was beginning to tell him about it. The great bull rages with which he had been wont to quell his council left him these days wheezing and shaken, and there had been, once or twice, a strange fluttering darkness; but he was not done yet, by Saint Anne. He stared down at his hands, which of late were not always so steady as he could have wished, and became aware through the sudden quiet of his brother's searching glance. Meeting it, he said with a disarming gleam, "I was thinking how things have changed. There's something here for you, Dickon, before you go. Will you bring the light nearer?"

He fumbled under the pillows; the parchment crackled as he drew it out. With the candle in his hand, Richard bent to look. His eyes swept the bold lettering and vivid seals, and lifted then, incredulous, to his brother's. "But this is—"

"Cumberland, the western Marches, all you've taken already from the Scots and whatever more of your personal judgment you see fit to take to secure the border—for you and your heirs forever. It goes to parliament tomorrow for ratifying," Edward concluded tranquilly. "You'll hold the north for me still, but this—this will be your own."

Richard said in a low voice, "You shame me to my soul. A minute ago I was thinking you clutch-fisted."

"It's only words now." Edward stared down at the yellowed sheet. "But in two or three years—maybe less—it will be real power, and no one can take it from you then. No matter what happens, you'll be safe with that."

"Ned"—Richard laid the parchment aside, his eyes on the pouched, lined face—"Ned, are you feeling quite well lately? I was speaking with Hobbes yesterday; I thought he seemed anxious."

"Hobbes is an old woman. He'd wrap me in linen and stuff his philtres down my throat till I gagged on 'em, if he had his way. No worry, no exertion, he says—body of Christ, I'd like to see him go to bed with that beside his pillow"—Edward jerked his head towards the bedroom, where the crown already lay—"and follow his own prescription."

"Perhaps that wasn't what he meant." Richard was looking without expression at a small object half-kicked beneath the couch; it was a lady's slipper, of that shade of blue especially favoured by Jane Shore. Edward saw the glance, and grinned impenitently. "Possibly it wasn't. But I'm not dead yet, your righteousness, nor doting either. Let the sermon go; you're behind with it by five and twenty years." He turned from his brother's tight-lipped silence to the armed chair before the glowing brazier. Voices came from the bedroom, where the knights of the body were assembling to see the King ritually undressed for the night; at a nod Richard opened the door, and Lord Hastings strolled in, rattling a dice box in his hand. The hour was not late, but there was a smell of wine about him already, and his shirt was undone to the thickly matted hair of his chest. He gave the King's brother a friendly greeting and waved forward an equerry, who cleared away the papers and put a replenished flagon on the table at Edward's side. Richard wondered if it could be true what Buckingham had told him: that they sometimes threw for Mistress Shore.

In the corner a lutist was tuning his instrument, and a slender youth, much painted, passed with a tossing of curls. Still playing with the counters, Hastings said cheerfully, "Will you join us, my lord?"

It would be, from all appearance, a good while before the knights of the body were called to their duties. Richard said shortly, "No, I thank you," and added under his breath, "Shall you be late, Ned?"

"Sinfully, Dickon," Edward returned blandly. He held out

his hand, amusement and a deep affection in his eyes. "Good sleep to you."

A few days later Lords and Commons rose, having ended their business with a ringing endorsement of the grants to the King's brother, and adding their own tribute to that prince and his captains in the late Scottish war. They voted a tax in support of its resumption, thriftily limited to aliens, who were not in a position to object. Heaven, it seemed plain, was once more about to demonstrate its overwhelming preference for the English point of view.

Soon after, Richard took his leave. He had been more than two months separated from his wife and son, but the spring lay temptingly before him, an interval of calm before his heralds rode again among the northern hills. This time he would wring from James the guarantees he had been in no condition to give before, with a good stretch of the turbulent Scottish Marches to hold the Stewart to his havering word; and by winter he could be turning his thoughts to Cumberland, the fallow promise from which henceforward all his hopes would spring.

From London the road stretched north and east, through Barnet and Saint Albans and branching beyond towards Coventry. To right and left the fields lay tilled for early sowing, and clouds of low-flying plover wheeled and circled above the furrows. The Duke's men rode with hawks on fists, and there was much laughter. "A fair prospect, cousin," Francis said contentedly. "Who would have believed it once."

"Not I, thirteen years gone in a fishing smack for Burgundy," Percy struck in. "D'you mind the time, Philip? It was a lean winter in Holland, that one."

"You've fattened since," Francis told him. Percy chuckled and spurred by, light-seated for all his girth. They were some miles yet from the town where they would sleep that night, but sunlight was lengthening across the meadows. Westward, the irregular mass of a Benedictine abbey sprawled against the colouring sky, and a chapman, done with his business in the village beyond, stood knocking at the gate. Philip nodded at the buildings as they passed. "Do you remember the monk in the house by Reading, that we met on our way to Tewkesbury? He's Prior at Colchester now. I stopped there by accident, the winter after I was back from Palestine: I had never thought to see him again."

"I remember he was the unlikeliest priest I ever knew. He

still owes me for some hours of sleep"—Francis grinned crookedly at the recollection—"but he knew how to physic a wound."

It was growing late. The riders picked up speed; the carts squeaked as they lurched after them down the rutted track. The last light, kindling on the spires of Leicester, followed them up the vale, and Market Bosworth dropped behind the shoulder of the hill.

In his palace at Westminster Edward of York was dying. He had fought it long, knowing how much undone there was that he must leave now to the fumbling hands of others, but the time had come when rebellion would serve no more. The anxious ministrations of Master Hobbes were a futile torment; impatiently he sent the distracted physician away and set himself to what, in the little space left him, he could still accomplish. It was scant enough: his will, the naming of its executors, all he could think of to ensure the peaceful succeeding of the twelve-year-old boy at Ludlow whom now, at the near limit of his waning strength, he confided to his brother Richard's care. With a desperate effort he gathered his nobles and his wife's kindred around him, and swore them to the friendship to which, alive, he had never been able to compel them. Weeping, they heard him and promised what he asked. Then there were only the priests, the viaticum, the cold touch of oils on his limbs and the pattered prayers.

The hour came when they left him in peace. They had lit tall candles at the foot of his bed; staring between the flames, Edward struggled with his thickening sight. The solicitous circle of faces wavered and swam away, and in the shadows other shapes moved. He knew them: Warwick, with his tall arrogance and hawk's stare, smiling a little, as if in irony at the impotence with which the dying man sought yet to hold the end away; Montagu, watching him with steadfast gaze—poor Jack, who had turned on him in a fit of temper and broken his heart for it on Barnet common. He heard the silk skirts of the Angevin queen, and saw her husband's mild, uncomprehending eyes. There were others he did not know so well, but they came too and stood looking, speechless, with folded hands.

The darkness pressed closer. He strove with it; the rows of solemn sentinels parted and something flashed brilliant, the dazzling brightness of many jewels catching fire in the floating points of light. Laughing, tossing a bauble in its hands, the last shade came and sat beside him and leaned down, mocking, to see his face. "Too soon is it, Ned? We all think that. I thought it when you had me in the Tower, but you never paused for that."

Laboriously, from behind unmoving lips, the sick man answered, "I never wanted to do you harm. I would have pardoned you if you had made submission: I promised it."

"How pleased you must have been that I didn't put it to the test. Well, it was a small thing to you, Ned, a life not your own, but it was all I had, once you'd stripped me of the rest. You might have left me that."

"How could I? I could deal with you—I always had—but there was the boy. I had to make it safe for him."

The shrill laughter sounded, high and darting as a swallow's flight. "And have you made it safe, Ned? Are you content? Have you settled with Louis, and bridled the barons, and got Henry Tudor from the Duke of Brittany's hospitable shores? You lack a little, Ned, of the perfect order you tried for."

The bright gawd flashed again, stabbing the dark. Edward turned his eyes from the hurtful gleam. "I've done what I can. Dickon must see to the rest; it's in his hands now."

"A right loving bequest. France, and Scotland, the Tudor in Brittany, my lady Elizabeth your goodwife at home—Northumberland at Alnwick, who does not love the Duke of Gloucester, and my lord Stanley in the west"—the smiling face came nearer—"who has a new wife. Would a miracle suit you, Ned? There's not much else to ask."

Stanley—Edward stirred restlessly, trying not to wonder where, in the schismatic turmoil his death would unloose, Stanley would elect to place himself. He had been too great to put down, so Edward had done the next best thing: cherished him, advanced him, made him an officer of his household and named him with the executors of his will. He had done well with Dickon at Berwick; perhaps after all there was no need to look doubtfully on him because of a new marriage, even if that marriage was with Henry Tudor's mother. Northumberland too was a question; and Buckingham, with his dangerous tincture of Plantagenet—who knew where that erratic dragonfly would choose to light?

The room grew tall; the candles receded, became small, were no more than outdistanced beacons in the soaring dark. Dickon—Dickon would take care of it. He closed his eyes.

CHAPTER SIXTEEN

Sitting in the ladies' gallery which overlooked Middleham courtyard, Anne of Gloucester withdrew her attention from the spectacle now terminating below, and loosened the fastenings of her mantle. The April day being sunny, it had seemed appropriate that the troupe of players taken lately under her husband's protection should set up their stage out of doors, but the sun's warmth had soaked into the castle walls, and the heat came in waves from the stone.

The actors were dismantling their platform, and an apprentice boy, the skirts of his heroine's costume kilted around his knees, was dragging the planks away. To at least one member of the household the performance had offered only fleeting interest, and when the space emptied the Duke's great stallion, White Surrey, appeared crossing the quadrangle from the stables, with the prince Edward of Gloucester upon his back. A mounted groom, one eye on the audience above, followed closely behind. Directly in front of the gallery the cortege halted and Edward looked up, waving a complacent hand in salute. There were smiles of acknowledgment from the observers, but Anne gave her husband an uneasy glance. "Do you think—?"

"Well, my heart, he must learn one end of a war horse from the other some day," Richard remarked. "I gave him leave: he's chaffing at hackneys now, and I've promised the bay colt for his name day if he can show himself able to manage him." He smiled an assent at his son, who was anxiously regarding him, and the boy turned his pacing steed towards the outer court. The portcullis was up; he crossed the square, the groom still attending, and trotted down the slope to the market place beyond. His mother listened to the retreating hoofs, a lingering disquiet in her eyes, and Francis turned from a desultory conversation with Ralph Assheton to say teasingly, "Ever the same tale, my lord. I shall be having the identical dispute with my wife, three or four years hence."

Richard was still looking towards the north gate. Beyond the jut of the chapel wall, he had heard other hoofbeats on the bridge; Philip, leaning quietly against the wooden gallery rail, saw him straighten with a frown. The horseman who clattered around the two sides of the keep into their view was plainly at a loss and in search of direction; he was mud-splashed to the thighs and caked with grime, but there was no mistaking the colours he wore. "Isn't that Hastings' livery?" Assheton said curiously. "What the devil is one of his fellows doing in such a hurry?"

The courier had slid from his mount, and they heard him shout, "The Duke! Where will I find the Duke?" The servant who took the reins pointed him the way he had come to the outer stair, but Richard was already hastening into the keep. They met in the great hall, and the messenger dropped on one knee to offer a sealed packet, saying huskily, "This to your grace from my master. The King is dead."

Hours later, when the confusion had died, the excited voices hushed, the solemn requiem in the chapel ended, came a whispering calm. Anne was in the south tower with her son; Richard had shut himself in his privy chamber, and no one who had watched his pale, graven face during the chapel service dreamed of intruding upon him. Groups of people lingered in the hall, conversing in subdued tones. Hastings' message had been brief and explicit: the King had named his brother Protector and left all in his hands; let my lord of Gloucester lose no time in securing the person of the boy heir at Ludlow, and bringing him to London. The ominous note of urgency was underlined by an otherwise total silence from Westminster. Elizabeth Woodville and her friends had not yet seen fit to inform the Duke of Gloucester of his brother's death.

"And may God damn her harpy's spite," Ratcliffe muttered, as the next day passed with still no word. "On my soul, I think the woman witless. What does she gain?"

"A great deal, she may hope," Philip remarked thoughtfully, and Francis gave a jarring laugh of agreement. "Doubtless. Oh, they'll be mightily occupied in London now, my lord Marquess and his dam, not to mention the rest of the tribe. I wonder if they've thought yet to put a watch on Hastings."

A squire touched Philip's sleeve, and, detaching himself from the angry little assembly, Philip followed the youth from the hall. At the solar door the boy left him, and Philip went inside.

The smell of melting wax received him. The Duke's secretary, Kendall, was sealing a letter while Richard sat at the table, turning a quill in his fingers. He glanced up as Philip entered, then took the missive from his secretary, and when the man had gone said abruptly, "Here is a charge for you, Philip. This is a letter to Lord Rivers, asking by what road he intends to bring my nephew to London, and at what time I want you to bear it to Ludlow for me and bring his answer as quickly as you can."

"Will you trust him for a straight reply?" Philip asked equably. Smiling grimly, Richard said, "I shall expect you to tell me if you think I may. Still—" He hesitated, his eyes pensive. "He's the Queen's brother, and without a doubt has brought up his charge in the belief that the house of Woodville was born to inherit the earth; but by his lights he's a gentleman. Which, of course, makes him the most difficult and dangerous of them all."

By mid-afternoon Philip had left Middleham with a party kept small for speed, striking south-west through the Yorkshire dales towards Lancashire and Wales. For that reason he failed to encounter on his way Lord Hastings' second courier, who came toiling up the hill from the village market-place shortly before nightfall. This time the Chamberlain wrote in more detail, but with a mounting desperation. The purpose of the Queen and her relatives had become clear: to get her son to London and crown him forthwith. A protector having no claim over a crowned king, it would be a matter then of setting a regent for his minority, and there was no reason, in Elizabeth Woodville's view, why that regent should be the protector King Edward had named. Already she was assuming the airs of the office herself; and was issuing proclamations, collecting taxes, mobilising the fleet and seizing her husband's treasure, which was instantly divided between herself and her eldest son, the busy Marquess Dorset. It had taken all his influence as the dead King's friend and councillor, Hastings wrote, to keep the escort from Ludlow to two thousand men; and he entreated the Duke of Gloucester, with an earnestness in which the first cracks of panic were beginning to show, to be sure he came south with not a man less.

It was now the middle of April. In London, Dorset and the Queen had pressed the browbeaten remnant of the late King's council into agreeing to set young Edward's coronation for the beginning of May. Clearly they hoped to have the thing accomplished before the Protector arrived; there was even the chance he might not yet have heard of the King's death. But of that hope, the Queen and her friends were quickly disabused. Immediately after Hastings' second communication reached him, Richard despatched a letter of condolence to the widow on her bereavement—a polite sarcasm, in view of her efforts to prevent his knowing about it—and sent by the same courier a longer one to the council itself. Reasonably and without heat, he pointed out that his designation as Protector was in accordance both with custom and his brother's wish. He would assume the duties which had been laid on him, having no desire but to serve the new King as honourably and loyally as he had served his father. The which faith and obedience, he trusted to find no less in them than in himself.

In succeeding days, although a multitude of directives and instructions went out from Middleham, there was nothing among them that concerned itself with the raising of the host Lord Hastings had so frantically urged. Richard's followers, at a furious pitch of resentment over Woodville doings, puzzled vainly over that singular omission; but to Francis, who was finally moved to expostulate, Richard said that he was not yet certain of Rivers' mind, and did not mean to worsen the strain of their first meeting by coming with an army at his back. A few days later a messenger arrived posthaste from the Duke of Buckingham, carrying the most cordial greetings to his cousin Gloucester and the offer of one thousand men. Richard answered that he would welcome the Duke of Buckingham's company on the road to London, but with an escort not exceeding three hundred persons. It was hardly more than a great lord's customary riding household; but it was all he was taking himself.

They were a small party who set off from Middleham, for Richard had sent to the bulk of the northern gentry who would accompany him, appointing York as their rendezvous. In the north courtyard he embraced his son, and across his hair met the mother's eyes. They had made their farewells the night before, and the ache of it was upon them still; never before had they parted in such doubt of when they would be together again. To her whispered question, "How long?" he had been able to say only, "I do not know. I will send for you when it is possible: I promise it." They were in the lady chamber, looking across the dales; his arm lying on her shoulder felt her tremble, and he knew she wept.

A great while after, she said, "I wish you would take more men. I am in such fear for you—is it too late to change it now?"

"I do not intend to do so." He had a lock of her hair wound on his finger; after a moment he slid it from his hand. "When you come to Westminster, it would be best that Ned remained here. He is happy in the north; let him stay so while he may, out of that sink." He saw her face, and drew her closer. "Believe me, I am thinking of him. He is young for that kind of torturing."

"Your brother did not consider you so when he brought you there. You were not much older."

A star fell, scoring the sky with light. "They were different times. He knew I was not too young to be shown what was expected of me: I'd been my life learning it. I was seven when they sacked Ludlow, and took my mother and George and me from the market cross where she had gone to protect her people. My father had had to flee into the hills, having been betrayed by Trollope; he could not take a woman and two children with him, but he thought old Buckingham would show her kindness, she being his wife's sister. He was mistaken. I tried to hide my face when the flames went up, but she bade me look, saying I would do better to see who were doing this, and to remember them. There was a girl ran by with her shift on fire, all the soldiers had left her when they'd done with their sport: she was the falconer's daughter, not twelve years old. And all that, because my father stood too near the King in blood for the liking of certain lords, who taught Henry to hate him for it. He had never thought of the crown then."

Philip Lovell joined the Duke's train as they were nearing Pontefract. He had with him Lord Rivers' reply, in which the Earl stated that he planned on leaving Ludlow shortly with his charge, and would be pleased to meet the Duke of Gloucester at Northampton. Richard scanned the letter, and sat gazing between the horse's ears. "Well, Philip? What do you think?"

"He'll be at Northampton, my lord. For the rest, I believe he's of two minds. He has a mighty following with him; I don't think he knows yet what he means to do with them.

He's an honourable man, but—the Queen is his sister."

"Just so. And without him her plans fall to nothing: I don't see Dorset playing the general." Richard rode on, looking thoughtful. He had in his pocket the latest of Lord Hastings' agitated communications, in which the Chamberlain enlarged upon his earlier warnings, and asserted that he went in fear of his very life for the opposition he had shown to Dorset and the Queen. The council, increasingly restive under the Marquess' daily hectoring, had let it be known that in their opinion the young King should be wholly separated from his mother's ambitious relatives during the years of his minority, but despite—or perhaps because of—these signs of rebellion, Dorset was despatching his brother Richard Grey to meet Rivers and the King.

At Nottingham they heard from the Duke of Buckingham, who was on his way from Wales. Richard sent word back telling the Duke of the day and place of the meeting with the King, and when in due course he entered Northampton, it was to find advance riders from Buckingham's troop awaiting him. The Duke, he learned, would be with him by nightfall. Nothing was to be seen of the Ludlow host, but enquiry at the inn elicited the interesting information that Lord Rivers and the King had reached Northampton very much earlier, and instead of pausing there had ridden straight through the town, continuing on the main road towards London. It was believed they meant to halt for the night in Stony Stratford, at the present rate of progress more than a half-day's march nearer London. Expressionless, Richard followed the bowing landlord into the dining parlour which had been cleared for his use; he was standing by the hearth, a foot on the settle, when a tumult in the street signalled further arrivals, and a moment later Earl Rivers walked into the room. Smiling, he explained that on second thought it had seemed to him the hostelries of Northampton might be hard-put to accommodate the royal train as well as my lord of Gloucester's men, so he had taken his nephew on to Stony Stratford, where His Majesty would eagerly await his uncle's coming next day. The account provided no explanation of why it had been considered needful for the King himself, as well as all his escort, to travel on to Stony Stratford, but Richard, after contemplating his visitor in silence for an instant, turned from the fire without comment, and presently invited the Earl to stay and share the supper now in preparation. Rivers affably agreed, and during the course of the next few minutes' conversation contrived to make clear to his non-committal host that he had already arranged lodgings nearby for himself and his handful of attendants, there being no plan for them to quit Northampton again that night. He then accepted a goblet of wine, exchanged pleasantries with those of the Duke's companions who were known to him, and settled himself with every evidence of composure to await the promised supper. The cook boy was just staggering from the kitchen under the weight of a gigantic platter of veal pasties, black puddings, and sausages when the Duke of Buckingham arrived, and after a confusion of greetings mingled with apologies for the delays of the road, the gentlemen sat down to dinner.

The candles were guttering before the supper party came to an end. Rivers, who had contributed his usual courtly share to the light chatter of the table, rose with a yawn and announced himself ready for his bed. An attendant fetched his cloak; another went to bring up the horses; Buckingham remarked gaily that they would all need to be up betimes next morning for the ride to Stony Stratford. Assenting, Rivers bade my lord of Buckingham a cheerful good night, picked up his gloves, and turned for a last word with the Duke of Gloucester.

"By God, I admire his nerve," Percy muttered in Francis' ear. "But whatever possessed him to come back to Northampton?"

"The only way to prevent Gloucester going after the King's party, I should think," Francis rejoined coolly. "Dorset's little improvisation, doubtless, as carried by Lord Richard Grey, but I marvel they expected to cozzen Gloucester with it. I suppose they never expected Hastings to be such a faithful correspondent."

An icy wind came blustering down the street as a servant opened the outer door. Rivers shivered as he stood on the step, and pulled his cloak more securely around him. Glancing at the man in the doorway behind him, he said with a smile. "A chill breeze. I found myself too English to be long happy from our island, but on such a night I could want myself in Italy again. You've travelled, Sir Philip? There is no place where spring comes softer: it is a golden land."

"Most fair, my lord," Philip agreed quietly. The Earl stood

for a minute, watching the scudding clouds, then drew on his gloves and nodded a friendly farewell. "Until morning, sir."

Philip watched him go briskly down the steps and vault into the saddle, a square, erect figure in his richly furred robes and jewelled collar. Even travelling, Anthony Woodville managed to outshine the rest of the world with his magnificence; it was symbolic, Philip was thinking, of that complex, irresolute personality that beneath all the splendour, the unvarying article of his attire was a hair shirt. "Characteristic," Richard had once bitingly observed. "He protests, even while he is persuaded. I tell you, Philip, my Lord Rivers is too great a gentleman for this common world." Philip had wondered at the savagery in his voice, until he remembered that when the bulk of the Duke of Clarence's estates were returned to the crown, there had been certain leavings for Rivers, as well as the brothers Grey.

Shortly before sunrise, a pale-face equerry knocked on the door of the bedchamber where Lord Rivers was sleeping. His whispered tidings brought the Earl from his bed, shouting for his squires; when, not long after, he descended hurriedly into the courtyard of the inn, it was to find the accuracy of his servant's report dismayingly confirmed. A cordon of guards had been flung around the building, the badges on their livery dimly illuminated in the cold half-light. White to the lips, Rivers swung round, seeking their captain, when the tap of hoof-beats brought him up short. He waited, rigid; the riders drew nearer, rounded a corner, and halted before him, looking down. Staring at the foremost of them, Rivers spoke with an effort at self-possession. "I presume there is an explanation for this, my lord of Gloucester?"

"An excellent one," Richard returned calmly. "I am on my way to Stony Stratford, my lord, where I trust to find my nephew not yet departed for London. You, I am afraid, will not accompany us. I have arranged for you to remain here in your lodgings for the present; the rest will depend upon what I find in Stony Stratford. If, as I believe, the purpose of your visit was to detain me here while Lord Richard hurries the King to London, it will be some time before you are at liberty again."

Rivers' hands knotted. "I question your authority for this, my lord."

"I daresay: by all I hear, your sister has been questioning

251

it too. It is not my intention that she continue to do so."

"In effect, I am your hostage!"

"You are a weapon I do not mean to leave ready to your sister's hand. It is for her to show she has renounced the use of it: for your sake, I earnestly hope she will." Gathering the reins, Richard touched a spur to his stallion's flank. "I wish you good day, my lord."

It was a fourteen-mile ride to Stony Stratford, where a force of two thousand men might still be found with the little King. The combined following of the Dukes of Gloucester and Buckingham numbered scarcely six hundred, but Richard did not stay for the whole of even that slender support. Leaving the baggage carts with the less well mounted of his attendants, he collected a picked group of knights and set off at top speed, Buckingham at his elbow and their small troop streaming behind.

Noon was striking when they clattered into the village which was their destination. A long train of riders was slowly wending from the town along the London road; before the house where the King and his half-brother had spent the night, a greater company waited; behind them, cumbersome wagons were being hastily readied for departure. A good many were stuffed with household goods; more still, piled high with armour and weapons of every kind, all crested with the Woodville arms. The young King was already on horseback with Lord Richard hovering impatiently at his side; it was Grey who first heard the beat of hoofs and, looking behind him, saw the approaching men. Momentarily he sat frozen, then jerked round in an uncompleted gesture whose patent intention at flight conveyed to his companions the first inkling of disaster. He had even laid a hand on the bridle of Edward's horse when the futility of the impulse was borne upon him, and the scalloped leather slipped through his fingers. In dead silence the Protector and his few attendants rode through the press of horsemen, dismounted, and knelt in homage to their bewildered sovereign.

Throughout the scene which followed, it seemed to occur to no one that the presence of two thousand men should have made an arguing point. Curtly they were dismissed; the boy Edward, amazed and affronted, was firmly requested to re-enter the inn for private speech with his uncles of Gloucester and Buckingham; and when, some while after, he emerged again, the last members of the glittering troop had drifted away. The deserted wagons were taken in hand by the Duke of Gloucesters' men; they would make a useful display for the London citizens, who had their collective opinion about the Woodvilles.

Richard had decided to return to Northampton with his nephew until he had more news from London. Without speaking Edward preceded his uncles down the steps, and accepted the assistance of one of Richard's knights in remounting his palfrey. His half-brother had disappeared, taken into quiet custody at the termination of the interview within the hostelry; his own knights and squires of the body had been relegated to the rear of the train; even his Chamberlain, kind Sir Thomas Vaughan, who had been such a friend of Uncle Rivers, was nowhere to be seen. Helplessly Edward scanned the deferential ranks of his new escort for a familiar face, and found not one. Richard's explanation, that the household at Ludlow had been all of Woodville appointing, and as such was unacceptable to the government King Edward had expressly devised for his son's minority, had drawn from Edward's son the retort that it was completely acceptable to him: a show of intransigence which brought him a long look, and not the slightest change in the new arrangements for his domestic well-being.

It was dusk when they reached Northampton. In the courtyard of the inn Richard paused, giving instructions for the safe bestowal of Vaughan and Grey, who were then conveyed to the adjacent lodging house where Earl Rivers had spent a thoroughly uneasy day. Relieved of the morning's uncertainties, Richard was disposed to think more tolerantly of Rivers, who had certainly been left to some very unpleasant conjectures; and when his Chamberlain appeared to announce the advent of supper, he told him to have a share of the landlord's best offerings sent to the Earl, with his assurance that all would yet be well. The gesture availed him little with Lord Rivers—to Francis, who was commissioned with the message, the Earl responded enigmatically that he had rather the dainties went to his nephew Lord Richard, being less accustomed than himself to the plunging of fortune's wheel—but Edward overheard the order, and during the ensuing meal there was a faint thawing of the royal reserve. Buckingham laid himself out to be entertaining; the dark-browed gentleman presented as Viscount Lovell had been, Edward knew, a notable favourite of his father's; and his kinsman, who seemed highly esteemed by the Duke, was discovered to have an infectious smile. Feeling more cheerful in spite of his misery of loneliness, Edward addressed himself to his supper with better appetite, and presently stole another glance at the man who sat by his right hand. Richard, who had been studying the fair face for some little time, gravely returned his nephew's gaze; he had been casting around for a way into the confidence of this half-child, half-youth who so plainly had been taught to mistrust him, and the forlorn expression which followed on realisation that the stranger kneeling with the brimming goblet was the new royal cup-bearer had not gone unnoticed. Waving away the attendant who was offering him similar replenishment, Richard said casually, "Your grace may be anxious about those gentlemen who came with you from Ludlow. There is no need; the officers of your household have been honourably provided for. Many of them, no doubt, you will see again very soon when they come to London for your coronation."

Swallowing, Edward rejoined unhappily, "Indeed I hope I may. They were my very good friends; I should not like to think they lacked for anything, being no longer in my service."

"It is seemly in a prince to have a care for such matters, certainly." Smiling at the depressed face, Richard added, "Being all new to your responsibilities, you may not have remembered that certain of your former servants are now entitled to reward. Your grace is the King: you have but to command."

Pink-cheeked, Edward considered. "There was my tutor at Ludlow," he said at last. "He will be in need of a new position, being a poor man, and there is a living vacant at Pembrigge. I should like him to have it, if that is possible."

"In orders, is he? Easily done." The tables were about to be cleared; Richard looked at an usher, who disappeared and came back shortly with John Kendall. When the landlord's henchmen had borne away the last of the crockery, the secretary drafted at his master's dictation the requisite writ and, at a nod from Richard, proffered it to the boy. It was the first such document which had come to Edward for his new signature, and he hesitated, looking down at the impeccable script. Philip leaned over to murmur something in the Duke's ear; his lip twitching, Richard slid a blank sheet across the table. Edward accepted it gratefully, and did a wobbling practice version before putting a large *"Edwardus"* to the warrant.

Richard picked up the parchment when his nephew had finished, and shook off the sand. *"Le Roy le veult,"* he observed, with a glance at the flushed countenance. "Intoxicating, isn't it? I remember the first writ I sent out: in Wales it was, and thought it went in the King's name, the seal was mine. I was four years older than you are now, but it was no less a moment."

Somewhat warmed by the unexpected confidence, Edward remarked politely, "They say your grace keeps a kingly state at Middleham."

There was a tiny pause. The inflection of the comment made clear where the information had originated: Elizabeth Woodville might have been standing at her son's shoulder. After an instant Richard said coolly, "Why so I do, for the greater honour of my sovereign, whose deputy there I have been." He hesitated, slowly folding the parchment. Staring at the table, Edward played with the discarded paper; Buckingham flung a leg before him on the settle and rested his chin on his knee, regarding them with his bright, intent gaze. Finally Richard laid the warrant down. "So much, then, for Master Geffrey: God and the Bishop of Hereford willing, he will soon be offering many prayers of thanksgiving in Pembrigge church for his prince's bounty. Is there no one else your highness would remember?"

Still examining the dog-eared sheet before him, Edward replied, "Yes: three. My lord, you have made many protestations of respect to me, but you have imprisoned my uncle Rivers, and my brother Grey, and Vaughan, who is their friend and mine: and you did this in my name although they never offended me. The best pleasure you could give me would be the release of these three men."

He faltered on the last words, for Richard's face had set like a stone. A whiplash rejoinder trembled on his lips, apparent for all the room to see; with an effort which was equally visible he fought it back. "If, as you say, I have shown my respect, it is to the King who commands my allegiance now, and to whom in years to come I will render my whole obedience. But for a little you must be advised by me. I could do you no greater disservice than to release and restore to you those men. I am aware of Lord Rivers' qualities, but his name makes him one with the rest of your mother's kindred; Vaughan is their creature, and you do not know as much as you might about your half-brother. You they may not have offended, but they have mightily offended your grace's subjects; they are cursed through the alleys of London and execrated in every corner of the kingdom. For what other reason, do you suppose, did your father exclude even the Queen your mother from the executors of his will? Their ambition is to rule through you, and if you permit them to do it, the day will come when your subjects will curse you too."

Impetuously Buckingham struck in: "Is your highness unaware they even laid a trap for the life of your uncle? They would have had him enter London with Rivers: How long after that, with two thousand men there before him, would the Duke of Gloucester have lingered in this life?"

"You have no proof of that, cousin." Mastering himself, Richard turned once more to the boy. "You are too young yet to know the measure of your father's achievement. How could you understand, having lived your whole life in what he wrought? We have a green land, where before was waste and despair; English ships are sailing west to discover what may lie beyond the sun; there is such music and building as these sixty years have not witnessed, and Caxton has come back from Flanders to set up his press. All this was your father's work; to preserve it he did not scruple to shed even his own blood, and when he was dying he looked to me to guard this so rich harvest during your young age."

Goaded, Edward flung back, "Did he look to you? I have only your word for that, Uncle."

"You may have Hastings', if you prefer it. As for your uncle and his friends, I have submitted their case to the judgment of the council. Will you be content with their decision?" Richard waited, his eyes on the sullen, averted face, then impulsively reached to draw the crumpled paper from his nephew's hand. He studied it for a minute without speaking, in his mind involuntarily comparing the uncertain signature at the top of the page with the other Edward's beautiful, intricate hand. Then, stooping, he wrote swiftly beneath it, *Loyaulté me lie*, signed it, and laid the paper for the boy to see. "My hand on it, kinsman. God judge me, if I fail in my sworn word."

There was a silence like snow falling. Curious, Buckingham lounged from his seat and came to look down at the written words. Smiling at length, he said cheerfully, "Your grace has another uncle present. Will you have my pledge too?" He picked up the pen, and after he had added his own name to the two already written, bent and touched his lips to his nephew's hand.

Beyond the fire, Francis glanced at Philip, met his eyes, and expelled a long breath. The other onlookers were wearing similar expressions of satisfaction; helpless before their approval, Edward struggled with his tears. It seemed the whole world had united in conspiracy to deliver him into the Duke of Gloucester's hands. Surreptitiously brushing his cheek, the boy rose, signifying his wish to retire, and one by one his uncles' followers made him a reverence before they filed from the room. Some of them, Edward thought drearily, he would no doubt find again in his chamber abovestairs, waiting to put him to bed. Engrossed with his own wretchedness and the effort to control the quivering of his lips, he did not notice the flickering appraisal in some of the respectfully lowered eyes; but not a few of the men present were remembering how young Edward of York had ridden with his father to Saint Albans when he was thirteen years old; and the Duke of Gloucester at eleven had put on his first armour to bring the western levies to Leicester for the King. There appeared little of his father's mettle in this shrinking lad, or his uncle's either; Philip, the last to depart, saw one or two heads shaken as the company trooped out.

As the room emptied, a deep quiet fell. Richard turned from the door, where he had gone with Edward to bid him good night, and came back to the fire. Some embers smouldered still in the grate; he stirred them with his foot, and said above his breath, "God have mercy on this unhappy land."

"Amen to that, cousin." Buckingham moved from the shadows. Tossing off a draught of wine, he set the cup on the table and added dryly, "Although it is in my mind that Heaven helps countries, no less than men, who help themselves."

Richard was still scowling at the fire. "I've sent messengers to Hastings; we'll soon hear from him how matters are going. All being well, we should be able to bring the boy into London by Sunday next."

"Sunday?" Buckingham's interest quickened. "The day the Queen had set for his crowning. Good: if the people only see him then, it will distract any suspicion at the post-ponement of the coronation."

Richard made no reply. Smiling slightly, Buckingham toyed with his goblet. "Cousin, in ancient times there lived a man who was called the fortunate prince. All things fell at his bidding: in war he had no equal, in peace his people called down blessings upon the justice of his rule. Being only a pagan, he began to fear the jealousy of the gods, and so he threw a precious jewel in the sea to break the chain of his fortune before another did it for him. But Heaven, rebuking him, returned him his treasure in the belly of a fish." A log cracked with a stream of sparks; a tongue of flame licked from the fissure. Slowly pacing, Buckingham came to the hearth and laid his fingers on the unmoving arm. "Cousin, it is in your hand. I mean, the crown."

Like the sea sound in an emptied shell, his voice lingered. After a moment Richard said quietly, "No," and drew his arm away.

There was a tramp of feet upstairs, and the scraping of bolts as the landlord secured his house for the night. Strolling back to the settle, Buckingham picked up his cloak and turned to the door. A faint frown, half annoyance, half bafflement, was beginning between his brows; Richard, looking up, encountered it, and gave him a quick smile. "Don't think me ungrateful for your kindness, these days past. Believe me, I shall remember."

The pleasant laugh came, with an affectionately mocking gesture. "Did you think I rode from Wales for that? Good night to you, my kinsman."

"Good night, Harry."

In the passage a squire waited to light his master to bed. Softly humming, Buckingham went upstairs.

CHAPTER SEVENTEEN

THE Duke of Gloucester entered London with his cousin the Duke of Buckingham and his nephew the King, to acclamation and bells. Grey, Vaughan, and Rivers had been unobtrusively sent north to Yorkshire, where they would be variously lodged pending the pleasure of the council, and the only reminder of the affair at Stony Stratford was in the piles of Woodville armour which were transported before the procession, and provoked high anger among the citizens. Richard left his nephew at the palace of the Bishop of London, where the young King was to take up temporary residence, and one by one the lords of the realm there presented themselves to offer their homage. A few days later they reaffirmed it, when the Protector, gathering city officials, lords, and prelates, swore them solemnly to their new allegiance. The coronation date was fixed, some six weeks distant; those gentlemen who in late weeks had prudently surrounded themselves with armed retainers from their country estates sighed in relief, and sent them home again; and by the middle of May Francis was writing to Philip that even the fleet, which Sir Edward Woodville had taken out in an effort to carry his sister's war with the Protector to sea, had proved a bankrupt hope. Sir Edward's attempts to hold his ships together had floundered into disaster when the armed bands he sent aboard his most cherished vessels, a pair of chartered Genoese merchantmen, had been first plied with liquor and then overcome by their rebellious hosts, following which the Italian masters weighed anchor and set sail for London. They were followed by all but two of Sir Edward's ships, Richard having offered unconditional pardon to officers and men alike, and Sir Edward escaped to France with only a handful of companions, and that portion of the Tower treasure with which Dorset had thoughtfully provided him. For Elizabeth Woodville, in tearful sanctuary at Westminster Abbey with her daughters and the little Duke of York, it was the wreck of her hopes. Lords and commons, church and council, had declared unequivocal preference for the Duke of Gloucester, of whom she shortly heard, weeping with rage, that he could not show himself in the streets without a crowd flocking after him, cheering and shouting his name.

Philip was in Calais, despatched thither with what he privately considered quite unnecessary pomp, where he was patiently trying to unravel the assorted claims of the English government's indignant deputy, Lord Dynham, and the French King's emissary, Monsieur de Crèvecoeur. The depredations of French pirates in the Channel were beginning to embarrass Louis as much as they had unfailingly maddened the victims, but it had taken all Philip Lovell's tact to bring the bristling principals into the same room, and his reply to Francis ended with the observation that if it were the Duke's pleasure he should become grey in his service, he had sent him to the likeliest place for it.

Although Francis grinned over that—he was acquainted with Lord Dynham—he frowned as he put the letter aside. It did not sound as if Philip would be quickly finished with his business in Calais, and Francis had been hoping that he would soon see his cousin in England again. An itching uneasiness worried at him: intuitively he felt that, somehow, something was going wrong.

People said there had never been so swift and bloodless an assumption of power. The incredible suddenness of the Woodville collapse, followed by Dorset's precipitate flight into sanctuary on his mother's heels—but he had since escaped, none knew where—was not astonishing in retrospect; the peaceful unanimity with which the late King's councillors had entered into alliance with the Duke of Gloucester and his adherents was, in view of past waverings, considerably more remarkable. Yet there they sat in the daily conclaves at Westminster, at Crosby Place, in the Tower; Russell, the popular, cultured Bishop of Lincoln; Hastings, near-garrulous with his first relief; the blunt John Howard, leaving no doubt as to his forthright satisfaction and already Richard's staunch partisan; Morton, churchman and politician, and Stanley, with his thin, inexpressive face. Even Archbishop Rotherham, who in the dawn hours which followed news of the coup at Stony Stratford had rushed after Elizabeth Woodville to offer her his Chancellor's seal, and then changed his mind and gone back for it again, had retained his seat on the council, with no more than a temperate reproof and the transfer of his office to Russell, a

change with which no one had any quarrel. The sole dis-
agreement had been over the fate of Rivers and his confederates; the discovery that Dorset had been augmenting his
uncle's activities with an attempt to raise an army against
him had brought from Richard a curt suggestion that the
three prisoners be tried on charge of treason. The proposal
found favour; it had remained for Russell to point out, in his
crisp, reasonable way, that the Duke of Gloucester had not at
that time been formally invested with the office of Protector,
and the plot had, after all, failed: one and all the lords temporal had refused point-blank to lift a hand for Dorset and
his mother. Naturally, the Chancellor concluded, there was
no question but that the three should continue in ward.
After a short inward struggle Richard conceded the point,
but there was some grumbling among those who had sup-
ported him, and the Duke of Buckingham, a new but ready
voice at the council table, cut rudely across Hastings' own
protests with a furious denunciation of Russell's temerity in
opposing the Protector's will. It was a long time since
William Hastings had been brushed aside in such a
fashion—even Dorset in the late King's time had not gone so
far—and Francis, about to add his objections to the rest,
caught a glimpse of the Chamberlain's expression and abruptly held his tongue. Richard interposed to say calmly that
nevertheless the Lord Chancellor was in the right with his
judgment, but if a rebuke was intended, neither Buckingham nor Hastings construed it as such. Rotherham,
whose mouth had flown open with astonishment, suddenly
remembered to shut it again; Stanley sat impassive, and
Morton, looking across the table to meet the Chamberlain's
wrathful eyes, shrugged, smiled, and spread his hands.

Some time after that, Francis, charged with the responsibility of escorting the Duchess of Gloucester to London,
rode to the Tower to take leave of Richard and receive from
him a letter for his wife. Crossing the green, he could see the
little King, lately removed from the Bishop of London's
palace to the more appropriate state of the Tower's royal
apartments, in solitary exercise at the butts; it looked a
lonely diversion, despite the group of attendants nearby, but
it was too much to expect of Elizabeth Woodville's son that
he would condescend to a match with the Lieutenant's
young lad. Hastings stood beside him, talking genially and
tallying the score. They seemed wholly absorbed in their

conversation, and Francis went on without pausing into the White Tower.

Richard was in the upper room which overlooked the green. He was standing at the window, watching the archery practice; Buckingham—inevitably, as it appeared these days—was with him. He was speaking in a low, confidential voice which fell silent at the creak of the door, but Francis saw him point outside, and heard Richard say, "Harry, let be. There's no evidence for it, none at all."

"By God, I'll find the evidence," Buckingham retorted. He looked round, impatient at the interruption, and vouchsafed his kinsman a distant nod of greeting. He was very full of his dignity now, having recently fallen heir to Earl Rivers' Welsh offices: an unquestionably suitable appointment, but Francis was not alone in considering he had had a surfeit of Harry Stafford lately, and even the faithful Howard had been heard to mutter something about plucking a peacock's feathers. Francis got himself away as quickly as he could, slipping Richard's letter into his wallet.

His designated associate on the ride north was Richard's Master of Henchmen, Sir James Tyrell: a disposition which Francis had received without conspicuous delight. He cared as little as most other members of the Duke's household for Tyrell: a tight-mouthed, brown-faced, burly man, with a savourless impassivity of manner which even after long experience Francis still found trying. Having neither warmth nor wit, he was difficult to be easy with, and the smaller boys, Francis knew from the years of his own tutelage, were afraid of him. After remarking town talk had it that Mistress Shore, to whose favours Dorset had briefly succeeded after the King's death, was now installed in Hastings' London house—an attempted sociability which met with silence, and what might have passed for a smile—Francis gave it up. He admitted to himself that their progress north was the more rapid for Tyrell's skill at organisation; he had a dull man's plodding preoccupation with detail.

Anne received her husband's messenger in the prince's tower, where young Edward was spending a week's mutinous convalescence: a slight fever, his mother explained, but the doctors thought him better in his bed for a few more days. The arrival of Lord Richard Grey and his warders some weeks before had created quite a stir; Francis had left Tyrell in the courtyard, dealing with the barrage of enquiry.

Richard's wife read through his letter swiftly once, and a second time more slowly, before she folded it and said after an instant, "I had not realised my lord of Buckingham was in London."

Francis said wryly, "Madam, he pervades the place." Her eyes glinted as they encountered his, but she made no further comment. Edward, who had been fretfully contemplating the sun-swept hills beyond the castle walls, turned suddenly to demand, "How does my father, Lord Lovell?"

"Carrying all before him, your grace, but sorely missing you and my lady. I was given more messages than I can remember."

The bright colour deepened. "Tell him I shall ride the bay colt to York for Michaelmas." Edward was dragging another pillow into position at his back; Francis went to help him, and was thanked with a smile. They had drawn the couch close to the window, where the boy could look across the moors and the long road winding south to the sky, but it was a tantalising reminder now that soon his mother too would travel it, leaving him once more behind. Presently the physician came with the patient's evening cordial, and Francis left the tower.

They set off next day, a small party of less than a hundred persons, Richard's wife being disinclined to wait upon the assembling of a more cumbersome train. It was a swift journey; barely a week later they arrived in Saint Albans, the last night's halt before London. Rising early next morning, they were not far out of the town when they overtook another, larger cortege, travelling in the same direction. Francis noted the escorting riders' livery, raised an eyebrow, and at a sign from Anne sent an equerry to investigate. When he returned with his surprising confirmation, Anne left all but a handful of gentlemen behind her and rode forward to the closed chariot drawn up by the roadside. There she dismounted from her palfrey. A thin, bony hand, veined with age, could be seen holding aside the mulberry curtains; Francis and his few companions withdrew a deferential distance, and the Duke of Gloucester's wife made reverent obeisance to the Duchess of York.

The escorts having merged, the journey was at length resumed, the younger woman's palfrey ranging close beside her mother-in-law's chariot. Francis, who had been summoned for a few words with Richard's mother, dropped a little behind the ladies and rode on, wondering. It was many years since Cecily of York had stirred from her privacy at Berkhamsted, although she had retained her formidable interest in the affairs of her sons. Edward, who most nearly resembled her, had suffered a raking lecture over his choice of a wife, and Clarence more than once braved a near-chronic disapproval to claim her as intermediary when relations with his elder brother needed patching. During Richard's absence in the north he had maintained a close and devoted correspondence with his mother, but Francis was speculating whether the present excursion might be the result of an invitation from her son—understandable, in view of the approaching coronation—or her grace's own determination to see for herself how matters were faring in London.

They entered the city late that afternoon, and there separated, the Duchess of York proceeding to her long-unoccupied residence at Baynard's Castle, the Duchess of Gloucester going on to Crosby Place. Richard was in conference with his advisers when they arrived, but he came instantly the word was brought, and, meeting his wife in the courtyard, kissed her and drew her in.

It chanced that Francis saw little of him in the next few days. He had been appointed to represent the Protector on Russell's committee in charge of coronation affairs, which sat at Westminster, and with the ceremony only a fortnight off, a mass of detail clamoured for decision. Hastings, too, was little in evidence; he appeared to be spending most of his time now at the Tower, in attendance upon the King. The days slipped by; a letter from Philip conveyed the cheering news that he expected to sail from Calais before the end of June. Russell was hard at work on his Chancellor's address for the opening of Parliament, in between increasingly harried meetings of his committee. Questions of protocol arose, and there were some contentious sessions; coming from one of them, involving the right of Lord Stanley's wife to the precedence of her Beaufort blood as opposed to her standing as the mother of Henry Tudor, Francis yawningly entered his apartments, and found a man of the Duke's from Crosby Place waiting for him. Lord Lovell's presence was required next day without fail, in council at the Tower.

Morning dawned fair with a dance of sunlight along the

river. Francis, travelling by water for the sake of speed, chatted idly with the bargeman, and pondered, without particular urgency, the reason for the summons to a meeting in London, when another one at Westminster had been expressly arranged for Russell and his associates that same day. Francis was the only one of them who had been called from it: true, as Richard's delegate to the committee he was the exception in a group of less prominent men, principally clerics, who had served on the previous council, but if there were important business afoot it seemed curious that Russell had been left out of it.

It was a small group which assembled in the great chamber of the White Tower. Buckingham was there, with John Howard and the young Earl of Lincoln, son of Richard's sister, the Duchess of Suffolk; Catesby, one of the new crop of lawyers lately beginning to take a hand in public affairs, who had been brought to Richard's notice by Lord Hastings, and was now firmly established in his service; and others of the Duke's northern following. Rotherham and Morton sat a little apart from the rest, with Stanley beside them and, next to him, an empty seat. Hastings, the last before the Protector to arrive, had come directly from the royal apartments, and sat down by Stanley without a word. Francis saw him look at Buckingham, who returned the stare half-smiling, and played with his rings. A moment later Richard came in.

His chair stood ready for him, but he did not use it. Resting his fingers before him on the table, he let his eyes move down the rows of faces to the four men at its foot. It was six weeks since he had ridden from Stony Stratford, and it struck Francis that the time had aged him. He looked nerve-worn and weary to exhaustion, the lines cut deep around his eyes and mouth; and in his temple a small pulse moved visibly under skin as pale and tightly stretched as parchment.

Since he had not seated himself, the others were forced to rise. The slow scrape of Hastings' chair was the last sound in the silence which descended, rustling, over the room; the level voice, when it began, was so low it seemed scarcely to break the quiet.

"My lords and sirs, a month ago you were pleased to approve the appointment of a protector for the minority of the King, and to vote that this regency be continued until he is himself of an age to rule. Since I had come unarmed among you, it appeared your willing choice, and your opinions at all times have been sought and heeded. Yet it seems now that this was not enough."

"Enough and to spare for most, your grace." It was Howard who had spoken, his deep rumble falling on a bewildered hush. Richard gave him a fleeting glance. "I thank you, my lord." He had a sheaf of papers in his hand; all at once he dropped them on the table. "I have here evidence of a conspiracy against this government. The heart of it is, of course, the Queen; Dorset, wherever he may be, is her agent; Rivers and Grey may be presumed also to have their allotted parts when they have been freed to play them. There is nothing new in this, save only in the fathering of the thought. But a way has lately been found for word to be carried to the Queen, and a reply brought again to her family and those others who have joined in this design—which, as I have had proof shown me, is to accomplish not only the overthrow of this government, but the deaths of those who have headed it. To meet this, I have sent Sir Richard Ratcliffe with letters to the city of York and some certain northern gentlemen, desiring the despatch with all speed of those men I had not thought necessary before to secure the peace of this realm." He paused, straightening the closely written documents beneath his hand. "These proofs will be laid before you and the lords spiritual of the council at an early date: at which time I intend to request that the sentence heretofore held in suspension over Lord Rivers, Sir Thomas Vaughan, and Lord Richard Grey, be implemented forthwith. There remains now the matter of their confederates."

Francis, following the direction of his eyes, felt a cold sickness of expectation. Lincoln recovered his voice first.

"Others in this, my uncle? What others, except the tribe of Woodville?"

"Others in this room." Richard, who had not looked at his nephew, continued to stare down the length of the table. "Lord Hastings, you have recently seen fit to take the woman Jane Shore under your protection. What if I should tell you that the messenger who was found to travel between Elizabeth Woodville and her lately made friends is that same harlot Shore?"

There was a grease of sweat on the Chamberlain's forehead. He said huskily, "My lord, I should say it was a lie."

"And what if I should say that Elizabeth Woodville has found not one new friend, but four? You, Hastings"—for the first time the icy blaze of his eyes shifted—"and you, Stanley, and you, reverend fathers in God Morton and Rotherham—" Stanley made a fractional movement; hard-faced, Francis barred the way. "Not just yet, my lord." The big man grew still again. Rotherham was making near-soundless little bleats of protest; Morton, his blandness gone, opened and closed a hand on his pectoral cross. Desperately gathering himself together, Hastings lifted his voice above the rest. "My lord of Gloucester, if any man has told you I desired your life, he has foully lied."

Richard said, very low, "Hastings, you know full true you had never accomplished your design without it."

"I deny that. It is true that I"—Hastings hesitated, and plunged—"that I would have seen certain changes in this government. You have gone far beyond whatever we— whatever the King your brother intended—"

"Have a care, my lord." There was danger in the soft voice, the taut threat of a bow strung to breaking, but Hastings rushed heedlessly on.

"—whatever he could possibly have meant. On my soul, you have power like a very king—you make and unmake at your pleasure and no man refuses you. I served long on this council, and now I find myself slighted and made little, great with offices I earned before you ever drew a sword, and smaller in voice than a scullion in my late master's kitchen—"

"You had a voice on this council like any other, my lord. Did you think to better your condition through this treason?"

"Who are you to call it so! I knew the King's mind—he was my dear lord, and more than any man I knew what he desired—"

"By Heaven, do you presume to tell me my brother's mind! You, who tempted him after you in your filthy pleasures, who took him in his youth and taught him to live in such a way that, had it been otherwise, he were here today—" Richard leaned forward. "You've owned your guilt, Hastings. Have a thought now for your soul." He wheeled, a command on his lips, but Catesby, obedient to the look, was already at the door. When he opened it, the Tower guards burst in. Hastings jumped back, fumbling for the poniard at his belt; he was a heavy man, powerful for his years, and it took two of them to hold him. Panting, he quieted at last, and Richard said harshly, "Take that man hence and see to it his head comes from his shoulders within this hour. For these other three, place them under guard and keep close watch on them. My lord Lieutenant, look to it."

White as his linen, Hastings strove futilely against the warders' grip. His tunic was ripped and the shirt torn from his throat in the struggle; Richard watched, immobile, as they dragged him out. Howard, wearing an expression of deep concern, started to speak, changed his mind, and with a glance at Francis turned to the door. Casually rearranging the lace at his cuffs, Buckingham murmured, "With your permission, cousin, I'll send a herald to quiet the city. The Lord Chamberlain had a certain following among the vulgar there."

Richard made no reply; he was looking down at the table, leaning his weight on tightly clenched hands. Buckingham went out, and by twos and threes the others followed him. Francis stayed behind the rest, waiting for he scarcely knew what by the half-open door. It was high noon and sunlight was pouring through the narrow windows, but the room seemed filled with shadows, robbing the lambent innocence of the day. His tongue felt stiff and unwieldy, wood shaped to no possible use.

In a shockingly brief time the Lieutenant of the Tower returned. Hesitating on the threshold, he regarded the motionless back; he was very pale, but he spoke firmly. "My lord, I have to inform you the prisoner has been despatched. Have you instructions for the disposal of the body?"

Richard did not turn. He said tonelessly, "When the late King my brother went to France, he deposed in his will that should mischance befall them, Lord Hastings was to be buried beside him. Carry him to Windsor and see it is done."

There was a pause. "And the others, my lord?"

"Have Lord Stanley conducted back to his house in the city and a guard set. Rotherham may remain here under your eye. Lodge him in comfort: he is old, and"—the grey voice checked momentarily—"somewhat foolish. As for the Bishop of Ely—" This time the pause was longer; Morton's face, smooth-jowled, inscrutable, hovered before them all. A tireless timeserver, implacably ambitious, he had moved from Lancaster to York with effortless aplomb; there was not much doubt in whose brain the conspiracy had hatched. What place in London was sure, what guardian would be proof against that subtle, persuasive tongue? After an interval Richard spoke with something of his former decision. "The Bishop of Ely is discharged into my lord of Buckingham's custody. Let him be kept here only so long as is necessary while his grace decides which of his manors will house him."

The Lieutenant bowed, impassive, and left the room. Francis, himself on the point of withdrawal, was abruptly halted. "Lord Lovell."

"My lord?"

"When you return to Westminster, tell the Lord Chancellor it is my opinion that the child York should be taken from sanctuary and brought to share the company of his brother the King. He has claimed no protection of the Church: his mother has no authority to keep him by her." A silence fell, during which Francis heard the sharp, restless tapping of his fingers on the table. "Tell the Lord Chancellor I will discuss this with him and his grace of Canterbury in full council tomorrow."

In the crowded antechamber little groups of men lingered, talking in varying defensive or troubled tones. "Attainder?" someone was saying in an argumentative way. "Why not attainder? It was treason, plain enough." ... "Rich pickings for a certain high-flying gentleman, then. By God, who'd have thought Hastings could be such a fool." A retainer in the Stafford livery strolled past; the discussion ended as if sheared with a blade. Crossing the room, Francis encountered Robert Percy; the big northerner was looking grim, but he said only, "Any word from your cousin, Lovell?"

"He expects to sail in time for the coronation." Francis kept his eyes on the floor. Percy grunted and said, "God be thanked for that. I suppose you're for Westminster again?"

He walked with the younger man to the outer door. Over the disjointed fragments of half a dozen conversations an earnest voice rose: "My lord, I entreat you, I must have speech with the Duke."

Francis looked back. He did not know the man, an anxious-appearing creature in cleric's dress, plucking at Howard's sleeve; but a vague impression of familiarity made him pause. "He'd better be careful if he means to break in on Gloucester now. D'you know him, Rob?"

Percy glanced perfunctorily at the worried petitioner. "I've seen him about, not for a number of years though: it's the Bishop of Bath. His name's Stillington."

CHAPTER EIGHTEEN

The Great Hall of Baynard's Castle was a large room; the few men assembled in it were swallowed by the vast gloom. A dry whisper of rushes caught by uneasily pacing feet, the river slapping on the water stairs beyond the windows, mingled with their subdued voices and rose, echoing, to the vaulted roof. Assheton, who had gone again to the door to peer out, returned muttering, "Plague on it, what's keeping them?"

Percy said imperturbably, "Patience, Ralph, it takes time to make a king. Moreover, you can't hurry the faithful Commons. They'll come."

Ratcliffe, just back from the north, hitched his belt and remarked in an academic way, "Since he's managing the business, I can't think why Buckingham didn't wait for the levies from York. He'd have been surer with them."

Francis kicked a log in the blackened fire pit. "Gloucester wouldn't have it. He said he wanted a free opinion, not one taken at pike's point."

Ratcliffe put up an eyebrow, and Assheton, nervous with strain, shrugged in exasperation. "A little too indifferent, surely!" Francis gave a short laugh. "Rest you: he's not indifferent."

Assheton had resumed his aimless roving about the hall; Percy broke open a nut on the table, and, using the point of his dagger, stolidly began to separate the meats from the shell. A short distance from the others a man leaned alone by the window; in the act of pouring himself a cup of wine, Francis hesitated an instant before he made a slight gesture with the flagon, saying carefully, "Philip?"

Philip replied briefly, "No, I thank you, cousin." He was resting one booted foot on the window seat, his travelling cloak bundled beside him. The Channel winds had held him in Calais several days beyond first expectation, and it was only that morning he had reached London. The pale light showed the unmoving lines of his profile like an artist's drawing; his steward's rod, loosely held, tapped a slow, intermittent measure against the ledge.

"I saw Stanley today, going off to Westminster," Assheton said idly. "He was looking pleased enough with himself. They say he sat with the Lords yesterday, very cheerfully adding his voice when they moved to offer the Duke the crown."

"Faith, I should look pleased too, had I got off as well as he did," Percy drawled. "Keeping his head and talking his way back on to the council in the bargain: quite an achievement for a man near-charged with treason two weeks since. Leave it to Stanley to smell the winning side."

The squeak of the door made them all start. A thin, sharp-featured man came busily into the room; he wore a plum-coloured doublet, much stuffed with bombast, and the Stafford knot was stitched on his sleeve.

"Gentlemen, we have word that a delegation from Parliament has left Westminster and is coming with a great body of citizens, to beg his grace of Gloucester to make us all happy by assuming the crown."

'Knyvet, your happiness is more than I can bear." Francis, who disliked on principle all the Duke of Buckingham's familiars, considered his grace's brother-in-law with distaste. "Do we sing a *Te Deum,* or have you more joy to impart?"

Knyvet returned the look with interest. "By your leave, my lord, I have instruction for you. When the people come, his grace of Buckingham will go out to address them—to ascertain their wishes, you understand. These being made known, he will return to wait upon the Duke of Gloucester, entreating him to hear the prayers of the people. This gallery here"—he nodded towards the long platform which opened from the hall to overlook the street—"will be a convenient spot. In which respect, it has been thought advisable that—saving of course, his grace of Buckingham—his grace of Gloucester should appear without attendants. I am therefore sent to command you to remain here, out of sight of the citizens. The impression will be a better one—there must be no suggestion of any contrivance, any threat of arms, to mar the free request of lords and commons."

"Jesu, I'm complimented," Percy murmured, with a glance at his half dozen companions, and Francis suggested irrepressibly, "Put him between a pair of holy fathers, Knyvet. That'll make an impression for you."

There was brittle laughter among his friends, but no one was looking amused. Clearly Buckingham intended no possibility of error about who was setting the crown on a grateful kinsman's head. From the window Philip asked coolly, "By whose authority are these orders sent, Sir William? The Duke of Gloucester's?"

Knyvet gave back stare for stare. "Sir Philip, by the authority of the most noble Duke of Buckingham."

"You do not surprise me."

There was a pause, while Knyvet weighed the comment. Philip had begun to gather up his cloak, conveying thereby, it appeared, his total disinterest in the day's further happenings; as if making up his mind, Knyvet said challengingly, "You are not merry, Sir Philip. Yet I think you have cause for cheer, like any other that is the Duke of Gloucester's true friend and servant."

"Merry?" Philip repeated. He straightened, the cloak swinging on his arm. "No, I am not merry. I left England sworn subject of King Edward, our late sovereign lord's undoubted son: I return to find I must acknowledge now King Richard, sometime Duke of Gloucester and Protector of his brother's child. I liked him better by his former titles—Lords, Commons, and the Duke of Buckingham notwithstanding."

"Did you indeed?" Knyvet smoothed his upper lip; the small eyes narrowed with sudden spite. "I am not astonished: it is men's work, the crowning of a king. I have heard you took a blow once, and from a Frenchman too."

All at once the room was emptied of sound. Francis saw the colour leave his cousin's face; it was an instant before he moved, but something made Knyvet step back. There was a cushioned faldstool behind him; he tripped over it, and as he struggled for balance Philip reached out, his hand fastening in the neck of the plum-coloured doublet. "You ditch-got slopsbearer to the most noble pander of Buckingham," he said, very quietly. "Men's work, do you say? I have done men's work for the Duke of Gloucester these fourteen years while you sat scratching on your Norfolk dunghill. There is not a man of Lords or Commons that cannot read your master's purpose, Knyvet: he would be a maker of kings even as the Earl of Warwick, not caring what shame or smirch he brings his kinsman's name, so there may be profit in it for Harry Stafford. But let him go softly. There was one tried the game with King Edward that was sorry for it; and the Duke of Gloucester is no man's instrument to play upon."

The tight fist opened so suddenly that Knyvet stumbled and snatched at the arras. His skin had gone yellow, and the veins netted beneath it were the colour of old meat. Pulling himself erect, he whispered, "My lord—my lord of Buckingham shall hear of this."

"Run to him quickly, before the account stales." Philip turned away, wiping his palms on his thighs. The sound of Knyvet's footsteps down the hall crossed with a light patter on the stair; a page appeared and came towards them. "Sir Philip, his grace of Gloucester will receive you now."

Francis began urgently, "Philip—" and halted. The warning hovered on his lips; swallowing it, he said at last, "I'll await you, cousin." Without answering, Philip stooped to pick up the cloak, lying where it had fallen. He flung it back into the window-seat, and with his staff of office in his hand followed the page from the hall.

It was a dark stair, narrow and twisting, the stones dank with a chill the heaviest hangings could not shut out. There was not much more light above, where a number of rooms had been partitioned from the old, larger ones. In the most commodious of them the Duchess of York spent her days; in another suite of apartments the Duke and Duchess of Gloucester less than a week before had, by invitation, established themselves. Few household servants were in evidence; all of them who were free to do so had swarmed out to the street to await the deputation from Parliament.

There were three rooms, each opening into the next. Philip went through the first two, and a gentleman usher let him into the third, the bedchamber which served also as the Duke's private closet and workroom. Except for the groom of the chamber who kept the door, Richard was alone; a little chest had been drawn near the bed with a dish of cherries on it, and he had a handful of them which he dropped back into the bowl when Philip entered. He was no longer wearing the mourning clothes in which he had ridden from Middleham; his doublet was purple cloth, slashed with silver, and there was a jewelled collar around his shoulders with his own boar badge depending from it. Cheerfully, he held out his hand.

"Philip, you are tardy. I have expected you these four days since; were you too comfortable in Calais to brave the winds?"

Philip bent to kiss the outstretched fingers. "Not overmuch, between Dynham and Crèvecoeur. Still, they've reached the talking stage at last, an improvement over what went before."

Chuckling, Richard remarked, "Dynham never loved a Frenchman. You've done well to bring him so far: they'll settle things soon enough between them now." He pointed informally to the bowl of fruit; he was smiling still, but his eyes evaded the hazel ones. Philip said deliberately, "I thought Dynham an able man, and sensible. A word from your grace might be in season: he is in fear for his post now, having been deputy by Lord Hastings' appointing."

The smile vanished. "He need not be." Richard looked down at his hands; they were sticky with juice, and he picked up a napkin to dry them. "I'm glad to see you, Philip. I have many around me, but too few I can call my friends. Those that are, I value the more: I have need of them now, every one."

Silence fought with silence; and then Philip said, "So you will truly do this? There is no changing what you have resolved?"

"Why should it be changed? It is mine by right. My brother was pre-contract to the Lady Eleanor Butler when he married Elizabeth Woodville: a secret oath, taken no doubt to shorten his path to the lady's chamber, but binding. He could not in law take any other wife, nor on any other lady father his true heirs. There is no questioning Stillington's word: he was witness to it."

Philip's lip twisted. "I have heard the tale. It was the subject of Friar Ralph's sermon at Paul's Cross last Sunday—'Bastard slips shall not take root', by grace of which God save King Richard. But I weary your highness; you were yourself present, I am told, to hear the friar."

"As you would have been present, if you had been here." There was an edge to the controlled voice. "I did not go there alone, nor was this step taken without the counsel of men who were many years my brother's loyal servants. Do you think me so greedy for his honours that I would have seized upon even so grave a hindrance to my nephew's claim, had I not been most strongly persuaded to it?"

"Oh, I believe you were persuaded. Did you know that while the bastardy of the late King's children was being preached at Paul's Cross, other holy men in the city were arguing a better claim? They were saying King Edward was not himself crowned by rightful descent from the Duke of

York, having been base-gotten on your grace's mother by the archer Blayborgne."

Richard had been moving impatiently about the room, but he checked at that. The restlessly swinging pendant in his fingers stilled; his face, incredulous, turned to the other man's. "Who—?" He stopped. There was only one person would have dared to prompt such sermonising. A dark colour crept into his cheeks; he hesitated, then walked to the door. The groom pulled it hastily open; looking beyond him, Richard addressed the usher outside. "Where is the Duke of Buckingham?" Even as the answer came, they heard through the open window Buckingham's voice in the gallery below. The representatives from Parliament had arrived.

Richard listened a moment before he came back into the room, banishing the groom with a gesture. He was deeply flushed; Philip saw his eyes go to the far wall of the chamber, beyond which his mother's bower lay. After an interval he spoke, jerkily and with difficulty. "I did not know this. I am amazed anyone could have thought I would countenance so crass a stupidity—"

"No one who knows you would suppose it, but the thing is done now. Oh, my lord, you will go elbow high in filth before you achieve this desire—"

"Desire?" Richard interrupted. "Survival, rather: Hastings taught me that. Believe me, I have no choice."

His brows lifting, Philip said, "Is that what they have told you? There was a time when you would have sickened on it."

"God's death, Philip, do you tutor me? Put a curb on your tongue, or for all that I have loved you—" The explosion died in a shock of silence. Philip, rigid, felt an object impede the instinctive doubling of his fingers; he looked down and saw the steward's staff, forgotten in his hands.

After a minute he held it out. He had known an impulse to break it across his knee; but he said instead, "It has been in my mind that your grace will require this service of me no more. The King's steward is his chiefest officer: it is unfitting I should act for you now over so many higher subjects." He laid it on the table, a finger's reach from the unstirring hand, and was withdrawing when Richard spoke.

"Philip, wait." He had turned to the window; it was no longer possible to see his face. "In all my life you never told me anything but the truth: I don't know why I should be angry with you for it now." His hand moved gropingly over the joining of the blocks, dug at it a while, and slowly made a fist which was pressed with desperate force against the gritty sill. "God witness me, I tried. If ever you believed a word of mine, believe me in this: I tried. Many will say I never intended anything else—when I left the north, when I took the boy from Rivers at Stony Stratford, when I swore myself his vassal and true kinsman; but it is not so. I meant to keep my word; I did not know—I had not begun to understand how impossible my situation was."

A murmur came from the street; there were shouts and clappings, and confused pattern of sound through which a golden voice wove itself: warm, persuasive, eloquent with conviction. The grey eyes flicked towards it with a kind of unconscious calculation, and as swiftly drew away.

"A regent governs by the consent of other men; he has power only so long as they can be bribed or coerced into accepting him. Neither crown nor chrism protect him; he is perpetual temptation to every noble with a troop at his back. Even supposing he survives the term of his office, what follows? What of the day when the borrowed royalties are yielded up, and my lady Elizabeth sits at her son's hand? The boy has hated me from the beginning for his mother's sake, and she—I doubt she has grown gentle since she dealt with Desmond and his sons."

There was cheering outside; Philip tried to shut his ears to the noise. "And Stillington? What if he lied?"

Richard was silent for a space, looking down at his hands. "I do not think he lied."

A rush of footsteps sounded in the outer chamber; the door burst open and Buckingham, radiant, appeared on the threshold. He came forward without a pause, his arms flung wide; the heavy angelica-scent he wore filled the room. "Cousin of Gloucester, the people wait. Do you come out, and tell them you will accept the crown." It seemed as though he would go down on his knees; he was reaching for his kinsman's hand when Richard forestalled him.

"In a moment, cousin: I would like to ask you something first. Was it you who set on some certain friars last Sunday to preach the bastardy of the late King and the dishonour of the Duchess of York?"

Caught unawares, Buckingham stopped short. His eyes

sweeping the room, settled on Philip, and the smile faded from his lips. "So you have returned, sir. I have heard it was so, and I am glad you are here: there is a matter which must be brought to his grace's notice." His gaze shifted to Richard. "I must complain of this—gentleman, cousin. He has handled my brother Knyvet very roughly, using the while such words as I would not affront you by the telling."

"Knyvet?" Richard repeated, momentarily deflected "Why in the world would you be flitting with that little rat, Philip?" There was oblique affection in the North Country provincialism: it was reminder of the shared years. Buckingham too apprehended it; and something leaped in his eyes. Unable to restrain a gleam of amusement—he was wondering how verbatim a report Knyvet had given—Philip rejoined tranquilly, "Perhaps his grace of Buckingham would rather tell you, my lord," and Buckingham, colouring, haughtily intervened. "I know not what liberties you allow your servants, cousin, but when they infringe on the dignity of the blood royal it is time to object." As he spoke, he ostentatiously smoothed the sleeve of his tunic: a gorgeous garment, conspicuously worked with the Plantagenet arms. Richard only waited, and Buckingham added lamely, "It was not only Sir William who was grossly insulted, but—in some part—myself."

Richard glanced at Philip, and back again to the younger man. Presently he said dryly, "I see. Well, Harry, since you will not be more explicit, there is little I can do. I am very sure Sir Philip needs no reminder of the respect due a nobleman; touching myself, you must permit me to judge what constitutes a liberty." His steady gaze compelled the unquiet eyes to his. "Meanwhile, you have yet to tell me what I have asked. Were they your creatures who slandered the virtue of the Duchess of York?"

At bay, Buckingham hesitated, floundered, and recovered. Kneeling, he spread his arms. "Cousin, I am at your mercy." The winning smile appeared, in which surprise, hurt, and a kind of whimsical contrition were variously blended. Distastefully watching, Philip thought he used his body like a woman: they were the same tricks and graces, the identical natural weapons of cajolement and tender raillery. He felt a prickle of embarrassment at the sight which seemed to communicate itself to Richard; almost imperceptibly he drew back.

"Harry, why? God above, have I not mired myself enough? Why would you shame me by publishing this lie in my name?"

Buckingham's face altered. The delicate lips thinned; he said boldly, "Whatever I have done, cousin, it was for your sake."

For an instant Richard stood poised; he looked ready to strike the smiling mouth. Then, slowly, the clenched hand fell. "You do well to remind me."

In the next room a clamour rose. Buckingham came to his feet, lightly brushing his knees, as the door opened to admit the Duke of Suffolk, with Lincoln his son, and Howard close behind. Suffolk was spokesman, a flush of excitement on his cheek. "My lord, will you come down? They are near-rioting below; they will not depart until you have shown yourself." Howard was beaming; Lincoln knelt to kiss his uncle's hand. Heartsick, Philip looked at them: upright men all, but Suffolk stood to become brother-in-law to a king, Lincoln no less a nephew; and Howard was near claimant to the dukedom of Norfolk, since the child heiress Elizabeth Woodville had seized for her youngest son had died. Buckingham, the storm forgotten, had tucked his arm through Richard's. "Cousin," he said gently, "will you dally still? It is to be the King."

A page hurried in, carrying a long over-gown; Philip took it mechanically from the boy and came to lay the robe over Richard's shoulders. The hubbub swelled around them, eager, congratulatory; through the laughing admonishments and assisting hands Philip whispered passionately, "My lord, think on it, only a little longer. It is a whole life of honour and an untarnished name you are offering here." Richard said roughly, "So be it, then," and went before them from the room.

The crowning day was fair. Early on a summer morning the King's train rode from the Tower, along streets made gay with hangings, loud with cheering and the clangor of bells. At Westminster the Abbot and his monks met them and received them in. Marshalling again next morning, the procession trod a ribboning scarlet carpet to the church with heralds and trumpeters crying before. The Earl of Northumberland carried the great sword Curtana with the blunted tip of mercy, the Earl of Kent and Viscount Lovell, the swords of justice spiritual and temporal; Lord Stanley followed, with Suffolk, Lincoln, and Howard's son, newly made Earl of Surrey, and behind them John Howard, Duke of Norfolk, with the crown. The Bishops of Durham and Bath walked to right and left of the King, supporting his arms, and Buckingham came after bearing his train.

Within the church lords and commons waited. A platform had been raised for the chairs of estate, and from its four corners the Archbishop of Canterbury four times showed the prince to his people. Their shouted assent crashed on the quiet, waking the echoes. There followed the offering and the oath of kingship, the long motionless prostration before the altar while the Litany was sung, the anointing. The Queen came with a whisper of silk to kneel beside her husband; the Abbot of Westminster unclasped his garments, and the Archbishop touched holy oil to breast, shoulders, and palms; the sacred chrism, oil of olive mixed with balsam, to his head. Then the crowns were brought, the sword offered, the mace and sceptre given; the attendant lords trooped forward, Buckingham leading, to be escort back to the royal seat, and the bishops who had enthroned him came each one to receive the sovereign's kiss. The silver voices of the choir children rose in jubilant *Te Deum*; incense mingled thickly with the smell of balsam and angelica; and the King's lips on Stillington's cheek were as cold as any stone.

There was feasting afterwards in Westminster Hall. The Duke of Norfolk rode about on a charger trapped with cloth of gold, overseeing the dispersal of uninvited onlookers, the arrangement of banquet tables, the bearing of dish after dish to the dais where presently the King and Queen took their places. Making his way to join the others chosen to serve the King, Philip glimpsed his sister's eldest stepson, Gilbert Secott, among the throng, and after a moment of quite irrational surprise—for Oxfordshire had never seemed so far—realised that Gilbert would have come from Stratton Audley in Lord Audley's train. Audley himself, with Francis and Robert Percy, was among those serving at the King's table; Philip, kneeling with the brimming goblet, caught his cousin's eye and understood from the distant look that he was still in disgrace with Francis. It was some days since they had met privately; Francis, to whom had fallen Hastings' old office of Lord Chamberlain, was preoccupied with his new duties, but the information, imparted by Richard, that Philip had refused both comptrollership of the royal household and election to the chapter of Garter Knights had brought Francis very speedily to his cousin's chamber, where he spoke his opinion with fluency and exactness. Philip listened patiently, but neither protest nor pleading had any effect upon an obduracy which Francis regarded bitterly as bull-headedness in its purest and most objectionable form. Clearly, his resentment was still rankling.

The afternoon wore on; in New Palace Yard the running conduits of wine showed signs of emptying, and shadows crept across the western sky. Downriver, the Tower guns roared a last salute, and the boy Edward, lately removed from the grandeur of its state apartments, wept at the sound. A new lieutenant was in residence now, Richard's Yorkshire follower Brackenbury; a kindly man, he did what he could to mitigate his charge's humiliation and grief. As wise as he was tactful, he did not force himself on the boy, and presently left him to the consolations of nine-year-old Richard of York, who comforted his brother with the assurance that Heaven would strike the usurper with a bolt of fire, and all would yet be well.

Not many days later the royal household travelled by barge to Greenwich. Disembarking at the water stairs, Philip encountered his cousin, but there was a suggestion of constraint in Francis' greeting, and he went quickly past. Philip experienced a twinge of guilt despite his amusement; he seemed to have mortally offended his kinsman, and he wondered contritely if Francis' own pleasure in the rain of honours now descending upon him had been seriously impaired by his exasperating relatives' refusal to share in them. The suspicion lingered depressingly through the rest of the day, and that evening in the great bedchamber, when Richard, noticing his abstraction and with a good idea as to the cause, commented humourously about it, Philip said ruefully, "I am in disfavour with my cousin, and it is something for him to cherish his anger so long. He thinks me the ungratefulest of all your grace's subjects."

"So do not I. Are you trying to apologise to me again? I want no slaves around me, but men for the weal of the kingdom who will speak me as honestly as they serve—not like poor Tyrell, who if I told him to leap from the top of Saint Paul's would hesitate only long enough to consider how he should ascend it." His chin in his hand, Richard regarded his companion with a smile. He looked comfortable and at ease, markedly changed from the pale man in the abbey church, but the lightly mocking tone only half-concealed a deadly earnest. "Not one jot, not one tithe of ill-gotten benefit will you accept from my hands. No, do not protest. For this time I am journeyman to my brother's work; if I fail not, in certain years I may earn what you will not concede me now."

It was late when Philip left the King's rooms; night had come, and in the maze of private chambers and crowded dormitories the household was composing itself for sleep. In the deserted passage Philip stood reflecting; he was trying to decide if he should pay his cousin a visit before seeking his own bed. But Francis would not be expecting him at such an hour, and it was quite probable that by now he would be enjoying the kind of company upon which a diplomatic cousin would not intrude. The flares guttered in their blackened sconces, and far off a voice was raised in shouted good night; shrugging, Philip abandoned the project, and was turning away when something made him pause. The step which sounded beyond the curve of the passage could have signified no more than the late retiring of another reveller, but there was an odd furtiveness about it, and it seemed to be approaching the door which gave on Buckingham's apartments. A shadow moved on the arras, leaped gigantically high, and dwindled to nothing under the torches which burned above the Duke's threshold. The light fell briefly on a muffled figure; Philip thought—and was certain by the incongruity of it that he must be mistaken—that it had looked like James Tyrell.

Richard did not remain long at Greenwich. He and his wife shortly departed for Windsor; and before the month was gone a great concourse issued from the castle gates, bound for the West Country and Yorkshire. It was Richard's intention to make as wide a progress as possible through his kingdom, and the brilliance of his entourage decorated the dun and russet roads with vair and ermine, gules and azure, rings and roundels and bezants of jewels winking in the sun. Laden sumpters trudged in their wake; busy purveyors scoured the route for provisions, thrusting inquisitively among the market stalls and reaping a harvest of denunciation for Paul Pry manners when their searching fingers turned up a soft head of cabbage, or loaves of less than proper weight. The local populations, long victimised by such practices, gave unanimous approval to their curiosity; embarrassed grocers and bakers did not.

It had been Francis' thought while conning the route at Windsor that the King and Queen should lie for a night at Minster Lovell. The proposal accepted, messengers were despatched to Oxfordshire, and early one afternoon the cavalcade poured into the courtyard where the lady of Minster Lovell waited to receive them. Francis appraised his wife's expression, and knew a belated doubt for the felicity of his suggestion. Anna, bidden to appear among the high-ranking ladies who attended the coronation, had refused on plea of indisposition, an excuse Francis elected to leave unchallenged at the time; in the end he had almost forgotten, but the memory returned now to warn him that, however much a distinction the rest of his dependents might consider the visit of King Richard, Anna Fitz Hugh was not overcome by the honour. She had her son by the hand, and her formal reverence was copied by the boy, but she kept her eyes lowered through Richard's conventional expression of thanks for the hospitality of the manor, and Will, Francis saw with annoyance, seemed to have wholly lost his tongue. Richard looked him over with a smile, remarking, "A strapping lad, Francis: he favours you," and the moment passed; but Francis had read the hostility in the small face, and his lips tightened. A minute later he dismissed Master William to the upper rooms. The remainder of the visit went without incident, but the edge of his pleasure had gone, and he was silently promising himself an interview with his wife at the first opportunity. It failed to materialise; their own great chamber had been naturally yielded to the King and Queen, and with the house overflowing, the apartment where they eventually retired together was, perforce, shared with several others. Declaring herself unutterably wearied by all the pother, Anna went—as it appeared—instantly to sleep. It was only the next morning, when the visitors were mounted again and turning their horses towards the east gate, that Francis, looking grimmer than she had ever seen him, was able to draw his wife aside.

"Madam, a word. For your labours in feasting your King and mine, I thank you; but you had better occupy yourself less in the larder, and more with our son. I know well what lesson he has been having and who gave it him, but look you: if it is your ambition that he have this place after me, let him show a different face next time King Richard honours this house. I would see my son stripped of every virgate of land and every title he is heir to, before I should know a false subject sits here to my shame and the disadvantage of his true prince."

As angry now as he, she replied bitingly, "Your true prince sleeps in the Tower, my lord Yorkist. Do you never think of him?" Before he could answer she turned from him, lifting her skirts over the cobbles to go back into the house.

The flat lands of Oxfordshire dropped behind them; the stone Cotswold villages rose on every hand. In Gloucester there were pageants and mummings; the castle windows blazed a welcome, and early in the summer dusk the huge train of the Duke of Buckingham was sighted streaming through the city gates. He was newly Constable, and the multiple affairs of his office had prevented his joining the King's progress; now he was journeying home to Brecon, where Bishop Morton had been earlier sent to genteel captivity, but it was unthinkable the Duke should not stay to join the night's revel. He had Sir James Tyrell with him, having incomprehensibly requested of the Lord Chamberlain the loan of King Richard's servant for the period of the delay in London; Francis, mystified, perforce granted leave, and received now a second spate of thanks for it. His business in London had not gone half so prosperously, the Constable smiled, without that loyal man.

It was a cheerful evening, made merrier when a pet monkey eluded the custody of its keeper to climb the tapestries, where it clung by the lintel, scolding and throwing orange rinds at the spectators below. The blushing yeoman retrieved his charge at last, conscious of the eye of the master of the royal beasts, who in turn was avoiding that of the Lord Chamberlain; but Richard, his fingers lightly joined with his wife's, had laughed with the rest. Through it all, Buckingham sat at the King's other hand. He had brought a new lutist, of rare and exquisite skill, all the way from London, only for the delight he had known to give his lord, and when supper was done he came with the knights of the body to linger through the evening ritual of undressing the King for bed. They must share a stirrup cup now, he explained gaily, for by daybreak he must be gone.

Next morning, very early, he rode away.

CHAPTER NINETEEN

In York Philip was overtaken by a groom of his household with tidings from Dame Alice: William Secott was dead. It was no matter for surprise, for he had been ailing lately besides being much afflicted with gout, but Kate was in distress and the house at all directions: Philip, his mother stated, must come at once. Philip knit his brows over that; he was in the middle of his eight weeks' daily attendance upon the King, and suspected the demand for his presence was prompted less by the trouble at Ipsden than his mother's curiosity about the coronation, and the triumphant journey north which had followed it. Francis, however, disposed of his doubts, promising he would set either Ratcliffe or Percy to take his cousin's place, and Richard said that of course he must go.

The weather held fair; within a fortnight Philip and Hugh arrived at Ipsden, where Gilbert Secott, very grave with his new responsibilities, received them. He spoke kindly to Hugh, voicing regret that he could not have been present on the burying day, and was overwhelmingly cordial to his uncle; they had not expected, he said, the condescension of Sir Philip's personal visit. Philip escaped as soon as he could; he found Gilbert's attentions oppressive.

Kate was in the bower, pale in her mourning hood; but she brightened when her brother entered, and, laying a hand on Hugh's head, told him he would be glad to greet his twin at supper. Roger, she explained, had come from Stratton Audley with Gilbert; he and Hugh would have much to talk of after so long. But when Philip presently left mother and son together, he discovered it to be himself that Roger was awaiting outside the door, clearly expectant and eager to bear his uncle to the kennels. Sir William's Irish wolfhound bitch, Fury, had whelped some weeks before, and Philip, sincerely admiring, was taken aback when the finest of the litter was pressed upon him for acceptance. As Gilbert appeared then in the stable door to approve heartily the suggestion, there was nothing for it but to take the offering, who wailed and closed her milk teeth on his glove. "A handsome Irisher, for all her sorrows," Philip smiled, with a glance at the mournful eyes. "I'm obliged to you, Roger." The pup, however, had found the glove to her liking, and seemed resigned to her new ownership. Philip took his present up to the chamber which had been provided for himself and Hugh, trying to suppress a certain amusement; but Hugh, informed he was to be nurse to a hound that night, relieved his uncle of the need for polite dissembling. "Am I? Good of Roger, I'm sure." Embarrassed, he stooped to fondle the bitch's drooping ears. "Have they been troubling you, Uncle? I'm sorry, I know Gilbert's a noddy but I never thought to see Roger copying him. You know what it is, of course: it's a great thing for him, Gilbert thinks, to have the King's friend for kinsman."

"That for my vanity, then," Philip remarked lightly. Hugh looked away; he was red to the roots of his sandy hair. "You know what I mean. Besides, I'd already said I wanted her for you; I knew you'd like her. I asked Gilbert, earlier."

A few days later they rode back to Willowford, but decency required that Philip remain long enough in Oxfordshire to observe the month-mind with his sister, and a letter from Francis reassured him that he might rejoin the household at Westminster after All Hallows'. Michaelmas came and went, and the mornings were sharper. Hugh was always with Philip now when there was business with the bailiff, or tenants to visit; it was becoming understood that one day he would be master there, and only Dame Alice continued unreconciled to her son's determined bachelorhood. Admonished, he said composedly that as his affairs were in excellent state, he had no need of a marriage dower to repair them, and slid expertly from the subject by launching on a description of the events which had been transpiring when he left York. Richard had had his son brought from Middleham so he might be created Prince of Wales in the Minster, and the splendour of the ceremony had been wonderful to see. "It was tiring for the lad; he was as white as his shirt by the time it was done, but there was no getting him to own it. He would only complain because he'd not been allowed to ride his colt from Middleham; the doctors wouldn't permit it."

They were in the solar beyond the upper hall, a comfortable room with tapestries between the painted buttresses. A carpet of Flemish weaving lay on a chest; silver and pewter gleamed on the cupboard, and the smell of new bread came pleasantly from the kitchens below. Philip lounged before the flaring hearth, his fingers moving absently behind the hound Deirdre's ears, his eyes on the rose-gold embers. He had good hands, flexible and well shaped, but they were ringless except for his seal; even his knight's collar he had put aside against his return to court, demanding, with a touch of impatience at his mother's representations, if she supposed him wanting to awe the pond trout. That earned a warm rebuking for unrespect which took some unqualified apology to abate; but the sun collar stayed in its press.

It was growing late; in his corner seat the manor clerk snored contentedly, his book of hours sliding from his grasp, and oil lamps bloomed to the taper by Dame Alice's loom. The clatter of hoofs in the courtyard was a surprise, for it was late for visitors; Philip looked round, and Hugh, busy restringing a bow, paused with the work in his hands. Footsteps sounded on the stair; the door flung open. From the threshold Francis said curtly, "Philip, what men can you muster here? Never mind arms, they'll be seen to. How many, this night?"

Philip rose quickly. "Tonight? No more than a score or two at Willowford—as many again with half a day to send to Tuttenham. What—?"

"There's no time, you must bring what you can to Banbury now, and the rest can follow. Buckingham's risen in Wales."

They could only stare at him, not believing what they had heard. Francis came into the room; he was stiff with weariness, and the dust had dried in sweat streaks on his forehead. He said jerkily, "I've been three days on the road from Lincoln: we had the news there. The King's named Leicester for the rendezvous, Tuesday next—Philip, he hadn't so much as a company of archers with him."

Philip turned to the cupboard. It was Friday, and there was only ale set out; he pulled the door open and groped inside for the wine flagon. Filling a cup from it, he brought the drink to his cousin and dragged round a chair, saying quietly, "Have you eaten?"

Francis took the cup, swallowed, and, ignoring the seat, went to throw an anxious glance out the window. "I can't stay. I've set the mustering for the shire at Banbury tomorrow, and there's an hour's light yet. Do you ride with me?"

Hugh was halfway to the door. Kicking off his shoes, Philip said over his shoulder to the boy, "Boots and a short coat, and the harness from my chamber. Send word to the stables—Francis, you'll want new mounts for you and your men. How many?"

"Half a dozen only, the rest have gone on to Banbury. Christ, if only we had a little more time." Francis rubbed his eyes, drank again, and put down the goblet. "Can you trust in your steward to see your fellows come after you straight?"

Philip nodded, tight-lipped. He had stripped to doublet and hose; in a moment Hugh reappeared, carrying a woollen jacket and thigh boots, with the steward in his wake. He had his instructions while his master dressed and Francis nervously paced the room, his eyes on the fading oblongs of light beyond the mullioned windows. Hugh, his squiring finished, scrambled out of his gay short gown; a groom came to say the horses were ready, and Philip turned to his mother. "With your blessing, Madam." Paunched and cassocked, his white hair spiking a nimbus around his tonsure, the chaplain drowsed stertorously on as they hurried down the stairs.

In the courtyard the horses stood saddled, the last packs strapped on. Minutes later the lights of the manor house had vanished behind them.

As they rode, Francis told the story. There had been news of trouble in the south, and Norfolk had been looking into it; the King was hardly out of London before the Woodvilles were stirring. "It seemed to be in Surrey and Kent; Fogge was in it—you remember, Rivers' kinsman that the King made Justice in Kent to show he meant fairly by every man. Much thanks he got for it. Then we heard that Stanley's wife was busy in London; she'd got through to Madam Woodville and her daughters in sanctuary, and next we knew no one was bothering about the prince in the Tower any more; it as all for Henry Tudor. I suppose the Beaufort harpy lost no time persuading the Queen to promise him one of her daughters to stiffen his claim. They say the Duke of Brittany has given him men and ships; he'll sail the first weather for it."

"And Stanley himself?" Philip interrupted. It was a crucial point; Francis laughed jarringly. "Making himself useful around the King: horribly embarrassed by his wife's doings in London! Thank God the King's kept the old fox by him in the north this while; I daresay Stanley would enjoy being stepfather to a king better than most, if he thought there was much to Tudor's chances. Well, the King sent out commissions of array and wrote to Buckingham in Wales to join him in putting down the rebels. Next day the word came that Buckingham was with them."

They were silent for a time while the dimming landscape flew past. A mist was rising, swathing the fields. Presently they slowed to a trot, and Philip muttered, "It makes no sense. Never was a man so loaded with treasure and favour—"

"Doesn't it?" Francis snarled. "We've been simple, Philip. Who stands next the King in blood but Harry Stafford? This is never for Tudor's sake, though he's raised Lancaster by pretending it. A jackal's trick, and a jackal's cunning—and he's had that serpent of a bishop with him at Brecon to stir the brew. As false as ever Clarence was, may they fry on the same grid— There was talk once he wanted his daughter matched with the King's son, but the King wouldn't have it. That may have started him thinking then."

Moonlight brightened on the edge of the hills, and the walls of Abingdon bulked before them, the watch lantern pricking the dusk. Philip said in a low voice, "How does the King?" and Francis, anguished, turned to meet his eyes. "I think it has broken his heart."

They slept that night at Abingdon, and reached Banbury the following afternoon. The fields outside the town were black with men, the Lovell talbot hound on their sleeves. Next day they broke camp for Leicester, arriving in good time to join the royal army before it set off for Coventry. Ralph Assheton had been named deputy constable, and a reward was out for Buckingham.

It was soon claimed. The Duke had left Wales with a great host, but he had not been too scrupulous about the manner of its recruiting; his men looked sullen in their enforced harness, and at the first opportunity began to steal away. No reinforcements came flocking from the English counties; it rained, and rained again. Buckingham woke one morning to find that Bishop Morton, whom he had brought with him for comfort and counsel, had vanished during the night, no one knew where. The King's forces were drawing nearer, and his own shrinking now by the hour; weeping with despair, Buckingham scrambled on his horse and fled. The family with whom he sought shelter was not rich, and the fugitive was worth a thousand pounds; the day after the royal army entered Salisbury, the Duke of Buckingham was brought in, still wearing the ignominious rags of the disguise in which he had been taken.

The King's men made camp on the great lift of Salisbury Plain. The household itself was lodged within the town in a big, gabled house facing the cathedral, the surplus of its members spilling into Wardrobe House which adjoined it. Everyone was very tired; although the threat from Wales had evaporated like breath in winter air, it had been a hard march from Leicester, and there was another before them yet, for the Woodvilles were still busy in Devon, hopefully awaiting Henry Tudor. The King's officers had Buckingham to thank for the extent of their knowledge; no one could have shown himself more anxious to explain and enlarge upon the probable activities of his sometime associates. It had been an access of helpfulness, embarrassing in its grovelling abjection, but it had not saved him. His trial before the constable's court was a summary one, short, by curt command, of all but the lawful essentials; a few hours later a scaffold was being thrown together in the market place.

Evening came, with a wing of shadow unfurling across the plain. The hammering in the square had ceased now, but while the sounds continued they had carried clearly to the house in the cathedral close, and the echoes seemed to hang still in the silent streets. The men who lingered in the hall conversed in undertones, conscious of the empty seat on the dais, and the shut door of the chamber above the hall. It was not long after supper when a yeoman came to whisper in the Lord Chamberlain's ear; Francis, in a state of savage depression, gave him a short negative, then, his attention caught by the respectfully persistent expression, swore softly and got to his feet.

Storerooms and wine cellars lay below; casks of butter and salt meat lined the walls, and there was a smell of malt. Francis, grimly following his guide, halted in mid-stride as a sound broke on his ear: a high, unearthly screaming, more howl than shout, deadened until now by the thick walls of the intervening chambers. "Mother of God," Francis said under his breath, and his companion rejoined expressionlessly, "Yes, my lord. Like that for the last hour he's been, since he learned the King wouldn't see him. We thought it best to send you word—not wanting his grace to be troubled again."

"You did well." They went on, their boots ringing on the flags. Beyond the stores, they entered at last a large room, with a bolted door at the end of it. The other warders were clustered before it, whispering among themselves; they parted thankfully when the Lord Chamberlain came in, and someone unfixed the bars. Francis said briefly, "Lock after me," and walked into the next room.

Buckingham was kneeling on the floor, by the couch they had provided for him. He fell silent when the bolts grated, twisting round to stare through the gloom; his knuckles were bruised and scraped from beating at the door, and a thin trickle of blood ran from the corner of his mouth where the lips had been bitten through. He sobbed when he recognised his kinsman, and began to crawl towards him. "Francis," he gasped, "cousin, thank God you've come. The whoresons won't carry my messages but you'll help me, I know you will."

He came nearer, putting out a trembling hand. Without moving towards it, Francis asked brusquely, "What do you want of me?"

Buckingham looked up at him with dilating eyes. "For God's sake, get me speech with the King. Only a minute—a little minute—just to speak with him, Francis. No one else will go to ask it for me, he'd not refuse if he knew—"

Suddenly, as if only then absorbing the cold abhorrence in the younger man's face, he reached up trying to clasp his knees. "Francis, I ever loved you, I meant great things for you—you'll not deny me this?" He snatched at the rigid hand, slavering it with kisses; violently recoiling, Francis threw him off.

"You whining Judas, the King's had your messages and he wants none of them. Were I in your place, I'd put a rope around my neck before I faced him."

"I want my life," Buckingham wept. "Only let him grant me my life—" He was groaning and pounding his head on his fists. Francis said softly, "You make my belly heave. Tell me: how long ago did you plan it? In London? In Gloucester, while you were bidding him good-bye?" Buckingham only crouched lower, mewling. Turning on his heel, Francis went to the door and kicked sharply against it; while he waited for the guard he rubbed his hand on his jerkin to clean it of the slobber. Behind him the high wail rose, keening, to a shriek. "I've done much for his sake, for his profit—I've served him well, but he's in it as much as I—let him sleep with that tonight—"

The guard came at last, fumbling open the door. When he had left the cellars Francis felt he could breathe again.

The Duke of Buckingham died next day in Salisbury market-place. The morning after, the army marched west, but the Woodvilles were already in flight. Henry Tudor appeared for a wary moment off the south coast, but a storm had scattered all but two of his ships, and the efforts of the King's men to tempt the Tudor to land—they shouted at him that Buckingham was everywhere victorious, and waited only to kneel at his feet—had no success. Even if it were true, without a full complement of troops Henry Tudor would not trust himself to the Duke of Buckingham. He lingered for a while, showing his sails off first one headland, then another, and finally turned back to Brittany. England, it seemed, would have to wait for another day.

CHAPTER TWENTY

It had been cloudy earlier, the sky dark with the overcast of impending snow, but an uncertain shaft of late afternoon sunlight was glancing from the roof tiles as Francis rode into the courtyard at Minster Lovell. He sat still for a minute, his eyes on the windowed front, conscious of the familiar lift in his spirits at sight of the lichened walls. He had other houses, of varying dimensions and comforts, distributed through a huge belt of holdings from Berkshire to York, but his roots were here, on the land where the men and women of his name had been coming and going for a dozen generations, and he would have seen the last ashlar of fairy-towered Rotherfield which Anna so infinitely preferred razed to earth, before he sacrificed a stone of Minster Lovell. It struck him that it was time young Will was learning something of his heritage: he himself had been younger when his father showed him the secret of the hidden chamber between the parlour and the hall, and told him how the second William Lovell had followed Lion Heart to Paynimrie, three hundred years ago. Well, perhaps this visit he would have time to talk a little with his son, to tell him about the men who had lived here before him, and the meaning of what, one day, would be his responsibility. He had a half-shy pleasure in the thought, and something of its warmth lingered in his greeting to his wife as she came down the steps. His men were tumbling wearily from their mounts around him; at the foot of the steps Anna paused, as if in doubt, and, swinging down, Francis went to kiss her cheek. "Have I surprised you, falling out of the sky like this? We heard talk that some of Tudor's agents were still about, west of here; I've been in Gloucester looking into it." It occurred to him then that the explanation might have been more tactfully phrased, but she said only, "Will you stay long?" She had a worn, burdened look, as if the bitterness of their last parting oppressed her still; with a feeling of compassion he slipped his arm around her waist. "A few days, I suppose. Where's Will?"

He had gifts for them both, purchased off a merchantman newly arrived at Bristol: a length of Italian silk for Anna, green woven with gold, and for Will a little dagger of silver gilt, the kind of toy which at seven would have delighted his own heart. He was pleased to see the knowledgeable way the boy handled it even as he murmured his thanks; it had not made him womanish, staying so close with his mother, though it was more than time they considered that too. Throughout supper—they took it by themselves in the parlour, out of the clatter of the hall—Francis continued to reflect on the question, and at the conclusion of the meal he broached the subject to his wife. Anna gave him a swift glance, and crumbled a wafer in her fingers. "I had thought—he is young yet, but I wondered when the time came if we might send him to my lord of Shrewsbury. It is a great household, and he would not be quite among strangers there, my lord being kin to me."

Francis bit back a retort. He was acquainted with Shrewsbury, who had always treated him with the distant courtesy due the husband of a kinswoman, but there was no love between them. The family was firmly Lancastrian, no matter how they had accommodated themselves to King Edward's government; the previous Earl had been John Lovell's friend, and Francis knew the present one would never see him as anything but a renegade to his father's cause. It was a fair guess what kind of instruction Will would have there. After an instant he said moderately, "We might bear it in mind, but I think I have a better suggestion. What do you say to Middleham? Come now, Anna"—he reached to lay a persuasive hand on hers—"I know, I know what grudge you think you bear the King, but his son is innocent, and one day he will be crowned by undoubted right. Will you deny Will the chance to make his way in his prince's service?" Her fingers had stiffened under his, but, surprisingly, the furious objection he had expected did not come. Relieved, Francis swung about in his chair and looked across the room at his son. They had been speaking in low tones, but the boy came at his gesture, standing very straight with his hands at his sides. "Will, we have been busy about your future. It is time you saw a little more of the world, and there are lands over the Trent you have never seen that will be yours one day. By the King's kindness you are to go to Middleham, to be schooled with the Prince of Wales."

Something flickered in his son's face. His eyes went to Anna's, and from there to the floor. "Yes, my lord."

It was not an enthusiastic response; smiling, Francis dropped a hand to his shoulder. "Yes, it seems a great way, and so it is. I wasn't much older than you—three or four years, maybe—when I went there, and I didn't care for the prospect either. I thought them all traitors, and meant to be sure they knew it."

The brown eyes studied him cautiously beneath their lashes. "Did you? I never knew that." And then, with abrupt intentness, "Why did you change your mind?"

A direct look answered him. "I found I was wrong. As you will."

Squirming free of the light touch, the boy said shakily, "I won't. I don't want the King's kindness—he is a warlock, he steals people from their true faith—"

"Hold your tongue!" Francis jerked to his feet, but the warning blew past like the wind. "No—he is foresworn, and God will strike him for it—" A hard grip pinned the childish wrist; the flood checked on a gasp.

"Now hark to me, Will," Francis said quietly. "You know only what's been put in your mouth, which is why I keep my hand from you now. But you are going to swear to me this instant never in your life to repeat those words again, and it will be your first lesson in keeping your word." There was a pause. "Well? I am waiting."

They measured each other. Francis felt himself flushing, even as the child's face paled and grew set. He knew the expression; it was Anna looking at him, from a model of himself. The silence stretched on; then Francis said tightly, "Go upstairs."

The great bedchamber lay above, with a small room through the antechapel adjoining it which overlooked the garden court. It was hardly more than a closet, but Anna had had a couch made up there for Will, an innovation Francis had disliked from the first, believing the lad would have been better off with the other youths of the household in the boys' dorter; but he was grateful for the seclusion of the arrangement now. When the parlour door had closed after his son he went over to the fireplace, leaning his palms against the breastwork to stare into the flames. Anna said in a constricted tone, "Francis, please—" but it was another voice he was hearing still. Presently straightening, he felt for the catch of his belt. It was a narrow one of soft leather, plain and unadorned with embroidery or metalwork. He unbuckled it, and without glancing at his wife walked from the room.

It was half an hour before he returned. The belt still dangled in his fingers; he threw it from him and sat down heavily on the settle, covering his eyes with his hand. There was an interval while neither spoke; then Anna made an instinctive movement towards the door. Motionless, Francis said, "Let him be, Anna. He's in bed, I've seen to it." She hesitated, and he dropped his hand to look at her. "Don't you think you have already done enough?"

She winced at the savagery of his voice, and bent her head as if to hide the tearstains on her cheeks. "I taught him what I believe to be the truth. Would you have done any less?"

Francis made no reply. A corner of his mind acknowledged the justice of the retort; too tired to struggle after refutation, he put it aside. "I'll send a groom off to Middleham tomorrow; they must have word to expect him. There's not much time if he's to be there before the weather breaks."

Her hands knotted in her skirts; he could hear the silk straining as she pulled and twisted it. "He is all I have left. Does it give you so much pleasure to take even that away?"

He answered wearily, "You were ever ready to judge me: if I said it was for his good you would not credit it. Are you accusing me for having been so little here? It never seemed to me you grieved for my absence; had I thought it, there were times I would have come."

"When you lacked a strumpet to tumble, no doubt. I marvel you have stayed so high in Crouch Shoulder's favour; they say he frowns on whoring."

She knew by his stillness that she had touched him at last. His eyes narrowed; in the dance of firelight his mouth and the planes of his cheeks were graven bronze. "If I had dreamed you cared, madam, I should have given the matter all my poor attention. But it is some time since you gave me to understand you found your chaste bed a lonely one."

She went white, and looked away. His rage was always quick, dying as swiftly as it was born, and as the tide of anger receded now he felt a sickness at himself that, out of the stored armoury of the years, he had chosen that shaft to wound her pride. He half rose, then sank back again. "I'm sorry, I'd no right to say that. Will you change forgiveness with me? I admit I have slighted you, but you should know why. Salt words and a face of stone: they're not much welcome to a man, Anna."

She made a slight motion of her head, something that could have been assent or denial, and he understood she wept. It came to him that she had not planned this quarrel, that the reproaches had sprung as unexpectedly to her tongue as they had fallen on his ears, an accretion of bitterness which had swollen beyond containment. But she had prepared otherwise for this evening, he thought; she had even dressed to please him, in the blue he had always liked to see her wear, saying it was like her eyes, near green, and yet not quite. Above it, her throat was a young girl's still, smooth and round, and softly pale as cream. It was long since he had known her—she had stung him too often, too deep—but he had the dynastic instinct to his bones, and it was her subtle magic that she alone could give him children of his name. She was a woman who seemed contented in pregnancy; he had used to say jokingly that it suited her, and the months following his return from Burgundy had been their happiest days. But no children came after Will, and he had not cared to let her know how it had hurt him: as if something in her body, even while it twined to his, had somehow rejected him.

A great log crumbled and fell apart on the hearth; the sparks flew up. He realised he had been silent too long, his eyes on her, and sensed with a sudden tingle the exact moment when she became aware of his gaze. He sat immobile, waiting for her to turn from it, but after an instant she leaned forward to pick up the wine flagon, poured from it into his empty goblet, and, rising, brought it to him. "Will you drink?"

He reached up; her fingers were cold as his hand closed over them, and her colour rose. He took the cup from her and set it on the floor, and brought her down beside him, whispering, "Anna. Is it too late, Anna?" She lay unstirring in his arms; he could sense the division within her, and the lurching of heart. He touched his lips to her brows, gently, from memory of the taunt that had gone before, and felt her slow yielding, the first prick of desire quickening to his like a spark in summer heath. Suddenly she turned her body full to his, and her arms clasped his neck.

A year or so later, as it seemed, he became aware that her headdress was bobbing under his chin. He worked at the pins, caught his fingers, swore, and laughed. "Why would a woman—?" Her eyes slipped impishly to his. "To please a man." The thick ropes of her hair burned copper in the leap of the fire; he kissed her, and the bright torrent tumbled down, laving her breast in flame. Running his hand through it, Francis said after a while, "Sweetheart, I've a thought. Couldn't we both ride north with Will? He would feel less strangeness at going, and you've not seen your brother at Ravensworth these fifteen years. Or—wait." He paused, frowning. "We'll have Christmas in a month, and Parliament sits after; I must be at Westminster for that. Listen then. It will be past Candlemas before they're done, and I go north on the King's business in the spring. You shall come with me, both of you; we'll take him to Middleham together, and go back to Askham Bryan afterwards, you and I; it's pleasant in Yorkshire in the spring. Would you like that?"

His hand was lying on hers, lean and brown, the short black hairs growing straight across the wrist. Without speaking she carried it to her cheek. As to one mind, remembrance fell upon them both: the first golden year after he had brought her to Minster Lovell. It had been a household joke then, which they had soon come to hear, that a closed door meant no welcome to intruders, no matter with what domestic calamity to excuse them past the threshold. Looking at her now, Francis thought it did not seem so long ago. His breath shortened, and he heard the breaking rhythm of hers as he lowered her to the cushions. His fingers sought within her bodice, and found her breast. Presently, when he had freed her mouth for a moment, she said softly, "Not here."

"Why not?" In imagination he was seeing already the white length of her stretched on the settle, warmed and gilded by the fireglow. She murmured, "Someone might come." Her cheek was burning as she turned it against his palm. "You—you could send upstairs, for my women to go away."

He was amused, but believed he understood. "*Les convenances?* Faith, love, you're prim." He got up, laughing at her blushes, and went out into the hall. It was settling for the night, the pallets for his men already being dragged out and meat, bread, and ale set by. He caught a frosty glance from Anna's chaplain, who was sitting with the steward and clearly annoyed at being so neglected by my lord, the first evening of his return. Francis found a yawning page and, under the smiles of half a hundred observers, despatched him upstairs to the great chamber where her tirewomen were waiting to attend his wife to bed. When he judged they had had time to take their leave he went back to the parlour.

A small lobby separated it from the hall, with the shadowed angle of a stair to the rooms above, lit by a single flare. Anna looked up as he entered; she had risen to her feet and was holding the abandoned cup, as if undecided how to dispose of it. He took it from her, drained it, to be rid of the problem, and put his arms around her. "You'll have me drunken. Sweet, they'll be gone now. Will you come up?"

The women had left candles burning, and put wine and wafers by the bed; the door beyond which they slept was shut. Francis closed the stair one, and drew her to him. She shivered a little when the cool air touched her body; there was a fire on the hearth to take the chill, but it had been warmer below. He brought a bedgown from the chest and wrapped her loosely in it, bending his face to her breasts. "Love, you're so fair. I've not been good to you." She answered something in a choked undertone, her fingers threading his hair. When, lifting his head, he turned her chin up for his kiss, her eyes flinched away; but the robe lay tumbled about her ankles, and he thought she was only shy.

Francis was not sure, later, what it was that roused him. One moment he had been asleep, plunged drowning-deep in that oblivion which comes from weariness and—he reflected with a drowsy smile—too much wine; the next he was broad awake, wondering confusedly if the wash of pallor beyond the window might be moonlight, or the struggling dawn. He decided eventually for the former, but when he moved his head on the pillow he was surprised to see by the weak gleam of the night candle that a few sands were still trickling through the glass on the chest beside the bed. He remembered turning it, for some reason or other, just before they had finally lain down to sleep; they had been sharing a last draft of wine—Anna's thought, although he had taken most of it. His mouth knew the taste of it still, less pleasant now than an hour ago, and there were the beginnings of a reminder in his head too. Well, he had the rest of the night to sleep it off. He settled himself deeper in the covers, and reached lazily to gather Anna nearer to him. It was only then he realised she was not there.

His first assumption was the common one. The garderobe tower was off the women's room, but there was a night stand drawn to the bed's foot; his eye had marked it, hardly noticing, when they first came into the bedroom. He lay waiting; then, when nothing stirred, raised himself quickly on his elbow. All at once he knew he was alone in the room.

Francis swung his legs over the side of the bed and groped on the floor. His clothes were as he had discarded them, but her bedgown, left where his impatience had dropped it, had disappeared. He dressed rapidly in shirt and hose and doublet, and knotted the points. When he stood up he hesitated, looking down the long room towards the women's dorter. Then he remembered Will, and went softly into the antechapel. His son's door at the other end of it was ajar as he had left it; the boy stirred at his step, sighed, and was still. A faint suggestion of perfume lingered in the air, but she was not here now.

Francis went back into the bedchamber. Moonlight pouring through the traceried windows parqueted the floor with shadows, and the coals in the fireplace had faded to glowing shell. He started mechanically towards the stair door, paused, and retraced his way. His armour glinted in the open press; reaching within, he detached from its chain the slender, wicked misericord slung from the baldric, and, sliding out the poniard, threw the scabbard aside. Even then he could have supplied no clear reason for what he was doing; something beyond thought was thinking for him, where his mind refused to look.

It was dark outside the bedroom, darker on the stair. The lobby too would have been in shadow, except for the stream of light which crossed it from the parlour. Francis halted, narrowing his eye against the gleam. A draft of air whirled against his face, piercingly cold; the window which opened into the north court was flung wide. He saw Anna standing before it, and with her the figure of a man. The candlelight shone on her profile, lifted to his; on the gaping blackness where should have been solid wall, opened now to the yawning hold of the secret chamber; and, as the man bent his lips to her cheek, on the undimmed foxfire of his tawny hair.

Francis moved then. He spoke aloud as he sprang, but was unaware of it until he saw the man jerk up his head and push Anna aside. Francis heard his wife's low cry, and a swift slither at his back; he spun instinctively, and the blow fell glancing. Then an arm like iron grappled his throat; there was a jab of a knee at his kidney, and something icy pricked his side. Close to his ear, a voice he knew spoke softly. "Lovell, I could have no greater pleasure in life than to skewer your hide, but it's an inconvenient moment. Do us both a service, and hold your tongue." No answer came; the needle point of the dagger prodded again. "Had you rather be trussed like a capon and left the night on your roadside? All one to me, but you might find it uncomfortable—undignified too. Promise me free leave-taking: I'll accept your parole."

Sharply twisting, Francis hooked his right heel backward. A booted foot shifted quickly in response; simultaneously his left hand came down hard, and the sting at his ribs vanished with a tinkle of falling metal. Like lightning the hold on his throat changed and moved higher; they strained together, and a hand inched along his outstretched arm to the poniard. The man who had first attacked him came scurrying from the shadows to help, and Humphrey Talbot gasped, "Davy, find me something to stop his mouth before he raises the hall. And get ropes from the packs—quick, Christ damn you, the whoreson's an eel."

His henchman bent over the nearer of the haversacks by the door, hesitated, and as if debating the priority of his tasks left off fumbling with the corded packs to slash down a length of arras. He began to improvise it hastily into a gag, found it too bulky, and knifed impatiently through the folds to start again. Humphrey whispered an oath; his foot had slipped among the rushes, spoiling his grip, and he heard the whistle of breath as his enemy filled his lungs. The shout was chopped off, none too soon; the next moment, through the panting quiet a light footfall sounded in the lobby, and Anna cried out, "Will, no, go back—"

The boy was already in the doorway, rosy with sleep, his wide eyes going from his mother to the wrestling men. Humphrey snapped, "Anna, get him out of this," and the man Davy, giving a final twist to the arras, dropped to his knees beside the pack and flung over his shoulder, "Master Will, come you to help me with undoing the ropes here, there is the good lad you are."

The sweet Celtic accents seemed to linger in the air; then

Humphrey's voice bit through the silence. The few words, which brought the blood to the Welshman's cheeks, had no meaning to Francis, being Cymric, but English would have come no clearer. He was conscious of nothing but the spill of light on his son's face, the poise of his body, impelled to the edge of movement, and the irresolution in his eyes.

Francis turned his head. "Wait—" The crushing pressure on his windpipe had slackened a trifle, and he was able to speak.

"Talbot, wait. I'll give you my parole." There was a pause, and the imprisoning arm fell away.

The boy was still standing on the threshold. Humphrey smiled at him, and rubbed his forehead. "You look as if you'd been seeing the wildman, my lad. What's the matter, have you never watched a friendly bout before? Yes, it's all right now: it was just you might have got hurt, being too near." Across his shoulder he added pleasantly, "You've got soft, though, Lovell; I couldn't have held you with that grip twelve years ago," and flicked a glance at his cousin. Anna came to touch the soft tousle of curls. "You should not be from your bed, Will. Did you have a dream?"

"No, I thought I heard something—" Doubt strove with relief; the explanation tailed off. Beyond the pool of light Francis leaned a hand on the chairback, fighting for breath, but the uncertain gaze stopped short before it reached him and focused abruptly on the floor. The strapped packs lay heaped before the window; Davy was surreptitiously knotting a loosened cord. As if just realising their import, the child darted across the room and clasped both arms around his kinsman's waist. "Are you going away, sir? Take me with you—I want to go with you and Davy—"

Over his head, Humphrey met the father's eyes. They looked nearly black now, with brown smudges under the lids. After a moment the red-haired man said mildly, "Well, I'm afraid you can't. I told you I'd be off again one day, didn't I? Well then. Now back to bed with you: good-bye, and—come, Will, only babes cry."

The dictum had its effect. Somehow they got him from the room; the catching sobs died away.

Meditatively contemplating Francis' motionless figure, Humphrey said at last, "I suppose you might say we are quits, Lovell." And then, roughly, "God's bones, what else would you expect! All he knows of you is his mother's tears, and she's had cause to shed them. Did you think to make a son by getting him?"

Francis became aware of an odd sensation in his hand, and realised he was still holding the poniard. The bones of his fingers felt broken to the shape of the haft; slowly he uncramped the stiffened joints and let it fall. "I do not require a reading of my son's character from you, Talbot."

Anna whispered, "Francis—" The clutched folds of the robe parted as her upturned palms went out; she would have gone to him, but he turned his head swiftly to look at her. "Cover yourself, my sweet lady. I am not presently in the vein."

Humphrey took a step forward, checked, and then, as pale as the woman, swung aside to put his arms around her shoulders. Her mouth was working, and she pressed a fist against it as he led her to the door. There he halted, taking her face between his hands. "Dear, in a little while I must be gone. Don't come downstairs again; we've run too close to luck as it is, and it could go ill for you if it were known at large you had sheltered me. God reward you, cousin, since I cannot. Now good-bye, and remember what I've told you: Shrewsbury is your kinsman. He'll hear from me." His eyes rested on her white face. "I have loved you since you took up your first spindle. Never grieve for me that you could not return it; I would not change one hour of those times for all the gold in France." He held her hand to his cheek, and watched her go; then gestured curtly to Davy. "Out, until I call. Lovell, I want a word with you."

Francis said harshly, "Don't try me too far, Talbot. I've promised you safe departure; I'll remember it while I can."

"Hold it in mind a little longer, my lord. There are two doors and I and Davy between you and your friends; open your mouth, and they'll be long in coming to be any good to you." Humphrey had retrieved the daggers. Sheathing the one, he flung the other one into the courtyard, pulled the window halfway to, and walked over to put his back against the lobby door. A detached fragment of Francis' brain noted that he had altered, despite the unmuted brightness of his hair; he was heavier in face as well as body, and something about his lips could have been humour when it was allowed. No trace of it showed now; his light eyes were blazing, and a muscle jumped beside his mouth. "Lovell, a minute ago I

had your life on a knife's point, and if you imagine I forebore out of regard for you or the snores in your hall, you're
in error. There's a thing I want more, about, than any other,
and that's my cousin's ease. I've slept hard and cold full
many a night since you helped me from England, and I'd
have given you your cuckold's horns in your own fine bed
with pleasure any time these seven days past; except the
fashion of your wife's love for me is not that of mine for her.
She gave me refuge out of charity and because I was like
her brother once; but there's no man for her now but you,
nor ever will be while you walk the earth, and from my
soul I pity her for it. Strange cattle, women"—his voice
lengthened savagely—"from your vast experience, don't you
agree?"

He pulled himself up, breathing fast. Francis looked down
at the black-out hearth, and stirred the ashes with his foot.
The words bounced around him like hail against a shuttered
pane: only their echoes reached him, and the sense of cold.
Humphrey gave an angry twitch to his doublet, and ran a
hand through his hair. "It was no doing of Anna's that you
found me here. I've been in Gloucester since before Buckingham rose, and there was some little business kept me and
a few others there after, until your fellows began to make
things warm. We should have made a run for Wales then,
but Davy let his horse put a foot into a rabbit hole one night
and got a bad knee for it: Oxfordshire was nearer. I knew we
could lie up here until he was right again, and I'd a wish to
see Anna anyway." He hesitated, examining his fingernails.
"For what further value the information may be to you, it
was accident that the boy learned of my presence here. He
caught us unawares one day—came in looking for his
mother, he's forever with her. Too much so for a lad his age,
if you don't want to make a young lady of him." He laughed
briefly. "He shows promise though. I don't see much of you
in him, bar the face."

Francis said colourlessly, "As you say."

Humphrey moved, cat-footed, to the window, and pushed
aside the curtain. Moonlight whitened the lawn, and there
was a glitter of frost along the wall. Time was getting on,
and he knew it, but it was Anna and her vulnerability that
moistened his palms. His mouth setting, he let the curtain
fall. Staring at the unresponsive profile, he said at last,
"What I've been trying to tell you, Lovell, is that you've no

quarrel with Anna for this night's work. Since it seems I've wasted my time, have this instead: take care how you use my cousin. She is not friendless, even in King Gloucester's England, and it will be a sorry day for you when the Earl of Shrewsbury hears his kinswoman has been abused. Remember it."

Francis slowly withdrew his gaze from the littered hearth. He appraised the strained face in silence for a space, and his lip curled in malice. "I deal with my wife as it pleases me, Talbot. Neither you nor Shrewsbury have a finger's length of right or power to interfere."

The pale eyes stared back at him, like pebbles scoured by the sea. "Not in law, maybe. But be careful, just the same. Oh, you're high now, Lovell—good dog Lovell, they call you in the houses I've stopped in, snuffing after your master's errands and wagging your arse when he throws you a bone. What would he have to say, do you think, if it came to his ears you had given Godspeed to a servant of Henry Tudor?"

"You flatter your importance," Francis said thickly. "King Richard knows very well who have been hosting Tudor's friends, thanks to Buckingham: I doubt he will break his sleep for your loss. As for me, Shrewsbury can spare his pains. The King will hear this by my telling before the week is done."

"Are you so confident? Now, I would not be, though I stood top to toe in a better innocence than yours. If voices might come past the grave, there are those of his own blood could give account of the mercy of Richard Plantagenet."

"Buckingham was a traitor taken in arms. Did he expect a kiss for treason?"

"Who spoke of Buckingham?" Humphrey came closer; his teeth shone like a wolf's. "They're cold, Lovell, cold as earth. Do you play the innocent with me? King Edward's sons lie under the Tower stones: Buckingham sent us the word from Wales three months ago. Why else, look you, would Madam Woodville have joined with us, if it were not to pull the murderer down?"

There was a ringing in Francis' ears. "It's a lie—"

"Do you tell me so? Never a man had his way so cleared for him as Henry Tudor, when my lady Stanley sent Lewis into Westminster sanctuary with that great good news. She had hardly hoped for her son until then."

Francis' hands closed. Rage like a sickness was drumming in his temples, a nausea of welling fury which ate through nerve and tissue to flush in acid to the aching skull walls; and like dumb separate bodies his fingers longed to kill. He thought of the hushed silence of Westminster and the light on the lifted crown; he remembered the road to Gloucester, lined with cheers, the shouts and garlands and Buckingham smiling down the board; and he saw Lincoln again, rain-swept under a wrack of clouds, and above the kneeling messenger a man's stricken, unbelieving face. But that had been only a foretaste, the mere first sip from Harry Stafford's bottomless poisoned spring.

There was a coolness against his brows, and the smooth feel of glass. He had no recollection of having gone to the window, and could not think how long he had stood there, gazing unseeing on the blighted death of the garden, his forehead to the leaded panes. He turned, and found he could speak once more.

"Get hence, Talbot. I did you wrong once, and I'll discharge the debt; run back to Brittany, I'll not hinder you. But never set foot to English earth again, for I promise I will hunt you down though it need a thousand men."

There followed then another blankness; he could not remember, after, what further passed between them before Davy was summoned, the packs gathered up, the garden casement pushed wide. He thought Humphrey spoke once more of Anna, but that too went with the rest, shadow voices against a wind of dark. From far away a hinge creaked; and he was alone.

The candles burned low, throwing him patterns on the wall, and the night breeze streamed in. Beyond the courtyard wall a horse whickered. Their mounts must have been hidden in some makeshift shelter in the woods; his grooms would have noticed if they had risked them in the stables.

He had a need for movement, for the absorption of small, preoccupying actions; slowly he crossed the breadth of the room, righted a footstool, and trod down carefully a scuffled heap of rushes. Davy had left the lobby door ajar; he was reaching to close it when he heard soft breathing in the blackness, and then, by a thread of light, the gleam of her feet, bare beneath the tightly gathered robe. He drew back, but she came from the stair, speaking his name and, when he made no answer, laying hold of his arm. His skin crawled

306

at her touch; yet he thought he had meant no more than to push her from him, until he saw the mark on her face.

The wall behind broke her fall. She leaned against it staring as if in wonder, her hand to her cheek, as he turned quickly back into the parlour. The door had bolts top and bottom for privacy; he shot the bars, and stood with his shoulder to the panel while the sound of hoofs, fading west, grew fainter and died away.

CHAPTER TWENTY-ONE

In early spring Gilbert Secott sent to Westminster for Hugh; he had concluded arrangements, he wrote to Philip by the same messenger, for his half-brother's marriage. It was a suitable match, the maiden being well dowered and not more than a year or so Hugh's elder besides. Philip saw his nephew off with a handsome bridegift for Mistress Margery, and regrets that he could not himself come to the wedding; Francis was in the north, and Philip being his cousin's deputy was needed at Westminster until his return. He missed the boy when he had gone, more than he would have believed possible, but the summons had been opportune, and he hoped Margery would prove taking enough to divert Hugh from more dangerous experimenting. Only a few days earlier Philip had glimpsed him making a cautious retreat into one of the curtained alcoves off the great hall, and not alone. The place being public with much coming and going from the hall, he had not then intervened, but he recognised his nephew's companion before her skirts vanished behind the tapestry, and Hugh, nonchalantly reappearing in his uncle's chamber at suppertime, got a scarifying lecture about the insanity of creeping into corners with the King's niece. The Lady Cecily, lately come from sanctuary with her sisters, was at court in her uncle's protection, and it was not to be presumed he would look with favour upon such antics with his brother's daughter. The interview closed with a quelling prohibition against recurrence; Percy, strolling in at its termination, later gave it as his opinion that Philip should have taken the skin from the offender's backside.

"Holy God, did he never think what it would have meant if he'd been seen? It would be said you'd put him up to it, and a fine turn out that would be for you! Many a man's gone whistling past the guard tower to climb over the wall: this would be pure gift to some here. I see Stanley smacking his lips."

"The devil fly away with Tom Stanley: he and his brother may carve up Wales and half the West Country between them and welcome for all of me, so they perform as they've promised. It's Hugh I'm thinking about; he's only fourteen, and there are quicksands that way he's too young to see."

"Five of 'em, to be exact," Percy yawned. "Well, young Mistress Cecily is promised already to my lord Welles, so I hear; if the King's wise he'll bestow the others just as fast as he can find sure men for them, beginning with the eldest. They say that Tudor's fit for binding hand and foot, to see the prize slipping from his reach."

"It's a snug armful to be wasted on that bloodless counting clerk, Rob; give you odds the lady's grateful to her uncle." Assheton had come up behind them as they entered the privy chamber; his appreciative eyes were on its farther end, where Elizabeth of York, the late King's eldest daughter, sat among the Queen's ladies. Her lids were lowered, her hands clasped meekly in her lap; but beneath her lashes were shadows blue as gentian, and the back-tilted headdress had slipped, as if carelessly, to show a coil of corngold hair. Percy grinned, and glanced aside in time to catch a gesture of greeting from a younger man who had followed them in. He came up when Percy spoke to him. "So you're back, Russell? I thought you were in York with Lovell."

"No, I've been to Oxfordshire, Sir Robert, to fetch my lord's son. He is going to Middleham for schooling, you know." Harry Russell gave Philip a cheerful salute. He was a fresh-complexioned young man, one of Francis' followers from the Yorkshire lands; his bright cheeks, flushed by wind and weather, gave him a youthful look unaltered from his squire's days. "We come with you, sir, when the King rides north, there's money for the cofferer from Lord Lovell to make it good. He meets his grace at Nottingham; I've letters for him from his steward. My lady is well, though queasy now and again of late, but I fancy this sickness will be pleasing to my lord as no other would be." He laughed at Philip's lifted brows. "Oh, there's not much showing yet, but I've two of my own and a third coming: I know the signs."

Will hovered behind them, very shy among all the company. Later, when he had made his reverence to the King, he would go with Russell to have his supper in the hall; only a chosen handful dined with the King in his privy chamber. Philip smiled at his godson, and would have talked with him for a little, but there was a stirring at the door of the inner chamber and hurrying ushers were taking the last of the company to their places. The King and Queen entered to the sound of trumpets and a rustle of obeisance. Philip had to content himself with a last friendly look; he thought the boy was probably miserable with loneliness, and it crossed his mind that he might find Russell afterwards, and offer a bed in his own apartment for the lad until they set off for Nottingham. Supper, however, was late; when it was over there was the ordering of the King's bedchamber to oversee, and the night's guard to set. By the time he was done the waits were piping the watch, and Russell and his charge had disappeared.

A few days later they left Westminster, an impressive cavalcade of riders and baggage carts, for the court was to lie at Nottingham until the summer's end. Henry Tudor was back in Brittany, besieging its veering Duke with appeals for help in embarking once more upon his English enterprise, and Richard had decided he could keep best watch from the Midlands against his enemy's coming.

Elizabeth of York and her sisters, not having been included with the departing household, were bidden a very kind farewell by their uncle, a proceeding which was observed with interest by not a few. Elizabeth Woodville's abrupt decision to abandon her refuge with the Abbot of Westminster and put her daughters in King Richard's hands had confounded everyone: it was not six months since she had been hysterically promising the eldest of them to Henry Tudor. Yet it had happened, and Philip at least suspected that the negotiations which preceded the event had included a private, most secret interview between Richard and his sister-in-law. There had been an evening when the attendant who slept across the threshold of the inner chamber was released from his post, with no reason given; that night even to Philip the door was shut, and he did not believe Richard had remained in the room behind it. Two days later King Edward's daughters were welcomed to their uncle's court, where the marked consideration which from the first had been shown them as still subject for comment. Even the baby Bridget, waving good-bye from her nurse's arms, drew a smile from the grave face, briefly lightening a mood which for months had been consistently sombre. Some said openly the King had never gotten over Buckingham's betrayal, and marvelled he should mourn so long for so poor a creature. Philip was not so sure, but he was aware without intermission of some inner disquiet. Like a blindly festering infection which cannot discharge its core, it threw up other things: picking up one day a slip of paper blown from Richard's work table, he found it to contain an idle, ironic tallying of benefactions to the men who propped his government. Northumberland and Stanley—enriched beyond measure, perforce, since Buckingham's fall: if they were not glutted now they were past sating—headed the list; midway down it was his cousin's name. Heartsick, Philip could only crush the scrap, and pray that Francis would never know.

It was bright spring weather, and the people came flocking to watch them by. All winter the land had been at peace; they liked their new king and were ready to cheer; but somehow the shouts straggled out. They were used to Edward's jovial response; it was difficult to wave caps in air in the face of a remoteness which took no note of their voices: which seemed, in fact, hardly to hear them. The great train rattled by with a clink of trappings and the squeaking of wheels; they stared after it, and went home, feeling obscurely disappointed.

"In God's name, what ails him?" Assheton muttered that evening, when Richard had once more withdrawn to his private chambers the instant supper was finished. Anne had not appeared at all; the journey was tiring her, and she had taken only a cup of wine before lying down to rest.

Percy shrugged his big shoulders. "God knows—and Philip Lovell, maybe." He tossed an apple in the air, speared it on his knife, and set to peeling it. "Sir James, if you've business with his grace, I should let it be this evening."

Tyrell had been speaking to an usher, looking the while towards the stair which led to the upper rooms. He paused when Percy spoke, his dark, impassive face turned to the younger man's. "There was the matter of the horses for tomorrow, Sir Robert. Her grace has commanded a litter, being fatigued still; the King should know, since it will change the ordering of the procession."

"Holy saints, will you bother him for such a trifle? He keeps household men for such matters. Speak to Lovell, if it's beyond nature for you to settle it yourself with the marshals."

Percy, who had made no effort to hide his contempt, went on paring his apple. Tyrell looked from his bent head to Assheton, playing amusedly with a pair of dice, and something stirred in the dull eyes. He said slowly, "I grow weary of Sir Philip Lovell. By what right does he fence the King's person from his body knights? What office does he hold, what service has he rendered, that he should be preferred before us all?"

There was a gape-mouthed silence. Tyrell had been an oddity and a butt for years; if a hall pillar had toppled or a stick of furniture given tongue, the astonishment could not have been greater. Several who had been conversing in careless undertones broke off to listen; suddenly grim, Percy met the dogged stare. "Philip has one sovereign virtue, Tyrell: he knows when his company isn't required. You should study him. For the matter of office, he stands as high as he wishes, and we all know what he might be any day he chose. I should find another quarrel, if you want to endear yourself to the King."

"There are others have served him as well—aye, better, and never even reminded him, never called themselves to notice for reward—I crave no permission of Philip Lovell, nor of you either, to present myself to my dear lord." Tyrell's jaw worked; he looked like a baited bull, head down and stupid with rage. Percy, his face changing, started to get carefully to his feet, and Ratcliff interposed calmly, "It is a friendship of many years, Tyrell: Rob meant only that Philip knows his grace's mind better than most."

For an unpleasant instant Tyrell seemed about to laugh. His head rocked back, mouth wide in silent mirth; then abruptly turning, he thrust roughly past them from the hall.

"Mad, pure and simple," Asshetone murmured, relaxing back in his seat again. "Dice you for it, Rob, that he's clapped into Bedlam in a twelvemonth"

The counters rolled again; summoned by the snapped fingers, a page ran forward with a flagon of wine. Dropping to the settle, Percy flung down a coin.

They reached Nottingham a week after, and Francis rode down from the castle rock to meet the King. Richard received him warmly; Philip, remembering the scrap of paper, wondered if there were self-reproach in the affection of his greeting, and was heartily glad of it. In any event, Harry Russell and Will had to wait their turn, and it was a while before Harry was able to draw the Lord Chamberlain aside. The packet from the steward was handed over; Philip saw them talking together for a short time, but was unable to read anything from his cousin's expression. Will, waiting diffidently upon his father's notice, was presently welcomed and informed briskly that the King intended to travel himself to Middleham next month, to see my lord the Prince of Wales: until the time of removal Master William would be pleased to conduct himself with decorum. The whispered assent was hardly audible; Francis looked down at the small face, and his own softened. He would be kinder, he knew, to send the boy on now with Russell, but it seemed foolish with so little a time before they were all to go, and the interval, he reflected, might well provide an opportunity for his son to review his opinions.

It was Lent, and sobriety overhung the activities of the court, but beneath it was awareness of change. Whatever broodings Richard had brought with him from Westminster seemed momentarily to recede with the prospect of the journey to Middleham; it was six months since he had seen his son. Then it was Easter, and chestnut and hawthorn bloomed to the city walls. There was hunting and hawking, and a troupe of players came; the days were drawing out and evening died with a fire of opal above the western hills. One night there were clouds massing purple over the keep; at dawn the rain came in a flood, and the wash of it was still running from the windows when a rider struggled up the slope, and, slipping from his horse in the outer ward, asked for the King.

They brought him into the great hall as he was, his cloak plastered around him. The Queen was sitting close to the warmth of the hearth with her ladies around her, one of them reading aloud; a little distance from them a pair of couples danced to rebec and tambourine, while Richard, half-attending, watched with a group of his knights from the dais. The courier knelt to a smile of recognition; he was a Middleham man, and there was not one of his son's household the King did not know by name or sight.

"Still more letters from my lord Edward? He must be patient yet a while: we do not ride from Nottingham for a fortnight more." He was holding out his hand, but the messenger made no answering movement. He was young, one of the squires Richard had carefully chosen to attend his son; he seemed to fumble with the words, getting them out. "I have no letter from the lord prince, your grace."

"From his chamberlain, then? There is hardly time to

answer, you must show a fine pair of heels to be before us, Robin—" Richard's smile faded. "Was there something—" And then, his voice changing, "Is my son—ill?"

Wetness glistened on the uplifted face: from the rain still, Francis instinctively told himself. They might have given him a napkin to dry himself before he came to the King. Then he felt Philip's hand on his arm.

The music faltered, interrupted in mid-phrase; the dancers paused, uneasy, then separated and slipped aside. Rain splashed against the sills. Richard said slowly, "Don't lie to me."

Still kneeling, the youth looked with sick appeal around the circle of taut faces. "Your majesty—" The drenched cloak fell apart, and they saw the mourning black of his clothes. The groan of horror which escaped them all was sound enough to tell him, groping now in his wallet, that his news was given.

Haltingly, now the worst was done, the story came. It had been the old illness, a fever, slight in itself, and the crippling weakness whose iron arms this time would not unloose. It seemed unremarkable in the beginning; he had stormed at the doctors who said the King should be told, swearing he would be at the gate to meet their graces when they came. But he lay more and more on the couch in the Tower, watching the long south road, and a morning came when he could not lift his head. He was tired, he said; he would sleep the day long like a sluggard, and rise the fresher for it. That evening, between vespers and complin, he died.

The hushed voice stammered to its end. Through it all Richard had not moved; tranced in stillness, he stood like one come face to face with the avenger who has pursued him far and found him weaponless. His lips stirred; those who were nearest thought he said, "Oh, most just God."

"My dear lord!" Tyrell lurched forward, thrusting in where no other dared intrude, to fling his heavy arm around the King's shoulder. Richard looked at him blindly; he seemed neither to recognise nor properly to hear, but with a violence which, had he been his brother, would have killed as it struck, he threw the man aside. Later, when they took away the wreckage of the faldstool where he dropped, they found it all spattered over with blood.

"Dickon—" It was his wife's voice, high with fear; and he turned as to an executioner. Her eyes had gone beyond him

314

to the courier and the untaken letter dangling against his crow's wing doublet; even as Philip sprang to catch her she swayed and crumpled, groping with outstretched hands towards her husband as she fell.

CHAPTER TWENTY-TWO

THEY had been at Scarborough, whence in July the fleet put
out to make an end of reviving Scots ambitions. James
Stewart called home his battered ships, and promised emis-
saries who would seal a lasting peace. "Another one?" Percy
drawled; but it was good hearing just the same. Henry
Tudor, it now seemed clear, would not sail that summer; he
had fled from Brittany only just in time to avoid renewal of
the tight guard under which he had lived in Rennes
throughout King Edward's time. The French court received
him, and temporised; Louis was dead, but the long-headed
Anne de Beaujeu, her feeble brother's regent, had an idea of
the use to which she could put such a convenient pawn, once
she had come to terms with her quarrelling nobles.

The Scottish danger removed, Richard travelled to
London, taking with him only a light riding household. Most
of the court remained at Nottingham with the Queen;
Francis himself was given leave for a brief journey into
Wiltshire. He was steward now for the Duchess of York's
holdings there, an office lately forfeited by the West Country
knight Colyngbourne when he fell under suspicion of being
too closely interested in Henry Tudor's affairs. Colyngbourne
had not stayed to face out his accusers; it was rumoured he
had gone to France.

In London Richard domiciled himself at the Wardrobe.
They were a small household, enlarged, however, by one new
addition: the King had brought from Pontefract John of
Gloucester, his bastard son. Tall and well-formed, older than
the dead prince by several years, he would have seemed a
living mockery of the father's grief. Yet Richard kept the
boy near him, watched him, and assigned small tasks which
were performed quickly and well, with an anxious eye for his
grace's approval.

About that time also it became known the boy's sister
Katherine had been betrothed to the Earl of Huntingdon.
An amiably compliant young man, Will Herbert accepted
gratefully the munificent dower Richard bestowed upon
his daughter, and from what accounts drifted back gave his

bride no reason to complain of him. Other considerations apart, the Earl was pleased enough just then to remove himself; to Robert Percy the peaceable peer confided that he would sit bare-arsed in a nettle bed more comfortably than he stood, these days, in his grace's presence chamber.

It had been more than a fortnight earlier, in the hour before the first light of dawn began to mark out the web of London's streets and alleys, that burgesses snoring above their shops by Paul's yard wakened to the sound of hammer blows falling rudely on the night quiet. One or two roused sufficiently to thrust out nightcapped heads, but by that time the noise had ceased; grumbling, they went back to their pillows, and the square of parchment tacked to the cathedral door continued to flutter there until daybreak, when scandalised watch officers found an out-at-elbows friar reading its contents aloud for a cluster of early-rising citizens. A sheriff arrived to tear down the offending document, and in due course delivered it to the Lord Mayor, who contemplated his trove in unhappy privacy for some days before deciding it would be better to take it himself to the Wardrobe before someone else reported him for possessing it. The gentleman usher who conveyed the sheet into the King's presence was no more cheerful; easing himself from one foot to the other as Richard ran his eye down the page, he was wishing that Sir Philip Lovell, a sure buffer, had not just then chosen to absent himself on a flying visit to the south coast, where the annual visitations of sea raiders were once more drawing clamorous appeal from the port towns.

But Richard did no more than glance at the scribble before he dropped it to the table. It was not the first time that week he had seen that gaily insolent hand, for whose owner his officers were even now searching, and the jibing lines that William Colyngbourne had affixed to Saint Paul's for all London to look at were only seasoning to his rage at a more bitter offence.

His household men did not attempt to copy his restraint; when Francis, who had encountered his cousin on their respective ways back to London, walked into the hall with Philip a few days later, the fire had grown to blazing. Percy, red with anger, turned from a knot of companions to beckon them over.

"Yes, there's a fine welcome for you. Have you heard the latest of Colyngbourne?"

Francis, to whom the question seemed addressed, indifferently responded, "Not in Wiltshire, certainly. Didn't he go to France?"

"He may wish he had. He's been writing Tudor instead; they've found a man that was to have been his messenger, and the letter with him. Making play of his late standing in the Duchess of York's service, Sir William begs to inform his master that he should sail with strength this autumn, and my lady of Beaujeu must hesitate no longer about supporting him, for King Richard means to make war upon her at his first convenience. This bearer having failed, the whoreson's doubtless repeated himself by another in the same style by now: and so farewell to Langton's efforts at persuading the Frenchmen to the contrary."

Philip whistled softly; he knew the hopes Richard had pinned to the French mission. It had been heavy going for Langton from the first; in France they still remembered how the Duke of Gloucester had opposed the French peace nine years ago.

Percy wheeled to snatch something from the table. "And that's not all: he's turned to rhyming too. Have a look, my lord, since it concerns you."

Unsuspecting, Francis took the tattered sheet. He read down it; Philip saw him stiffen, and moved to look over his shoulder. Beneath a rough caricature of Richard's boar emblem a pair of lines were scrawled:

"The Cat, the Rat, and Lovell our Dog
Ruleth all England under an Hog."

There was a brief silence. Ratcliffe, studiously impassive, was paring his nails; beyond him William Catesby's prim little features could be seen, scarlet to the hair. Francis' colour was beginning to match them; taking grapes from a bowl, Philip remarked, "Cousin, one of us has been overlooked."

Someone on the edge of the group laughed nervously. Wadding the sheet to a ball, Francis said stonily, "I think not," and added after a minute, "Colyngbourne had better get himself beyond seas. He's running up a long reckoning."

It was all the comment he made, but he had been got on some raw of hurt, and Philip knew it. Later, when they were parting for the night, he lingered within his cousin's door to say quietly, "It's spite, Francis, no more: you have his

Wiltshire offices. Will you trouble yourself for that gadfly?"

Francis shrugged, shook his head, and after a momentary hesitation pulled a folded letter from his doublet. "I didn't tell you: I had this while I was in Wiltshire. I suppose it would be appropriate for you to offer good wishes."

There was a brittle note in his voice. He kept his back turned while Philip read through the missive: a discreetly worded communication from the steward at Minster Lovell, tendering respectful felicitations on my lady's safe delivery of a baby girl. There was something odd about the cautious phrasing: the steward had managed to include the salient points, without himself appearing as informant of the event. If Anna's clerk had received no instructions for a letter to her husband, the tactful officer was betraying no knowledge of the omission. The letter ended with a query as to his master's pleasure for the uprising of my lady, which—she being weak still, for the babe had come hard, although untimely by a month—would probably not be until Saint Lawrence's feast.

Francis had gone to the cupboard, where fruit and wine were laid out. Putting down the letter, Philip said calmly, "I'm wondering what you want me to say."

"Why, nothing. The child's mine; had you supposed anything else? In spite of the small embarrassment of the dates, I have complete faith in my wife's honesty in that particular."

"Good of you," Philip could not prevent himself remarking.

"I assure you, it's more than many a husband might care to wager on." Francis came from the cupboard, handed him a goblet, and stood gazing satirically at the neatly inscribed pages. "There was a place where I stopped on the way to York last winter, for example: she was very hospitable, and by chance her husband was from home. When I saw him in Leicester last month he was drinking to the approach of his heir—a simplicity of trust which strikes one dumb. Of my own experience, I doubt the strumpet could swear who had fathered the brat."

A silence fell. Philip swirled the wine gently in the goblet, his eyes, unreadable, on the younger man's profile. Presently smiling a little, he drained the cup and, having replaced it on the table, lightly clapped the other's shoulder. "It's late. Sleep well, coz."

319

The room seemed quiet when he had gone, for all the noises of the inner room where the attendants of the chamber were making up the bed. Through the half-open door Francis could hear the squires laughing among themselves, and Harry Russell, seriously overseeing all. The shadow of the tented bath arched against the bedroom wall, with the boys' lesser ones coming and going before it, and there was a smell of herbs.

Sighing, Francis let his eyes return to the steward's letter. He had not answered it yet, and he must see to that in the morning; it could not be postponed longer. His mind went back to the time which had followed Will's birth: the feasting with the house full of guests; the elaborate churching—he had ordered Anna a velvet robe furred with sable for that, in defiance of sumptuary laws. She could have worn it by right now.

Picking up the letter, he held it to a candle, and when the flames leaped high he dropped the blazing fragment to the floor and ground it to powder. Next day he wrote to the steward, telling him to do as my lady commanded, for he himself could not be present for his daughter's baptism. He would have her named Maud, after that distant ancestress who had founded the priory beside which the first Lovells of Minster had built their home.

That done, he tried to put the thing from his mind. But as the days passed he found scraps of the letter coming back, teasing him by the imperfectness of his recollection. It had been a curious, strained communication; but apart from the embarrassment which breathed in every line something else worried at him, a subconscious feeling of omission. For weeks, desultorily, he pondered it; then suddenly he knew what was missing. It was the babe, Maud herself; nothing had been said of her beyond the bald statement of her birth. That was unusual, surely; particularly in such an instance the steward might have been expected to gloss his discomfort with more than the customary compliments about the child. The strangeness of it, once seized upon, grew with the days. Towards Martinmas, when the court had once more settled at Westminster, he made occasion to ride into the west on his affairs, and when he had finished in Wiltshire he let his companions know that the return journey would take them by Minster Lovell.

It was early afternoon when he arrived. The bulk of his

followers he had despatched ahead to the assigned lodging of the night; he had sent no notice of his coming, and there were only a handful of pigeons in the courtyard to greet him. He was glad to avoid encountering Anna, but he missed Will's face peering around the screens; he had sent the boy for schooling in the Earl of Lincoln's kind, capable hands. Richard had lately named the young man his heir, passing over his brother Clarence's child, the pathetic boy Warwick, in favour of his sister Elizabeth of Suffolk's son; and Francis knew there were those who had laughed when Will was delivered to Sheriff Hutton, saying that Francis Lovell was bound on getting his boy into the favour of the next king, whoever he might be. Francis turned a bored shoulder to the amusement; he liked and respected Lincoln, and knew his son would do well in his keeping.

The steward appeared, exclaiming that my lord had come without warning and found them all unready. Francis brushed that aside, explaining that he did not mean to lie that night at Minster Lovell, and had travelled out of his way only to bring a gift for his daughter. His ear discerned a faltering in the heartiness which accompanied him to the lobby stair, but the servant's changed expression told him more.

He took the stairs rapidly, leaving his servants below. The nursery lay through the women's room, and he was hoping as he opened the door that Anna would not be there. She was not; there was only a nurse, dozing beside the big oak cradle. She started guiltily at his step, but he spoke no reproof, and she left when he signed her out, squinting inquisitively at him over her shoulder as she went.

Crossing the room to the cradle, he looked down. She was half-sleeping too, a fist curled beneath her cheek, tinier than he had imagined after Will's sturdy size. Her hair was a dark brown fuzz, fine, straight, and every way now, but it would be thick later, heavy and shining; he had a childhood's memory of seeing his mother's so. That too surprised him a little, he did not know why he should have thought she would be fair. He had time to notice that much before she stirred, squirming round in the tangled clothes; her hand slipped down as she turned on her back towards him, and his heart stopped. She was birthmarked from brow to chin, half her face splashed across with a great, obliterating stain of purple-red. Even her neck was flecked with it.

He stood frozen, fighting a wave of sickness. All his life he had had a horror of deformity; he hated even the court dwarfs, and the worst wounds of the border wars had repelled him less than maimed beggars by the road, showing their hurts for alms. He used to throw them coins hastily to have them gone. But he could not pay this to go away.

He had been leaning over the cradle, but instinctively now he drew back. The gold chain around his shoulders clinked with the movement, and the sound woke her. She considered him solemnly, blinking at the light but quite unalarmed by the strange face; Will, he recalled, had been shy of him for all Anna's coaxing. The sun sparkled on the collar's metal links and she reached, crowing, for the swinging brightness. Half in shame for that moment of recoil, he put down a finger; she clasped it firmly.

Francis stood for what seemed a long while, thinking. He could endow her so no marriage, hardly, would be too great for her, no estate too high; but it turned him cold, conceiving it.

Well, it must be the church then. That was the answer, of course; nothing was safer than those great houses. He would found an abbey for her: fetch some of those do-nothing sisters from Shropshire—what was the name of the place? It was in his gift anyway—and she should have the ruling of it so soon as her years allowed.

He felt better for the decision, and stooped, trying gently to pry her hold from the finger she was still clutching. Her face crumpled; he heard himself explaining absurdly that he must go, that he could stay no longer this time, but he would come again with a present for her if she would be good now. He had one below already: a scarlet coverlet for her bed, embroidered with his Garter arms. It made him wince, imagining the colour against those hideous marks. He would get it out of the way and think of something else; meanwhile, to quiet her he undid the collar and strung it with its great flashing George across the foot of the cradle. He was careful to secure the catch tightly; babes, he had heard, ate everything. The arrangement pleased her; he straightened, and turning saw his wife in the door.

For months there had been not a line of communication between them; clearly she had not known of his coming now, and was as disconcerted as he. She looked at him for an instant, and then at the child, laughing again and stretching up her hands. Following the glance, he said awkwardly, 'Does it hurt her, do you supose? It looks so angry—"

She answered in a strained tone, "They say not." She came nearer the cradle; she was wearing a loose-bodiced gown, the kind he had seen her in after Will was born. He had protested when she sent away the wet nurse he had found for her, and his reluctance at conceding the point had contained, perhaps, a grain of jealousy, but he was glad she was showing no less fondness this time. "Poor little wight," he muttered. "She will curse her life one day, and us too for giving it. Better, maybe, if she had not lived."

She picked up the child quickly, holding her to her breast. "You would think so, of course. You cannot boast in your cups of this one's getting."

His face closed, like a door slamming. He swung on his heel; she heard his boots crossing the women's room and, minutes later, the clatter of his men below as they followed him from the hall.

Francis rode back to London, the set of his lips a warning his retinue was not slow to interpret. He reached Westminster to learn that Colyngbourne had been taken, and that he himself had been named to the body of peers and justices who would try him.

A week later they did so, with Norfolk and Stanley heading the commission, and all Philip's representations could not save him from the special agony of a traitor's death. Richard said curtly, "It is the law. Shall it be amended for such as him? Others have suffered so, and better men than he; I will not forgive one stroke of it."

So Colyngbourne died, castrated and disembowelled; and that evening at Westminster the supper ceremonial was marked, as by deliberate design, with the full complement of music and dancing. Contrary to her habit of late, the Queen remained throughout, sitting in a high-backed chair on the dais. She had been ailing, it sometimes seemed, half her days since her son had died, and there was no counterpart for her in the toil her husband had turned to like an opiate which could drug him to forgetfulness. Time, said the barons' visiting wives, scrutinising the thin, wasted face with the skin stretched so tight on the bones that the colour seemed to burn right through it, time will help; and the women of the court agreed, although less quickly now than a few months ago. For time passed, and summer changed to autumn and the chill sleeting rains of early winter fell, but there was no difference in her of the kind they looked for: only the hollows grown deeper under the bright, fiery cheekbones, the shadows darker beneath her eyes. She had surprised them all this night by staying to view the wearisome ceremony of the hall, but the occasion had another colour for her presence, a bloom of normalcy which flushed over recollection of the cruel scene on Tyburn heath. Philip, who had witnessed it, thought he was seeing hardly less gallantry here as she sat, smiling on them all and watching John of Gloucester follow his father about the room like a young, loyal ghost. Her eyes encountering his, she made a small gesture and pointed to the stool by her chair; he came at once and sat beside her, saying gently, "Aren't you tired? They will be hours yet; it has served the purpose that you stayed as long as this."

She shook her head, the smile going from her lips. "I can do this much. It is very little." She looked at his profile as he stared down the hall. "Did you see it done?"

"Yes. What is there to be said? It is the law. But it was another way he ruled the north, and got their love."

She coughed, weakly at first and then with harsh, racking violence. He turned in time to glimpse her hand go to her mouth and come away to drop in a hurried, secret way to her skirt. Leaning swiftly forward, he caught her wrist and forced up the palm; she tried to free herself, but he had already seen.

After a long moment Philip took out a handkerchief and wiped the blood away. Slipping the linen into his doublet, he said softly, "Madam, how long has this been so?"

She pulled her hand from his; he could feel all her bones through the flesh. "A little while, I can't remember. It's worse some days than others. I burn the handkerchiefs, my women would notice the marks." Her eyes entreated him. "I want to spare him while I can. He will know soon enough."

"But the doctors? This is madness, they have cured worse ills—"

"Dear friend, I have doctors in plenty since it eases my husband's heart. But you know well there is no person here that does not now live in the sure expectation of my death, save only him."

She fell silent abruptly, leaning back in her chair. The musicians were striking up; across the hall Elizabeth of

York was talking to her uncle, her lovely, flower face lifted to his. A sudden suspicion shot through Philip's mind, something at once so impossible and so gross that imagination revolted to protect the lie. Then he realised that Richard, unmindful of the girl, was looking past her at his wife. She, catching his glance, smiled in return; in just such a way Philip had seen them exchange a message in the hall at Middleham, with the evening only half gone, and the minstrels tuning in the gallery for their best offerings, saved to the height of the revel for the pleasure of their lord. With a grief too sore for tears, Philip thought: He knows.

Winter was early that year; in the north snow fell, and fog thickened on the Thames from Westminster to the Tower. There came a day when the doctors, taking courage from numbers, told the King he must no longer share his wife's bed for fear of infection. He turned on them in agony, calling them liars and fools in the bargain that could not even heal a little cough; but she said if his grace would pardon her weariness, she might rest better so. He submitted then, in torment that it might be true.

Christmas was upon them, and throngs of nobles arrived from their country holds to join in the feasting they expected as their due. They had it, and the Lady Elizabeth was the gazing glass for all their eyes. One night she appeared for dancing in robes cut from the same stuff as the Queen's. The newly come barons gaped, but Philip was not the only one who was beginning to read that diamond purpose, and guess its prompter. Elizabeth Woodville, defeated and dispossessed, saw greatness waiting for her daughter; and across the sick body of her supplanter she was already reaching for it.

The year turned, and the clear voices of the children of the chapel winged upward in the Epiphany Feast. "*Ecce advenit Dominator Dominus—*" Stiff silks whispered to the movement of many bodies, and the pointed flames of the candles swayed and steadied on the altar. "Give to the king thy judgment, oh God: and to the king's son thy justice—" Not a muscle stirred in the graven face; the waxy hand on the missal beside him was quiet on the leaves. Beyond the jewel colours of the windows the snow drifted silently, covering pond and meadow, fair manor and shepherd's croft, from the chalk Channel coasts to Sheriff Hutton church, where the body of the King's son lay.

Not long after, she took to her bed. The doctors hovered, exchanged glances, and went away again; there were daily visitors, and daily her husband's anxious, careworn face. Philip was constantly there, bringing a book, or a lutist with a song that might please, new from Flanders. In February he made a special journey to Cambridge and came back with drawings to show how work was going on the college to which she had given moneys, when building flagged for want of a patron.

Winter broke with a cracking of ice on the river, and the black boiling waters carried its softened masses out to sea. The sky was lapis by day, by night a white blaze of stars. Scholars with their astrolabes watched them, and prophesied marvellous things.

There was stillness in her rooms now, the books and scrolls put by. One day, very early in the afternoon, Philip came to the King's cabinet and said quietly, "My lord, will you come?" The doors were always open now between the apartments; as they entered, they met the priests coming from the inner chamber.

She seemed sleeping, but her lashes lifted at the known step. Richard sat on the bed, whispering, "How is it, my heart?" and she answered with drowsy content, "Well, now you are here." Her hand moved wanderingly to find his. Philip would have left them together then, but she turned her head with difficulty to look at him. "Dear friend, there is no need for you to go."

Of a sudden the light faded in the narrow windows; from the antechamber came an exclaiming of women's voices, and a shadow fell across the sun. "It is nothing," Philip said, to the question in her eyes. "The wise men have been telling of some such thing to come; it will pass soon."

She sighed and murmured, "I should like to have seen so great a wonder. Is the sun quite gone?" Richard said steadily, "Not quite gone."

She was quiet then, for so long they thought her sinking already into the foresleep of death; but all at once her eyes opened to the set face above her. "I have been thinking," she said with a little smile. "Do you remember, when my lady mother was with the nuns after Barnet, and kept so strait? You sent to bring her into the north to an easier house, which by the King's favour he granted you, although she had been ruled by his ordering. It was the kindest thing

326

anyone had done for her after my father died, and she has ever loved you for it." She moved restlessly, and tears coursed down her cheeks. "Oh, I have put you in such danger. If I could have given you a son to live and be your heir— Do you think I have not known how it placed you, a barren wife and only Lincoln to come after you, with poor simple little Warwick to stand before him if anyone chose to urge his claim—"

"Hush now. Lincoln is all I need, a true man and a lion heart. Shall I hale him from Sheriff Hutton to swear his allegiance at your foot?" He was stroking her forehead. She answered with a gleam, "But you used to say, more valour than tactics."

There was silence again, broken only by the rasping labour of her breath. He raised her in his arms to ease it, and the torchlight leaped in her eyes. She said softly, "How black it is. I would not have thought it could be so black, and yet be day." Her face twisted. "Dickon—" The ragged whisper broke. Her hand clenched on his, then slowly fell away.

Turning to the doorway, Philip looked at the jostle of attendants and wordlessly gestured them out. All the light had gone; in the outer chamber there were women weeping, but from the room behind him no stir nor sound: only stillness, and the baleful dark.

CHAPTER TWENTY-THREE

A KING must have an heir: that was the council's perpetual clamour, and for a man not yet three and thirty it was absurd a nephew should content him. It did not content the King's subjects, that much was certain: the King must marry again. So his advisers said among themselves, although they had not nerved themselves to plead it to that haggard face. Caught in a suspension of doubt and anxiety, they waited for the moment when they might urge it upon him. Meanwhile, hardly less pressing, there was the matter of the late King's daughters; one of them had been safely married to Viscount Welles, but four others remained for whom husbands must be quickly found to put them out of reach of Henry Tudor. He had already sworn his troth to the eldest, and his followers had done homage to him for it: above all, the Lady Elizabeth must be married.

Wearily Richard suggested they name a bridegroom. It must be a man who could equal her in blood; he would not demean his brother's daughter by bestowing her otherwise, and he had given his word, besides, that he would match his nieces as became their birth. He would not retract that now, though Henry Tudor intend a very harem for himself of King Edward's daughters.

The argument gave them pause, for eligible bachelors of proven loyalty did not abound for choosing. Balked, the council returned on another tack. If she was not to be married, then something must be done to make sure she was not spirited off to France, a spectre that had haunted them while the little Duke of York was still in sanctuary with his mother. They had scotched the hazard there, finally, but now it was the Lady Elizabeth: she was too free, she wandered the court at will, it must surely be possible to find safer housing for her until Tudor should be disposed of. Failing a husband for her, John Russell said firmly, she must be sent to join her brothers in the Tower.

It was a reasonable proposal: the Tower was the most securely garrisoned of all the royal palaces, and could offer quite as comfortable living quarters as most; but Richard, who had flung away from the table, his hands at his temples to ease the din of voices, spun at the words to show a face that shocked them to silence. He stared at them, his mouth working; but when he spoke it was to the Chancellor alone in a voice cracked and threaded through with a dreadful ghost of laughter: "Reverend father in God, you would persuade me to an ungracious course for the lady who is in daily hope of becoming my wife."

Some of them exclaimed at that, with a dismay which should have warned him that, long aware of Elizabeth Woodville's intention, they had been uncertain only of his. But he had already gone, and upon Francis, the ranking lay member of the council, was imposed the disagreeable task of finding out if it was the King's purpose to seek dispensation from Rome to marry the girl. Francis went, telling his associates impartially as he left that they were a parcel of fools to suppose such a thing, for what in God's name had the wench to recommend her but her person, and hardly a man living was less susceptible to that particular form of persuasion. On his heels followed Catesby, quaking with terror at the bare thought of the crowning of Elizabeth of York, who would surely find a way to avenge the deaths at Pontefract of her uncle Rivers, and her half-brother Richard Grey, upon the men who had urged it. From those unlike messengers, one angrily embarrassed, the other in stark fear, Richard learned that what had come to him through the slow length of days with a loathing which still crept on his flesh, was being gossiped about and added to in every corner of his court: that not only did Elizabeth mean him to make her his queen, but that he himself had looked upon his brother's daughter, and found her fair.

He denied it, first privately, then publicly, with a passion of sincerity that reassured his council and shamed the talkers. But the rumour ran lightly on, defying capture; Archbishop Rotherham, who had been pardoned his share of the Hastings conspiracy in time to assist with the new king's coronation, and regained his old place on the council at the same time, wrote spitefully to Henry Tudor that the marriage was intended in very truth. In a panic, Henry started looking around for another bride. But the Lady Elizabeth, far from being plunged into nuptial preparations, was packed off to join her sisters at Sheriff Hutton, where—Ralph Assheton observed—she could palliate the disappointment

by trying out her tricks on her cousin, the little Earl of Warwick, who was simple enough just possibly to enjoy them.

It was June now, and Richard was at Nottingham. Francis
had gone to Southampton, where he was watching the Channel with the fleet; Norfolk was raising the eastern counties,
Sir William Stanley acting for his brother in the west. That
summer, Henry Tudor came.

They had known since Christmas that he would sail that
year. He had a few hundred English exiles, a promise of
French ships and money, and the further contribution of
two thousand Frenchmen, criminals freed from prison on a
guarantee of enlistment in Tudor's service. "God help our
poor folk when that rabble's loosed among 'em," Percy commented, when the word reached them. He had come into
Philip's room after supper, looking more than ordinarily
thoughtful; he made sure Hugh was beyond earshot before
adding softly, "Is it true what I hear, that Stanley has asked
leave to join his brother in Shropshire—"

Philip was checking the laces in a heap of armour. Pulling
out a frayed thong, he slid in another, tested it with a tug,
and threw the piece aside. "It's true. The King has granted
it."

"God defend us, is he from his wits?"

"Yes, I think so. Not as you mean." Philip swept the
harness aside. It had been more to provide occupation for his
restless hands than from any kind of necessity, and Hugh
was hovering jealously. He let the boy take the stuff away
and leaned back, considering his companion's troubled face.
"If the Stanleys mean to play traitor, there's no preventing
them. What's the point of holding one of them while the
other goes free in the west?"

"The best reason of all to keep the one we've got!"

"Not quite: his brother has the men," Philip said grimly.
"Oh, it's an argument, of course. Stanley's son comes to replace him here, and Stanley knows well why the King
has—requested it. It's all we can do."

"And Northumberland at our backs, watching to see
which way the cat jumps, if I'm not mistaken," Percy said
slowly. "I mind the time the King flayed him for letting in
the Scots, that summer after Tewkesbury. Well, it's a weak-
livered bastard. We'll see."

In due course Lord Strange presented himself: a soft-jawed
young man, unimpressive of appearance despite his own

great holdings, with nervous eyes. For good reason too, Philip reflected. He was received with honour, and stood at Richard's right hand while Stanley bade his sovereign and his son a smooth farewell. Then there was nothing to do but wait.

The wind which blew against the English fleet carried Tudor and his followers far around the Southampton lookout to Wales. Four days later the news was in Nottingham, where Richard promptly despatched letters to his captains naming Leicester as the place of meeting. It took twenty-four hours for his message to get to the Duke of Norfolk, another twelve to reach Francis in Southampton. Lord Stanley, the nearest of them all, was his own time about replying, but they heard from him finally. He said he would come as soon as he was able: at present he was sick. "I don't doubt!" Lincoln laughed harshly. That night Strange tried to creep away, and failed. Brought back, he wept, begged for mercy, and confessed that his uncle, who should that moment be guarding the Welsh passes against the invader, had long been in confederacy to join him, as had Strange himself. But his father should come: only let him write, he pleaded, and he would surely come.

They gave him leave. Under the hard eyes of Ralph Assheton and Philip Lovell the frantic man scrambled off a wild entreaty to Lord Stanley, saw it sanded, sealed, and given into the bearer's hands. Then they lodged him under guard, and left him with his prayers for company.

Francis quitted Southampton the day the summons from Nottingham arrived. The southern levies were breaking camp behind him to march next morning; they would rendezvous with his Midland contingents at Banbury. In a last-minute change of mind as they rode, he told Harry Russell to make straight for the mustering there, and turned off himself for Minster Lovell.

The courier he had sent before him had been swift; the manor strength was marshalled and waiting when he rode into the courtyard. Running an eye over the drawn-up ranks, Francis nodded approval to the steward, and then—for the grooms were bringing out fresh horses from the stables, and it would be a few minutes before they were saddled and the gear shifted—he dismounted and entered the house by the south door.

He had not seen Maud since Easter, and she had grown

again. She knew his step now and trotted wobblingly to meet him, showing three teeth in a wide smile. The nurse followed attentively, but she was a light-footed child, slender and very quick, with none of the bumps and grazes which had been Will's unfailing lot. The few minutes Francis had allowed himself stretched to a quarter hour; hurrying then, he did not notice as he was leaving that the door to the women's room was ajar. It had not been so when he came into the nursery, and for an instant he had paused, thinking of the great chamber beyond; now, in haste to be gone, he left by the way he had come without looking behind him.

Her hand on the latch, Anna listened to him go. She had been poised there, waiting for what seemed hours, and if he had hesitated even a moment she would have opened to him. But he did not, and she could not think if anger or indifference would have thrust with the keener pain. His steps faded. Suddenly she flung open the door and, disregarding Maud and the astonished nurse, ran through the nursery and on to the tower stair; but there were voices below, and then the sound of a door closing. She had never believed he would go like that, without one word. Sobbing, tripping on her skirts, she hurried up the steps to the wide upper chamber which overlooked the gate.

The courtyard lay in a block of shadow, a tangle of spears rising from it, each with its square pennon flattening in the wind. A babel of noise swept up like a wave: the clang of weapons, the blowing of horses and scrape of their hoofs, called-out farewells from the women who had crowded out to see their men away. Her husband moved among them, a smile or hand-clap on the shoulder for each; she could see their affection and pride in him as they followed him with their eyes. Light glimmered dimly on his cuirass, and the blazoned standard flamed like sunfire barred with blood.

Someone brought up his horse; now—oh now, he must turn. He did, but the window was too deep for her to lean from it, and she was half-hidden by the buttress. He sat for a moment, the breeze stirring his hair, looking up at the house with that peculiar, indrawing absorption which had so often baffled and eluded her—for a man must be born somewhere, and what was it after all but stone and mortar, and some of that the worse for weathering? Then his face changed and lightened, for the nurse had carried Maud to the window to wave good-bye. He kissed his fingers, bowing as to some great lady, then wheeled and lifted a hand to the waiting troop. The long line of men swung about, the horsemen going before; hoofs rattled in the cobbled passageway, and the gate closed after them.

Francis overtook the Duke of Norfolk beyond Banbury, with Surrey and all the strength of the eastern counties. They entered Leicester a little before the King, but by sunset his advance riders were passing through the city gates, and shortly afterwards Richard arrived. He had had word from the Earl of Northumberland that he was following close behind with his northerners; in such haste had he gathered them, the Earl wrote, that they were too tired to catch up with his grace that night, but assuredly he would be in Leicester tomorrow. Richard passed the scribbled note to Norfolk with a shrug, smiling faintly as he met the older man's eyes. Before he left Nottingham he had heard from the mayor of York, who was enquiring anxiously why his grace had sent no request to the city for men to repel his enemies. Northumberland should have summoned them long since; but Northumberland was bringing no troops with him who would set Percy below Plantagenet. Richard sent a calm reply to the mayor, telling him only that he should send his men to Leicester, but it was questionable whether they could arrive now in time for the encounter with Tudor. Swearing bitterly, Norfolk threw the Earl's letter across to Francis, and Richard said wryly, "They say pigeons come homing, Jack. I think we shall have to do without my lord of Northumberland."

Apart from Northumberland and the Stanleys—from whom had come no acknowledgment of Strange's passionate appeal—they judged their numbers somewhat overmatched Tudor's. He had not added much to his forces as he marched through Wales; an apathetic countryside saw him pass, and the best recruiting he had was with Rhys ap Thomas and his followers. Thomas, sworn to King Richard, had been set with a mighty host to guard the southern approaches, but Tudor, hearing of his near presence, sent to tender him the lieutenancy of Wales. Thomas promptly closed with the offer, and brought in his men.

The Earl of Northumberland presented himself as promised, still full of explanations about the exhaustion of his troops. He hoped the King, in view of it, would let them form the rearguard of the army when they set forth next morning. "Or perhaps they might lie in bed here the day long, and await news of how the battle goes," Francis suggested dulcetly, and was rewarded with a stare of mingled suspicion and hauteur. In the end Northumberland was allowed his way, and, the hour being late, they sought their beds.

They mustered very early, when the first streaks of light were creeping above the city walls. Norfolk and his son had the van, with Richard following; Northumberland rode beside him, his northerners far back of the rest. A press of townspeople watched them go by. As they crossed Bow Bridge the King's foot struck hard on a stone which jutted from the parapet, and an old woman cried out that his head should lie lower before tomorrow eve. A lull had fallen; the thin piping carried clearly. Some of the household knights pulled up, hardly believing what they had heard; one of them cursed and spurred back to catch her by the shoulder. She came unresisting, the horrified crowd parting to let her captor through as he dismounted and pushed her across the bridge.

At the other end the King waited. Bewildered by the suddenness of what had befallen, she stared up at him in fear, her hands knotting in her skirt. He spoke quietly, bending down to look into her face. "Do you have the sight?" But she had gone dumb, and only plucked at the cloth, shivering and blinking her eyes. Presently straightening, Richard signed the knight to release her and turned away.

A number of them held she should be punished, but he shook his head and urged his horse forward again. Sedately keeping pace, Northumberland said, "You have madwomen in the south, my lord."

It was known now that Tudor was striking south from Stafford. In Shropshire he had been joined by the Earl of Shrewsbury's uncle, who brought a good part of the Talbot strength with him; they seemed now to be making for London, an advance the King's course was designed to intercept west of Leicester. Somewhere between them the double force of the Stanleys hesitated, shifted, and finally came to a halt, by the scouts' reporting, not far from the village of Market Bosworth.

They pitched camp hardly a mile from Sir William Stanley's pickets. Not much south of him his brother's standard fluttered, well to the other side of the highway down which,

334

if he cared now to meet his enemy, Henry Tudor must come. As the sun sank westward, far down the road the first banners appeared.

Dusk fell, and the men settled for sleep. Richard went among them, speaking to those he knew; there were many, for lords from the north had come with their meinies independently of Northumberland, and they had long served him on the border. He had swung his camp athwart the Tudor's line of march, leaving his own left like a guarding arm across Lord Stanley's emplacements. Another message to Stanley that afternoon bidding him join the royal army had brought a shuffle of excuse. Richard knew now that both the Stanleys had met and talked with Tudor on the way.

He went back to his tent to rest, and Philip, who had been seeing to the disposition of his own men, found him there soon after, sipping a cup of wine while his squire saw to a last-minute burnishing of the King's armour. The boy departed at a nod, and Philip went over to inspect his handiwork. A golden circlet lay near the helm, and he chuckled as he observed, "Your grace changes no custom. The knights of your household have cursed the coronet of Gloucester many a day, for drawing the whole field on them horse and foot."

As if thinking aloud, Richard said idly, "Philip, how long have I reigned?"

Something in his voice made Philip look at him. "Two years. By the favour of Heaven to us all."

The grey eyes were amused. "You turn courtier." He was silent for a time, stretched on the couch with his arms beneath his head. "I've had only one Parliament. But it was a good one, there are laws now for the people they had not before. They are the better for it, and Lincoln will be too." He saw Philip's face change, and laughed. "I am only looking ahead. He is my heir, and some day he must deal with what I leave him. God send he has forgiven me by now for leaving him to ward the north; he thought poorly of me for it, but I'd no mind to strip the border in Tudor's honour."

Strolling to the loosened tent flap—for the night was warm, and barely a breeze stirred—Philip said carelessly, "I saw Oxford's banner next Tudor's while they were making camp. I wonder if he remembers now that his wife would have been in want these dozen years, only for the pension you granted her from your private purse."

"She was the Earl of Warwick's sister; there was no reason

she should suffer for her husband's persuasions. As for Oxford, he has served Lancaster all his days, and chose imprisonment and exile rather than be foresworn of his oath. He is the only general Tudor has: I promise you, I fear him." Richard leaned on his elbow, propping his chin in his fist. "Tell me, Philip: Do you believe in the mercy of God?"

"Yes. How else is a man to endure his own knowledge of himself?"

"I do not. I believe in judgment, and a bound beyond which the unpardonable is damned into eternity."

"The unpardonable is a personal conception, the best that is in a man accusing his worst. But the soul of man and the sins of his soul are not in his right to acquit or condemn. He can only bear them, which are witness to his mortality." Philip looked round briefly to meet the steady gaze. "We are responsible, but there is not one of us that is not still the measure of a thousand souls from God: so once someone said to me. I was angry when he called me arrogant, so I know it was true."

"A priest? Well, I could believe he spoke truth for you." Richard reached to reverse the glass beside his couch and lay back, watching the slow trickle of the sands. "I have done evil in my life of my own will, and more has followed where I had not designed nor wished. For all that, I cannot clean myself of it."

The light was going; beyond the massif of Ambien Hill the abbey bells were ringing vespers. *Recessus Dei*: the departing of God. Shivering, Philip came back into the tent, letting the flap drop after him.

The candles threw amber shadows on the tent walls, lighting the disorder of papers on the chest and turning the heaped armour to massy gold. He stooped to pick up a piece which had rolled from the rest, and Richard watched him, toying with a ring on his thumb. "I had a letter from my sister in Flanders a week ago, Philip. Erard de Brezy is dead." He saw the outstretched hand freeze in its movement, and after an instant shifted his eyes. "I had meant to tell you before; you knew him, I remember. He had been ill for some years, and lived wholly retired on his estates—tended with great devotion, I understand, by his wife." He turned the ring again. "It is some time since my sister visited England. I have it in mind to send inviting her, and I wondered if you would care to go to Malines for my messenger."

Philip put the armoured gauntlet down. The clatter of it rocking among the other pieces made his teeth set, he covered the litter roughly with his palm, and the silence lengthened. After a long time he said, "You know then?"

"You must admit when we left Saint Omer I had grounds for conjecture. Francis was unhelpful, but my sister has had a long fondness for Madame de Brezy." It was mildly spoken, but the blood rushed into the other man's face; against it the tiny scars on his cheek showed pale as bone. Richard directed a brief glance at the rigid profile, and dropped his eyes. "I am not trying to pry. But you have not married, and it is absurd that a man of your substance should have no heirs of his body to follow him. It is not too late for you to think of it still, if you care to."

"I have promised Willowford to Hugh—" The words came slowly, groped for through a still working daze of shock. "The other lands too— He would never hold me to it, but I—I could not disappoint him now."

"Hugh will take no loss: my word on it. For the moment think for yourself."

Philip looked down at his hands. They were shaking, and he rested them on the chest, clenching his fingers hard against the wood. Barely audibly, he said, "It is the wish of my heart, but if you must know I am sore afraid. She was hardly more than a child: she has had ten years to understand the quality of what I did to her and him, that summer."

"A long while," Richard agreed calmly. "Well, people change: you would be foolish not to think of that. But I believe you should go and see." He hesitated, choosing his words with care. "Her marriage, naturally, is for the Archduke Maximilian to approve, but you would have my sister's voice, and he might be glad of a sure man, being already in difficulty with some of his wife's nobles in Flanders. I see no obstacle in that particular, although you would have to divide your time between England and the low countries henceforward."

"Do you suppose I would touch a hide of Erard de Brezy's land? I'll bring my wife to England, if she will have me: the Archduke may bestow her husband's property where he wishes."

Richard studied him thoughtfully; it was a minute before

337

he replied. "You may find that is impossible." A stubborn silence answered, and he stood up, impatiently kicking aside the cushions as they tumbled after him from the couch. "For God's love, Philip, let it be. Erard de Brezy is dead, and if there is any pity in Heaven for our human state he sleeps very sound. His life was many years a burden to him, he would not thank the man who called him back to it. He fell ill not—not long after he returned from the Duke's business in Lorraine; he was thought recovered in a fashion, but then he lost the boy—Auguste, was his name?—at Nancy, the winter you were in Palestine, and that was his end. For eight years he lay in his bed, stirring neither hand nor foot, washed and fed and tended like a babe in the cradle—even his speech gone. He must have desired death as his dearest friend."

After an interval Philip said, "It was when he came back from Lorraine that he was first stricken? How long—after the night I saw him?" The pause answered him. "I see."

He moved to the door of the tent, and mechanically lifted the flap. Night had come, and campfires winked through the dark. It was choppy ground; here and there a thicket of scrub loomed against the wavering light. He halted beneath the curtain, staring out, and Richard came to stand beside him.

"What's done is done, Philip. If men could know the future they would have no need of prayers." He was holding two sealed parchments from the chest; he looked down, lightly weighing the scrolls in his hand. "While I think on it, I am charging you now with a commission. This letter is for my sister in Flanders; what else may be to go you can have later, but this is for her by my private hand. This other"—it was a thicker roll, tied loosely with ribbon—"is for you. It is a charter for some certain lands, late of the crown, which lie not inconveniently far from Willowford, given under my seal to Baron Lovell for long service. It could be useful when you are dealing with Max; he sets store by such things. You have long refused gifts of me, and I do not force them on you now: thus far only Lincoln and I know of this, and Kendall, who wrote it out. Think on it, and decide after tomorrow what you want to do." He put the rolls in Philip's hand, and stood gazing at the flickering watch-fires. "It grows cold. The sky is clear though; we'll have the sun."

Philip left him shortly after. Hugh would be waiting for

him; but Hugh, and the polished weapons over which he was still undoubtedly labouring, and the whole of the camp could not have been farther from his thoughts. As with an arm long bound when the cords first drop away, he could not immediately realise the fetters were gone; feeling returned only slowly, and with it, the renewed experience of pain.

He had not so much willed himself to forget her as slammed a door on part of his mind; suddenly it had been unlocked, and all the agony and crushing finality of loss, the unbearable which must somehow be borne, met him again with her beloved ghost. He had built strong walls against those biding presences; but remorse and shame for the grief he had caused her and the injury to the man who had been his friend, the danger he had let in and the punishment he had left her to face alone: these he had neither submerged nor penned. The horror of those last hours in Saint Omer was still, as then, a nightmare confusion he could not clearly remember; he knew Francis had stood between him and the outer door of their chamber, inflexibly promising either to rope him to his bed, or send for a squad of the Duke's men to mount guard on the threshold, before he saw his cousin go seeking again for Erard de Brezy or his wife. He meant it too, and relented in the end only so far as to guarantee delivery of a message to the Duchess of Burgundy. Her response was no more than a seconding of Francis' arguments; the only service he could do his unhappy lady now was to remove himself from Flanders, and he might rely on her to see Madame came to no hurt. The wisdom of that was beyond denial, but he used to wake at night, sick with terror and hearing her voice. Autumn passed into winter; a secret letter to the Duchess at Lille, begging news of how Margaret fared, elicited the reply that she did very well, and would continue to do so if he would forbear meddling. It was that, finally, which drove him on his travels; he could not trust himself in England, with Burgundy so close across the narrow seas.

Twigs cracked beneath his nervously pacing feet; in his doublet he felt the stiff rustle of the parchments. A crescent moon swung above the trees, white as a woman, the shadow of the old moon curved between the horns. He stopped short, saying aloud, "Meg." If she could forgive him, if he could make her care again, if only he could forgive himself.

There were murmurings to his right, and a glow of fires

painted, the lion standard of Norfolk tawny-gold. His wandering had brought him far beyond the King's battle, and they were Howard men that kept watch here. They passed him through, grinning at his absorption, and he climbed the farther slope to look across the fields to Market Bosworth. The Benedictine monastery lay between, a darker bulk against the tussocky meadows, its church tower prodding the sky.

Chance had brought him, travelling on his affairs into Essex, to spend a night with the monks at Colchester not long after he came home from Jerusalem; he had been frequently in the town as a young man, dealing with shipmasters who were carrying the Woodstock sarplers to market in Calais: less often in later years, when the Duke of Gloucester's business was engaging him and he had agents to ride from Woodstock to London and Colchester, getting the wool away. So it had been a while since he had claimed the brothers' hospitality; and nothing in his life had been less welcome than to discover there the one-time monk of Reading. Surgeon or priest, he had an eye before which evasion failed. "I wish you good speed on your journeying, sir," had been his farewell. "You will have need of it, to outrun what travels with you." Well, he had not outrun it.

There was a light still over the abbey gate. He slid the cloak from his shoulders: twenty minutes' walk, each way, but it would be hours before the men were stirring for tomorrow's array. A night-walking spearman, as disinclined for sleep as himself, promised to take a message to Hugh that he was to get himself to bed. Then he swung the cloak across his arm, and started down the hill.

Some time after midnight a breeze sprang up; the moon set, and the air quickened with the promise of dawn. Strolling quietly about the camp as the King's officers began to rouse, Francis sensed, rather than saw—for it was still thick dark—a figure crossing the stubbled common towards him. It came nearer into the gutter of torchlight, and he recognised his cousin. "Up early, Francis? I didn't think to find you abroad yet."

"Like yourself. I looked in at your tent a few minutes ago, and wondered where you might be."

"At the abbey, hearing lauds with the brothers." Philip nodded over his shoulder, stretched, smiled, and smothered a yawn.

"Good hearing, from all appearance," Francis observed, a trifle dryly. He stared curiously at him. "Has someone made you a present?"

"The best in the world." There was movement around them; shouted commands rang out as the sergeants strode among the sleeping men, and a luminous pallor showed on the eastern rim of the plain. Philip said, "I'll go arm," and touched his kinsman's shoulder. "Good fortune, Francis."

He found Hugh already awake, dancing with excitement, and sorting and resorting his uncle's gear. Sword and axe lay near, honed and glittering; Philip tested the murderous edges with his finger and said with a smile, "I could be shaven with either. Have you been all night toiling over them?"

His padded doublet had been put ready for him, and the leg binding, and the thick cap for under the helm. He surveyed the heap with distaste, thinking of the heat of the coming day. "My father had the sense to fight ham-high in snow at Towton," he remarked, as Hugh got him into them. "I hope Tudor fries." Disregarding the comment, Hugh gave the quilting another remorseless turn about his uncle's calf, and Philip watched the flushed, absorbed face with amusement. "You put me in mind of young Will before Barnet. When you, I must remember, had done scarcely more than see the light of day."

"Sir William was here, earlier," Hugh volunteered. "He was looking for you, and my lord Chamberlain was too."

"Yes, I know Will's here. And Zouche, and Greystoke, and Scrope of Bolton—it's a roll call of the north. Hugh, do I seem old to you?"

Astonished, the boy sat on his haunches to stare up; the question was only half in laughter. "Old, sir?"

"I'm seven and thirty: many men are grandfathers by such a time. Does it seem a great age?"

"No," said Hugh stoutly, and spoiled the effect by adding loyally, "Anyway, you've not got a great belly like Sir Robert."

"Thank you. Praising Heaven for unspeakable mercies, we'll have the breech."

An obscure joke was, apparently, intended. In silent dignity Hugh laced the guard mail around his uncle's narrow hips, and reached for the cuirass.

Outside the sky was turning milky; the arming done,

Philip quenched the torches and stood in the doorway of the tent, watching the growing light. He could feel the shape of the papers rolled in his doublet: a minor encumbrance, but he must not leave them about before he had talked with Richard again, and spoken acceptance of his gift. The scrimmage with Tudor lay between, exasperating to his new impatience, but, he told himself, it would be over in a few hours. Then—then he could go.

A number of men were gathered around the King's tent when he reached it: Norfolk and his son; Brackenbury, the lieutenant of the Tower, with his thin, serious face; Francis, Percy, Ratcliffe and Assheton, and the northern lords. Of all the faces Philip saw, there was hardly one that had not been known at Middleham. That led his mind inevitably to Sir James Tyrell; it was strange he should be absent on such a day, but he was captain of Guisnes Castle now overseas at Calais, and had long left the body of the King's knights. Philip was not sorry for it. Still vivid in his memory was the Master of Henchmen's face when Richard struck him down at Nottingham; there had been a morning shortly after when one of the pages crept to his place in hall with tear-stained cheeks, cradling a wrenched and swollen arm that had been whole, Philip knew, when the child went to his duties in Sir James' chamber the night before. A few days later Richard relieved his officer of custody of the wards and henchmen and sent him to serve with the Calais garrison, and Philip knew himself justly blamed by Tyrell for it. In his heart he pitied him: it was his private belief the man was mad.

Kendall came from the King's tent, the quill and tablets he carried incongruous against his armour. There had been quite a business when Richard knighted his faithful secretary; even Francis had lifted an eyebrow and murmured something about clerks in harness. He was the first king's secretary to be made member of the Privy Council, but he looked more at home in his gear than Catesby, whose stomach for tactics was limited to the strategy of the commons chamber.

A herald took the letter from Kendall and rode off towards Lord Stanley's camp; one of the scouts appeared to report that Oxford was rousing his men. Francis hummed to himself, " 'Oh Sweetheart, will you lift your skirt, And lie with me a while?' " The royal standard snapped against the slowly colouring sky. Assheton said quietly, "My lords and sirs, are you ready?" and Richard came out.

He spoke to each of them, one man after another moving forward to kiss his hand. For Philip he had a quick smile; answering a query from Francis, who thought he looked weary, he said lightly that he had dreamed a good deal, and had a restless night for it. To Brackenbury, who was last, he gave both his hands, and it seemed as if a message passed between them. Then he turned away; a squire brought his helmet, and someone led up his horse. Philip was nearest, waiting to help him mount, but he stood an instant, fingering the reins. "When the Earl of Warwick was at Barnet, his officers refused him his horse out of fear he might betray them. I wonder where they thought he would run?"

Their shocked expressions made him smile. He looked round the circle of troubled faces: northern men, most of them, who had come to serve him because they had known and loved him in the northern years. He knew how few from the rest of England had come of his personal summoning. To them, through those years he had been only a fable, the valiant soldier-brother who had loved the King. But the image had cracked like a sword flawed from the forge, and they could not kindle to the man who had supplanted it. The patness of it nearly made him laugh. He knew—who better, havin gloved the Earl of Warwick?—how impossible it was to put back the gilt on clay.

A lark broke from the trees and fluttered up, singing. He mounted, the household knights forming escort behind. Norfolk and Surrey had gone to lead out the van, and the King's men fell in after them. North of the central position where Norfolk had spent the night with his troops they met the Earl of Northumberland, who gave it as his opinion that it would be as well if he remained where he was, to watch Sir William Stanley; from the heights of Sutton Cheney they could see him slowly marshalling his men, far north of, and discreetly flanking, Tudor's forces. His brother occupied a similar situation to the south.

Ironically measuring Northumberland's stolid countenance, Richard gave his consent. It would cut his available forces by a third, but he could still overmatch Tudor's strength. Norfolk was already marching rapidly on Ambien Hill, the thrusting outcrop which overlooked the enemy camp: a discomfiting confrontation for Oxford, who was hastily mustering Tudor's motley of followers at the foot of the slope. Warily Norfolk took his men a short way down the hill, leaving room for the King to establish himself with the reserves on the crest. It was while Richard was still seeing to the deployment of his rearguard that the herald returned from Lord Stanley. To the King's curt command—less softly phrased than before—that Lord Stanley join the royal host and redeem by his good offices the life of his traitor son, Stanley replied viciously that he had other sons. "Stepson, he means," Ratcliffe muttered, his eyes on the plain below. Back of Oxford's array, on a little hillock planted with the gawdy banner of Cadwallader, they could make out the slight figure of Henry Tudor, surrounded by a bodyguard of several hundred men. White with passion, Richard spun round; a few of his attendants, reading the order that trembled on his tongue, half-moved towards the wretched Strange. Ringed with warders, he was sobbing again and holding out his hands in supplication. For a minute Richard gazed at him; then, his lip lifting, he turned wordlessly away.

Far below the trumpets shrilled. The first rush of men were swarming up the slope; a cloud of arrows from Norfolk's flanking archers darkened the sky, and the splintering shock of collision echoed to the crest. The two forces met, engaged, and melted into a single writhing line.

At the top of the hill Richard stood watching. They could see now that Oxford had committed nearly all his men to the first assault; it was his only hope, for if he could not show an initial success he knew well the Stanleys, for all their promises, would never help him. The resultant advantage of numbers was beginning to tell on Norfolk; narrowly appraising his vanguard's situation, Richard detached a few hundred men from his shrinking reserve and sent them down to Norfolk's support. The line straightened and steadied; and the watchers on the hill drew a long breath.

The sun was well up now, and blazing. The wild movement of the surging melee was slowing with heat and exhaustion; Richard nodded grimly to Ratcliffe, who marched out another group of billmen. The towering banners of Oxford and Norfolk crashed together, and a courier came labouring up the hill, shouting that the Duke of Norfolk was slain. Surrey had taken over his father's command; north of the heaving line sunlight flickered suddenly on a stir among Sir

William Stanley's troops. Cavalry all, he was bringing them closer to see.

Richard was staring down the slope. Oxford, heartened, was forcing his advantage. Through a ragged gap in the rear of the battle some men came out, carrying a body by its armoured legs and arms; a lad in squire's dress followed, weeping. A little way back of the press they laid it on the turf, and went down the hill into the fight again.

Shortly after that, Richard said quietly, "Oxford is nearly done. He's no fresh men." He looked back at his thinned reserve, and beckoned a herald. "Go tell my lord of Northumberland to bring up his men."

"My lord, why trouble?" Francis demanded impetuously, as the courier raced off. "We've numbers enough to finish Oxford: Why let Northumberland share in the pleasure?" Richard said only, "I want his answer."

They had it, in not many minutes. The Earl of Northumberland respectfully submitted that he must stay where he was, to hold Sir William Stanley in check.

"Gelded, on my honour," Percy whispered. "And by his own hand." He was pale with the shame of it; the man was of his blood.

Of them all, Richard showed the least emotion; he was thoughtfully regarding the lie of the plain below, the shifting sway of the battling men, and the long, clear path around them to the little hummock where the dragon of Cadwallader fluttered against the sky. A flick of colour caught his roving glance: the bright tabard of a herald, riding full tilt from Oxford's line back to the dragon standard, carrying the news to Tudor, doubtless, of the Duke of Norfolk's death. They saw him pull up, dismount, and go forward; a squire who watched a moment longer said in a hushed voice, "Your grace, he takes obeisance of him like a king."

Richard had turned to speak to one of his officers, but he wheeled round at that. He looked after the pointing finger, and a spark leaped in his eyes. "By my soul," he said softly, "he shall have homage enough."

The officer was returning; he had gone to the horsepark and came back now leading the King's war charger, White Surrey. There were only a handful of mounted men left among the reserves, but they were sufficient, Richard said composedly, for his intention. The seesaw struggle on the hillside might go on for many hours while the Stanleys debated whether to intervene; there was only one way to make a swift end. He was going after Henry Tudor.

They followed him without a word. Quickly the remaining horses were brought up, the plan of advance explained. Visors snapped shut. It was Philip who took the King's axe from the squire and handed it up to him; then he swung up to his own horse beside him. Last of all, the royal standard bearer took his place.

They moved quietly down the hill, without fanfare, out of care to conceal their purpose as long as possible from the enemy below. Rounding the locked northern wing of the battle, they could see Surrey holding his own worthily. Then they were past it, and the sound of trumpets broke on the morning air. The pace quickened from canter to full-out gallop; pennons stretched in the wind—Percy and Lovell, Assheton, Brackenbury, Scrope of Bolton, the modest ensign of Sir John Kendall. The tufty levels of Redmore Plain flattened before them, to right and left the solid phalanxes of the Stanleys, watchful and waiting; and clear ahead, screened by several hundred horsemen, the dragon standard of the Tudor.

The bewildered ranks of Tudor's guard buckled before them. They clove through it, a few score men against as many hundred, White Surrey and the lightly-armed standard-bearer outdistancing all the rest. A quiver passed through the poised files of Stanley's cavalry, and Sir William, mounted at their head, slowly lifted his arm. Swerving to avoid a horse, felled and screaming in his path, Philip caught the shiver of movement and shouted to Francis, "For God's sake, get to the King! Stanley's moving!"

A roar as of many waters drowned the cry, the swelling thunder of two thousand horsemen. The scarlet-jacketed riders flashed by, sweeping the slender barrier of defenders from their way like straw scattered in the wind. Philip saw Kendall go down, and heard Francis' voice raised desperately to rally the blocked-off remnant of the King's knights. Far ahead, the royal standard had reached the banner of Cadwallader. Trying frantically to force a way through the mob, they glimpsed the dazzling arc of Richard's axe as it whirled, fell, and rose again. The mass of Stanley's cavalry thickened between; and when it parted again the wheeling blade was gone. The scarlet and gold banner toppled like a chopped

346

reed; a last brilliance gleamed as the bright circlet fell, sparkling and tumbling, dashed from the helm of the man who had worn it. Then there were only the bays of triumph, a forest of spears and axes plunging forward to the death, and the astonishing, stripped blankness of the empty sky.

More horsemen were pouring past; wild with victory, ignoring the shattered remnant of Richard's knights, they were making for the wallowing confusion around Tudor's standard. An armed rider spurred after in hopeless pursuit, battering vainly against the intervening wall of men and horses, and Philip cut his way to his side. "Francis, come away. It's finished, can't you see it's too late?"

His cousin seemed not to hear. Motionless, he sat gazing with the sick eyes of unbelief at the chaos; from the hillside Surrey, a soldier to the last, was sounding the retire. Around the dragon standard against which Henry Tudor had at last shakenly dismounted there was only slight movement now: the occasional, indifferent lift and drop of an axe, the prod of a spear at what lay at the foot of the banner of Cadwallader.

A group of riders, helmets discarded, were cantering slowly from the scene. Francis shouted hoarsely, "Stanley! You whoreson Judas, will you turn?" and lunged towards them. Mildly contemptuous, Sir William glanced over his shoulder. He could afford his ease. His companions were already galloping to meet the attack; some foot soldiers scrambled from the path of the oncoming horseman, and one of them jabbed upward with the bloodied hook of his bill. There was an instant's check as the frightened destrier plunged and sidled against the slackening hand; then the reins went free, swinging like ribbons as the rider slid from the saddle, and Stanley's stroopers rode over him.

The impetus of their chargers' rush carried them past; for the result, they did not even wait to see. In an uncaring turmoil of fleeing men Philip threw himself from his horse and, catching one of the frenzied passers by the scruff, halted him long enough to secure a hand's help in getting first Francis, and then himself, up on Francis' trembling stallion. Blood drenched the housing, and the unstirring heaviness of the weight against him struck at his heart. With his own charger's reins noosed about his wrist, he made for Ambien Hill. Blurred faces passed him, showing the white-lipped panic of running men; many of them with his own or his cousin's badge tried to stop him, begging to be told what do to. To each one he shouted the same thing, that the seneschals must get them home. As he breasted the slope he was searching anxiously for sight of Hugh, and at the crest of the hill he found him, slumped over the barrel of an abandoned cannon with Gregory Traynor pulling an arrow from his arm.

There was nothing for it but to leave Traynor to his task. Easing his unconscious burden to the ground, Philip fumbled at the armour lacing, throwing the pieces heedlessly aside as he stripped them from the flaccid limbs. His cousin's face was sallow; one leg was like a cushion below the knee, and from the thighs down he was soaked with blood. The thrust had gone beneath the fauld and its underskirt of mail, deep into the groin; what horror the barb had wrought as it was dragged out again Philip dared not even think. He stanched the wound as best he could and bound it with the discarded leg padding, thinking it make-shift work, but it would serve until the brothers at the abbey could do better. The broken leg was easier; he used arrow shafts to splint the limb, and was wondering how to improvise a litter when Traynor came over to say, "There's a cart here, sir; he'll do better in that, while we get him down to the monks."

It was a rough thing, some farmer's forgotten wagon and beast for supplies long taken away, but they made it as comfortable as possible with the horsecloths, and lifted him in. Hugh, pale but determined, had violated flat instructions to lie still, and was standing on the lip of the hill looking down at the field. Suddenly he exclaimed aloud, and Philip, half-knowing already, came swiftly to his side. On Redmore Plain some of Tudor's men were mobbing an archer. So far away it seemed a play of puppets, the rope swung up; the tree shook as the horse was flogged from under it, and only the doll's figure remained, twisting and turning in its bright Howard livery. In a little while the kicking legs were still.

"Philip—" It was Francis' voice, as dry and hoarse as the rustle of dead leaves. Philip went back to the cart and, bending down, answered gently, "I am here." It was only then he realised he had his sword still futilely gripped in his hand. He laid it on the ground, and Francis, watching him, said, "What is it?" Rolling the discarded arming doublet into a pillow, Philip slipped it beneath his head as he replied, "Nothing to trouble you." He was telling himself they had better be quick, getting him down to the monastery, before the riot spread over the hill. When he looked at Traynor, he could see he was thinking the same. As if they had spoken aloud, Francis said weakly, "The abbey's a mousehole. They'd drag me from the steps of the altar, and you too—" Philip wondered how much, after all, he had heard. Helpless, he said, "What, then? Francis, you need tending. I've done what I can, but there will be doctors and a bed for you with the monks—"

"And Tudor's hangman at the gate." His eyes closed; Philip saw his fingers cramp in the horse blanket. After a minute he whispered, "Take me to Tichmarsh."

Across the cart, Philip met Traynor's eyes. It was thirty miles; and the castle itself had been falling into ruin for a hundred years. He glanced at the sky, which was clear now, but it could change by nightfall, and they would be less than half the way there. Minster Lovell was not much farther; but he did not ask why his cousin had not named it, nor asked the nursing of Anna Fitz Hugh.

The cries of men came faintly from below, a mingling of French, Welsh, and English, as Tudor's soldiers ranged the field. Mounting his tired destrier, Philip signed to Hugh to take the hurt man's charger, and pointed Traynor to the seat of the cart. "To Tichmarsh, then," he said.

CHAPTER TWENTY-FOUR

THEY were three days accomplishing the journey, a distance a hale man could have travelled in one.

In dreams, after, Philip relived those days. There was nothing like a main road; the jerking of the cart over the ditched and muddied track made his heart flinch with pity, and he was thankful when very soon the sick man fainted. In frequent halts he inspected the bandages, sodden with blood which was oozing still, and retightened the splints; and, when the first night found them near an outlying farm, risked asking a bed and some wine and clean cloths to wash and dress again his cousin's wound. Their hosts were satisfied with few questions; although it would be some days before Henry Tudor was proclaimed from the remoter village market crosses, they plainly thought it wiser to know as little as possible of their guests, and saw them away next morning with clear relief. The heat which had been at first a blessing by noon was torment worse than the flies; Hugh, rapidly tiring, from the second afternoon was persuaded to lie with Francis in the cart, his hurt arm in a sling.

Tichmarsh village lay midway between Northampton and the Lincoln fens. For more than two hundred years the Lovells had held the land, and the great church remained, unmoving witness to the power and wealth which had endowed it; but the castle had long fallen into decay, and there was only a bailiff's house now, walled and closed with gardens, of roughcast limestone with a slated roof. The officer himself met them at the gatehouse; he had a stained clout around his head and looked weary, having been home no more than a day from bringing the Tichmarsh levies away from Bosworth; but he said at once that my lord must have his own good bed, and, shouting for servants, brought them warmly in. About his wife Philip was less easy; her eyes glanced sideways, furtive with anxiety, and she was in plain terror for her husband. He felt for her, but his first concern was with his cousin. Equally little did he care for their situation; Tichmarsh lay in a backwater of marl and oolite villages, near-roadless if it came to running, and bare of the simplest defence. In time, he knew, for his reputation's sake Henry Tudor must get control of his men; but intruders could mean only danger until the Tudor's grip was sure. So soon his mind was accepting, it, what a scant week before had been impossible as the phoenix.

A man of the bailiff's household sent next day to Leicester was back the evening after, pale-faced and laden with news. Only the day before his arrival there had been more hangings, this time in the city: William Catesby, King Richard's councillor, and a yeoman farmer and his son of whom nothing could be learned but that they had fought at Bosworth. Sir Robert Brackenbury, the Lieutenant of the Tower, had died in the battle, as had Ratcliffe and Kendall. Assheton, escaping, was believed to have fled north to his family in Lancashire; Percy had been carried from the field by his men, his spine crushed by the hoofs of Stanley's cavalry. Of Richard himself, the rough voice shook to speak. Stripped, mutilated, haltered like a thief and flung over a horse ridden by one of his own heralds, the dead king had been paraded back to Leicester. In the house of the Grey Friars the body lay two days naked on the paving stones, before the brothers were given leave to bury it in an unmarked grave.

When the first birds began to sing in the early dawn, Philip knew what he must do. To Francis, briefly lucid between fever and broken, uneasy sleep, he said no more than that he was unsatisfied with the nursing to be had in Tichmarsh; but in his heart he knew there was only one place in England he could believe safe now to leave his kinsman. The bailiff provided a horse litter, and Hugh, buoyantly recovered, protested to final defeat the tranquil hackney supplied for him. Then they set off, moving by slow and gentle stages across the Cambridgeshire marshes, and so south again to the Benedictine abbey of Colchester on the salt-blown mouth of the sea.

Next morning, perforce, he had to take his leave. Dom Martin, his examination done, told him Lord Lovell would be many weeks healing, and Philip, having just come from a parting look at him, could well credit it. There had been no farewells, the Prior's opium having done its work; and the stretched immobility of the body in its linen wrappings appeared to him more of death than life, so unbreathing was the quiet beneath the coverlet. He would send word, the

Prior said; and with that Philip—desperately anxious, but knowing how urgently he must be required in Oxfordshire—was compelled to be content.

They travelled slowly to spare Hugh, who still had the bandages around his arm, and it was another week before they reached Ipsden. Philip had had no way to get a message to his sister, who he knew would be wild with fear for the boy, unless Dame Alice had sent one of the returned men from Willowford to reassure her. There had been no one from Ipsden at Bosworth to bring her news.

Gilbert was at home, and met them in the hall. They exchanged a few words; queries on Philip's part for Kate and the rest of the household were acknowledged, and followed by correct, although guarded words of commiseration from Gilbert. He asked politely after Lord Lovell, voiced regret at his hurts, and trusted they were not serious.

"Grave enough," Philip responded mechanically. "I left him"—something made him pause—"in good hands, but it will be a time before he can be moved."

"Ah? Somewhere near Bosworth, I suppose?" The curious eyes drifted to Hugh, who returned a guileless stare of incomprehension. Philip had not even looked at him. "Not too near, brother Gilbert. We rode for a while—I don't remember how far, I'd a scratch myself, you see, and it made me stupid."

Gilbert only nodded, and shortly after dismissed his half-brother with instructions to attend upon his mother in her bower. The slight swagger of the retiring shoulders plainly spoke the weary soldier, home from war.

Philip made no attempt to follow him. It was becoming clear to him that his presence in Gilbert Secott's house was an intrusion and an embarrassment; and it was not hard to guess why. With a slight colour in his cheeks—he was remembering the effusions of previous visits—Philip made his farewells. Hugh, of course, must stay at home under his mother's eye, the next little while; he would be in communication with Gilbert later, he said, when it was time to discuss the boy's resumed service at Willowford. He could not resist a parting thrust: "I still have the hound you gave me, Gilbert. A fine bitch and of quite unswerving fidelity: I am never absent but she welcomes me as from a ten-year pilgrimage." Gilbert did not even blush; in all probability, Philip reflected, he was unaware of any reason why he should.

The sight of Willowford land cleansed his mouth of the taste of Gilbert Secott. He reached it late in the afternoon, skirting the bridge and hermit's hut beside it to splash through the shallows of the ford. Willows grew thick along the banks, and the trampled horsetrack was lined with velvet cat-tails, solid to the sight, but perishing at a touch.

Beyond the lift of the far bank the outer lands spread before him, as familiar and untroubled as if Bosworth had never been. Some tenant farmers were cocking corn, and a ploughman was leading his team into the winter field. They came running when they saw him, shocked he had journeyed from Leicestershire with no escort but squire and groom, and astounded when he told them he had seen neither Welsh nor French marauders on the way. There had been scores of callers, they said: gentlemen returning to their own lands with their scatterings of retainers, seeking his opinion and counsel. Even the bailiff had been unable to identify all the badges.

Philip rode on. Something primitive was quickening within him, a deep, primal instinct of possessiveness, a fierce satisfaction no less for being lately born, in the rich earth which stretched on either hand. Though the broad holdings Richard had meant for him had vanished, ploughed under—with a piece of his heart beneath the clods of Redmore Plain, this remained; and Henry Tudor was not England, although he had his foot on it. Princes lived and died, but they were older than many kings, these hills which had seen Caesar come.

What code of conduct, he wondered, governed the victor's attitude towards the followers of his defeated enemy? For all the savageries of Bosworth and Leicester, here in the innocent Oxfordshire sunlight he was unable to believe that terms could not be reached. To the depth of his soul, Philip hoped it would be so; he could not see Lincoln—honest, sober, loyal and devoted to his uncle as he had been—unseating Tudor now. Henry could keep his crown, and Philip Lovell would try to forget how he had used the body of his friend. He would be his unrebellious subject; he would swear his fealty though it choke him, and even serve him with his sword if need arose, for his honour's sake; if only he need never go to Westminster and see the Welshman sitting in Richard's place.

The desolation of loss struck again with a pain that was

physical; but even in his flinching the thought of Margaret put up a green shoot in the waste. It was a modest estate he would be offering her after the opulence of Hainault, but she might be as weary as he of courts and princes; and she would understand that Hugh must be secured in his rights, having been so long promised them. There would be her widow's jointure, and although if he had his way it would be no more than the dower she had had from England, that of itself could be no trifle. He would not be robbing their children for his nephew's benefit.

His mother's face when he rode into the courtyard reproached him for the involuntary lifting of his heart. She came from the house as he dismounted before it, and when he touched her he felt her trembling. All the wretchedness which had been her portion when her husband took up arms for the Duke of York, all the uncertainty and danger of those evil days had returned a thousandfold to terrify her for her son. He did his best to comfort her: it was a different case then, he said; the Duke of York, no matter how great his wrongs, had been in arms against his king. But she only clutched at him, murmuring, "What will befall? What will befall?" And then, with a surge of the old bitterness, "Gilbert Secott did not go to Bosworth. He kept to his own lands, and your sister does not look now to have the roof pulled from her head. Oh, did I not tell you how it would be?"

He had to close his teeth on the rejoinder; and in a moment he was able to pity her. She had shared in nothing of his golden years but the land, and if he was prosperous now, it was as much due to her as the bailiffs and their swarms of underlings. Now she was old, and saw no reward but to be put from her home. It was not only his fortune he had risked: it was hers too.

Since there was no reasoning with her fear, he worked to distract it. The ensuing days supplied the means in full measure, for it was harvest time, but mixed with the business of reaping and necessity of providing food and sleeping room for the extra roll of workers, he was burdened with the worry of what might be passing at Minster Lovell. He sent a groom with a brief note of reassurance for Anna the day he returned, meaning to follow himself as soon as he was able; but the man came back saying there was a strange gentleman visiting at Minster Lovell, Lord Talbot he was called, my lady's kinsman, newly reinstated in his father's lands. It would have been illogical to feel surprise—where else should Humphrey Talbot go but to see his cousin, the instant he could get leave from his service?—but Philip could not suppress a twinge of revulsion. Although Anna's distraught reply spoke her impatience for full particulars of her husband's circumstances, he postponed the journey to his cousin's home. He was not yet able to imagine himself exchanging civilities with a servant of Henry Tudor.

A few days later, rising from the supper table in the great chamber above the hall, Dame Alice turned to bid the page call to clear away, gripped her side, and fell headlong across the board. They carried her to her bed, but next afternoon, before the sun had quite gone, she died. Philip stayed with her through all the night and the day before she passed, save for the time when she asked for the chaplain to hear her confession. She dictated her will, and gave instructions for the ordering of her funeral. Then she lay still among the pillows, too habit-grained even then to yield to the weakness of groping for her son's hand. Philip offered it without the asking, and held the roughened fingers until she was gone. Watching through the slow night hours, it grieved him that he could feel nothing more hurtful than compassion, and a profound sadness that, so many years before, his soul had separated from her, whose body had conceived his life, and gone its different way.

He sought after belated atonement in the next days by seeing her wishes were scrupulously followed. A bedeman walked before the coffin to the church, ringing his little bell; the dozen mourners in new black hoods came after, and alms for the peace of her soul went to the parish churches of Willoford and Little Barking. There were bequests for Kate—half the crop of the dower lands, her bed with its hangings of arras, and a purse of twenty pounds—and for the grandsons, Hugh and Roger Secott. These he could only annotate, trying the while to believe it was Gilbert's doing that neither Kate nor anyone else had come from Ipsden for the burying day.

On the evening of the seventh day of remembrance, for the first time since his return he dined in the great hall. His own chair alone at the high table seemed the more solitary for the crowded boards below; he missed Hugh behind him, and his mother's chair by his. The hound Deirdre lay at his foot, chin on paws, thumping her tail when he dropped her a piece from his plate to nose for in the straw. His page was just offering ewer and basin at the meal's end when the porter ran in to say there were riders at the gate—"The Sheriff of Oxford, so he says he is, and a troop of men."

Philip sat motionless, his hands above the bowl. The Sheriff of Oxford had been a frequent guest at Willowford in other days; Since the porter had not recognised the present caller, it seemed apparent another officer had replaced his old friend. He could feel, in that instant of silence, every eye in the hall fixed upon him; the page had gone pale, and some drops from the jug slopped on the tablecloth. Philip looked at him, and the small hands steadied. Water splashed into the basin. Rinsing his fingers in it, he said, "Tell them to enter."

He was drying his hands on the napkin when the tramp of boots sounded at the door. They crowded in, two score men or more, all armed; their numbers filled the hall. At their head was a stranger who could only be the Sheriff of Oxford: a well set-up man with a sunburned neck and pale, protuberant eyes. In his right hand he carried an unsheathed sword. While the household folk sat like statues in their places, he came halfway down the hall towards the high table and stood foursquare before it, hooking a thumb in his belt. He did not give his name, although it would have been courtesy to do so. For a heartbeat the light eyes rested on the hazel ones; then Philip rose, passing the towel to the page, and the other man spoke.

"You are Philip Lovell, sometime body knight to the Richard Plantagenet?"

Philip answered levelly, "I had that singular honour." The hairs of his nape were pricking like an animal's before a natural enemy; the wolfhound Deirdre, sensing his anger, came to her feet with a snarl.

The Sheriff glanced over his shoulder, first at the hushed lower tables, then to one of his officers. "Clear this gaggle," he said briefly, and turned again to the dais. "You are attainted upon charge of treason, Sir Philip. Your lands and goods are forfeit; it is the King's pleasure that you be taken to London forthwith, and lodged in the Tower."

The frightened manor people were being herded past the screens to the kitchens; they had no chance to resist, having been taken weaponless. With a curt gesture Philip sent the whimpering page after them and strode round the table to stand before it, Deirdre padding watchfully at his heels. The ranks of men drew closer, as by a silent command; the movement pulled his eyes, and the furious question died on his tongue. Gilbert Secott was among them, and close behind he thought he saw Hugh. An instant later he knew better: not Hugh, but Roger.

The boy coloured at his uncle's look, but Gilbert stood unmoved. His eyes on the young man's stolid face, Philip said slowly, "You have been a long time coming for me, Sir Sheriff: it's more than a month since I was with my king at Bosworth. Were you one of those here before, that my bailiff did not know? I suppose you had to wait then for someone to send you word when I could be found at Willowford." He could feel nothing but a cold disgust. It's not even malice, he thought; he doesn't bear me any grudge. He just wants to be certain no one thinks to blame him for being kin to me; and he brought my sister's son with him to witness this to make doubly sure.

The hound pushed her muzzle against his fingers, whining. He touched her head to soothe her; the trivial reminder of her presence helped him command his voice. "Upon what grounds am I charged with treason?"

The answer came flat. "Upon the grounds of having been in arms against your sovereign lord Henry, whose reign began on the eve before Bosworth fight."

"On the eve *before*—?" It was grotesque. Philip leaned against the table, staring at him, but there was not a flicker of a smile in the heavy face. Suddenly, helplessly, he began to laugh; it was that or howl like a dog at the ingenuity of man. His shoulders shook, and he dragged a hand across his cheek to wipe the angry tears. "You must pardon me, sirs," he managed to say at last. "I have had small reason to be merry these weeks past, but Henry Tudor has given me the best joke ever told a man. He should have explained the case to King Richard when they came near meeting on Bosworth field: I doubt not my king would have been happy for the matter to be made so clear to him. Upon the eve before Bosworth—!" His voice began to tremble again, and he stopped short, controlling it. His eyes swept the room, lingering an instant on the piled manor rolls lying on the dresser; only that morning he had been going through them, while he told the steward that he lands must be his charge that autumn, it being his purpose to sail very soon for Flanders.

Presently he looked away. "Well. In the circumstances, sir, I am not sure whether you or I should be considered host. Is it your wish to lie here tonight, or do we make shift on the road to London?"

"There is another thing first." Light winked on the bared blade as it swung idly in the owner's hand. "Other persons besides yourself are to be named in this bill when Parliament sits—some thirty, all told. Most of them are either dead or in custody, but a few have still to be fetched in. I should like to know where we can find Lord Lovell."

Philip met his eyes, and something cold brushed his spine. It was strange that such full, moist things could be as dull and hard as stones. After a short silence he said, "I daresay you would. I can't help you."

"I have been assured you can. Come now"—the abrupt cajolery was made more repellent by the unchanging coldness of the man's gaze—"Come now, think a little. You are in evil case, Lovell: you face years of imprisonment. Some help from you in this may dispose his grace to a more clement view."

Philip looked again at Gilbert, and his hands clenched. He thought of Rob with his wife and children at Scotton, crippled to the end of his life; he thought of Francis; and all the impotent fury of the dispossessed broke into conflagration. "Henry Tudor," he said evenly, "may apply his royal clemency to the spot he sits upon. Am I plain?"

"Plain enough, but perhaps I have not been so! You're not the mayor of the palace now, Lovell: you'd best get accustomed to your new condition. You'll give answers when I ask questions, or I'll have them from you in a way you'll take no pleasure from—" One of the younger officers leaned over to whisper, and fell back, repulsed by a roughly disregarding arm. "God's teeth, I care not who he is! He'll speak full soft and meek before I'm done, and we'll have my lord Viscount's bolthole from him or he swings from a beam of his own hall tomorrow morning! Now then!" Beckoning a few after him, the Sheriff mounted the dais. He moved lightly for so big a man. "And as extra measure for insolence—" For an instant he stared grimly; then he jerked his head towards the lower hall. "Fetch him down."

Resistance was as instinctive as it was futile. Even as he sprang back, snatching for the knife at his belt, Philip heard other steps behind. He spun to meet them, but hands laid hold of his arms, pinning them to his sides; a heavy fist smashed against his mouth, and with a roar the hound leaped past him. The drawn sword caught her in midflight. She screamed once, and the blade, hacking downward, withdrew, a coil of entrails spilling after it as her body pitched to the floor of the hall below. The scuffle died into silence, and there was a sound of retching.

"May God damn you, Gilbert," Philip panted, "get the boy out of here. What tale is he to tell himself before he sleeps this night? Get him out!" Roger was leaning against a pillar, green-faced and wiping his mouth. A nearby officer—it was the man who had spoken to the Sheriff earlier—turned to look at the pallid countenance, raised a brow in derision, and went over to seize his arm. "Belly sickness, codling? come on then." He led him to the door; as he kicked it open someone shouted after them, "Put his head under the pump, Nick."

In the courtyard Roger hung over the horsetrough. His keeper stood sardonically watching, and presently, as the paroxysms lessened, he strolled to the well, filled a dipper, and brought it back to fling the contents ungently over the bowed head. Gasping for breath, the boy pushed himself erect, muttering, "I'm sorry—I'm all right now, sir."

"Are you, forsooth," was the drawling rejoinder. "Well, it's more than your uncle will be claiming for himself the next little while, if I'm any prophet. He is your uncle, isn't he?"

"What—what are they doing to him?"

"What they choose. Oh, don't distress yourself, bantam. They'll leave enough to hang in the morning."

Roger leaned against the trough, looking up at him. He was blond, hard-faced man, slightly built, with very blue, mocking eyes. Somehow Roger's own fell before them. "He shouldn't have come back," he said huskily. "He should have known better—how could we have warned him? First thing, we'd have been in trouble ourselves—" And then, angrily—for the ironic eyes were still regarding him—"What am I supposed to do about it? We never thought they would—hurt him, but we're only two, Gilbert and I—"

Picking up the dipper, he went to the well, dipped from the bucket on the curb, and swallowed. His companion observed him in a detached way, and his lip curled. "You flatter yourself. I should rate the pair of you as considerably less than one." Turning on his heel, he walked back into the house.

The Willowford cellars lay beyond the high table of the hall, under the parlour from which a turret stair led to the great chamber above. Having seen his prisoner finally conveyed below, the Sheriff got his men bedded in the hall and with his officers retired upstairs; but it was long past nightfall before the house settled into quiet. The moon came up against the hall windows, patterning the sleepers on their pallets with a fretwork of light, and the shadow of an owl crossed the silver trackway, swooping on silent wings. After a great time, soft footsteps sounded on the upper stair. Descending to the arched entry which gave on the parlour, they hesitated while someone listened, and continued on down to the cellar.

The door was a stout one, barred top and bottom, with a flare burning by the lintel. Without noise the man slipped the bolts, and held a taper to the spluttering torch; the light sank and brightened again as he drew the spill down. Shielding it with his cupped palm, he pushed open the door and stepped inside.

It was a long room, the windows high and narrow, with a vaulted roof and the feel of damp and earth. As he entered something leaped and rustled, peering at him with red, malevolent eyes; he kicked at it and the thing fled squealing. There was an iron sconce on the wall near the door, with a blackened flambeau in it from which he made a light, and by its glow he could see to the room's farther end. A dark object was lying there; as he went forward he saw it move.

They had bound him and left him face down, his arms dragged behind his back. Working clumsily in the blot of his own shadow, the man turned the limp body over; it stiffened at his touch, and he said under his breath, "Softly now, while I see." Something harsh brushed his hands: the thickness of a rope knotted close round the neck and left trailing, as a reminder of the morning. Swearing, he got it off and slid his hands within the torn shirt. He felt a wince, but presently, grunting in satisfaction, he got up, crossed to the huge bulk of a wine vat, and, returning, knelt with a brimming pannikin. "Can you drink?"

Philip swallowed without answering. The wine stung his cut lips; after a sip or two he turned his head away. Putting the vessel aside, the man lowered him back to the floor. The squat shape of the house's inner well showed dimly beyond the casks; he went to it and brought back a dripping clout which he wrung before using it to wipe crusted blood and dirt from the discoloured face. Then, reaching behind, he slit the cords. "So. As far as I can judge, the principal bones are whole, though you may be feeling otherwise just at present." He sat on his heels, moving a little so the light shone on both their faces. A faint, quizzical smile hovered about his mouth. "Nicholas Ferrers, Sir Philip. I don't suppose you remember me?"

"Ferrers?" Philip repeated the name tiredly. "There was a Ferrers died at Bosworth—a very gallant gentleman."

"No kin, I assure you. It's some years since we met, but I was obliged to you once for some kind words you were under no call to offer, and the gift of a horse." He pushed back a lock of fair hair, his smile deepening. "The nag got me home to Wiltshire, where—taking your advice—I remained. You, I believe, rode on to Tewkesbury."

Philip looked at him. It was coming slowly back to him: the tavern where he had stopped with Francis in Gloucester, the hostile landlord, arguing and angry, and a boy slumped across the common table, sobbing for the lost cause of Lancaster and Margaret of Anjou's son. "I remember," he said at last. "And you reminded me I had forgotten Henry Tudor." With a twinge of ungovernable bitterness, he added, "My compliments on your prince, Ferrers. He has not let his hour spoil for waiting."

"That, you mean?" Ferrers jerked his thumb at the ceiling. "A king's followers cannot be all of the same cloth, sir. Had King Richard no such men in his service?"

After a little silence Philip said, "I'm sorry. Yes, your captain put me in mind of another man I knew once. I remember I thought he too was mad." He rested his shoulders against the buttress and rubbed his numbed wrists. "Oh God, what is a party or a cause? It was neither a soul to be saved nor a body to be beaten: it is only men, and there is no word in human tongue can be a name for two of them. In France they will tell you Englishmen are born with tails." He laughed jarringly, and broke off because the slight movement brought a lance of pain through his side. The blood was beginning to run again in his deadened hands, and he was conscious of an excruciating sensation in the left one, where someone had set a boot heel in the palm. He wrapped the wet cloth round the swelling, and turned his head to regard the younger man. "It was good of you to come,

361

Ferrers; this is a—a long night. I've been trying to think, these past hours—why a man lives, what right he has to buy his life, or let it go. Gilbert Secott might be able to tell me; he at least seems to know what he wants. Only he seemed always a joke to me—" His shoulders lifted. "Do you remember the host at Gloucester? I suppose he has painted his sign again. The stuff of laughter—like Gilbert—but indeed they inherit the earth."

"A piece of it, maybe," Ferrers said quietly. "It's as much as they understand." He got up, walked to the foot of the high window behind them, and surveyed it thoughtfully. It was the full height of a man above his head. After a minute he turned to the wine butts; one that was nearly empty yielded to the thrust of his shoulder, and he pushed it under the sill. Standing upon it, he could just reach the heavy shutters. He forced the catch, and, leaving them swinging, jumped down from the vat. "That should do for explanation. There's a horse outside the walls, sir: Are you fit to ride?"

Slow to understand him, Philip said, "You—you are setting me free?"

"Why else should I be here? I'll be open with you, Sir Philip. My king has seized your lands and your friends', and for that I see no blame to him. How is he to secure himself, else? But of all the servants of Richard of Gloucester, to my mind you are the least deserving of"—he glanced briefly at the knotted rope—"this. Well, it's the way of things, often as not, but I'm no philosopher. All I know is, I won't be party to it."

"You'll be in trouble."

"I doubt it." He was busy fraying the ends of the severed cords. Finishing, he eyed the result critically, and flung the pieces from him. "Now then. It's a wretched business, sending you on your way in this state, but there's no help; and by the way, it would be as well, maybe, if you didn't try to hide up with any of your friends. People have been known to change their opinions. You've a six-hour start before the hue and cry is out: I recommend you make for the coast and find a ship to take you beyond the seas. Are you all right?" Philip had staggered slightly as he came to his feet. He braced himself against the buttress while the wheeling darkness steadied; in a moment he said, "Quite all right," and went to the well. The water cooled his temples, and he dipped the rag in it before fastening it more securely about his maimed hand.

Ferrers went to the door, pulled it softly open, and looked outside. Nothing stirred. He waited for Philip to join him, then quenched the light and shut the door, fixing the bolts firmly after him.

They went up the stair on their toes' ends, Ferrers leading. A door in the parlour led into the rear court; under a bush of ilex the postern opposite was ajar. Clear moonlight gave the yard a noon brightness; they moved across it warily, clinging to the shadowing angles of the walls. Once Philip halted, for the smothering faintness had swept over him again, but the freshness of the air revived him, quick and sweet after the sour closeness of the cellar. The mare was saddled in a copse beyond the gate, a neat chestnut from the Willowford stables, with a cloak thrown across her back to keep off the chill; she had been tethered there since dusk. A skin of wine and some food had been left near her, with a heap of clothes.

"Robbed from your own great chamber," Ferrers explained with a grin, as he helped Philip struggle into them. There were shirt and hose, boots, doublet, and a warm jerkin. While Philip contended with the points—clumsily, with his one good hand—the younger man detached a purse from his belt. "You'll need coin to buy your passage. I'm afraid they've already been at your strong box; call this repayment for the landlord's beast."

"You've already paid for that several times over." A little flushed, Philip took the purse. He half-turned to look back at the house, hesitated, and said, "Nick, I've forgotten something. Will you wait for me here, or—it might be better if you went back first and got to your bed. There's something I must take with me."

"Take with you?" Ferrers echoed blankly. "You don't mean to go strolling back for keepsakes now, God save the mark!"

"I must. Believe me, I wouldn't risk all your efforts if it weren't important." He had already taken a step towards the gate; with a stifled imprecation Ferrers came after him. "You can't go back there, they're bedded down all over the house. What is it? Tell me, and I'll go."

Philip tried to shake off his hand, failed, and succumbed. "It's in my private cabinet, next the solar. In the coffer there, not the money box—some parchments, rolled with a ribbon. There are two of them tied together."

"I'll find them." His footsteps died away.

Philip leaned against the wall. He was feeling sick again; his hand seemed an alien thing, a misshapen embodiment of agony shooting arrows of fire to his shoulder. The fingers were stiff and unmovable. He made a sling with the shreds of the discarded shirt, and was trying to slip it over his head when a twig cracked in the thicket, and he heard voices.

The crumpled linen fluttered in his hand. Overpoweringly weary, he let it fall; of a sudden the thing seemed wholly unimportant. The Prior would look to Francis, somehow, and Richard would have understood he had done his best. So let it go, he said to himself; it's not worth the trouble. But I hope Nick keeps himself clear of it.

He stood waiting; a shadow crossed the patchy moonlight, and his heart leaped. "Hugh?"

"Uncle—sir!" The boy pushed through the trees, halted in midrun to whisper over his shoulder, "It's all right, Gregory, he's here," and came on again at a rush. Traynor's lank figure materialised behind him.

"Gregory, what the devil—? I thought you shut up with the others in the kitchens." Philip surrendered his right hand to Hugh, who was gripping it as if he supposed him ready to vanish under his eyes. Traynor smiled at him slowly over the boy's head. "Went up the chimney," he said briefly. "You were saying only yesterday, sir, that the top needed new bricking—it's fair smashed open now. I was on the way to fetch my lord Audley, him not being one to see his friends took off without argument, as you might say, when I came on Master Hugh. You're—you're sound, sir?"

"Sound enough, Gregory." Disengaging his hand from Hugh's passionate clasp, Philip gave it to the groom.

"Some men came to Ipsden today, a whole troop of them," Hugh was saying. He had kept his hold on his uncle's sleeve. "I didn't know about it until they'd gone, but the talk after was they were coming for you. Then I heard Gilbert had ridden out, and taken Roger with him. Sir"—he stared up, all the youth pinched from his face—"sir, Gilbert didn't come here—did he?"

Philip looked at Traynor, and silently thanked him. "No," he said deliberately. "Why should he come here? A landowner's affairs take him about, Hugh: you know that. You don't flatter your half-brother, nor Roger either, by what you're thinking." It had been more difficult than he cared to admit, but he had his reward in the changing eyes. And it's safe enough, he thought; I doubt Gilbert will want to brag about it. He likes a good opinion, if it comes cheap.

Impatiently he shut his mind on Gilbert Secott. "Gregory, this falls out well. I've been at my wits' end, wondering what to do—you know someone must take word to Lord Lovell. I was thinking to go myself, but if they pick up my trail I'll lead them straight to the place they want above all others to learn of—besides which, it will be weeks yet before my lord can travel, and I am known there: I couldn't be all that time at the abbey, chancing some gossip to draw Tudor's men. For you too, it will be best you get yourself gone from Willowford: any moment now someone may remember you were with me after Bosworth. Listen then. Go to the monks, and tell the Father Prior what has befallen. Tell him I've business in Flanders, and will refuge there until Christmas; and do you stay with the brothers to wait for me. If"—he hesitated—"if for some reason I cannot come, at least my lord will have been warned. Tell him this was my message: let him get from England . . . You're horsed? This to travel with then, and God be with you. I shall see you again by Saint Nicholas'." He pressed silver into the groom's hand, and watched him from sight. Then he turned to the boy.

"Hugh, good-bye. What special madness you had planned when you rode here from Ipsden, I do not know, but I'll remember you came. For the rest, I doubt we will meet again, unless you come to Flanders one day, a fine gallant with plumes and a sword. But in case that does not happen, one last thing. You may hear it said that this need not have happened—that I could have made my peace with King Henry, and after a space in prison I might even have had my lands restored to me, and so to you after—I meant you to have them, you know. But the price of that was a man's freedom, maybe even his life, and I could not pay so high. Since what I sacrificed was as much yours as mine, tell me: Was I wrong?"

His eyes on the trampled earth, Hugh said, "You couldn't have done anything else. No one could."

"Good lad. When you look around you in the next months and years, you will notice a good many men you knew in King Richard's court, coming to right fair terms with Henry's England. When you see that, be careful of your judgments. Remember, I was free to choose. But if I had a wife and babes whose bread depended upon how I shaped my tongue, I cannot guarantee that—setting aside the matter of Lord Lovell—I should not be doing the same."

"I'm coming with you," Hugh said stubbornly. "Do you think I can stay here while they drive you forth? Sir, take me with you, we'll take ship for Flanders together—"

He wanted it—wanted it desperately—and thrust it from him as a man in fever would turn from the cup. "Because I served one prince and fell out with another because of it, does that make a true cause for you? Believe me, they are not so slightly come by. King Richard was my friend; that does not mean King Henry may not rule well, and be honourably served."

"But—"

"Hugh, don't be a trouble. I do not go holidaying in Flanders: it will be worry enough to feed myself, without being burdened with a schoolboy too." The shock of hurt in the young, vulnerable face cut him to the heart, but he dared not temper it. He heard Ferrers' step again in the courtyard; the enormous pressure of time leaned at his back, hurrying him on. "I can think of much now that I should have taught you, but it seemed to me it was better you should come on these things yourself, to see and learn in your own way—well, it's too late now. Be faithful, speak the truth, have charity— Commend me with all my love to your lady mother, and tell her I shall pray for you both, as I would have you do for me. So now, good-bye."

"You taught me one thing," Hugh said thickly. "The measure of a man." The tears were pouring down his cheeks. They embraced, and Philip put the boy from him. "Go now, and God keep you."

He stood listening for a time while the steps grew faint among the trees. Then they came no more; and never in his life had he felt more alone.

He did not know how long after it was that Nicholas Ferrers touched his arm. "Are you ready, sir? I have what you wanted." The rolls were in his hand, still tied as they had come from Bosworth. He glanced at the seals, clear in the moonlight, and then, his face sharpening, at Philip. "I am in some doubt of this, if you want the truth. If this should bring trouble—"

"No trouble, Ferrers," Philip said wearily. "They will not bring him back to life again." He took the papers from the

reluctant hand and slipped them inside his jerkin. The sling
was lying on the grass; he stooped to pick it up and put it
round his neck. Ferrers said slowly, "I shall never understand
how a man like you could have called him friend."

"How should you understand? You never knew him."
Philip turned away. Beyond the scrub the fields slept under
the moon, and the steep pitch of the barn roof showed black
against the sky. They had already the remoteness of things
which are being looked at for the last time. At the foot of the
slope the brook chattered and murmured; he had often gone
there with his line, in the days before Richard Plantagenet
had held out his hand across the years to call him to his
service. He thought of the chimney he had meant to have
mended, and the new mill planned for when spring came.

Ferrers spoke quietly. "Sir, the time is passing. You must
go."

"Yes." Mounting, Philip gathered up the reins. As if to
himself, he said, "I was born here." But there was no profit in
that. He leaned down to grasp Ferrers' hand, and, straightening, touched the mare's flank with his heel. The beast
moved off obediently, circling the trees to the twist of path
beyond. At the turn he looked back, lifting his arm; then the
track bent away and carried him from sight.

CHAPTER TWENTY-FIVE

In the Duchess of Burgundy's court at Malines, a shabbily dressed gentleman was no sight for remark. Many such had come to her out of England since Bosworth; she welcomed them, thanked them in her brother's name, and spoke of a better day. Her own state had become a private one, the throngs of courtiers gone after Maximilian in Germany, or to push their fortunes anew in France; looking round the great, half-empty hall, Philip realised there was not a soul he recognised from Charles of Burgundy's mighty days.

He was brought presently to the princess, who rose from her seat to give him her hand. He kissed it and gave her Richard's letter, and would have withdrawn then for her to read alone, but she halted him with a gesture. Seating herself once more, she turned aside in her chair as she broke the seal: a big woman with Edward's jaw, inclining now to jowliness, but the lines had been exquisite once. The paper rustled as she spread it.

It seemed long before he heard the parchment whisper again. Lifting his eyes from the velvet covering of the dais, he discovered her regarding him, and he saw with a jolt of pity that her eyes were filled with tears. After a silence she spoke. "Do you know the contents of this letter, sir?"

He answered, "It was not addressed to me."

Touching a finger to her cheek, she brushed the tears away. "God have mercy upon him. He had none for himself." She made the letter into a roll again, and sat fingering it for a time before she held it out. "Will you have this to read, sir? I know you were his friend."

She had put the parchment in his hand. He held it without speaking, looking down at the broken seal, then slowly returned it. "I never spied on him in his life. He meant it for you, madam: let it be as he wished."

There was a fire burning. At her sign he kindled a brand and brought it to her, and she held the roll to the light. Together they watched the flames gather and grow. The parchment curled as the fire licked down it; here and there a line of the known, erect hand worked through. When it was nearly gone she dropped the last scrap to the floor, and he put his foot on it.

Sighing, she said, "Well, it is done. And you, Sir Philip? What do you mean to do now?"

It was the question he had been dreading. With an attempt at lightness he responded, "You will allow there is not a great range of choice. My first business is, of course, my cousin; I must bring him safely from England before considering anything else. After that—" Her eyes were still on him; he turned his own away. "I met a mariner in Bristol once, a Genoese I think he was, though he preferred the Spanish tongue. Some prentices were shouting at him for a Jew—I don't know if it was true, but he had some skull-caps in his party, which may have started it. They are clever at navigation, I'm told. Anyway, I was able to be of service, and we fell to talking—he having no English, in very ill Latin. He was on his way back from Iceland then, but he'd a scheme afoot for finding a sea route to the Indies, and I have heard he is now in Spain and like to get sponsorship there. It was in my mind that he might be glad of a man who could write a fair hand, and use a sword too."

Her brows rose. "Have you such a taste for wandering?"

"Madam, I must get my bread." There was an edge to his voice; repenting it, he achieved a smile. "A man newly landless is like a sea creature that has lost its shell—soft, helpless, and in some surprise at the altered light of day. Having been reared for very little that is of use to me now, I don't have much choice of occupation—short of seeking a position in one of the German companies. But I've always liked to know the reason for it before I set out to kill a man: I prefer the ventures of Master Cristóbal Cólon."

Hesitating, she began, "I might have a place about me—" She was looking at the bandaged left hand, still in its sling. Hotly colouring, Philip said roughly, "If the day comes when I must take charity to feed myself, I had sooner beg of strangers than my friends. I ask your highness' pardon," he added perfunctorily.

"Breath of Christ, sir, only just in time!" She had stiffened dangerously. Their eyes fought; then, surprising him, she smiled. "Pest on it, man, never kill me with a look: it was not my intention to offend you. God above, I remember how my poor brother strove to help you forward, and to how little purpose. But see now: I will speak plainly. It was my belief

369

there was one very weighty anchor to hold you fast in Flanders, if I may call a lady by such a name— No, do not look away. Has the case so changed with you that this is no longer true?"

His face answered her. Leaning back in the chair, she pointed to the seat beside her; Philip took it silently, but she only waited. Forced to it, he said at last, "You must surely see how it is. Only a few weeks ago I was thinking in truth to come here, to ask her if she would come back to England with me and be my wife, but you must know how I am situated now. I cannot go riding into Hainault to entreat her to share my beggary."

"You need not go so far, sir," the princess joined dryly. "She is not in Hainault at this moment: she is here."

He went white; but she was frowning and studying her hands. "I cannot see so immense a difficulty. Madame de Brezy has not been left poor, Sir Philip, nor is the Archduke unreasonable. His position in Hainault is a strong one; while Madame must of course marry again, he would be willing to allow her her preference, provided it were at all suitable. Particularly in the circumstances—he is a romantic, Max, when business doesn't get in the way."

"He would need to be," Philip said colourlessly. "Hold me excused, madam. If any man helped Erard de Brezy to his grave, it was I: do you seriously suppose me ready now to steal his lands, to line my pockets with his revenues and take duty of his vassal to my own aggrandisement? It concerns my honour." He saw it was goodwill that had moved her, and his mouth softened. "Let your highness believe I am grateful. But I have no cause to think that—that Madame de Brezy has held me in remembrance, and however once I wished to call myself to mind with her again, I have no right to do so now. It was long ago, it is finished, let it rest. She has great—kindness: I will not have her bound now by pity and a false sense of obligation."

"Obligation!" The eloquent hands spread, and fell helplessly. The silence was deadlock; studiedly regarding the cloth of estate behind her chair, Philip was surprised at the indifference of tone when she spoke again. "Well, it is your affair. So you return to England for your cousin? Surely this is a second trifling with fortune's favour!"

Relieved at the abrupt change of subject, Philip explained about Francis. She listened, nodded absently, and remarked

"I remember him: a gay lad, and my brother's faithful friend. I doubt Bosworth is a finished thing for him—as it is not for me. God's body, when I think of that posturing mountebank sitting in Dickon's place—" She broke off, her hand clenching on her knee. "Look you, sir, I should like speech with Lord Lovell when you two come again from England. Tell him—" She reflected, her eyes brooding. "No, I must think first. Withdraw a while, sir; I shall have a message for you to carry anon."

It was a window alcove, half-curtained with arras, to which Philip betook himself, not altogether easy in his mind. He was not anxious to linger, being afraid that any moment might bring Meg into the hall, but the Duchess had beckoned her steward, and they were deep in conversation. People came and went; with every stir at the door he felt a new lurching of his pulses, but no one came near him except presently a page, who approached to enquire shyly if messire would take wine. He had it with him, in a beautiful silver cup inlaid with the joined arms of Burgundy and York. It crossed Philip's mind that the princess might have despatched this small henchman to keep him while she sent to Meg, and he was anxiously searching the hall with his eyes when he became aware that the page was scrutinising him with unremitting interest. It was the sling which had drawn his fascinated stare, and Philip smiled involuntarily, remembering Hugh a few years ago. Encouraged, the boy demanded, "Did you get it in battle, messire? They say you were at Bosworth."

"No, it didn't come from Bosworth, I'm afraid." Disappointment was clear; considering some rescue necessary for his standing, Philip amended gravely, "But I had a wound once in the field—at Barnet, where the Earl of Warwick fell."

The bright eyes quickened. "Tell me about it, please. Was he a noble knight, the"—he struggled with the foreign title, and gave it up—"the Count of Warwick?" He noticed Philip's fleeting glance towards the dais, and explanatorily added, "It's all right, you know. Madame said I was to talk to you while she was busy."

With a last wary look around the room, Philip resigned himself to the offered entertainment. Leaning against the embrasure, he pointed to the window-seat. "It's too much a story for just now; suppose you tell me about yourself instead. Have you been long in the Duchess' household?"

Setting the brimming cup on the sill, the boy perched on the seat, restraining with obvious effort the temptation to swing his legs. "Not very. I like it, it's better than at home with tutors. Had you to do Latin when you were young, messire? My lady mother says no gentleman is without it."

But Philip was no longer listening. It was not the medallion hanging against the page's tunic which chilled like a drench of icy water, although the Brezy antelope was as familiar to him as the rose of York. The hand spread casually on the cushions was slender and well-shaped, but there was a markedly disproportionate breadth between thumb and forefinger; and the eyes lifted to his were not brown, as he had thought, but hazel.

"Are you ill, messire?" The voice reached him from leagues away. He made, he thought, some reply; a detached sensation of pain told him his bound hand had struck roughly against the wall. He paid no attention; all externals had dimmed and receded before the need to grapple with this one impossible fact. He remembered the little shop—they sold salves and compounds of herbs; the old man who kept it spoke good French for all his Flemish gutturals, being used to visits from court gentlemen who required more secret drugs. He remembered the phial he had come away with, and he look of recoil when he put it in her hand; his own voice came back to him in passionate testament for his disbelief— "It's to prevent a woman untimely conceiving a child." But she had hated and loathed it: how could he have failed to guess she would put it by, postponing from day to day, until the time came when she could be in doubt no more? And by then he was far away.

"Messire?" The boy was standing now, and reaching again for the wine. Philip looked down at him; his mouth was dry, but he found he could speak almost normally. "What—what is your name?"

"Simon de Brezy. I thought you knew, messire: Madame said you were a friend of my father's."

"Yes. A long time ago."

The direct eyes measured him. "He is dead, you know. He was sick a long time, as long as I can remember."

"Yes," Philip said again. "Yes, that also I know."

Somewhat awkwardly, for it was a heavy thing, the goblet was proffered once more. Stooping, Philip adjusted the uncertain hold. "Take it this way, under the handles. Then it can be received easily— I was taught so, when I was the Earl of Warwick's squire at Middleham." He had to demonstrate unhandily, hampered by the sling; the slight fingers accommodated themselves deftly to the altered grip, managing with a tactful quickness which made light of the instructor's impediment. The two identically shaped hands touched; then Philip drew his away like a guiltful thing. When he straightened with the cup he saw the Duchess of Burgundy watching, a faint amusement in the curve of her lips. He could have hit her for it, the woman who had lied to him that all was well with his love.

"Simon—" Infinitesimally the mothwing brows lifted; Philip understood abruptly that the Brezy name would have accustomed him to rather less casual address. "—Simon, will you be my messenger? Madame your mother—will you go to her, and ask her if she will receive a—a visitor?" A dozen phrases trembled on his tongue, but he discarded them all. He could not use the lad to plead for him. He thought, and said baldly, "Tell her it is someone from England." And then, when the boy waited, courteously enquiring, he added, "My name is Lovell. Thank you, Simon."

When he had gone there was nothing to do but wait. The minutes stretched by, each one a bottomless cleft in time, dark and inscrutable; alternatively he dreaded and perversely longed for the moment when Simon would return. His heart thumped sickeningly, and a damp coldness gathered in his palms.

"Messire?" It had been a long while by any reckoning. With a great effort Philip compelled himself to turn; the boy's face was grave. "Madame says, will you be pleased to come this way."

He followed him from the hall, into another chamber, through an entrance passage. More rooms, a flight of stairs, another door. The suite which they finally entered was of ample size, the rooms light and spacious; even as a guest, Erard de Brezy's widow kept considerable state. An hour since he would have shrunk from it, but now he hardly noticed.

There were pages and some ladies and grooms of the chamber in the first room; more ladies and a clerk in the second, with a jongleur who seemed just finished entertaining them. The door to the third chamber was closed; Simon knocked, and opened them without waiting for a reply. "Will you enter, messire?"

A narrow passage lay beyond, giving in turn on a broad room. The hangings at the far window had been drawn close against the light, but a thin crack of sun flashed through and blazed against his eyes. There were no attendants: only herself standing rigid before the carved fireplace, her face a white blur in the checkered shadows.

"Meg—" The silence accused him; he could not for his life have gone another step. "Meg, I didn't know, before God I swear it. Do you think I would not have come? She wrote me you were well—"

He heard the sound of her breath, like a whispered cry. "He told me—he said it was—I thought it was your cousin, come to tell me you were dead."

Her hands went blindly out to him. It took him forward as the moon pulls the tides; what he next clearly knew was the feel of her fingers locked in his, and the stiff crushing of her skirt against his face.

"Madame—" They had both forgotten the boy. He was staring at them, astonishment and a faint, burgeoning hostility in the expressive eyes. Flushing, Margaret withdrew her hands, saying with a shaking smile, "*Attends—attends dehors*, Simon." The lad hesitated; Philip, rising, turned to speak and thought better of it. Under his breath he murmured, "Does he understand English?"

"A few words."

The door closed on a last, flying glance. Philip said unevenly, "He is your very self, Meg—I was mad not to know, the instant he spoke."

She answered, smiling again, "A little like, maybe: it was more so when he was younger. But every day I see more of you."

He shuddered, and gripped her close. After a while he spoke against her hair: "Tell me." And then, when she whispered in protest, "Tell me, Meg. How can I bear not to know?" He drew back, tilting up her chin to see her eyes. "I used to dream sometimes— Did he lay hands on you?"

"I can't remember—how should it matter now? And he was weak with the sickness coming on—"

"Yes, I heard about that. It was the night he saw me last that it began, wasn't it? Go on."

"He came to my room where I was tending Marthe, who

was crying from the hurts of his questioning. He stood in the door and accused me—I told him it was true. I don't know what I hoped, that he would kill me perhaps. It was what I wanted; I thought I should never see you again, and it did not seem possible to live." She was silent for a moment, but Philip said only, "I know."

"He had hold of my arm—I forget what he said. But then he fell, in a faint it seemed, and the doctors came. We stayed in Saint Omer for weeks while he mended, and when he began to get back his strength we went to Brussels. While we were there I learned he meant to adopt Auguste for his heir, having no other. By that time I knew it was true, what I had prayed for"—her voice faltered an instant—"that I was with child to you. I told him it was his, since before he went to Lorraine; he said he would credit me if I swore it on my knees over holy relics, and I swore.

"We went back to Hainault, and Auguste came with us. I didn't blame him for hating me. He never believed me, and if it should be a boy and Erard owned him, he stood to lose everything. All that winter and spring he watched me—it was he that told me what had passed between you and him in Saint Omer. He asked me how I liked my lover now. I used to lie awake at night, wondering what Erard would do if the child should be so in your likeness that even he must see it—he was still very lame, but he could walk if he had a stick, and someone's arm.

"When Simon was born, he came to look at him and went away without a word. There was no telling, and he knew it. From that time I never left Simon in his cradle at night; the nurse took him into her own bed, and in the days he was never from my sight. I knew what Auguste was saying. Then the Duke went on campaign again; Auguste rode with him, and died at Nancy. They brought the news to us at Len-aertsdijk—it killed Erard, but left him breathing."

All at once she stopped, turning away to hide her face in her hands. "I had not let myself understand, until then, what I must seem to him. The doctors said he would never move again; they had told him the same. When I went into his room, I could see in his eyes what he expected of me. He believed I would take that time to be revenged upon him for what he had made me fear for Simon—"

There was a chair near. Philip led her to it and knelt beside her, holding her hands. The patchy light showed how the years had marked her; the faint lines beginning between her brows, the thinness of her temples where the pulses moved. But her mouth was the same, as firm and tender as when he had first known its warm sweetness under his in the candle-light of Saint Omer.

"He was so proud—and to be reduced to that—the servants were a torment to him, staring and fumbling. He could just lift two fingers, and I learned to understand him by that; after a while his speech came back a little, though very slurred and slow, and it was easier then. But it is a bitter thing to be handled so, and not in love. I never brought Simon near him, but one day he asked me to fetch him. He only looked, and signed for me to take him away, but in a few weeks he asked for him again. Children change quickly in the early years; I could guess what he was watching for. It was already plain to me, and growing more so every day. One afternoon when Simon had gone away, he lay looking at me. So I told him—how you had tried to keep faith with him, and about the medicine you gave me so that wrong at least would not be done him. I said if he wished he might repudiate Simon, who had no right to his name; I would send him to England and my father would make provision for him. As for me, the law would uphold him in whatever he wished to do. But he only closed his eyes as he used to when he wanted to be alone. I thought he would never want Simon to come into his sight again, but many days after he asked for him. He was three then— You've seen his hands? Erard whispered to me to bring him close to the bed, and I could see what he wanted. I put Simon's hand in his, and he turned it over and spread it, and looked. Then he said, 'He could have killed Auguste', and—and he wept."

Stiffly rising, Philip unclasped her fingers and walked slowly to the window. Outside a loosened shutter tapped, and scattered trebles from the jongleur's instrument drifted from the antechamber, with intervals of silence where the lower notes fell. He stood listening in an unthinking way, and with her eyes on his profile Margaret said, "There is no soul alive but you and I and Madame of Burgundy that knows now Simon is your son. Of his own wish Erard acknowledged him, and when he was dying he had him brought so he might take leave of him before all the household, blessing him for his child and heir." A faint colour stained her cheeks. "It was plain also to him that I must marry again; Simon is too young for such an inheritance, and there would be danger in another lord's holding so great a power in trust for him. My husband must be his regent, and the portion that is my jointure ceded to him in right of his marriage to me."

Philip replied in a strained voice, "I understand that." The space of the room lay between them. He hesitated, then crossed the tiled floor to sit beside her in the big chair, closing her in his arms. "Meg, I am poor. Worse than poor: I have nothing, can you realise it? The clothes I am wearing, some few crowns that must feed me and get me back to England for my cousin again—all the rest is gone. It would shame your standing to be given to such a man, like some unvalued person—"

Margaret touched the sling, which he had pushed impatiently aside, and stroked her fingers down his arm to the thick bandages. "You've hurt your hand, love." His cheek rested on hers; she could not compel his eyes. "Beloved. They are fair lands, Saint Aubin and Lenaertsdijk and the rest, and they are Simon's while he can hold them. Even now do you suppose there are no covetings? A child's heirship is nothing, and the Archduke knows it. Either he gives Simon's ward and me to a strong man who will keep his peace, or they go to one who can take them. Dear heart, I have no fancy to be a prize of war." Sunlight lay in moted, dusty bars across the curtained dusk; she watched it, while the pause went on. "If I had been your true wife and it happened that your lands were lost, would it have so troubled you that there was only my dower left?"

A silence followed, during which Philip, having opened his mouth on the instinctive rejoinder, became aware of the net arranged for him. Between despair and laughter he turned her face to his, saying, "Oh, guileful. You know well you were never else to me." Her lips smiled back, as simply offered as in her childhood's days. He bent his head, speaking with catching breath her name.

CHAPTER TWENTY-SIX

It had begun snowing at daybreak, and the flakes were still drifting down. The noon sun was only a diffused brightness above the church tower, and dried stalks of rue and valerian in the Abbot's garden thrust up feathered goblin shapes through the white: a chill day for travel, but the man standing by the open door watched indifferently, his cloak bundled over his arm. He was still there, leaning against the jamb, when there was a brush of robes in the room behind, and the Prior came in.

"My lord, your cousin is here."

"He's prompt." Francis turned slowly, swinging the cloak around his shoulders. "Well, Father, I'm obliged to you: for what my life may be worth I owe you for its preserving, and for some months of shelter besides. I'm sorry I cannot offer more than words in repayment."

A disclaiming gesture answered him. Inscrutable, the priest said, "I shall pray for you, my lord."

The dark eyes came up sharply, meeting the older man's. After a moment Francis said pleasantly, "It's your business, isn't it?" He bent over the Prior's hand, and went out into the passage. There was a halt to his step yet; Philip, coming with a smile to meet him, perceived it and was concerned. Scanning his cousin's face, he found it thinner than he would have liked, and beneath the waxy colour was a look of eroding weakness. When they had embraced he said involuntarily, "Francis, I should have thought. A litter would be easier for you—"

"Yes, the heralds going before to proclaim our passage. I'm quite well, Philip, don't trouble yourself." Francis glanced from the liveried squires, respectfully waiting, to the page holding a folded scarlet mantle, and his brows rose. "Faith, you're in some splendour. Have you fallen on prosperity among the Burgoners, only a dozen weeks out of England?"

"Very considerably," Philip admitted. He had coloured in spite of himself. "I'm married, Francis, these two months past. Will you give me good wishes?"

"You're—" Francis stared at him; then, comprehending, he began to laugh. "Oh, I see. Little Madame? Yes, I thought as much. I heard her—her husband was failing, and I wondered— Well, well. All credit for your patience, coz, it was a long wait! I look forward to making my compliments to the bride; for yourself—" He gripped the other's hand. "I'm heart glad for you, Philip. You deserve your joy."

It was the ungrudging pleasure in his voice that struck Philip with a pang. The contrast was too great; he was embarrassed to the soul by his own richness of felicity, remembering all Francis had lost. Journeying up from Tilbury he had not dared in his foreign guise enquire too particularly about affairs in England; hardly a whisper had reached him of what was happening at Minster Lovell since King Henry had made a gift of it to his kinsman, the Tudor Earl of Pembroke, and he knew only that Anna and her children lived there no more.

It had stopped snowing by the time they set out, Dom Martin walking with Philip behind the others to the outer gate. Wih his eyes on the man ahead of them, the monk said in an undertone, "There was no ship here, then?" and Philip shook his head. "None: I sent to the harbour last evening, but the sailing weather is uncertain now, and there was no waiting here for it to change. We must make for Tilbury; I've a ship there that brought me. From the look of my cousin I wish we had a nearer port, but I could not risk it in case it had become known he was in sanctuary here."

"Sooner or later, it will be," the Prior said quietly. "You are wise to get him gone." He hesitated. "There has been word put about, I know not how widely, that Lord Lovell would be received with honour at Westminster if he chose to be reconciled with the King. It may be a trap to draw him from where he is hidden."

"Maybe." Philip looked at him sideways. "Has my cousin heard this?"

"Yes. He laughed."

In the outer court the horses stood saddled; Francis, already mounted, was looking round for him. It was the hour of prime, cloudless and smiling; as they rode out the sound of bells followed cheerfully, and some robins were picking crumbs under the kitchen wall.

They laid a deliberate trail south to Maldon, where the bulk of Philip's Walloons and Flemings were to make rendezvous with them by another road. Within the hurly of that busy port the last traces of King Henry's great fugitives were swallowed up; the two squires and little page were left at a house of Franciscans with money and certain others of their countrymen to await with patience a ship for Flanders; and in the upper room of a discreet hostelry Philip assumed the sober dun gown and flapped cap which, a half-day before him, the leader of his train of servants had conspicuously worn through the town gates. There departed unhurriedly from Maldon next morning the seeming trader who had entered it, pausing by the way to thank, in halting Low Country speech, the friendly gateman who pointed the Burgoner folk on their road.

They lay that night beyond Chelmsford, where the highway, swinging inland, forked south to London and the estuary ports. Two days later they smelled the sea.

The shipmaster was lodged in a tavern by the harbour, and chafing to be gone; his cargo was loaded and for three days the wind had been fair. They went aboard before it was light, and sailed with the morning tide. Francis sat on a bale, watching the land drop away; the sun came up, and a peal of bells drifted over the water. With a glance at his companion he remarked ironically, "Good lack, to think I'd forgotten. It's King Henry's wedding day." He stretched and leaned back, his cheek on his hand. "And it will be as fine, doubtless, as if his grandam crazy Katherine had gone to bed with Tudor her groom by the church door. I'd a fancy once to take myself to London to see the sight, but—" He was fingering the dagger at his girdle. "Well, it was a fool's thought: I've better now. I shan't want houseroom of you long, Philip: not if the Duchess of Burgundy is of the mind I think she is."

"For God's sake—"

"Well, cousin?" Francis stared up, his mouth like adamant. Philip's eyes rested on the white, inflexible face, and he felt himself wrung with that which was neither fear nor pity: only despair, and the anguish of a grief foreknown. "This quarrel will be your death. If you care nothing for that, will you think of those you take with you to the same end?"

"I take no one that is not willing. Is it so hard for you to imagine there can be those that are? You were not so laggard once; but then, you had less to lose."

He stopped, vividly flushed. Philip said slowly, "Will you restore the dead to life? If you can do that I will come with you gladly." There was a short silence, and then Francis bent forward, hiding his forehead against his knees.

"I'm sorry, I didn't mean that. If ever a man had a right to his peace it is you—"

"It's nothing, let it go. It doesn't matter."

The sky was turning cobalt as the sun edged higher, and rainbows danced in the creaming wake. Shivering, Francis hugged his cloak around him. "Philip. What happened to the boys?"

"The boys?" It took a moment to understand. Francis said, "The princes: young Edward and his brother. Do you know?"

Expressionless, Philip answered, "I can tell you what happened to the boy John of Gloucester, that no one ever claimed to be anything but the bastard of a king. He was shut up after Bosworth and starved to death. Tudor believes in nipping his dangers young. He had to call the princes lawful when he promised to marry their sister: What do you suppose he would do with them?" It was the extending pause which made him turn. "Why ask me? How should I know, better than any other?"

Looking up at him, Francis met his eyes full. "Then you don't know," he said at length. "I thought you at least surely must; he told you everything."

"I assure you, he did not." The words came slowly, divided like infinitely precious things. "Will you tell me what you mean?"

"I mean the princes. The story is they died two years ago—before ever Buckingham rose." There was a stifled sound from Philip; getting to his feet, Francis folded his arms on the rail. "I came on it first not long after Buckingham was executed in Salisbury; I thought it a lie then, put about by Tudor's friends. Later there began to be gossip in London but I didn't regard it; it was the kind of thing that would be said if they weren't much seen. But last summer—no, you weren't there. It was one day in council, when Russell wanted to send the lady Elizabeth to the Tower to stay with her brothers, as he said, until Tudor was out of the way. I saw the King's face—I knew then it was true."

"True—how? That they were dead? Or that he had commanded it?"

Francis said steadily, "Do you believe that?"

The wavelets splashed and lapped against the bow. Staring into the eddying deeps, Philip remembered Bosworth eve, and the feel of an agony of spirit he could neither comprehend nor aid. "Christ shield us," he whispered. "So that was it." The light on the water was dazzling; he put a hand to his eyes against the bright gleam. "No. I don't believe it."

"I thought sure you must know the right of it," Francis said again. "It might have been sickness took them, or even an accident maybe, or—" His fingers moved along the rail. "There are always men around a king wanting his favour. Something might have put it into someone's head that he would have been glad if— He was a long time from London, that first summer. Brackenbury couldn't be always at the Tower: it could have been done, and the King never known until he came back from Salisbury."

The wind, which had slackened, blew fresh again. Philip looked at the younger man; there was a blue tinge to his lips, and his fingers trembled as he groped for the fastenings of his cloak. "Francis, come below. You're ill yet, it's too cold for you here."

Shaking his head impatiently, Francis eased himself down once more to the sack of wool. His movements were slow and unsupple still, but Philip knew better than to offer a hand to help.

"It's past Epiphany," Francis said quietly. "We kept it at Westminster last January, do you remember? Oh God, was it only a year ago." He huddled his knees against his chest. "Here's a jest for you, Philip, that I had from the monks—they're great gossips, the brothers, and get travellers' news as quickly as any folk in the kingdom. Tyrell has made his peace with Tudor." He laughed at his cousin's face. "Yes, faithful Tyrell that loved King Richard so well—he gets back his Welsh offices, and keeps all his goods besides. Does it make you smile?"

Philip said at length, "Give him joy of his winnings. I remember how he used to wait about the King, only wanting the chance to pick up a cloak or offer the cup— He was fixed to Buckingham's heels for a while: the comfort of vicarious association, probably. Buckingham was just the man to play on it. I wonder what Tyrell made of it when his great patron fell."

Yesterday was too much with him again. Absently, with a gesture that had become near habit, he cradled his left hand in the right, trying to heal the ache with warming it. The bones had knit in a fashion, although he would be clumsy with it to the end of his life, but sometimes it hurt him still: some days, as now, when he was tired or dispirited or too much gripped by remembrance, he could feel again the boot heel in his palm.

The ship drove on, and the chalk scarp of Foreland head rose against the sky. South lay the shadow of the French coast, with Flanders beyond, invisible yet beneath the dark sea-rim. Philip smiled at his cousin and pointed, but Francis was looking back towards England.

THE Yorkist defeat at Stoke, two years after Bosworth, was the last battle of what have become known as the Wars of the Roses. After savage fighting the forces of Viscount Lovell and the Earl of Lincoln, a mixture of Irishmen and German mercenary troops supplied by the dowager Duchess of Burgundy, were put to flight by King Henry's general the Earl of Oxford. Lincoln was killed on the field; Lord Lovell escaped, swimming the river Trent on horseback, and was not seen alive again.

More than two hundred years later, the residents of the manor house at Minster Lovell, undertaking alterations, caused to be broken open the walls between several of the lower rooms, and discovered a hidden one. In it were found the bones of a man who was suppositiously identified as Francis Lovell; it has been assumed he took refuge there after the rout at Stoke, hidden by servants who were faithful to him still, but the manner of his death, whether of wounds, or exposure, or by some mischance starvation, is unknown.